U0439668

本书是国家留学基金资助项目（20153012）和
中国博士后科学基金资助项目（2016M601481）的阶段性成果。

IMAGES OF THREE
PROTAGONISTS IN HAWKES'
TRANSLATION
OF HONG LOU MEN

A CORPUS-BASED STUDY ON EXPLICITATION

追寻霍克斯笔下的
红楼主人公形象

——基于语料库的显化翻译研究

姚琴 著

中国社会科学出版社

图书在版编目（CIP）数据

追寻霍克斯笔下的红楼主人公形象：基于语料库的显化翻译研究/姚琴著.
—北京：中国社会科学出版社，2017.12

ISBN 978-7-5203-1236-3

Ⅰ.①追… Ⅱ.①姚… Ⅲ.①《红楼梦》—英语—文学翻译—研究
Ⅳ.①I207.411

中国版本图书馆CIP数据核字（2017）第260348号

出 版 人	赵剑英
责任编辑	王 琪
责任校对	张爱华
责任印制	王 超

出　　版	中国社会科学出版社
社　　址	北京鼓楼西大街甲158号
邮　　编	100720
网　　址	http://www.csspw.cn
发 行 部	010-84083685
门 市 部	010-84029450
经　　销	新华书店及其他书店
印　　刷	北京君升印刷有限公司
装　　订	廊坊市广阳区广增装订厂
版　　次	2017年12月第1版
印　　次	2017年12月第1次印刷
开　　本	710×1000 1/16
印　　张	18.5
插　　页	2
字　　数	285千字
定　　价	78.00元

凡购买中国社会科学出版社图书，如有质量问题请与本社营销中心联系调换
电话：010-84083683
版权所有　侵权必究

前　言

自小酷爱《红楼梦》，我和翻译结缘，始于对《红楼梦》的喜爱。

记得十几岁时读《红楼梦》，还学着金圣叹在书上圈点、在页边空白处点评，现在想来，可叹可笑。

多年前无意在网上看到一篇题为《莎士比亚眼里的林黛玉》的文章，提到西方人把林黛玉翻译为"black jade"（黑皮肤荡妇），甚为吃惊，作为《红楼梦》第一女主角，作为一个极具美学含义的小说人物，她那含露带愁的绝世姿容、超逸灵秀的神女风度、热烈深挚的坚贞情感，渗透着诗情的个性特征，时时刻刻萦绕在读者心头，她在西方世界中被翻译成了一个怎样的形象，这成了我的牵挂，我特别为之心焦。

此后不久，上海外国语大学的红学翻译研究专家冯庆华老师来教授我们博士课程中的"语料库翻译学"，冯教授是红学专家，经常引用《红楼梦》的例子，这更激起了我研究英译《红楼梦》的人物形象的冲动。

经冯老师指点，我选择了在学界和普通读者中都得到了广泛认可的《红楼梦》的一百二十回英文全译本——杨译本和霍译本作为研究对象，在研究过程，非常欣喜地发现，这两个译本都废弃了"black jade"这个译名，分别改为拼音"Lin Daiyu"和"Lin Dai-yu"。

更令人激动的是，我发现学界对英译《红楼梦》人物形象的关注度尚不足，正如文军和任艳两位学者的研究发现：自1979年至2012年，国内学者对英译《红楼梦》的研究论文多达782篇，然而，其中研究人物形象的只有7篇。

而之后，我的一篇论文《基于平行语料库的〈红楼梦〉意义显化考察——以霍译本林黛玉人物特征为例》由外语类权威期刊《外语教学与研究》发表，这对我是一个极大的鼓舞，于是诞生了研究英译《红楼梦》人物形象之念，然虑及时间和精力有限，遂先行研究英译《红楼梦》的主人公形象。

下面谨以自创小诗结束前言：

幻渺
梦里情痴抱恨长
梦外悲喜千般同
我
在中英文中旅行
摇动梦的风铃
讲
三个漂洋过海的可人儿
音容笑貌、爱恨情迷
给你听

姚　琴
2017年1月于英国剑桥大学

目 录

导 论 …………………………………………………………… (1)

第一章 霍克斯笔下的林黛玉人物形象 ………………………… (54)
 第一节 语料采集与基本数据比较 ……………………… (54)
 第二节 分析与讨论 …………………………………… (85)
 第三节 小结 ……………………………………………… (97)

第二章 霍克斯笔下的贾宝玉形象 ……………………………… (99)
 第一节 语料采集与基本数据比较 ……………………… (99)
 第二节 分析与讨论 …………………………………… (141)
 第三节 小结 …………………………………………… (157)

第三章 霍克斯笔下的薛宝钗形象 …………………………… (159)
 第一节 语料采集与基本数据比较 ……………………… (159)
 第二节 分析与讨论 …………………………………… (171)
 第三节 小结 …………………………………………… (175)

第四章 霍克斯显化翻译红楼主人公形象的多维动因 ………… (177)
 第一节 翻译活动所受制的特定社会文化背景 …………… (177)
 第二节 翻译活动的赞助人 ……………………………… (181)
 第三节 译者的主体性 …………………………………… (183)

结 语 …………………………………………………………… (189)

附录一　林黛玉人物形象语料库数据 …………………………（194）

附录二　贾宝玉人物形象语料库数据 …………………………（212）

附录三　薛宝钗人物形象语料库数据 …………………………（263）

参考文献 ……………………………………………………………（267）

后　记 ………………………………………………………………（280）

导　　论

"开谈不说《红楼梦》，读尽诗书也枉然。"

——（清）得舆

一　选题缘起

（一）《红楼梦》人物形象英译的研究现状与问题

《红楼梦》是"一部从某种意义上说可以象征中国整个文化的作品"①，"古代文学作品中，没有哪一部有《红楼梦》这样丰盈的文化包容量。我们从《红楼梦》里几乎看到了整个中国文化。特别是我们民族的人文意识和人文传统，可以说尽在其中了。《红楼梦》作为一种文化现象，它所流露的文化精神，很多可以称为整个中华民族的历史文化精神"②。《红楼梦》所包含的文化内容，不仅表现于生活物质等有形物的直接描写中，而且通过作品中的人物及其性格特征的描写，来表现中国人的文化性格。

在我国，以研究中国古典白话小说巅峰之作《红楼梦》为己任的"红学"，成为十分热门的学问，"与'甲骨学'和'敦煌学'并称我国上古、中古、近古三个不同历史时期的'三大显学'"③。

---

① David Hawkes, "The Disillusionment of Precious Jade", in John Minford & Siu-kit Wong (ed.), *Classical Modern and Humane: Essays in Chinese Literature*, Hong Kong: The Chinese University Press, p. 268. 原文如下："a book that in some sense epitomizes their whole culture."

② 刘梦溪：《传统的误读》，河北教育出版社1996年版，第298页。

③ 吕启祥、林东海主编：《红楼梦研究稀见资料汇编（增订本）》，人民文学出版社2006年版，第528页。

作为"整个中国文学里最流行的书"①,《红楼梦》及其英译本作为研究对象的价值毋庸置疑。

近年来,对于《红楼梦》英译的研究,人们或引用借鉴中国传统的翻译理论即文艺美学的理论;或采用西方翻译理论,如从文化学的视角来研究;或运用当代语言学的一些研究成果。前人对《红楼梦》的研究从视角上讲可以归纳为文化学视角②、语言学视角③和接受美学视角④三个研究视角,凸显出多学科研究的特色,我国《红楼梦》英译研究进入了真正的繁荣时期,不少论文研究的广度和深度得以加强。"但是仍然有重复选题,甚至重复思路,出现了不平衡的现象……"⑤

对1980—2003年20多年中13种外语类期刊上刊登的所有有关《红楼梦》英译的50篇文章⑥、1980—2006年26年中11种外语类核心期刊上刊登的所有以《红楼梦》英译本为研究对象的52篇文章⑦以及1979—2010年30年中CNKI期刊上刊登的所有以《红楼梦》英译本为研究对象的782篇文章的分析结果,证实了《红楼梦》英译研究在选题方面存在不足和缺陷。

到目前为止,《红楼梦》的人物形象翻译研究并没有受到应有的重

---

① David Hawkes (trans.), *The Story of the Stone* (Volume I – III), London: The Penguin Books Ltd., 1973, p. 25.

② 详见王宏印《〈红楼梦〉诗词曲赋英译比较研究》,陕西师范大学出版社2001年版;刘士聪《红楼译评——〈红楼梦〉翻译研究论文集》,南开大学出版社2004年版;李磊荣《文化可译性视角下的〈红楼梦〉翻译研究》,上海译文出版社2010年版;邱进、周洪亮《文化视域及翻译策略:〈红楼梦〉译本的多维研究》,西南师范大学出版社2011年版;陈可培《译者的文化意识与译作的再生》,载刘士聪《红楼译评——〈红楼梦〉翻译研究论文集》,南开大学出版社2004年版,第363—374页。

③ 详见谭载喜《翻译学》,湖北教育出版社2000年版;任东升《语篇翻译与译者的写作》,载刘士聪《红楼译评——〈红楼梦〉翻译研究论文集》,南开大学出版社2004年版,第205—215页;洪涛《女体和国族——从〈红楼梦〉翻译看跨文化移植与学术知识障碍》,国家图书馆出版社2010年版。

④ 冯庆华:《红译艺坛——〈红楼梦〉翻译艺术研究》,上海外语教育出版社2006年版;冯庆华:《母语文化下的译者风格》,上海外语教育出版社2008年版。

⑤ 刘士聪:《红楼译评——〈红楼梦〉翻译研究论文集》,南开大学出版社2004年版,第482页。

⑥ 闫敏敏:《二十年来的〈红楼梦〉英译研究》,《外语教学》2005年第4期。

⑦ 陈曜:《〈红楼梦〉英译史及其在英语文学中地位初探》,《湖北成人教育学院学报》2007年第3期。

视。在语料库研究方法兴起之前，情况已然如此；在语料库研究方法兴起之后，也鲜少有人问津这一领域。自1979年至2010年，人物形象研究"这个领域的研究文章只有七篇"①。

《红楼梦》被誉为一座艺术丰碑，而人物形象塑造是成就这座艺术丰碑的关键。"据统计，《红楼梦》里共描写了774人，有名字或有绰号的，如果连没有名字的也算上去，就有975人。"② 上至皇帝妃子，中有国公大臣、各级官员衙役，下至仆人丫鬟、市井走卒、村夫村妇，各色人等。"各人的面目、性格、身份、语言，都不相同。"③ 其语言鲜活生动，让人如睹其况，如闻其声，如见其人。

曹雪芹怀着深挚的情感和同情，用他的诗情画意，用饱蘸着他全部美好理想的笔墨，塑造了一群集"山川日月之精秀"的红楼女儿。翻开《红楼梦》，各种各样的艺术形象就会向我们走来：贾宝玉、林黛玉、薛宝钗、凤姐……数不胜数的人物以其个人的风采各呈异彩，展现给读者的有宝玉的怪诞、黛玉的任性、宝钗的贤淑、湘云的憨直、凤姐的泼辣、袭人的柔顺、晴雯的率真、可卿的妩媚、探春的果断、惜春的才情、妙玉的孤芳、宝琴的艳丽、香菱的秀逸、鸳鸯的刚直、紫鹃的慧诚和平儿的坚忍，等等。其笔下人物"人有其性情，人有其气质，人有其形状，人有其声口"，迥然有别又栩栩如生。

以《红楼梦》人物形象翻译作为研究对象，在《红楼梦》英译研究中属于新兴话题，据笔者在中国期刊全文数据库搜查，国内最早可以追溯到《从文学文体视角看林黛玉形象在翻译中的再现》④。

从那时算起迄今，相关文章数量极为有限，研究零散难成系统，专项研究更是门可罗雀。下面从文章、专著、学位论文三个方面逐一观之。

1. 文章情况

相关文章笔者搜集到11篇，作者、题名等信息见表0-1。

---

① 文军、任艳：《国内〈红楼梦〉英译研究回眸（1979—2010）》，《中国外语》2012年第1期。
② 冯其庸：《红楼论要——解读〈红楼梦〉的几个问题》，《红楼梦学刊》2008年第5期。
③ 吴世昌：《红楼梦探源外编》，上海古籍出版社1980年版，第1页。
④ 魏瑾：《从文学文体视角看林黛玉形象在翻译中的再现》，《安徽文学》（下半月）2007年第5期。

表 0-1　　　　　　　《红楼梦》人物形象翻译论文

作　者	题　名	期刊名称	年/期
姚琴	基于平行语料库的《红楼梦》意义显化翻译考察——以霍译本林黛玉人物特征为例	《外语教学与研究》	2013/03
韦妙、韦合	《红楼梦》英译审美中人物外貌的再现与缺失	《河北民族师范学院学报》	2013/01
杨春花	不同的译者不同的形象美——以《红楼梦》中林黛玉的文学形象再现为例	《长春工业大学学报》（社会科学版）	2012/02
朱耍霞	从人际功能评析《红楼梦》英译文的人物形象	《贵州师范大学学报》（社会科学版）	2011/03
张妍	浅谈《红楼梦》茶文化翻译与人物性格塑造	《内蒙古农业大学学报》（社会科学版）	2010/06
王田	简析霍克斯英译版《红楼梦》中林黛玉形象的裂变	《红楼梦学刊》	2010/03
宋华、刘晓虹	《红楼梦》外貌英译的审美建构	《红楼梦学刊》	2008/02
魏瑾、汪小英	译者介入与《红楼梦》人物形象变异	《南华大学学报》（社会科学版）	2007/06
邓宏春	杨译《红楼梦》中王熙凤语言的翻译及其形象的再现	《考试周刊》	2007/38
张小胜	评《红楼梦》杨译本中王熙凤形象的重塑	《现代企业教育》	2007/18
魏瑾	从文学文体视角看林黛玉形象在翻译中的再现	《安徽文学》（下半月）	2007/05

11 篇文章内容介绍如下：

（1）《基于平行语料库的〈红楼梦〉意义显化翻译考察——以霍译本林黛玉人物特征为例》通过对《红楼梦》的霍译本与其所据原著程乙本进行平行语料库的源语/目标语语际对比和分析，考察《红楼梦》霍译本中有关林黛玉人物描写的翻译特征。语料库研究表明：对林黛玉的人物特征，霍译本以释意、增添等方式进行意义显化翻译。

（2）《〈红楼梦〉英译审美中人物外貌的再现与缺失》就《红楼梦》的英译本——杨译本和霍译本中对人物外貌词汇的重组、外貌词汇的模糊化翻译、外貌词汇差异的误读和外貌审美差异下的增译，说明了译者强烈的审美心理活动对文学翻译起着重要影响。

（3）《不同的译者不同的形象美——以〈红楼梦〉中林黛玉的文学形象再现为例》就杨宪益、戴乃迭和霍克斯在再现《红楼梦》中主人公林黛玉的外貌美、服饰美和语言美时，采用了不同的翻译方法所塑造出的林黛玉的文学形象美进行了探讨。

（4）《从人际功能评析〈红楼梦〉英译文的人物形象》从功能语法的角度对我国古典名著《红楼梦》中的人物对话及杨宪益和戴乃迭翻译的人物形象以其中的人际意义模型进行了语篇分析研究。

（5）《浅谈〈红楼梦〉茶文化翻译与人物性格塑造》选取其中两个主人公——黛玉和妙玉之于茶事对霍、杨两英译本进行对比分析，借述茶事刻画人物形象，表明人物身份地位、体现人物复杂关系、显示人物学识修养、塑造深化人物性格。

（6）《简析霍克斯英译版〈红楼梦〉中林黛玉形象的裂变》选取霍译本其中有关林黛玉人物形象翻译实例，认为经霍克斯的翻译后，我们很难再从中复原出那个拥有着高贵气质、温文尔雅的林黛玉形象，留在我们脑中的更多的是活泼、张扬、泼辣、野蛮又略显强悍的黛玉形象。

（7）《〈红楼梦〉外貌英译的审美建构》以《红楼梦》英译本中人物外貌的英译为切入点，探讨分析审美趣味、审美心理和审美态度作用下译者对人物外貌英译的重新建构与变异现象，认为杨译本的译者与源语文化背景相同，所以更重直译，其笔下的人物外貌英译更多地体现出中华民族的审美观和审美趣味；而霍译本由于受西方审美意识和态度的影响，更重意译，导致了译本中人物形象的变异。

（8）《译者介入与〈红楼梦〉人物形象变异》选取七例对比和分析《红楼梦》的霍、杨两英译本，从译者的个人情感倾向、审美想象的不同运作以及译者文化取向三个方面，揭示译者的介入不可避免地作用于翻译效果，使人物形象产生不同程度的变异。杨译本中尽可能尊重原文和原文文化，霍译本考虑更多的是读者的需求和接受水平。

（9）《杨译〈红楼梦〉中王熙凤语言的翻译及其形象的再现》援引

数例《红楼梦》原著中王熙凤的语言,从机心、辣手、刚口三方面分析了她复杂的性格。同时结合杨译本中王熙凤的语言的相关翻译,采用纽马克翻译理论做出适当评价,认为杨译以"语义翻译"为主,兼顾"交际翻译",成功地再现了王熙凤这一不朽的艺术形象。

(10)《评〈红楼梦〉杨译本中王熙凤形象的重塑》从杨译《红楼梦》的选词、句子结构以及翻译的叙事角度对译本进行分析,发现译文中王熙凤泼辣、粗俗、直率的鲜明个性减色不少,认为杨译本对王熙凤这一典型形象的重塑有所欠缺。

(11)《从文学文体视角看林黛玉形象在翻译中的再现》通过从文学文体角度对《红楼梦》两种英译本四处实例进行对比,认为从文体效果上看,杨、霍两译本在塑造林黛玉这一形象中都有得失。

由文章观之,有关《红楼梦》人物形象的英译研究历时不长,若从2007年算起,只有几年。在2007—2015年八年间可以说刚刚起步,研究基本处于零散状态,远未成系统。

2. 专著情况

就笔者收集资料来看,有关《红楼梦》英译专著,迄今国内共出版16部,其中港台3部,大陆13部,分别是:《〈红楼梦〉西游记》[1],《〈红楼梦〉诗词曲赋英译比较研究》[2],《〈红楼梦〉管窥》[3],《红译艺坛——〈红楼梦〉翻译艺术研究》《母语文化下的译者风格》《思维模式下的译文词汇》《思维模式下的译文句式》[4],《霍译红楼梦回目人名翻译研究》[5],《〈红楼梦〉概念隐喻的英译研究》[6],《〈红楼梦〉与诠释方法论》《女体和国族——从〈红楼梦〉翻译看跨文化移植与学术知识障》[7],

---

[1] 林以亮:《〈红楼梦〉西游记》,台湾联经出版事业公司1976年版。
[2] 王宏印:《〈红楼梦〉诗词曲赋英译比较研究》,陕西师范大学出版社2001年版。
[3] 范圣宇:《〈红楼梦〉管窥》,中国社会科学出版社2004年版。
[4] 冯庆华:《红译艺坛——〈红楼梦〉翻译艺术研究》,上海外语教育出版社2006年版;冯庆华:《母语文化下的译者风格》,上海外语教育出版社2008年版;冯庆华:《思维模式下的译文词汇》,上海外语教育出版社2012年版;冯庆华:《思维模式下的译文句式》,上海外语教育出版社2015年版。
[5] 赵长江:《霍译红楼梦回目人名翻译研究》,河北教育出版社2007年版。
[6] 肖家燕:《〈红楼梦〉概念隐喻的英译研究》,中国社会科学出版社2009年版。
[7] 洪涛:《〈红楼梦〉与诠释方法论》,国家图书出版社2008年版;洪涛:《女体和国族——从〈红楼梦〉翻译看跨文化移植与学术知识障》,国家图书出版社2010年版。

《〈红楼梦〉中英文语料库的创建及应用研究》①,《文化可译性视角下的〈红楼梦〉翻译研究》②,《文化视域及翻译策略:〈红楼梦〉译本的多维研究》③,《〈红楼梦〉亲属称谓语的英译研究》④,《〈红楼梦〉英译艺术比较研究——基于霍克斯和杨宪益译本》⑤。

上述 16 部专著中,除了《〈红楼梦〉中英文语料库的创建及应用研究》中收录了刘泽权、朱虹先前发表的一篇文章,即《英译刘姥姥形象的对比研究——以话语的人际功能分析为例》(收入该书时题目有改动)与人物形象翻译有关外,其余均未涉及《红楼梦》的人物形象翻译,更遑论人物形象翻译专项研究。

3. 硕博论文情况

有关《红楼梦》人物形象显化翻译的硕士论文尚未查到,笔者只收集到 6 篇与人物形象翻译有联系的硕士论文,即《〈红楼梦〉人物描写及其翻译中的隐含的语用分析》⑥《从语境对等论〈红楼梦〉两英译本中王熙凤的性格塑造》⑦《〈红楼梦〉中个性化人物语言风格在译文中的再现》⑧《美的传达——论〈红楼梦〉杨译本中的人物外貌描写》⑨《跨文化视角的〈红楼梦〉中涉及人物塑造的隐喻研究》⑩《霍克斯〈红楼梦〉人

---

① 刘泽权:《〈红楼梦〉中英文语料库的创建及应用研究》,光明日报出版社 2010 年版。
② 李磊荣:《文化可译性视角下的〈红楼梦〉翻译研究》,上海译文出版社 2010 年版。
③ 邱进、周洪亮:《文化视域及翻译策略:〈红楼梦〉译本的多维研究》,西南师范大学出版社 2011 年版。
④ 严苡丹:《〈红楼梦〉亲属称谓语的英译研究》,外语教学与研究出版社 2012 年版。
⑤ 党争胜:《〈红楼梦〉英译艺术比较研究——基于霍克斯和杨宪益译本》,北京大学出版社 2012 年版。
⑥ 陆梅:《〈红楼梦〉人物描写及其翻译中的隐含的语用分析》,硕士学位论文,广西大学,2004 年。
⑦ 田婧:《从语境对等论〈红楼梦〉两英译本中王熙凤的性格塑造》,硕士学位论文,广东外语外贸大学,2005 年。
⑧ 徐文臻:《〈红楼梦〉中个性化人物语言风格在译文中的再现》,硕士学位论文,中国石油大学,2008 年。
⑨ 梁艳:《美的传达——论〈红楼梦〉杨译本中的人物外貌描写》,硕士学位论文,上海外国语大学,2009 年。
⑩ 付红丽:《跨文化视角的〈红楼梦〉中涉及人物塑造的隐喻研究》,硕士学位论文,湖南师范大学,2011 年。

物话语翻译艺术研究》①。

以下是上述6篇学位论文具体介绍：

（1）《〈红楼梦〉人物描写及其翻译中的隐含的语用分析》摘选了《红楼梦》人物描写的一些典型片段作为例子，在对每个例子进行个案分析后把所得到的有关其语用隐含的论证应用于评论部分现有译文的得失，通过从语用学研究所囊括的语境、预设、会话隐含、话语行为等各个研究角度对案例中某些典型隐含进行分析。该文对有关译文的评论重点在于两个方面：①译者在多大程度上传达了有关隐含的语用意义；②原文中语用隐含的模糊性在多大程度上在译文中得以传达。

（2）《从语境对等论〈红楼梦〉两英译本中王熙凤的性格塑造》以哈蒂姆和梅森基于篇章语言学研究的交际翻译论作为理论框架，通过对杨宪益与戴乃迭的译本和大卫·霍克斯的译本中对王熙凤的性格塑造的译例进行对比与分析，从在译文中重建语境对等的角度，探讨了两位译者不同的翻译策略以及由此导致的两个译本在王熙凤性格塑造方面的不同的翻译效果。

（3）《〈红楼梦〉中个性化人物语言风格在译文中的再现》以杨宪益、戴乃迭译文和霍克斯译文为文本，以小说文体分析为基础，对两个英译本主人公对话所采取的翻译策略进行对比分析，由此分析人物对话风格传达对人物性格塑造的影响，评价对话译文风格是否与原文保持一致，认为：《红楼梦》的上述两个英译本在不同的文体类型翻译中各有千秋，基本实现了译文人物语言韵味、风格的传达。

（4）《美的传达——论〈红楼梦〉杨译本中的人物外貌描写》以《红楼梦》杨宪益、戴乃迭夫妇的英译本为研究对象，通过对原文本中有关人物外貌描写的翻译，聚焦于杨译本中对相应描写的翻译，以服饰、肖像为经纬，对典型译例进行分析评价。对服饰的翻译研究主要集中在服饰颜色和服饰材质及款式上，对人物肖像的翻译研究则集中在小说的三个主人公——贾宝玉、林黛玉和王熙凤的肖像描写上。通过对以上相关翻译段落的评析，总结出杨译本所体现出的一些突出特点：杨译本对文化内涵深刻的意象持完全保留的态度，尽力在译作中保持文化信息的

---

① 孙洋：《霍克斯〈红楼梦〉人物话语翻译艺术研究》，硕士学位论文，山东大学，2012年。

原貌；而对于文化印记较淡的表达，则采取了更为灵活的译法，以能让译入语读者获得同样的审美感受为第一要务。

（5）《跨文化视角的〈红楼梦〉中涉及人物塑造的隐喻研究》选用《红楼梦》及杨宪益、戴乃迭夫妇和大卫·霍克斯的《红楼梦》的英译本作为研究的主要语料，对比英汉涉及人物塑造的隐喻的异同。作者在前人研究成果的基础上，将不同的翻译方法划分为六个不同等级，随机选取了《红楼梦》的两个英译本的前八十回中212个涉及人物塑造的隐喻，对它们进行分组归类，进而对各个类别组的翻译等级做了统计，考察了两译本中体现出来的英汉隐喻的相似性与相异性。

（6）《霍克斯〈红楼梦〉人物话语翻译艺术研究》通过对霍克斯人物话语翻译艺术的分析，认为霍克斯通过在语言各个层面的操控，促使译文中的人物话语比原文中的人物话语更具个性特色，虽然这样做在语言层面违背了原文，但却通过话语成功传达了人物个性，所以广义上做到了对于原文的忠实。

另外，就博士论文而言，笔者遗憾地发现相关研究几乎无处寻觅。但值得一提的是，博士论文《〈红楼梦〉拟声词及其英译研究》在第四章第一小节"揭示人物性格"中单独辟出一个标题来探讨人物形象话题[①]，但只从拟声词的独特视角探讨了其在塑造人物形象中的作用。

综上所述，就硕博论文情况而言，《红楼梦》的人物形象英译研究，在研究《红楼梦》的硕博论文中有过零星论述。这些论著中的零星成果，给我们进一步研究提供了一定的借鉴，虽然这类零星成果不乏真知灼见，但缺乏系统，讨论也不够深入。

4. 国外研究情况[②]

西方对我国古典白话小说《红楼梦》的关注由来已久。据资料显示，英美红学始于1842年德国传教士郭士立（Karl Gutzlaff，又译郭实猎）发表在《中国丛报》上的一篇文章，题为《红楼梦》[③]。该文主要将原著故

[①] 黄生太：《〈红楼梦〉拟声词及其英译研究》，博士论文，上海外国语大学，2011年，第53—75页。

[②] 此处"国外"主要涉及英国和美国等西方英语国家。

[③] 《中国丛报》（*The Chinese Repository*），又译《中国文库》。题为《红楼梦》的那篇文章，英文名称是"Hung Lou Meng"，或"Dreams in the Red Chamber"。

事梗概介绍给西方读者。从19世纪中叶迄今研究势头日趋强劲,现已有西方红学、欧美红学、英美红学(姜其煌语)或英语红学(葛锐语)等不同称谓。

总体而论,西方红学的成长深受国内红学发展影响,两者有着十分密切的关系。从总体上来看,比起《红楼梦》英译,西方学者似乎对原著更感兴趣。有关西方红学研究对象及热点,可以概括为九个方面:"《红楼梦》里的哲学思想;传统评点研究;女性主义文学、性别、性和女性研究;叙事结构和技巧;虚构型作品《红楼梦》;情;人物研究和比较研究;《红楼梦》的清代续书;还有一些非主流特殊话题诸如表亲婚姻、饮食文化和园林美学"①,而有关《红楼梦》人物形象英译的讨论很少见到。

笔者利用 ProQuest 学位论文库提供的资源②,分别输入 Hong lou meng、The Dream of the Red Chamber、the Story of the Stone、zhonghui novels、Chinese classical/vernacular novels 等关键词后搜索出国外与《红楼梦》相关学位论文仅1篇与本书研究有关联,具体内容如下。

黄国彬(Laurence Wong)博士论文③——《红楼梦文学翻译研究——以大卫·霍克斯英译本为中心》(*A Study of the Literary Translations of the Hong Lou Meng: With Special Reference to David Hawkes's English Version*),以英、法、德、意四种语言译就的11种《红楼梦》译本为讨论霍译本的参照对象,通过分析原作个性化语言(idiolect)、方言(dialect)、语域(register)和风格(style)等文学特色在这11个译本中的体现情况,其中第三章"个性化语言"和第四章"方言"及第五章"语域"提到《红楼梦》众多人物如刘姥姥、李贵、冯紫英、马道婆、张太医、北静王、史湘云、贾元春、贾政、贾雨村、甄士隐、贾宝玉、蒋玉菡、秦钟、贾母、薛蟠、焦大、林黛玉、王夫人、茗烟等个性化语言的

---

① 葛锐:《英语红学研究纵览》,《红楼梦学刊》2007年第3期。
② ProQuest 学位论文全文库是目前国内唯一提供国外高质量学位论文全文的数据库,主要收录来自欧美国家2000余所知名大学的优秀博硕士论文,目前中国境内可以共享的论文已经达到304781篇,涉及文、理、工、农、医等多个领域。
③ Laurence Wong, *A Study of the Literary Translations of the Hong Long Meng: With Special Reference to David Hawkes's English Version*, Graduate Department of East Studies, University of Toronto, 1992, pp. 212-305.

翻译对人物形象的塑造的重要性。

但是，黄文仅限于呈现翻译现象，而未就其展开深入探究，譬如人物形象采用何种方法译出、人物形象译出是否体现原著特征等。

可见，令人遗憾的是，《红楼梦》人物形象英译问题迄今没有深入研究资料面世，对于英译人物形象的关注远远滞后于《红楼梦》英译研究中其他领域探究。

综合国内外文章、专著、学位论文所述，目前的《红楼梦》人物形象英译研究当中主要存在着以下问题。

（1）研究方法单一，研究者采用"感悟式"和"印象式"分析方法，绝大多数研究以定性为主。只是在近年来开始有文章将语料库介入相关研究[①]，为《红楼梦》人物形象英译研究提供了定性定量相结合的可能性。

（2）有关《红楼梦》人物形象英译研究仍然处于零散状态，相应专著迄今空白，对于英译《红楼梦》作品人物形象的塑造过程缺乏研究，对霍译本中出现的大量"增义显形"现象迄今尚未纳入研究视野。

（3）从语料库翻译研究方法被介绍到国内至今已有十多年的时间，国内的相关研究经历了从介绍综述到理论探讨与实证研究的快速发展。平行语料库建设已经具备一定规模，基于平行语料库的《红楼梦》语言对比与翻译研究也取得了较为丰硕的成果，但对《红楼梦》基于语料库的研究大多就《红楼梦》的语言表述、文化现象翻译等对一个或几个译本进行研究，包括叙事标记语英译[②]、译者风格[③]，也有应用系统功能语言学的人际功能理论分析《红楼梦》人物话语和人物塑造[④]，而从显化翻译视角研究《红楼梦》人物形象的鲜有涉及，《红楼梦》人物形象翻译是

[①] 姚琴：《基于平行语料库的〈红楼梦〉意义显化考察——以霍译本林黛玉人物特征为例》，《外语教学与研究》2013年第3期；刘泽权、朱虹：《〈红楼梦〉中、英文本中刘姥姥形象的对比——以刘姥姥话语的人际功能分析为例》，《翻译季刊》2007年第44期。

[②] 刘泽权、田璐：《红楼梦叙事标记语及其英译——基于语料库的对比分析》，《外语学刊》2009年第1期。

[③] 刘泽权、闫继苗：《基于语料库的译者风格与翻译策略研究》，《解放军外国语学院学报》2010年第33期。

[④] 刘泽权、朱虹：《〈红楼梦〉中、英文本中刘姥姥形象的对比——以刘姥姥话语的人际功能分析为例》，《翻译季刊》2007年第44期；刘泽权、赵烨：《〈红楼梦〉人物"哭态"探析》，《河北学刊》2009年第29期。

红学研究中尚待探讨的重要课题。

(二)《红楼梦》的中英文版本研究

版本是翻译研究的基础,正如欧阳健指出的那样:"版本乃红学之本,关系到千百万读者以哪个本子为《红楼梦》的真本,作为阅读、鉴赏、研究对象的大问题。"①

"《红楼梦》的创作,经历了'增删五次'的过程,有人认为这五次增删,都可能有各自的版本流传于世。而它的流传情况,又增加了其复杂性。《红楼梦》的最后一次定稿,完成于乾隆庚辰年(1760),而书的付梓,却是在乾隆辛亥年(1791)。在此之前,它一直是以抄本的形式,在读者中流传。作者的增删,抄手的讹误,后人的校改,使它的版本现象变得极为错综复杂。"②

关于《红楼梦》的中文版本,根据冯其庸、李希凡先生主编的《红楼梦大辞典》③所载,就有146种(其中包括一些未见版本)。

《红楼梦》中文版本分为两大系统:一是八十回抄本系统,因为大多带有脂砚斋、畸笏叟等人的批语,所以习惯上称为脂本系统;二是一百二十回刊印本系统,最早由程伟元、高鹗整理刊印,所以又称程高本或程本系统。

抄本系统包括甲戌本、己卯本、庚辰本、列宁格勒藏本(列藏本)、有正本(戚序本)、蒙府本、南图本、靖藏本、甲辰本(又称"梦序本")、梦稿本(又名"杨藏本")、己酉本(舒序本)、郑藏本等。

印本系统包括程甲本、霍底本、东观阁本、抱青阁本、藤花榭本、三让堂本、王希廉评本、妙复轩评本、王姚合评本、王张姚评本、王蝶合评本、中华索隐本、亚东初排本、亚东重排本、商务本、世界本、开明洁本、作家本、人民文学本、艺术研究院新校本、浙江文艺本、江苏古籍本、齐鲁本等。

《红楼梦》作为一部文学经典具有恒久的魅力,它在中国文化里产生、流传,在异域文化里也得到传播,这主要是通过它的译文得以实

---

① 欧阳健:《眼别真赝 心识古今——和蔡义江先生讨论〈红楼梦〉版本》,《红楼梦学刊》1994年第3期。

② 郑向前:《〈红楼梦〉早期抄本研究综述》,《红楼梦学刊》1991年第3期。

③ 冯其庸、李希凡:《红楼梦大辞典》,文化艺术出版社2010年版。

现的。

《红楼梦》在风行海内的同时，很快流传到海外各地。"早在乾隆五十八年（1793）便走出国门，传入日本，这时，距程甲本的印刊只有一年多。19世纪，有了英、日、俄文的摘译本和英文节译本。到20世纪，陆续有了日文、英文、俄文、法文、西班牙文、捷克文、缅甸文、朝鲜文、越南文、蒙古文等世界上主要语言文字的全译本，以及德文、荷兰文、意大利文、匈牙利文、罗马尼亚文、泰国文的节译本。"①

《红楼梦》历经160多年，产生27种外文语言的83个外文译本，仅英译本就有19种之多。②

据《英语世界中国古典文学之传播》一书记述③，《红楼梦》英译史如下：

（1）《红楼梦》的英译发端于1830年以英汉对照方式发表的第三回中"西江月"词二首，译者是英国人J. F. Davis。从那以后，在报纸杂志上陆续出现《红楼梦》片段英译，如E. C. Bowra译前八回（1868—1869）。（摘译）

（2）1846年，收入各种选集的有R. Thom所译《红楼梦》第六回的部分片段译文。（摘译）

（3）1864—1869年，E. C. Bowra摘译《红楼梦》第八回。（摘译）

（4）1885年，H. A. Giles译《红楼梦：述宝玉的故事》。（摘译）

（5）以单行本出版发行的由H. B. Joly所译《红楼梦》一至五十六回（上册，1892年；下册，1893年）。（节译）

（6）1927年，王良志的节译本《红楼梦》分九十五章在纽约出版。（节译）

（7）1928年，E. Hudson译第四回，名为"一个老而又老的故事"，

---

① 王宏印：《〈红楼梦〉诗词曲赋英译比较研究》，陕西师范大学出版社2001年版，第1页。
② 陈宏薇将《红楼梦》英译事业分成三个阶段，但只阐释了9种英译本，而江帆在其博士论文中阐释了11种英译。参见陈宏薇、江帆《难忘的历程——〈红楼梦〉英译事业的描写性研究》，《中国翻译》2003年第5期；江帆《他乡的石头记：〈红楼梦〉百年英译史研究》，博士论文，复旦大学，2007年。
③ 黄鸣奋：《英语世界中国古典文学之传播》，学林出版社1997年版，第127—128页。

主人公为宝玉。(摘译)

(8) 1929 年,王际真的节译本《红楼梦》分五十九章出版,次版分六十章在 1958 年出版。(节译)

(9) 1933 年,袁家骅、石明的节译本《红楼梦:断鸿零雁记选》(中英对照) 出版。(摘译)

(10) 1946 年,高克毅所译《刘姥姥》。(摘译)

(11) 1958 年,F. McHugh 和 I. McHugh 姐妹根据 F. Kuhn 的德文译本转译的围绕宝、黛、钗三个人物的剪辑故事,分五十章出版。(节译)

(12) 1964 年,杨宪益、戴乃迭译《红楼梦》第十八回至第二十回、第三十二回至第三十四回、第七十四回至第七十五回和第七十七回。(节译)

(13) 1965 年,Ch'u Chai 和 Winberg Chai 所译《红楼梦》第四十一回。(节译)

(14) 1968 年,英国传教士神父班索尔翻译但未出版的《红楼梦》全译本[①]。

(15) 1972 年,C. Birch 所译《红楼梦》第六十三回至第六十九回。(节译)

(16) 1973 年,张心沧以"葬花"为题译第二十三回。(节译)

(17) 1991 年,黄新渠出版了他的缩写译本《〈红楼梦〉:一个中国贵族家庭的长篇故事》。(节译)

(18) 《红楼梦》的全译本由 David Hawkes 与 John Minford 的合译本(1973 年),共五卷,总书名为 *The Story of the Stone*,由英国企鹅出版集团 (The Penguin Group) 出版。Hawkes 翻译了前三卷,包含了《红楼梦》的前八十回,后又指导其女婿 John Minford 翻译了后两卷,包含了《红楼梦》的后四十回。第一卷名为 *The Golden Days* (1973 年);第二卷名为 *The Crab-Flower Club* (1977 年);第三卷名为 *The Warning Voice* (1980 年);第四卷名为 *The Debt of Tears* (1982 年);第五卷名为 *The Dreamer Wakes* (1986 年)。(全译)

(19) 1978 年,杨宪益、戴乃迭伉俪的合译本,译名为 *A Dream of*

[①] 另见王金波、王燕《被忽视的第一个〈红楼梦〉120 回英文全译本——邦斯尔神父〈红楼梦〉英译文简介》,《红楼梦学刊》2010 年第 1 期。

Red Mansions，共三卷，由中国外文出版社出版。（全译）

除了以上的19种正式出版的译本以外，还有未经面世的译本值得一提：传说中的Thomas Francis Wade（威妥玛）译本，新西兰人Edward T. C. Werner（魏纳）曾于1927年发表论文，比较此译本和乔利译本①，但这一译本始终未曾正式出版。吴世昌先生在《红楼梦探源》的附录《〈红楼梦〉西文译本和论著》中也指出，由于该译本未曾出版，因此未将其列入书目。②

（三）对《红楼梦》英译本及其底本的选择与语料库的建立

《红楼梦》的一百二十回英文全译本——杨译本和霍译本的出版，"不论在文化交流的意义上或是译事的发展上都是有里程碑意义的大事"③，其问世在《红楼梦》英译史上具有划时代的意义，为中国与世界的文化交流做出了巨大的贡献。

霍译《红楼梦》由企鹅出版公司出版后，"顿时成为经典译著"④，受到了学者的一致赞叹。

1980年霍克斯《石头记》第三卷《哀世之音》出版之时，英国《泰晤士报》（*The Times*）评论道："《红楼梦》这一中国文学中最伟大的爱情故事在霍克斯的英译本中得到了完美的艺术再现。这部译者全身心译介的作品流畅生动，是一部真正的杰作。"⑤

《纽约书评》（*The New York Review of Books*）赞誉霍译为"一部光彩夺目、生动逼真的杰作……无愧于原作的深刻"⑥。

美国汉学家葛浩文（Howard Goldblatt）是世界首席翻译家之一，他

---

① E. C. Wener, "Correspondence: The Translation of Chinese", *The China Journal*, Vol. VI, No. 4, April, 1927, pp. 175 – 177.

② 吴世昌：《书目甲·红楼梦的西文译本及论著》，载吴世昌《吴世昌全集第七卷·红楼梦探源》，河北教育出版社2003年版，第380—385页。详见第385页"我未见威氏译文，未列入本书目"。

③ 王宏印：《〈红楼梦〉诗词曲赋英译比较研究》，陕西师范大学出版社2001年版，第2页。

④ 刘宓庆：《文化翻译论纲》，湖北教育出版社1999年版，第5页。

⑤ David Hawkes (trans.), *The Story of the Stone*, Harmondsworth: Penguin Books, Vol. 3, 1980, the cover.

⑥ David Hawkes (trans.), *The Story of the Stone*, Harmondsworth: Penguin Books, Vol. 1, 1973, the cover.

评介霍克斯的《石头记》"没有辜负几乎来自各个大洲的汉学家、评论家和读者的期望。他的译文权威、精湛、优美……完全胜任把中国这部 18 世纪的伟大世情小说的方方面面向英语世界读者传达的任务"①，译本在很大程度上"能使人获得接近阅读原著的享受"②。

许国璋对霍克斯翻译《红楼梦》评价道："我觉得最可重视之点，在于他注意到文化情境之移植，使西方读者不仅读到两个世纪以前的一部中国小说，而且看到中国社会的一个侧面，领略其中风光与人物。其翻译贴切处，为近时兴起的社会语言学提供了最好的例证。"③

戴乃迭，作为《红楼梦》在英语世界最早全译本的完成者之一及牛津大学汉学科学士学位的第一位获得者，于 1980 年在《伦敦大学亚非学院学报》发表书评高度评价霍克斯《石头记》前八十回译文。书评从三个大方面肯定了霍译本的独特与价值所在。认为：首先，在版本处理上明智、合理；其次，在丫鬟姓名意译处理上对西方读者帮助巨大；最后，摒弃注脚，通过增译原文来使引用或典故清楚明白，也有助于霍译本再现原文的文学风味。故而，最终评价道："霍克斯的伟大成就在于以优美的英文使得这部中国名著能够为西方读者所阅读"，并认为自己的译本 *A Dream of Red Mansions* 与之相比恐怕只能是提供语言学习的直译本。④

其实与霍译本几乎同时代出现的全译本，即由杨宪益、戴乃迭夫妇翻译的 *A Dream of Red Mansions*。称为"杨译本"和"霍译本"的这两个全译本可谓各有千秋，在学术界和普通读者中都得到了广泛认可。

本书的研究译本只采用由霍克斯翻译的《红楼梦》的前八十回，原因如下：

《红楼梦》的前八十回是曹雪芹所写，后四十回是由高鹗等人续写；

---

① Howard Goldblatt, "(Untitled Review) Cao Xueqin. The Story of the Stone. 1: The Golden Days. 2: The Crab-Flower Club. David Hawkes (tr.), Bloomington, In Indiana University Press, 1979", China, *World literature Today*, Vol. 54, No. 2, Spring, 1980, p. 333.

② 林煌天：《中国翻译辞典》，湖北教育出版社 1997 年版，第 1044 页。

③ 许国璋：《借鉴与拿来》，《外国语》1979 年第 3 期。

④ Gladys Yang, "(Untitled Review) David Hawkes (tr.): The Story of the Stone. A Novel in Five Volumes by Cao Xueqin. Vol. I: The Golden Days. Vol. II: The Crab-flower Club. Bloomington, Ind.: Indiana University Press, 1979", *Reviews Bulletin of the School of Oriental and African Studies*, University of London, Vol. 43, No. 3, 1980, pp. 621-622.

相似的是，对于《红楼梦》的英语翻译，前八十回由霍克斯本人亲自完成，后四十回由闵福德在霍克斯的指导下完成的，考虑到原著作者的创作和译者的翻译的一致性，本书的研究译本采用由霍克斯翻译的《红楼梦》的前八十回，以力求中英文研究语料的典型性和对应性的完整。

本书的对比译本采用由杨宪益、戴乃迭夫妇翻译的《红楼梦》的前八十回，原因如下：

由于这两个全译本均产生于20世纪七八十年代，所以译本比较方面的研究亦多为共时性的。杨氏夫妇是译著等身的杰出翻译家，曹雪芹原著所融合的中国几千年的文化传统在杨氏译本中得到了较为忠实的再现。杨译本在准确传达信息的同时，保存了源语文化特色。Baker认为两个类比语料库"必须涵盖相似的领域、采用相同的语言、有着相似的时间跨度并具有可比的文字长度"①。霍克斯翻译的《红楼梦》的前八十回和杨宪益、戴乃迭夫妇翻译的《红楼梦》的前八十回刚好满足上述条件，因此，两种译本具有很强的对比性。

在选定了进行比较研究的译本之后，就需要确定译本使用的底本。在大多数情况下，翻译的底本至少在文字上是固定不变的，尽管其意义可能因人而异。然而，《红楼梦》这部中国古典小说却存在诸多不同中文版本，因此译者在建立语料库过程中首先遇到的问题就是对译本底本的选择。而要对《红楼梦》的译本进行研究，了解和确定译者当时所根据的底本无疑成为研究工作的首要步骤。因为如果没有确定译者所遵循的底本，那么对译本的评论研究就成了无源之水，无本之木，对译者的评价也必失之公允。

首先，关于《红楼梦》霍译底本，学界众说纷纭。

Hawkes自己在"导言"中说：

It is somewhat surprising fact that the most popular book in the whole of Chinese literature remained unpublished for nearly thirty years after its author's death, and exists in several different versions, none of which can be pointed to as definitely "correct". (Hawkes, 1973: 15)

---

① M. Baker, "Corpora in Translation Studies: An Overview and Some Suggestions for Future Research", *Target*, Vol.7, No.2, 1995, p.234.

中国文学中最受欢迎的这部小说竟然在作者死后近三十年才得以公开发行,并且还存在着不同的版本,甚至没有一个版本可以说是绝对"正确",这多少令人吃惊。(笔者自译)

即使在霍译《红楼梦》第一卷"序言"部分,霍克斯自己就底本所做的两处简短说明已经显示前后不一:

a. This translation, though occasionally following the text of one or other of the manuscripts in the first eighty chapters, will nevertheless be a translation of the whole 120 chapters of the Gao E edition.①

本书所译前八十回虽然间或参照这个或那个抄本,但是整本翻译还是以高鹗一百二十回本为底本。(笔者自译)

b. In translating this novel I have felt unable to stick faithfully to any single text. I have mainly followed Gao E's version of the first chapter as being more consistent, though less interesting, than the other ones; but I have frequently followed a manuscript reading in subsequent chapters, and in a few, rare instances I have made small emendations of my own.②

翻译这本小说,我感觉根本无法忠实参照某个单一版本。比起别的版本来,高鹗底本虽然不太有趣,但由于前后更为一致,故在第一章翻译中我主要还是以这个本子作为蓝本,在其后章节翻译中,我不断参照抄本,有时还自己做一些小修订。(笔者自译)

在上述两处引文中,高鹗底本在霍克斯《红楼梦》翻译中的参照比重实际上自相矛盾。如果根据 a,高鹗底本为主要参照蓝本;而如果依据

---

① David Hawkes (trans.), *The Story of The Stone* (Volume Ⅰ-Ⅲ), London: The Penguin Books Ltd., 1973, p.18.
② Ibid., pp.45-46.

b，高鹗底本只在第一回作为主要参照蓝本，而整部书所参照底本应该是一个百衲本，且经过译者加工的本子。因此，目前译界对于霍译底本有三种观点。

第一种观点认为霍译底本是一个具有"独创性"的底本，如王宏印在《试论霍译〈红楼梦〉体制之更易于独创》① 中对霍克斯上述言语做了如下阐释：

> 然而，最为重要的还是霍克斯第一卷"序言"中的最后一段话②，其中不仅讲了他所谓《石头记》的译本，实际上是一个译者参考众多资料经过重构而产生的一个理想译本的底本，而且说明译者的翻译宗旨，是尽可能传译出这部未完成的艺术杰作中的一切思想的和艺术的东西。

第二种观点认为，由于霍译本参照底本的复杂性，不可能也没必要去寻根究底。如范圣宇在其专著《〈红楼梦〉管窥》中认为：

> 要准确无误地指出霍克斯在翻译时究竟哪一段参照了哪一种底本似乎不太可能，也没这个必要，因为如果底本文字相同，探讨他究竟是依据哪种底本显得没有什么意义，如果底本文字有出入，以英文翻译为准则就可以知道他参考的是哪一种底本了。③

第三种观点是在学界占主流的观点，认为霍译本主要参照底本为程本。

姜其煌在《〈红楼梦〉霍克斯英文全译本》一文中明确写道：《红楼梦》霍克斯英文八十回全译本，主要根据程高本译出。④

洪涛认为，"既然已知道霍克斯是以程本为主，那么，他多据程本来

---

① 王宏印：《试论霍译〈红楼梦〉体制之更易与独创》，载刘士聪、崔永禄等编《红楼译评——〈红楼梦〉翻译研究论文集》，南开大学出版社 2004 年版，第 77 页。
② 此处指上面引文 b。
③ 范圣宇：《〈红楼梦〉管窥》，中国社会科学出版社 2004 年版，第 26 页。
④ 姜其煌：《〈红楼梦〉霍克斯英文全译本》，《红楼梦学刊》1980 年第 1 期。

翻译，这是不言而喻的事"①。

从霍克斯的翻译笔记看，我们知道他主要的翻译底本是以程本为底本整理出来的"旧行本"②。在注释中洪涛对"旧行本"做了解释：

"旧行本"指曹雪芹、高鹗《红楼梦》，人民文学出版社，1964。按照周汝昌主编《红楼梦辞典》的"凡例"，这个本子简称为"旧行本"（相对于1982年人民文学出版社的"新校本"而言），广东人民出版社，1987。

霍克斯本人谈到翻译底本时说：

最初以最通用的120回本为底本，当脂砚斋评批本提供了更好的文字时就依脂本。③

但后来我才开始对本子之间的差异等问题感兴趣，原因是你开始认真工作的时候，所有的问题，比如故事的不一致、情节的混乱、本子之间的差异，等等，都冒出来了，当然，那些书和资料也都是逐渐出版的，我很迟才得到那个乾隆抄本。开始工作的时候我没怎么考虑版本问题，开始的时候只有人民文学出版社的本子和俞平伯的80回校本，后来书才慢慢多了。④

1998年访谈中霍克斯提到版本问题时谈得最清楚：

我开始时没有太考虑版本问题，我以人民文学出版社的《红楼梦》（四卷本）着手翻译，但那时手中也有俞平伯的《红楼梦八十回

---

① 洪涛：《女体和国族——从〈红楼梦〉翻译看跨文化移植与学术知识障》，国家图书馆出版社2010年版，第128页。
② 洪涛：《〈红楼梦〉翻译研究与套用"目的论"、"多元系统论"的隐患——以〈红译艺坛〉为论析中心》，《红楼梦学刊》2010年第2期。
③ David Hawkes, "The Translator, the Mirror and the Dream—Some Observations on a New Theory", in John Minford & Siu-kit Wong (ed.), *Classical, Modern and Humane Essays in Chinese Literature*, Hong Kong: The Chinese University Press, 1989, p. 159.
④ 转引自范圣宇《〈红楼梦〉管窥》，中国社会科学出版社2004年版，第27页。

校本》。①

可见，霍克斯翻译中依从最多或者叫作翻译底本的就是人民文学的四卷本即霍克斯所谓的高（鹗）本，参阅最多的是俞平伯的八十回校本即霍克斯所谓的脂本或抄本。这一点弟子兼女婿及《红楼梦》后四十回的译者闵福德说得更为清楚：

> 霍克斯的书架上当然有俞平伯八十回校本，甲戌、庚辰本，和新近抄本的程高影印本，但他工作的脚本一直是人民文学出版社由启功注释的四卷本。他做过记号的书目前还保存在岭南大学的图书馆。②

笔者查了1964年人民文学出版社出版的《红楼梦》本子，从"关于本书的整理情况"这一章节中，找到了此版本的底本说明："本书整理，系以程伟元乾隆壬子（1792）活字本（校记中简称'乙'本）作底本"③，说明霍克斯翻译时所依据的这个人民本大致就是程乙本。在霍克斯英译笔记中前半部分多以人民本称之，后半部分多称为程本。

综上，在创建霍译本汉英平行语料库时，本书可以选取《红楼梦》"旧行本"，即曹雪芹、高鹗所编的由人民文学出版社1964年出版的《红楼梦》，即程乙本，作为底本对应。令笔者欣喜的是，由企鹅出版集团授权上海外语教育出版社出版的英汉对照的霍译本④已然面世，这为创建霍

---

① Connie Chan, "Appendix: Interview with David Hawkes", *The Story of the Stone's Journey to the West: A Study in Chinese-English Translation History*, Conducted at 6 Addison Crescent, Oxford, December, 1998, p. 327.
② 转引自范圣宇《〈红楼梦〉管窥》，中国社会科学出版社2004年版，第27页。
③ 曹雪芹、高鹗：《红楼梦》（共四册），启功注释，人民文学出版社1957年版，第1页。
④ 本次汉英对照版《红楼梦》，前八十回的英文部分以霍克斯先生翻译的企鹅出版社《石头记》（*The Story of the Stone*, Penguin Books）1973年版第一卷、1977年版第二卷、1980年版第三卷为底本，参照霍克斯先生《红楼梦英译笔记》（香港岭南大学文学与翻译研究中心，2000年）及相关日记、书信，对现有译文做了全面系统的校订。中文部分则以人民文学出版社1964年竖排版（启功校注）为底本，主要参校《红楼梦八十回校本》（俞平伯校本）、《脂砚斋重评石头记》（庚辰本）、《脂砚斋甲戌抄阅再评石头记》（甲戌本）、《戚蓼生序本石头记》（有正本）、《乾隆抄本百廿回红楼梦稿》（梦稿本），这些都是霍克斯在翻译过程中主要参考过的本子。

译本汉英平行语料库提供了便利。

其次,关于《红楼梦》杨译本底本。

根据杨译本"出版说明",其有关参照底本有下面一段文字:

> Our first eighty chapters have been translated from the photostat edition published by the People's Literature Publishing House, Peking, in September 1973 according to a lithographicedition printed by the Yu-cheng Press, Shanghai, in about 1911. This Yu-cheng edition hadbeen made from a manuscript copy kept by Chi Liao-sheng of the Chienlung era. The lastforty chapters are based on the 120 – chapter edition reprinted by the People's Literature Publishing House, Peking, in 1959 from the movable-type edition of 1792. The ChiLiao-sheng manuscript of the first eighty chapters is one of the earliest copies extant. In our translation certain minor errors and omissions made by the man who copied the original manuscript have been corrected according to other versions. ①

参照译文如下:

> 我们的译本前八十回译自人民文学出版社 1973 年出版的影印本,这一影印本的原本是 1911 年左右上海有正书局出版的石印本,该石印本是乾隆年间戚蓼生保存下来的一种抄本。后四十回译自人民文学出版社于 1959 年校勘重印的 1792 年一百二十回活字印刷本。戚蓼生保留的前八十回手抄本是现存最早的版本之一。在翻译中,我们参照其他版本,修订了抄本中的错误。②

---

① Cao Xueqin & Gao E. , *A Dream of Red Mansions*, Yang Hsien-yi and Gladys Yang (trans) . , Beijing: Foreign Languages Press, 1978, p. ix.

② 陈宏薇、江帆:《难忘的历程——〈红楼梦〉英译事业的描写性研究》,载刘士聪、崔永禄等编《红楼译评——〈红楼梦〉翻译研究论文集》,南开大学出版社 2004 年版,第 57 页。

大中华文库《红楼梦》汉英对照本"前言"中也有类似文字说明：

> 本译本为一百二十回，其中前八十回以"戚蓼生序本"有正大字本为底本，后四十回则以人民文学出版社1974年出版印行的"霍底本"为底本，并参照其他版本对个别地方作了校改或补正。①

依据上述出版说明，杨译本所参照的中文底本前八十回参照"有正本"，即戚序本，后四十回则译自人民文学出版社校勘重印的程乙本。

但作为杨译本审校的著名红学家吴世昌先生以《宁荣两府"不过是个屠宰场而已"吗？——论〈红楼梦〉英译本的"出版说明"》为题撰文，批驳《人民日报》1979年5月8日刊登的报道中将杨译本底本说成是"有正本"和"程乙本"的观点：

> ……译者明明告诉新华社记者说，他们根据北大图书馆的"脂京本"②译出前八十回，而出版社却偏偏说是用"有正本"的复制本译出前八十回。译者明明说，后四十回是据"程甲本"译出，而出版社偏偏说是据"程乙本"。③

该文中他依据自己审校结果，认定杨译本参校的是"脂京本"（"庚辰本"）和"程甲本"。

12年后，这一观点得到呼应：

> 英文120回《红楼梦》全译本，可以我国著名学者、翻译家杨宪益先生及其英籍夫人戴乃迭先生的合译本为代表。此译本前八十回据庚辰本译出，后四十回据程甲本译出，由北京外

---

① Cao Xueqin & Gao E., *A Dream of Red Mansions*, Yang Hsien-yi and Gladys Yang (trans.), Beijing: Foreign Languages Press, 1978.

② "脂京本"即庚辰本，是吴世昌先生"为了批评胡适而提出来的"，后来遭到红学家冯其庸的质疑，详见冯其庸《石头记脂本研究》（人民文学出版社1998年版，第148—151页）"关于所谓'脂京本'的名称问题"一节。

③ 吴世昌：《红楼梦探源外编》，上海古籍出版社1980年版，第487—488页。

文出版社分别于1978年和1980年出版。①

21世纪初，洪涛在《红楼梦》汉英对照本中屡屡发现"张冠李戴"以及原文与译文之间无法对应的现象后，再次对杨译本中文底本提出质疑，并依据文字校对推测杨译本有可能根据"庚辰本"来翻译：

> 查戚序本中无"蚩尤"，亦无"刘庭芝"，庚辰本等抄本却有。杨氏夫妇应该是根据有"蚩尤""刘庭芝"的本子来翻译的。②

但洪涛又认为，第九回金荣的那段秽语在"庚辰本"中被保留，而在号称"洁本"的"戚序本"中却被删，且杨译文并未译出，据此看来译者此处又是依据"戚序本"来译的。

有关杨译本底本的"有正本"和"庚辰本"之争，范圣宇就回目的翻译判断杨译本所参照的底本应当是有正本而非庚辰本。

> 所以，更可能是《人民日报》的报道出了差错，而"出版说明"则是对的。③

另外，在《〈红楼梦〉管窥》脚注中，范圣宇就杨译底本做了更为详尽的阐述：

> 关于杨宪益小说使用的底本究竟是哪个本子，杨先生自己的说法就不甚一致。如上所述，他在英译本"出版说明"里说的是有正本；但在《银翘集》④ 中却说是《脂砚斋重评石头记》；而在他的回忆录《漏船载酒忆当年》中，他说的是吴世昌

---

① 王丽娜：《〈红楼梦〉在国外的流传、翻译与研究》，《国家图书馆学刊》1992年第1期。
② 洪涛：《评"汉英经典文库本"〈红楼梦〉英译的疏失错误》，《红楼梦学刊》2006年第4期。
③ 范圣宇：《〈红楼梦〉管窥》，中国社会科学出版社2004年版，第24页。
④ 如水：《记杨宪益先生》，载《银翘集》，天地图书公司1995年版，第126页。

先生帮助他与戴乃迭参照了多种手抄本和印刷本，择善而从，编成翻译的本子，这样看来他的译本又是一个"百衲本"了。综合这几种说法，并仔细校读译本，笔者认为它在翻译过程中使用的主要是有正本，并主要参照庚辰本对其中的讹误做了校正。也就是说"出版说明"的说法是准确的。①

语料库整体的设计和语料的汇集对于"基于该语料库的研究的信度和效度都具有十分重大的作用"②。它直接影响到语料库所设计的研究目标能不能有效实现。

霍译本汉英平行语料库创建步骤：

第一步：语料的采集。

语料的采集有两种方法：一是通过光电扫描或键盘输入制作电子文本；二是利用网络上已有的电子文本，并将其转化为所需的格式。由于目前网上《红楼梦》霍底本③有现成文本文档，本书在保证质量的前提下采用后一种方式，这样不仅避免简单的重复劳动，又可以降低语料库的建设成本，提高效率。霍译本电子版是扫描并校对得出④，并且依据上海外语教育出版社出版的英汉对照的《红楼梦》霍译本进行核对。

第二步：语料的格式化。

除了语料质量，还应保持语料库中语料存储的规范性。从网上采集的原始语料需加工为统一的格式后才能进入到语料库中。为了保持语料的纯洁性，将各种语料统一转化为纯文本（text）格式，即以". txt"文件的形式存储，以借助 text 文档中不含任何页面显示标记的特点避免"脏字符"对语料内容的干扰。

第三步：相关语料提取。

利用汉字分割软件（ICTCLAS 2008）和语料检索软件（WORD-

---

① 范圣宇：《〈红楼梦〉管窥》，中国社会科学出版社 2004 年版，第 28 页。
② Kennedy, G. D., *An Introduction to Corpus Linguistics*, London/New York: Longman, 1998, p. 60.
③ 程乙本电子版来源：http://bbsopenow.net/showthread.php?s=c12211171cb4d4d5299ca6a32fdf6756&t=43473。
④ 杨、霍译本电子版均系冯庆华教授携同众位弟子合力扫描并校对后得出，在此一并致谢。

SMITH 6.0.0），提取相关语料并建立平行语料库。

杨译本汉英平行语料库与霍译本汉英平行语料库创建步骤类似，但在第一步"语料的采集"上，由于没有可供编辑的《红楼梦》汉英对照本中文 Word 文档，将程乙本第一回至第八十回与纸质版《红楼梦》大中华文库汉英对照本中的中文进行逐一对照核查，包括标点符号、段落划分和空行等文本特征，将核对结果输入电脑，建立了可供编辑的杨译底本电子文档。

至于语料格式化和语料提取方法与霍译本平行语料库的创建相仿，此处不赘述。

二 显化翻译研究综述

（一）翻译共性与显化假说

目前，基于语料库的翻译研究做出的最突出的贡献在于对"翻译共性"的研究。所谓翻译共性（translation universals），亦称翻译普遍性或翻译普遍特征，是指翻译语言作为一种客观存在的语言变体，相对于源语语言或目标语原创语言从整体上表现出来的一些规律性语言特征，指"翻译文本而不是原话语中出现的典型语言特征，并且这些特征不是特定语言系统干扰的结果"[①]。Mauranen 等指出，Baker 所著《语料库语言学与翻译研究：意义与应用》一文确立了"语言学翻译共性思想在翻译研究核心中的一席之地"[②]。

Chesterman[③] 将翻译共性划分为两大类：源语型翻译共性（S-universals）和目标语型翻译共性（T-universals）。前者是基于原文与译文之间的关系，关注译者对源语文本的处理方式。后者是关于目标语中

---

① M. Baker, "Corpus Linguistics and Translation Studies: Lmplications and Applications", in M. Baker, G. Francis and E. Tognini-Bonelli (ed.), *Text and Technology: In Honor of John Sinclair*, Philadelphia & Amsterdam: John Benjamins, 1993, p. 243.

② A. Mauranen & P. Kujamaki (eds.), *Translation Universals: Do They Exist?* Amsterdam: John Benjamins, 2004, p. 1.

③ A. Chesterman, "Beyond the Particular", in A. Mauranen and P. Kujamaki (ed.), *Translation Universals: Do They Exist?* Amsterdam: John Benjamins, 2004; A. Chesterman, "Hypothesis about Translation Universals", in G. Hansen, K. Malmkjar and D. Gile (ed.), *Claims, Changes and Challenges in Translation Studies*, Selected Contributions for the EST Congress, Copenhagen, 2001, Amsterdam: John Benjamins, 2004.

翻译文本与原创文本之间的关系，重点放在译者对目标语语言的处理方式上。柯飞所提出的"翻译共性"则属于前者，是指"译文中呈现的有别于原文的一些典型的、跨语言的、有一定普遍性的特征"①。Baker 所谓的"翻译普遍特征"属于后一类，她将其定义为"翻译文本而不是源语中出现的典型语言特征，并且这些特征不是特定语言系统干扰的结果"②，即指翻译语言作为一种客观存在的语言变体，相对于目标语原创语言，在整体上表现出来的一些规律特征。这一定义有两重含义：第一，翻译共性是特定语言模式的概率性分布特征，主要在归纳的基础上获得；第二，翻译共性由翻译过程本身造成，与两种语言系统之间的差异无关。

Baker 在前人③的研究成果基础上，首先提出了基于语料库的翻译普遍特征（universal features of translation）的假设，包括六个方面：（1）译文显化程度显著提高；（2）译文中消歧和简化；（3）合乎译文语法性；（4）通过省译和词汇重设避免重复源语词汇；（5）超额再现目标语语言特征；（6）某些语言特征在译文中表现出特定的分布类型。④ 就翻译共性种类而言，Baker 明确提出至少四种可能构成翻译普遍性假说的特征：显化（explicitation）、简单化（simplifieation）、规范化（normalization）、整齐化（leveling-out）。⑤ 简而言之，Baker 提出的翻译共性具体包

---

① 柯飞：《翻译中的隐和显》，《外语教学与研究》2005 年第 4 期。

② M. Baker，"Corpus Linguistics and Translation Studies：Lmplications and Applications"，in M. Baker，G. Francis and E. Tognini-Bonelli（ed.），*Text and Technology*：*In Honor of John Sinclair*，Philadelphia & Amsterdam：John Benjamins，1993，p. 243.

③ R. Vanderauwera，*Dutch Novels Translated into English*：*The Transformation of A "Minority" Literature*，Amsterdam：Rodopi，1985；S. Blum – Kulka，"Shifts of Cohesion and Coherence in Translation"，in J. House & S. Blum-Kulka（ed.），*Inter-lingual and Lntercultural Communication. Discourse and Cognition in Translation and Second Language Acquisition Studies*，TüBingen：Gunter Narr Verlag，1986；M. Shlesinger，"Interpreter Latitude VS Due Process：Simultaneous and Consecutive Lnterpretation in Multilingual Trials"，in S. Tirkkonen-Condit（ed.），*Empirical Research in Translation and Lntercultural Studies*，Tübingen：Gunter Narr Verlag，1991.

④ M. Baker，"Corpus Linguistics and Translation Studies：Lmplications and Applications"，in M. Baker，G. Francis and E. Tognini-Bonelli（ed.），*Text and Technology*：*In Honor of John Sinclair*，Philadelphia & Amsterdam：John Benjamins，1993，pp. 243 – 245.

⑤ M. Baker，"Corpus-based Translation Studies：The Challenges That Lie Ahead"，in H. Somers（ed.），*Terminology*，*LSP and Translation*，Amsterdam：John Benjamins，1996，pp. 176 – 177，180 – 185.

括：显化、消歧和简化、合乎语法性、避免重复、凸显目标语语言特征及其分布六个方面。相关的实证讨论又增加了传统化、标准化、范化、净化等讨论，后来主要集中在显化、简化和范化三个方面，近年来又增加了独特项假设、干扰、非典型搭配、不对称假设等。这些分别以不同语对或语种的语料库为基础，以语际对比或语内类比为模式的实证研究，既有对原有假设的支持，又有不同程度的背离，引起研究者对现有研究的反思。2001 年在丹麦哥本哈根举行的第三届 EST 大会和在芬兰萨翁林纳举行的关于翻译共性研究的大会上，与会者就这一话题进行了深入探讨。①

显化假说被纳入翻译共性研究范围内，成为该家族中的重要一员。"虽然显化研究开展时间不长，却是目前翻译领域中得到最为全面研究的现象之一。"②

"显化"这一术语最早是由法国学者 Vinay 与 Darbelnet 从对法语和英语进行文体对比研究角度提出的。它作为"一种文体翻译技巧"，指"在目标语中对原语中隐含的但可以从语境或情境中推断出的信息加以明确说明的过程"③。Nida 和 Taber 指出，好的译文往往会比原文长，主要因为在翻译过程中译者会通过明示原文中的隐含信息，在一定限度内增加译文的冗余度。④

对显化最早进行系统研究的当属 Blum-Kulka。她于 1986 年提出了著名的"显性假说"，即"译者对原文的解释过程可能导致译文比原文冗长。这一冗长现象表现为译者提高了译文在衔接层次上的显化程度"⑤。

---

① 参见 G. Hansen, K. Malmkjer & D. Gile (eds.), *Claims, Changes and Challenges in Translation Studies*, Amsterdam: John Benjamins, 2004; A. Mauranen & P. Kujamaki (eds.), *Translation Universals: Do They Exist?* Amsterdam: John Benjamins, 2004。

② Elisa Perego, "Evidence of Explicitation in Subtitling: Toward a Categorization", *Across Languages and Cultures*, Vol. 4, No. 1, 2003, p. 68.

③ Jean-Paul Vinay & Jean Darbelnet, *Comparative Stylistics of French and English: A Methodology for Translation*, Translated and edited by Juan C. Sager & M. J. Hamel, Amsterdam & Philadelphia: John Benjamins, 1958/1995, p. 342.

④ E. A. Nida, & C. Taber, *The Theory and Practice of Translation*, Leiden: E. J. Brill, 1969, pp. 164 – 165.

⑤ Blum-Kulka, S., "Shifts of Cohesion and Coherence in Translation", in J. House & S. Blum-Kulka (ed.), *Inter-lingual and Intercultural Communication. Discourse and Cognition in Translation and Second Language Acquisition Studies*, Tübingen: Gunter Narr Verlag, 1986, p. 19.

在她看来，显化现象的产生绝大部分是由翻译过程对原文的阐释造成的，即翻译过程本身固有的特征，而不取决于不同语言对（Language pair）的具体差异（如语法体系差异、文体偏好差别）。

Baker 最初对于显化做了这样的论述："相对于特定原语文本以及原创文本总体而言，翻译文本显化程度显著提高"[1]。随后她又指出："在翻译中，（译者）总体上往往会将各种情况加以详细说明而不是将含糊不清的地方保留下来。"[2]

Séguinot 认为，显化不仅仅指原作中不存在而译作中添加的表述，也包括仅在原文中暗示或只有通过预设才能认识到的信息在译文中加以明示，还包括原文中的某些成分在译文中通过凸显、强调或词汇选择等手段而加以突出的现象。[3]

贺显斌认为，只要译文中的词句意义比原文更清楚、明确、具体、易懂，逻辑关系比原文更明晰，或中心意思比原文更突出，就算发生了明晰化转换。[4]

柯飞进一步指出："作为一种翻译现象，显化（以及隐化）不应只是狭义地指语言衔接形式上的变化，还应包括意义上的显化转换，即在译文中添加了有助于译文读者理解的显化表达，或者说将原文隐含的信息显化于译文中，使意思更明确，逻辑更清楚。"[5]

Pym 也对 Blum-Kulka 的"显性假说"发表过类似看法。他认为，首先，该假说只局限在语篇衔接层次，从严格意义上讲未涉及所有语篇或语篇部分以外的语言使用，更不用说涉及文化方面的问题；其次，该假说"只见树木，不见森林"，看到的只是译本语篇衔接标记的不必要重复，而不是信息从隐化变成显化的完整过程。[6]

---

[1] M. Baker, "Corpus Linguistics and Translation Studies: Implications and Applications", in M. Baker, G. Francis and E. Tognini-Bonelli (ed.), *Text and Technology: In Honor of John Sinclair*, Philadelphia & Amsterdam: John Benjamins, 1993, p. 243.

[2] M. Baker, "Corpus-based Translation Studies: The Challenges That Lie Ahead", in H. Somers (ed.), *Terminology, LSP and Translation*, Amsterdam: John Benjamins, 1996.

[3] Candace Séguinot, "Pragmatics and the Explicitation Hypothesis", *TTR Traduction, Terminologie, Redaction*, Vol. 1, No. 2, 1988, pp. 106–113.

[4] 贺显斌：《英汉翻译过程中的明晰化现象》，《解放军外国语学院学报》2003 年第 4 期。

[5] 柯飞：《翻译中的隐和显》，《外语教学与研究》2005 年第 4 期。

[6] Anthony Pym, "Explaining Explicitation", http://www.fut.es/-apym/welcome.

匈牙利学者 Klaudy 等对显化类型进行了最为系统的分类，提出了强制性（Obligatory）、选择性（Optional）、语用性（Pragmatic）、翻译本身固有（Translation-inherent）四种显化类型。① 其中，"强制性显化"由不同语言在形态、句法、语义方面的差异所致，如从俄语翻译成匈牙利语时必须加冠词，而相反方向要省略冠词。"选择性显化"依赖语言的使用，取决于目标语文本的不同文体取向，即"为了创造出语法正确、自然、近似本族语的句子，译者可能选择使用更为显化的表达方式"②。以上两种显化类型，都涉及目标语中插入语言成分。"语用性显化"由文化差异所致，为了跨越原语与目标语之间的文化鸿沟，译者往往要在译文中加以解释说明。例如，译语读者可能对源语读者熟知的文化概念或地理名词一无所知，因此译者需要在译文中明确该概念或名称。而"翻译本身固有显化"既"不取决于源语与译语间结构、形式或文体方面的差异，也不受制于具体文化特征的语篇成分，而是由翻译过程本身的性质决定的"③。具体来讲，目标语对源语中的思想和想法进行二次加工和整理过程可能会影响译文的长度，因为译者要遵循不同于源语的思考方式，采取更为复杂的认知途径。

显化研究从对比模式上也可分两类：一类是指翻译过程中在译文中添加或明示原文中隐含（implict）语言成分的过程，目的在于更清楚地传达原文中的语法和非语法信息；另一类是指翻译文本相对于译语中非翻译文本所表现出的显性程度（explicitness）提高。前一种显化是源文本与目标文本之间的语际对比基础上的显化，简称语际显化（inter-language explicitation）；而后一种显化是目标语内翻译文本与非翻译文本的比较所表现出的语内类比显化，简称类比显化（comparable explicitation），此二者都应作为显化研究的对象。

显化研究从影响因素方面，又可分为强制性和选择性两种，前者是语言系统影响的结果，后者则取决于译者、翻译过程、目标语规范等多

---

① K. Klaudy & Krisztina Károly, "Implicitation in Translation: Empirical Evidence for Operational Asymmetry in Translation", *Across Languages and Cultures*, Vol. 6, No. 1, 2005, pp. 13 – 28.

② Elisa Perego, "Evidence of Explicitation in Subtitling: toward a Categorization", *Across Languages and Cultures*, Vol. 4, No. 1, 2003, p. 69.

③ Ibid., p. 70.

种因素。而从译者角度,又分为有意识的策略和下意识语言选择的结果。

黄立波和王克非认为,汉英/英汉翻译中的显化可做出分类(如表0-2)。①

表0-2　　　　　　　　　　显化的分类

显化类型		
语内对比ᵃ ($T_1 - T_2$)	形式上(T_1相对于T_2)	强制性
		非强制性
	意义上(T_1相对于T_2)	强制性
		非强制性
语际对比 ($C_{st} - E_{tt} \backslash E_{tt} - C_{st}$)	形式上(E_{st}相对于C_{st}/C_{tt}相对于E_{st})	强制性
		非强制性
	意义上(E_{tt}相对于C_{st}/C_{tt}相对于E_{st})	强制性
		非强制性

注:语内对比也称为类比。T_1=翻译汉语;T_2=原创汉语;C_{st}=汉语原文;E_{tt}=英语译文;E_{st}=英语原文;C_{tt}=汉语译文。"强制性"显化=语言系统差异导致的显化;"非强制性"显化=翻译过程导致的显化。

(二) 前语料库时期的翻译显化研究

因为基于语料库的显化翻译研究离不开对前人研究成果的传承,笔者参照 Laviosa② 和 Olohan③ 的做法,以 Baker④ 的 "Corpus Linguistics and Translation Studies: Implications and Applications" 一文为界,将翻译共性研究划分为前语料库(pre-corpus)和基于语料库(corpus-based)两个时期加以评述。

前语料库时期的翻译显化研究,主要是从语际对比的角度出发;而

---

① 黄立波、王克非:《翻译普遍性研究反思》,《中国翻译》2006 年第 5 期。

② S. Laviosa, *Corpus-based Translation Studies: Theory, Findings and Applications*, Amsterdam: Rodopi, 2002.

③ M. Olohan, *Introducing Corpora in Translation Studies*, London & New York: Routledge, 2004.

④ M. Baker, "Corpus Linguistics and Translation Studies: Implications and Applications", in M. Baker, G. Francis and E. Tognini-Bonelli (ed.), *Text and Technology: In Honor of John Sinclair*, Philadelphia & Amsterdam: John Benjamins, 1993, pp. 233 – 250.

在基于语料库的翻译研究范式下,翻译显化研究呈现出多样化,既有语内类比基础上的研究,又有以语际对比为模式的研究。

这里所谓"前语料库时期"就是指大规模机读翻译文本用于翻译研究之前,通过人工采集原文与译文文本,并对与翻译有关的语言现象进行人工对比、分析和统计的时期。这一时期的翻译共性研究主要表现为从词汇、句法和文体等语际对比的角度关注显化问题。

在语料库翻译方法提出之前,有关显化的研究主要有 Vinay 和 Darbelnet、Nida 和 Taber、Vanderauwera、Blum-Kulka、Klaudy 等。

Vinay 和 Darbelnet[①] 是从对比文体的角度提出这一概念的,他们将显化和隐化视为一组对立的文体翻译技巧,常与信息的获得和损失相联系。所涉及的显化包括词汇显化和信息显化两种,这两种显化表面上都是语境或情境要求的结果,但从本质上讲依然是语言系统差异造成的,属于强制性显化的范畴。

Nida 和 Taber[②] 指出好的译文往往会比原文长,主要是因为在翻译过程中,译者会通过明示原文中的含蓄信息在适当限度内增加译文的冗余度。他们主要是从语言文化差异和方便译文接受者理解原作的角度来探讨翻译中的新信息现象。

Vanderauwera[③] 指出了译者常用的 10 种显化策略,这些技巧均不在语言系统差异影响之列,但与译者的个人文体偏好不无关系,这在一定程度上为后来用语料库研究译者的文体奠定了基础。

Blum-Kulka[④] 从翻译中衔接与连贯的转换入手提出了显化假设(the explicitation hypothesis):翻译过程会使译文相对于原文更加冗长,其表现

---

① Jean-Paul Vinay & Jean Darbelnet, *Comparative Stylistics of French and English: A Methodology for Translation*, Translated and edited by Juan C. Sager & M. J. Hamel, Amsterdam & Philadelphia: John Benjamins, 1958/1995.

② E. A. Nida & C. Taber, *The Theory and Practice of Translation*, Leiden: E. J. Brill, 1969, pp. 164 – 165; E. A. Nida, *Toward a Science of Translating*, Shanghai: Shanghai Foreign Language Education Press, 1964/2004.

③ R. Vanderauwera, *Dutch Novels Translated into English: The Transformation of a "Minority" Literature*, Amsterdam: Rodopi, 1985.

④ S. Blum-Kulka, "Shifts of Cohesion and Coherence in Translation", in J. House & S. Blum-Kulka (ed.), *Inter-lingual and Intercultural Communication. Discourse and Cognition in Translation and Second Language Acquisition Studies*, Tübingen: Gunter Narr Verlag, 1986, p. 19.

形式为衔接方式的显化程度提高。这一假设有两个特点：第一，将显化视为翻译过程内在的属性，摆脱了语言系统差异的影响，使显化研究具体化；第二，从句法的非强制性转换入手，将译者的文体偏好作为参数之一。Blum-Kulka 的论断为后来基于语料库的翻译共性研究提供了重要思路。

Klaudy[①] 将显化分成强制性显化、非强制性显化、语用显化和翻译内在显化四类，各类之间尽管存在一定程度的重合，却让我们认识到显化现象的多样性和多层次性，在此基础上能对翻译共性做出更加全面的认识。

前语料库时期的翻译显化研究主要是指在语际对比基础上翻译文本相对于源本文表现出的形式方面的特点，都是 Baker 基于语料库的翻译共性研究直接或间接的思想来源，研究内容与方法在之后的语料库显化研究中都有不同程度的体现，其共同点是关注翻译文本中的规律性语言使用模式。与 Baker 方法不同的是，这些研究都是以源文本为标准来衡量译文。

相对于基于语料库的方法，前语料库时期的翻译共性研究表现出以下问题：（1）每个研究都是从不同视角，如对比语言学、文体学或翻译研究的角度出发，在对个别概念的认识上存在一定的偏差；（2）在关注焦点上，词汇、句法、文体等层面均有涉及，但缺乏统一的指导原则；（3）对共性的研究主要以语际转换为基础，即相对原语而言译语的普遍特征，限于探讨译文与原文之间的关系，这种二元对立的做法常常将译文视为原文衍生物，在此基础上的理论研究本质上依然是对译文质量的回溯式评估。

尽管如此，这些前期研究为基于语料库的翻译共性研究奠定了基础。

（三）基于语料库的翻译显化研究

语料库翻译学也是对原有翻译研究范式的传承，所不同的是着眼点和方法。前语料库的研究以"源文本"为中心，采用人工的文本对比方法；而基于语料库的研究则以"目标文本"为导向，采用计算机数据提取、统计与分析技术，将关注焦点放在翻译语言上。

语料库用于翻译研究可以追溯到 20 世纪 80 年代，[②] 但当时文本采集

---

① K. Klaudy, "Explicitation", in M. Baker (ed.), *Routledge Encyclopedia of Translation Studies*, London: Routledge, 1998.

② See S. Laviosa, *Corpus-based Translation Studies: Theory, Findings and Applications*, Amsterdam: Rodopi, 2002, p.1.

的规模通常较小,并且多以手工统计为主。20世纪90年代初期,平行对齐的语料数据开始应用于机器翻译。Baker 的《语料库语言学和翻译研究:启示与应用》① 一文,倡导用语料库方法研究翻译,标志着基于语料库的翻译研究范式的诞生。

基于语料库的翻译显化研究打破了前语料库时期研究建立在内省数据基础上演绎式、规定性的规则系统,由规定转向描写,以翻译本体为研究对象,由大规模翻译文本或翻译语言整体入手,采用语内对比与语际对比相结合的模式,对翻译现象进行描写和解释,探索翻译的本质。根据 Baker② 等,翻译共性研究目的在于识别翻译文本的典型语言特征,这样不仅可以揭示"第三类语码"的本质,更重要的是能认识影响翻译行为以及隐藏于此类独特语言形式之下的各种具体的制约因素、压力和动机,从而达到对翻译现象的深层解释。

Baker 对显化的最早界定是"与特定源文本或(目标语中)原创文本总体上相比较,(目标文本)所表现出显性程度的显著提高"③。从这一界定可看出,Baker 当时所讨论的各种翻译共性既有单语内类比(comparable),也有语际对比(inter-lingual)。

单语内类比模式的第一类是对形式词汇或标记的考察,如 Olohan 和 Baker④ 通过对叙述动词(如 say, tell)后选择性"that"在翻译英语语料库(TEC)和英国国家语料库(BNC)中的频次进行考察,发现英译文本中"that"的使用频率要远高于其在英语文本中的使用频率。就此得出结论:英译文本可能更倾向于使用显化程度高的句法形式。

Olohan 考察的同样是对形式成分的选择性显化,具体切入点包括补语标记词 that、关系代词 wh-/what、动词补语小句中的 to be、that 从句中

---

① M. Baker, "Corpus Linguistics and Translation Studies: Implications and Applications", in M. Baker, G. Francis and E. Tognini-Bonelli (ed.), *Text and Technology: In Honor of John Sinclair*, Philadelphia & Amsterdam: John Benjamins, 1993, pp. 233-250.

② Baker, Mona (ed.), *Routledge Encyclopedia of Translation Studies*, Shanghai: Shanghai Foreign Language Education Press, 1998/2004.

③ M. Baker, "Corpus Linguistics and Translation Studies: Implications and Applications", in M. Baker, G. Francis and E. Tognini-Bonelli (ed.), *Text and Technology: In Honor of John Sinclair*, Philadelphia & Amsterdam: John Benjamins, 1993, p. 243.

④ M. Olohan & M. Baker, "Reporting That in Translated English: Evidence for Subconscious Process of Explicitation", *Across Languages and Cultures*, Vol. 1, 2000, pp. 141-172.

should 省略与否等选择性句法成分和词汇成分在翻译文本和目标语非翻译文本中的使用情况。① Olohan 认为翻译文本中对选择性句法成分的过多使用，目的在于明示各种语法和词汇关系，对选择性词汇，如人称代词的使用频次低，说明译文为了明示语义信息往往会以名词化结构代替原文中的人称代词形式。

Olohan 在 TEC 和 BNC 的基础上，对英语翻译文学和原创文学中各类缩写形式（contracted forms，如 's, 'll, 'd, 've, 't, 're 等）的种类和频次考察发现，翻译文学在两方面均低于非翻译文学，说明翻译文本表现出显化的倾向。②

单语内类比模式的第二类是对句法形式的考察。如 Puurtinen 通过对翻译芬兰语的语言特征以及意识形态规范进行考察发现：非翻译芬兰语作品中非定式结构的出现频次低，而译自英语的翻译作品中，非定式结构的使用频次明显高于当代非翻译芬兰语作品。③

胡显耀与王克非④利用"通用汉英对应语料库"⑤考察了翻译汉语区别于汉语原创语料的词汇使用特征。他们发现，无论是文学语料还是非

---

① M. Olohan, "Spelling out the Optionals in Translation: A Corpus Study", *UCREL Technical Papers*, Vol. 13, 2001, pp. 423 – 432; M. Olohan, "Leave It Out! Using a Comparable Corpus to Investigate Aspects of Explicitation in Translation", *Cadernos de Traducao*, Vol. IX, 2002, pp. 153 – 169; M. Olohan, "Comparable Corpora in Translation Research: Overview of Recent Analyses Using the Translational English Corpus", http://www.iff.unizh.ch/cl/yuste/postworkshop/repository/molohan.

② M. Olohan, "How Frequent are The Contractions? A Study of Contracted Forms in The Translational English Corpus", *Target*, Vol. 15, No. 1, 2003, pp. 59 – 89.

③ T. Puurtinen, "Syntax, Readability and Ideology in Children's Literature", *Meta*, Vol. 43, No. 4, 1998, pp. 524 – 533; T. Puurtinen, "Genre-specific Features of Translationese? Linguistic Differences Between Translated and Non-translated Finnish Children's Literature", *Literary and Linguistic Computing*, Vol. 18, No. 4, 2003, pp. 389 – 406; T. Puurtinen, "Nonfinite Constructions in Finnish Children's Literature: Features of Translationese Contradicting Translation Universals", in S. Granger, J. Lerot & S. Petch-Tyson (ed.), *Corpus-based Approaches to Contrastive Linguistics and Translation Studies*, Amsterdam: Rodopi, 2003.

④ 胡显耀：《基于语料库的翻译小说词语特征研究》，《外语教学与研究》2007 年第 1 期；王克非、胡显耀：《基于语料库的翻译汉语词汇特征研究》，《中国翻译》2008 年第 6 期。

⑤ "通用汉英对应语料库"由北京外国语大学中国外语教育研究中心的王克非主持建设。该语料库库容量达 3000 万字词，由翻译、百科、专科对译语句四个子库构成。其中，翻译文本库容量为 2000 万字词，英译汉占 60%，汉译英占 40%，分别含文学和非文学语料。全部语料进行了句对齐和词性标注，可分类检索和考察词频、搭配等。文学语料中以小说为主。

文学语料，与原创汉语相比，翻译汉语具有虚词显化、指代方式显化、常用词频率增加等特征，从原创汉语与翻译汉语对比的角度验证了 Baker 提出显化假设。

同一时期，以平行对应语料库为基础的语际对比模式从语言转换入手，双向考察语际显化。

语际对比模式第一类主要是从词汇或句法双向转换入手。

Schmied 和 Schffler 以克姆尼茨英—德翻译语料库（Chemnitz）为基础，将英—德翻译中的显化分为结构显化和非结构显化两类，分别体现在词汇和语法两个层面。① 这项研究表明英→德和德→英两个方向上均表现出显化，初步说明显化确是翻译过程的共有特征。Schmied 和 Schffler 继而从认知和信息加工的角度对显化现象的原因进行了解释。

Øverås 以英语—挪威语平行语料库（ENPC）为基础关注了词汇衔接现象，结果表明从翻译方向上看，总体上英语→挪威语方向上的显化要比挪威语→英语方向上更为突出②。这一发现，与 Schmied 和 Schffler 的发现不完全一致。Øverås 的研究表明尽管两个方向上都表现出显化，但程度有差异，说明具体语对是一个重要变量。Øverås 特别指出，语际显化的研究结果可以作为类比显化的必要补充，因为翻译文本相对源文本显性程度的提高并不一定能够说明翻译文本就比目标语中的同类原创文本显性程度高。这一研究初步将平行与类比两种模式联系了起来。

Perego 以两部匈牙利语电影及其意大利语字幕为考察对象，从类别和形式上证实了电影字幕中翻译上存在显化现象。③ 从类别上，显化现象被划分为"文化"（Cultural）、"符号间转化"（Inter-semiotic）、"基于简化需要"（Reduction-based）三类。从形式上，显化现象表现为"添加"（Addition）和"具体化"（Specification）两种。具体来讲，前者指在译

---

① J. Schmied & H. Schffler, "Explicitness as a Universal Feature of Translation", in M. Ljung (ed.), *Corpus-based Studies in English. Papers from the 17th International Conference on English Language Research on Computerized Corpora (ICAME 17) Stockholm, May 15 – 19, 199*, Amsterdam: Rodopi, 1997, p. 21.

② L. Øverås, "In Search of The Third Code: An Investigation of Norms in Literary Translation", *Meta*, Vol. 43, No. 2, 1998, pp. 568 – 588.

③ Elisa Perego, "Evidence of Explicitation in Subtitling: Toward a Categorization", *Across Languages and Cultures*, Vol. 4, No. 1, 2003, pp. 63 – 88.

文中添加有别于原文中使用的语言学（语法、词汇或句法）成分，后者指用语义更为详尽和明晰的词语替换语义较为笼统和宽泛的词语。

柯飞以英汉—汉英平行语料库为基础，对汉语特殊句式"把"字句在英汉转换中的分布特点进行考察发现：翻译汉语作品中的"把"字句要比非翻译汉语中的"把"字句频次高，文学类作品比非文学类作品频次高，由于"把"字句适于表达复杂和细微的意思，因此"把"字句的频次说明了翻译文本中的显化现象。①

语际对比模式第二类研究属于纯形式的对比。

贺显斌对 O. Henry 的短篇小说 *The Last Leaf* 及其汉译文采用了定量和定性的分析，发现汉译文中显化的倾向较为明显。该倾向具体表现为：在原文全篇 134 句中，译成汉语后显化程度提高的有 79 句，占汉译文全篇句子总数的 59%。②

王克非根据汉英—英汉平行语料库的 4 个子库（汉译英文学、汉译英非文学、英译汉文学、英译汉非文学）中句对应抽样检索发现，无论是英译汉还是汉译英，译本都呈现出字数扩增的现象，而且不同类型的译本在扩增程度上有差别。③ 他认为广义的显化现象可能是导致译本字数扩增的原因之一。

Frankenberg-Gacia 以葡—英双向平行语料库（Compara）为基础，以定量分析的方法证明了翻译文本中词汇数量的整体增加表明译文往往比原文更为明晰，而且这并不受制于两种语言之间的差异。④

Klaudy 和 Károly 在对英译匈和匈译英文学文本两个方向上报告动词（reporting verbs）进行考察的基础上提出了显化的"非对称假说"（A-symmetry Hypothesis），⑤ 指出译者在 L1→L2 方向进行了显化处理，在相

---

① 柯飞：《汉语"把"字句特点、分布及英译研究》，《外语教学与研究》2003 年第 12 期。
② 贺显斌：《英汉翻译过程中的明晰化现象》，《解放军外国语学院学报》2003 年第 4 期。
③ 王克非：《英汉/汉英语句对应的语料库考察》，《外语教学与研究》2003 年第 6 期。
④ A. Frankenberg-Gacia, "Are Translations Longer Than Source texts? A Corpus-based Study of Explicitation", 2004, http://www.academia.edu/3260827.
⑤ K. Klaudy & Krisztina Károly, "Implicitation in Translation: Empirical Evidence for Operational Asymmetry in Translation", *Across Languages and Cultures*, Vol. 6, No. 1, 2005, pp. 13 – 28.

反方向却并不总会进行隐化处理。通过对从 3 部（1 部英文和 2 部匈牙利文）小说中随机抽取的各 100 个报告动词及其匈/英译词进行对比分析，从不同报告动词数与报告动词总数的比率以及仅出现一次的报告动词数与报告动词总数的比率分析后，Klaudy 和 Károly 认为"译者更愿意使用显化操作，而不使用选择性隐化操作"①。

柯飞通过对北京外国语大学从宏观和微观角度对语料库中的汉英互译实例进行分析，发现翻译中显化（和隐化）现象的发生由语言、译者、社会文化等多种因素造成。他认为显化现象"不应只是狭义地指语言衔接形式上的变化，还应包括意义上的显化转换，即在译文中增添有助于译文读者理解的显化表达，或者说将原文隐含的信息显化于译文中，使意思更明确，逻辑更清楚"②。

Gumul 将同声传译中是否存在显化现象作为研究对象。③ 通过分析 14 位波兰语口译者同声翻译的 2 篇英语演讲稿的录音及其对自己口译结果的回顾式评论（Retro-speetive Comments），Gumul 发现同声传译中也存在显化现象，并且在绝大多数情况下该现象属于口译者下意识的行为，而并非他们有意采取的策略。

Englund-Dimitrova 综合采用"有声思维记录法"（Think Aloud Protoeol）和对译文分析的研究方法，发现显化技巧的使用与译者专业水平有关。④ 专业译者下意识使用显化技巧的程度最高，语言学生往往有意识地采用显化技巧解决实际翻译问题。相对于前两类译者而言，翻译专业学生显化技巧的使用，表现为下意识、有意识兼而有之。

这一时期，在研究对象和研究方法方面还存在许多不统一的地方，语际共性与类比共性的讨论兼而有之。此后，单语类比模式与双语平行模式的翻译共性研究同步发展。

另外，也有通过语内类比与语际对比两种途径兼而用之考察显化现

---

① K. Klaudy & Krisztina Károly, "Implicitation in Translation: Empirical Evidence for Operational Asymmetry in Translation", *Across Languages and Cultures*, Vol. 6, No. 1, 2005, p. 14.

② 柯飞：《翻译中的隐和显》，《外语教学与研究》2005 年第 4 期。

③ Ewa Gumul, "Explicitation in Simultaneous Interpretation: A Strategy or a By-product of Language Mediation", *Across Language and Cultures*, Vol. 7, No. 2, 2006, pp. 171 – 190.

④ Birgitta Englund-Dimitrova, *Expertise and Explicitation in the Translation Process*, Amsterdam/ Philadelphia: John Benjamins Publishing Company, 2005.

象的，如 Papai 使用平行语料库和可比语料库研究文学/非文学文本，从逻辑—视觉关系、词汇—语法、句法、语篇—超语言因素（Extra-linguistic）四个层次综合考察了英译匈显化技巧的具体运用，比较了匈译语与匈非译语中文本显化特征的分布。① 研究结果证实译文中运用了显化策略，译文中显化程度高于非译文。

基于语料库的显化翻译则以"目标文本"为导向，采用计算机数据提取、统计与分析技术，将关注焦点放在翻译语言上。为了区别于前语料库时期的源文本—目标文本的语际对比模式，基于语料库的显化翻译发展初期主要采用目标语中翻译文本与非翻译文本比较的单语内类比模式，在初期以类比语料库（comparable corpus）为基础建立了目标语单语类比模式，即对比目标语中翻译文本与非翻译文本的文本特征。"在不考虑所涉及源语言或目标语言的情况下，识别翻译文本中的特定语言模式，探索翻译本质。"② 类比模式的语料库显化研究主要是对 Baker 所倡导模式的应用和验证。

描写翻译研究是 Baker 语料库翻译学思想的另一个重要来源，这一研究学派抛开"对等"和源文本，以"规范"（norms）为核心概念，关注目标语文化中的"翻译"事实，并对翻译事实进行客观描写。描写翻译研究跳出"对等"的局限，将关注点放在翻译文本整体尤其是对翻译行为规律性的描写上，而不是关于源文本和目标文本关系的个案研究或对比分析上；强调建立独立的学科分支、完善的方法论和明确的研究步骤，强调翻译行为的概率性，并对此做出合理解释；同时这一研究过程具有可观察性和可重复性。③

总的来说，基于语料库的共性研究呈现出四个特点：（1）大多数研究都是以共时语料为研究对象，主要依靠计算机技术分析数据，如平均

---

① Vilma Papai, "Explicitation: A Universal of Translated Text", in A. Mauranen & P. Kujamuki (ed.), *Translation Universals: Do They Exist?* Amsterdam/Philadelphia: John Benjamins Publishing Company, 2004.

② M. Baker, "Corpora in Translation Studies: An Overview and Some Suggestions for Future Research", *Target*, Vol. 7, No. 2, 1995, p. 234.

③ M. Baker, "Corpus Linguistics and Translation Studies: Implications and Applications", in M. Baker, G. Francis and E. Tognini-Bonelli (ed.), *Text and Technology: In Honor of John Sinclair*, Philadelphia & Amsterdam: John Benjamins, 1993, pp. 240–241.

句子长度、类符/形符比率、词汇密度等手段对词汇多样性、信息负载度等方面进行考察；(2) 以对共性的验证和描写为主，解释较少；(3) 理论阐述与实证研究相结合；(4) 主要以单语类比语料库为基础，探究相对于目标语原创文本而言的翻译文本特征。这项研究总体上经历了一个由单语类比语料库范式向单、双语结合语料库（包括单语参照库和双语对应库）综合发展的过程，研究内容由词汇向句法、语篇层次延伸，宏观与微观、理论阐述与实证性研究并举。

基于语料库的显化翻译研究较少关注译者"对源文本的反应方式"[①]。"大多数研究都是以共时语料为研究对象，主要依靠计算机技术分析数据，如平均句子长度、形符/类符比率、词项密度等手段对词项多样性、信息负载度等方面进行考察……主要以单语类比语料库为基础，探究相对于目标语原创文本而言的翻译文本特征。"[②] "采纳的多是翻译产品/目标语取向（product/target-oriented）的视角，着重探讨翻译文本相对于非翻译文本而言所表现出来的语言特征。"[③]

尽管 Baker 所倡导的单语类比模式是翻译描写研究的一个新视角，但在对所描写现象的解释中，源文本还是一个不容忽视的重要因素，否则就只能说明翻译文本与非翻译文本有差异而已。

首先，在方法论方面，语料库翻译学的初衷是要建立一套有别于单一源文本—目标文本对等与否的回溯式研究模式，而以目标语文本为取向，将翻译文本整体视为研究对象，考察翻译文本不同于非翻译文本的特征。但实际研究中，源文本不可能完全被忽略掉。例如，Baker 对显化的最早界定是"与特定源文本或（目标语中）原创文本总体上相比较，（目标文本）所表现出显性程度的显著提高"[④]。从这一界定可看出，Baker 当时所讨论的各种翻译共性既有语际对比，也有语内类比。

Bernardini 和 Zanettin 认为基于语料库的翻译共性研究存在的问题主

[①] Saldanha Gabriela, "Translator Style: Methodological Considerations", *Translator*, Vol. 17, 2011, p. 27.
[②] 王克非：《语料库翻译学探索》，上海交通大学出版社 2012 年版，第 49 页。
[③] 胡开宝：《语料库翻译学概论》，上海交通大学出版社 2011 年版，第 108 页。
[④] M. Baker, "Corpus Linguistics and Translation Studies: Implications and Applications", in M. Baker, G. Francis and E. Tognini-Bonelli (ed.), *Text and Technology: In Honor of John Sinclair*, Philadelphia & Amsterdam: John Benjamins, 1993, p. 243.

要表现在对共性概念的界定和所采用的方法论两方面。① 关注的对象不同，所采用的研究模式就会有差异。在翻译共性研究中存在两种对比模式：（1）原文文本与译文文本的语际对比模式；（2）目标语中译文文本与原创文本的语内类比模式。

之后一些学者②建议将含有"源文本"的平行语料库重新引入语料库翻译研究中，作为对类比模式的补充。黄立波、王克非认为："脱离源语文本而仅对译文做纯形式的语料库统计对于翻译研究而言意义不大……要关注译者如何在翻译文本中来表现源文本中的某些特征。"③

黄立波、王克非也认为显化翻译应"在指导原则上，以平行语料库为基础，在翻译研究中重新引入源语文本"④。"脱离源语文本而仅对译文做纯形式的语料库统计对于翻译研究而言意义不大……要关注译者如何在翻译文本中来表现源文本中的某些特征。"⑤

"在方法论方面，单语类比语料库研究法存在明显的局限性，具体表现为：（1）排除源语文本而孤立地讨论翻译问题；（2）目标语内翻译文本与原创文本可比性的缺乏……导致研究结果信度与效度的缺乏……基于语料库的普遍性研究需要打破类比语料库研究模式的垄断，重新将源语文本因素纳入其研究的视野。"⑥

其次，根据 Baker⑦ 等，翻译共性研究的目的在于识别翻译文本的典型语言特征，这样不仅可以揭示"第三类语码"的本质，更重要的是能认识影响翻译行为以及隐藏于此类独特语言形式之下的各种具体的制约

---

① S. Bernardini & F. Zanettin, "When is a Universal not a Universal? Some Limits of Current Corpus-based Methodologies for The Investigation of Translation Universals", in A. Mauranen and P. Kujamaki (ed.), *Translation Universals: Do They Exist?* Amsterdam: John Benjamins, 2004.

② D. Kenny, *Lexis and Creativity in Translation: A Corpus-based Study*, Manchester: St. Jerome, 2001; D. Kenny, "Parallel Corpora and Translation Studies: Old Questions, New Perspectives? Reporting That in Gepcolt: A Case Study", in G. Barnbrook, P. Danielsson & M. Mahlberg (ed.), *Meaningful Texts: The Extraction of Semantic Information from Monolingual and Multilingual Corpora*, London & New York: Continuum, 2005.

③ 黄立波、王克非：《语料库翻译学：课题与进展》，《外语教学与研究》2011 年第 6 期。

④ 黄立波、王克非：《翻译普遍性研究反思》，《中国翻译》2006 年第 5 期。

⑤ 黄立波、王克非：《语料库翻译学：课题与进展》，《外语教学与研究》2011 年第 6 期。

⑥ 黄立波、王克非：《翻译普遍性研究反思》，《中国翻译》2006 年第 5 期。

⑦ M. Baker (ed.), *Routledge Encyclopedia of Translation Studies*, Shanghai: Shanghai Foreign Language Education Press, 1998/2004.

因素、压力和动机,从而达到对翻译现象的深层解释。对此,吴昂、黄立波提出了质疑:一是对研究对象的界定;二是对各种变量的关注与控制。① 以译者因素为例,一方面可就不同译者对同一原作或同一作者作品的翻译加以考察,这种研究属于译者文体或翻译文体学范畴;另一方面则是译入还是译出的问题,即将外语文本翻译成母语,还是将母语译成其他语言,同时涉及翻译方向因素。目前,英译汉文本大多属于译入,即由以汉语为母语的译者完成,而汉译英文本中的情况可以分为汉语母语译者、汉英合作译者和英语母语译者三类,后两类所占比例较小,这也是影响语料平衡性的一个因素。

Toury 提出,对翻译共性的研究既不应过分具体化,也不可层次过高,而应当采用概率思维方式对其加以认识,并以条件式表述方法加以描写和解释;翻译共性研究并非一个存在与否的问题,而是一个解释力问题,即如何借助各种概念工具对翻译现象进行更好的解释。②

三 研究内容、方法及创新点

(一) 研究内容

1. 研究假设

曹雪芹在《红楼梦》的开篇中,曾批评"满纸潘安、子建、西子、文君"的"佳人才子等书",皆为"通共熟套之旧稿"。而他在《红楼梦》中对人物的塑造,虽传承着民族艺术传统的创作特色,着重于传神的性格刻画和深邃的内心世界的描写,但也并不忽略描写形貌,而是使人物创造的"写形"与"传神"相互照应,特别是对男女主人公——贾宝玉、林黛玉、薛宝钗以及王熙凤的典型性格的创造,更是将其容貌特征融合在性格特征的创造里,使之形神兼备、各具风采,令人过目不忘。③

贾宝玉、林黛玉、薛宝钗是《红楼梦》的主人公,也是其中三个最

---

① 吴昂、黄立波:《关于翻译共性的研究》,《外语教学与研究》2006 年第 5 期。
② Gideon Toury, "Probabilistic Explanations in Translation Studies. Welcome as They Are, Would they Qualify as Universals", in A. Mauranen & P. Kujamaki (ed.), *Translation Universals: Do They Exist*? Amsterdam: John Benjamins, 2004.
③ 李希凡、李萌:《"可叹停机德"——薛宝钗论》,《红楼梦学刊》2005 年第 2 期。

成功的艺术典型,其一颦一笑、一言一行都显示着不同的个性,反映着各不相同的社会人生意义和美学价值,霍克斯是如何显化翻译这些不朽的艺术典型的性格生命的呢?

黄国彬认为在众多的《红》译本中,"霍克斯的翻译是最出色的,在准确性、想象力和创造力上都超过了其他本子,最值得仔细研究,也包含了更多的翻译技巧"[①],"当之无愧是曹雪芹巨著的好伴侣"[②]。

黄立波和王克非认为,汉英/英汉翻译中的显化可依据不同的语料库类型将显化分为语内对比显化和语际对比显化两类。前者是基于目标语中翻译文本与原创文本的对比研究;后者则是源语与目标语文本比较分析的结果。[③] 任何语言类型通常都包括形式和意义两部分,在此基础上,它们又进一步分为形式上和意义上的显化两类。

通常认为,翻译转换中所表现出的一些特征完全是语言系统具体差异的结果,但基于语料库的实证研究[④]表明,翻译中的显化在许多情况下确属一种非强制性策略,并非译语文本的绝对要求,即译者在译文中添加信息或明示隐含信息,均不是译文语言系统所强制要求的。

本书以黄国彬关于霍译本的观点为假设前提,以黄立波和王克非的显化分类为基础,提出霍克斯对《红楼梦》人物形象进行了非强制性显化翻译。

本书充分考虑到语料库设计中的可比性、研究中的参数选择与文体类型选择、翻译方向、译者因素等会对研究结果产生很大影响的因素,因此,以语料库设计中的可比性、研究中的参数选择与文体类型选择、翻译方向为控制变量,在上述变量相同的情况下,就译者因素提出如下假设(见表0-3)。

---

① Laurence Wong, *A Study of the Literary Translations of the Hong Long Meng: With Special Reference to David Hawkes's English Version*, Graduate Department of East Studies, University of Toronto, 1992, p. 10.
② Ibid., p. 517.
③ 黄立波、王克非:《翻译普遍性研究反思》,《中国翻译》2006年第5期。
④ L. Øverås, "In Search of the Third Code: An Investigation of Norms in Literary Translation", *Meta*, Vol. 43, No. 2, 1998, pp. 571–588; M. Olohan & M. Baker, "Reporting That in Translated English: Evidence for Subconscious Process of Explicitation", *Across Languages and Cultures*, Vol. 1, 2000, pp. 141–172.

表 0 - 3　　　　　霍译本对《红楼梦》人物形象显化的假设

显化类型	显化内容	形式上	意义上
显化类型	语际显化 （霍译本—原著）	+	+
	类比显化 （霍译本—杨译本）	+	+

假设 1：从语际显化方向上看，霍译本在形式和意义上均突出原著《红楼梦》主人公人物形象。

假设 2：从类比显化方向上看，霍译本在形式和意义上均比杨译本突出原著《红楼梦》主人公人物形象。

假设 3：霍译的显化翻译乃有意识的策略，而非下意识语言选择的结果，即霍克斯对《红楼梦》主人公人物形象进行了非强制性显化翻译。

2. 研究检测项

本书的考察语料库是由霍克斯翻译的《红楼梦》前八十回，对比语料库是由我国翻译家杨宪益及其夫人戴乃迭（Hsien-yi Yang 和 Gladys Yang）翻译的《红楼梦》前八十回。参照语料库是他们各自的《红楼梦》的原著前八十回。

为了便于表述，下文分别将以上语料库简称为霍底本、霍译本、杨底本、杨译本。

语料库翻译研究的关键在于如何将研究假设与语言层面的表现形式联系起来，以具体的语言检测项为切入点来考察翻译现象。"在实证研究中，如何将高层面的显化概念转化为低层面可供语料库检索的数据，成为基于语料库研究的关键。"①

Noel 指出，语义本身是不能够直接观察的，而译文是译者对原语中构式 A 的语义的判断，如果构式 A 在相当规模的语料库中都译为另一种语言中的构式 B，而构式 B 是明示了某语义 [S] 的，便可以认为构式 A

---

① 刘泽权、侯羽：《国内外显化研究概述》，《中国翻译》2008 年第 5 期。

也含有语义［S］。这种证据是具有心理现实性的直接证据。① 据此，笔者认为：其一，若源文本中的人名前后有构式 A 在霍、杨翻译语料库中都译为构式 B，且若霍译语料库中构式 B 是明示了某语义［S］的，则源文本中的人名前后构式 A 也应该含有此语义，若源文本中的人名前后构式 A 没有含有此语义［S］，则霍译语料库可视为显化翻译；其二，若霍译语料库构式 B 是明示了某语义［S］的，而杨译语料库构式 B 没有含有某语义［S］，则霍译语料库可视为显化翻译。

故本书的检测项是源文本中的"人名"和它在霍、杨翻译语料库译文中的对应"人名"，通过寻找"人名"的前后词项确立平行语料库语言之间的对应构式，通过比较对应构式的语义对应程度来考察源文本中的人物形象在译文中的显化现象。

3. 研究步骤

第一，运用 ICTCLAS 对霍、杨底本进行分词处理，并运用 WORD-SMITH 6.0.0 的 CONCORD 检索功能，分别对考察语料库和参照语料库及对比语料库中《红楼梦》人物的出现次数和该词的左右语境词进行初步观察。

第二，利用 WORDSMITH 6.0.0 的 COLLOCATE 工具分别为考察语料库和参照语料库生成 Word Cloud 搭配词云图，直观地得出"人名"左右的搭配词序列，从这些词中选择拟作为例证的形式，"将搭配序列作为研究单位是必要的策略；搭配序列的异同对比直接指向双语短语单位的对应关系；只有当被比单位的形式、意义和功能特征都相同或相似时，它们才可能具有最大程度上的对等"②。

第三，选择拟作为例证的形式，主要依据为：在霍底本和霍译本中都高频出现，形式构成特征较为明显，便于深入分析。"平行语料库显示的翻译对等是对比研究切实可行的出发点，而反复出现的翻译对等（recurrent translation equivalent）……揭示了双语词语一个侧面的对等关系，

---

① D. Noel,"Translation as Evidence for Semantics: An Illustration", *Linguistics*, Vol. 4, 2003, pp. 757 – 785.

② 卫乃兴：《基于语料库的对比短语学研究》，《外国语》2011 年第 4 期。

因此是最重要的对比依据。"①

第四,根据 WORDSMITH 6.0.0 提供的搭配词频数,确定考察语料库和参照语料库典型对等形式,然后再从对比语料库中,找出杨译本的相同序列搭配词,再以搭配序列为研究单位,考察并确定能够展现人物形象的词项。

第五,数据提取。运用 WORDSMITH 6.0.0 的 CONCORD,以上述典型形式为节点词分别从霍底本和霍译本及对比语料库杨译本抽取符合要求的索引行,从平行语料库显示的复现翻译对等出发,考察它们在双向翻译过程中的语义对应关系和互译数据。

第六,分析与讨论。主要包括:根据考察语料库和参照语料库及对比语料库中的对应数据,分析霍、杨译本对人物形象翻译的策略;对翻译策略进行分类和讨论。

(二) 研究方法

语料库是研究的工具,语料库的使用也需要先进的工具,"能使我们简洁、有效地进行编码,能使我们查询并获得大量的数据"②。本书运用中国科学院的 ICTCLAS 汉语词法分析系统和牛津大学出品的 WORDSMITH 文本处理与分析软件,为语料库在切分、标注、统计等方面提供极大的方便,使研究过程更具直观性,研究结果更具信度与效度。

基于语料库的翻译研究,"是近十多年随语料库语言学发展起来的新学科分支,包括方法论或工具层面上的应用研究、描写性研究和关于翻译特征的抽象性理论研究。它在研究方法上以语言学和翻译理论为指导,以概率和统计为手段,以双语真实语料为对象,对翻译进行历时或共时的研究,代表了一种新的研究范式,产出了一批研究成果,加深了人们对翻译现象的认识","语料库翻译学以电子文本为基础以计算机统计为手段,对各类翻译现象进行大范围的或特定范围的描写,在充分描写的

---

① W. Teubert, "Directions in Corpus Linguistics", in Halliday, M. A. K., Wolfgang Teubert, Co-lin Yalop & Anna Germakova (ed.), *Lexicology & Cor-pus Linguistics*, London & New York: Continuum, 2004.

② M. Tymoczko,, "Computerized Corpora and the Future of Translation Studies", *Meta*, Vol. XLIII, No. 4, 1998, pp. 1 - 8.

基础上，探究两种语言及其转换的过程、特征和规律，分析和解释翻译现象或验证关于翻译的种种假说"①。

借助语料库开展显化研究，能全面快速检索语料，以实证的手段对各类文本的翻译特征进行定量描写和定性分析。"大规模语料库（包括原文及译文）将为翻译研究者提供前所未有的机会，让他们能够直接观察自己的研究对象，探索翻译不同于自然生成语言或其他任何文化互动形式的原因。"②

语料库翻译学"通过理论阐述与实证研究相结合，展示语料库研究方法正在发展成为一种连贯、综合、丰富的范式"③。

"双语语料库有助于翻译对等的研究"④，"帮助研究者洞悉翻译的本质"⑤。"使用双语语料库数据分析为译者提供不同语言中可能的翻译单位或者对等篇章单位的集合，提高译者的翻译意识，即对翻译难点的处理意识和对翻译策略的运用意识，有助于改进翻译的终端产品。"⑥

基于语料库的翻译研究方法至少有两大特点：可观察性（observability）和可重复性（replicability）。这一研究模式面对的是实实在在的语料，从假设出发，在各种语言中不断加以验证和置疑，周而复始，使得研究逐渐深入。Chesterman 指出，"一门科学只有通过在单个个案之间寻找其相似性并从中加以归纳，才能达到对未来研究或尚未研究个案的预测，

---

① 王克非、黄立波：《语料库翻译学的几个术语》，《四川外语学院学报》2007 年第 6 期。

② M. Baker, "Corpus Linguistics and Translation Studies: Implications and Applications", in M. Baker, G. Francis and E. Tognini-Bonelli (ed.), *Text and Technology: In Honor of John Sinclair*, Philadelphia & Amsterdam: John Benjamins, 1993, p. 235.

③ S. Laviosa, "The Corpus-based Approach: A New Paradigm in Translation Studies", *Meta*, Vol. 43, No. 4, 1998, p. 474.

④ Geoffrey Leech, "Teaching in Language Corpora: A Convergence", in Gerry Knowles, Tony McEnery, Stephen Fligelstone & Arme Wichman (ed.), *Teaching and Language Corpora*, London: Longman, 1997, p. 22.

⑤ Susan Hunston, *Corpora in Applied Linguistics*, Cambridge: Cambridge University Press, 2002, p. 128.

⑥ Noelle Serpellet, "Mandative Constructions in English and Their Equivalents in French: Applying a Bilingual Approach to the Theory and Practice of Translation", in Bemhard Kettemann and Georg Marko (ed.), *Teaching and Learning by Doing Corpus Analysis*, Proceeding of the Fourth International Conference on Teaching and Language Corpora, Amsterdam & New York, 2002, pp. 359 – 360.

从而取得进步"①。

本书对象都是真实使用的文本,本质上都是假设检验(hypothesis testing),具体包括七个步骤②:(1)提出假设;(2)设定研究目标;(3)检验假设;(4)分析数据;(5)对发现进行理论阐述;(6)将假设精确化;(7)在前六项基础上为将来的研究提出新假设,研究对象都放在语言的规律性特征上,方法上以文本对比为基本模式。

1. 双语平行对比与单语平行类比相结合

Bernardini 和 Zanettin 认为基于语料库的翻译共性研究中存在两种对比模式:(1)原文文本与译文文本的语际对比模式;(2)目标语中译文文本与原创文本的语内类比模式。③

前语料库时期的翻译显化研究主要是从语际对比的角度出发,而基于语料库的翻译显化研究既有单语内类比基础上的研究又有以双语语际对比为模式的研究,但以单语内类比研究为基础的显化研究较集中。在方法论方面,单语内类比研究语料库研究法存在明显的局限性,具体表现为:(1)排除源语文本而孤立地讨论翻译问题;(2)目标语内翻译文本与原创文本可比性的缺乏。这些都导致研究结果信度与效度的缺乏。一些实证性研究的结果④已经证明,基于语料库的显化研究需要打破单语内类比语料库研究模式的垄断,重新将源语文本因素纳入其研究的视野。国外新近研究已经证明双语语际平行语料库在双语对比和翻译研究中的

---

① A. Chesterman, "Beyond the Particular", in A. Mauranen and P. Kujamaki (ed.), *Translation Universals: Do They Exist?* Amsterdam: John Benjamins, 2004, p. 33.

② S. Laviosa, *Corpus-based Translation Studies: Theory, Findings and Applications*, Amsterdam: Rodopi, 2002, p. 2.

③ S. Bernardini & F. Zanettin, "When is a Universal not a Universal? Some Limits of Current Corpus-based Methodologies for the Investigation of Translation Universals", in A. Mauranen and P. Kujamaki (ed.), *Translation Universals: Do They Exist?* Amsterdam: John Benjamins, 2004.

④ L. Øverås, "In Search of the Third Code: An Investigation of Norms in Literary Translation", *Meta*, Vol. 43, No. 2, 1998, pp. 571–588; D. Kenny, *Lexis and Creativity in Translation: A Corpus-based Study*, Manchester: St. Jerome, 2001; D. Kenny, "Parallel Corpora and Translation Studies: Old Questions, New Perspectives? Reporting that in Gepcolt: A Case Study", in G. Barnbrook, P. Danielsson & M. Mahlberg (ed.), *Meaningful Texts: The Extraction of Semantic Information from Monolingual and Multilingual Corpora*, London & New York: Continuum, 2005.

有效性。① 本书所采用的汉英/英英平行语料库将双语语际平行模式和单语内类比平行模式结合起来，如图 0-1。

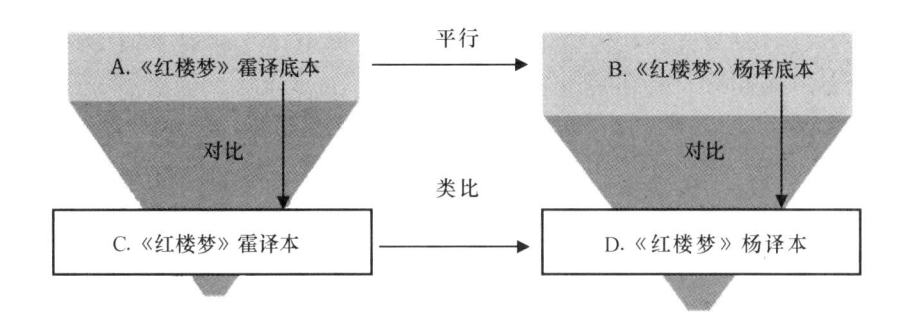

```
     A.《红楼梦》霍译底本  —— 平行 →  B.《红楼梦》杨译底本
           │                              │
          对比                            对比
           ↓            类比               ↓
     C.《红楼梦》霍译本  ──────→  D.《红楼梦》杨译本
```

图 0-1　双语语际平行模式与单语内类比平行模式相结合的对比模式

如图 0-1 所示，本书所用的语料库包括《红楼梦》霍译底本、《红楼梦》杨译底本、《红楼梦》霍译本及《红楼梦》杨译本四类。其中，A—B 和 C—D 分别为单语平行对应关系；A—C 和 B—D 分别为双语平行对应关系；A—C 和 B—D 方向上的语料之间为对比关系；C—D 方向上的语料之间为类比关系。以平行语料 A—C 和 B—D 对比翻译中的语际显化过程，以平行语料 C—D 类比翻译中的译者显化策略和手段的差异，构成了一个复合的平行和类比对应关系，既考察中文源语文本和英文翻译文本之间的关系，又对比两个英文翻译文本之间的特征，对《红楼梦》霍译本人物形象翻译现象进行三维考察。

2. 定量与定性分析相结合

"语言学领域内每一次重大的范式转换大都由该学科领域对基本数据看法的改变而引发。"②

---

① H. Hasselgard, "Using Parallel Corpora in Contrastive Studies: Cross-linguistic Contrast of Future Referring Expressions in English and Norwegian", *Foreign Language Teaching and Research*, Vol. 1, 2012, pp. 3-19; S. Johansson, *Seeing Through Multilingual Corpora: On the Use of Corpora in Contrastive Studies*, Amsterdam: John Benjamins, 2007.

② Michael Stubbs, "British Tradition in Text Analysis from Firth to Sinclair", in M. Baker, G. Francis & E. Tognini-Bonelli (ed.), *Text amd Technology: In Honour of John Sinclair*, Amsterdam & Philadelphia: John Benjamins, 1993, p. 24.

本书不仅关注单一类比模式（the comparable mode）下霍译文本与杨译文本之间的差异，而且也将源文本作为分析和解释翻译文本中特定人物形象转换现象的一个维度。

本书的研究范式在内容上既包括语际转换中译文相对于原文的语言特征，也包括目标语内部译文文本之间的语言特征。采用的方法包括对比分析、单语类比语料库模式、双语平行语料库模式等。研究性质以实证性描写为主。借助语料库工具，以实证的手段对各类文本的翻译特征进行定量描写和定性分析，遵循"让语料说话"的原则，关注源文本和目标文本中的"翻译"事实，并对翻译事实进行语料数据的采集和统计等定量研究，强调翻译行为的概率性，将关注点放在翻译文本上，尤其是对《红楼梦》人物形象翻译行为规律性的描写上，对特定语言形式转换现象的大规模观察与分析，以定量分析的方式揭示了不同译者对《红楼梦》人物形象翻译的倾向，总结译者的人物形象翻译策略。

在此基础上，本书结合显化翻译理论，对研究对象、语料选择、数据描写做出合理分析和解释，对隐藏在数据表象背后的因素进行定性研究。

3. 描写与解释相结合

本书是在实证基础上的描写，但描写的最终目的是对翻译现象做出合理解释，从可观察的现象入手，对翻译文本进行描写，逐步达到对各类深层关系的认识，并最终达到对无法直接观察的过程的重构，通过描写达到最终对翻译现象的解释。

本书所采用的基于语料库的翻译研究建立在两块土壤之上：语料库语言学（Corpus Linguistics）和描写翻译研究（Descriptive Translation Studies）。语料库语言学从语言研究角度为语料库翻译学提供理念和方法上的依据，以文本对比为基本模式，从假设检验入手，关注典型的翻译语言模式，注重概率性统计分析。描写翻译研究则是从翻译研究角度提供具体研究对象和理论方面的支持，对真实文本进分析和描写，达到对语言现象的客观认识。

基于语料库的翻译研究为双语平行对比与单语平行类比描写研究提供了一个强有力的数据支持，先有针对性地进行描写和分析，然后再上升到整体归纳和解释。本书在对显化翻译人物形象的现象进行充分描写的基础上,不仅从翻译活动内部尝试在源语文本中寻求对这些发现的解释,更从外部如译者主体和社会文化等视角对其做出合理的解释。柯飞在考察汉英/英汉翻译中的隐和显时指出:翻译中的隐和显可由语言、译者、社会文化、文本类型等多种因素造成。① 若将这些方面综合起来进行考虑,就可以尝试建立一套对翻译普遍现象的解释机制,加深对于翻译本质的认识。

本书将《红楼梦》前八十回霍克斯与杨宪益英译《红楼梦》人物林黛玉、贾宝玉、薛宝钗形象的全部语料加以梳理归类,进而从不同的角度摘引出霍译显化所在。通过大量的语料事实证明霍克斯的英译存在着显化的特点,再通过对典型译例的阐释,说明这些显化的翻译策略符合译者对读者的认知考虑,并阐明认知中复杂的社会文化语境,及文本语境和翻译活动的赞助人对译者的要求。

(三) 创新点

1. 研究内容创新

自 1979 年至 2012 年,国内学者对《红楼梦》英译的研究论文多达 782 篇。② 然而,这 782 篇文章中对人物形象"这个领域的研究文章只有七篇"③。迄今为止,对《红楼梦》的人物形象英译研究只有过零星论述,虽然这类零星成果不乏真知灼见,但缺乏系统性,讨论也不够深入,研究内容针对《红楼梦》主人公林黛玉、贾宝玉和薛宝钗形象翻译的尚不多见。

2. 研究方法创新

大规模原文和其对应译文的电子语料库以及相关语料库技术所提供的大规模数据检索与提取为本书从海量的语料存储中获取自己所期望的重要信息提供了新方法。

"《红楼梦》长达一百二十回,多达七十余万字,共描述了四百四十八个有血有肉的人物,客观上讲,研究者面对如此庞大的文本信息量,

---

① 柯飞:《翻译中的隐和显》,《外语教学与研究》2005 年第 4 期。
② 文军、任艳:《国内〈红楼梦〉英译研究回眸 (1979—2010)》,《中国外语》2012 年第 1 期。
③ 同上。

没有合适的统计工具,单凭手工统计,很难进行全面的数据提取和分析验证,而应用语料库,能很好地解决这一问题。"①

正如王宏印在"全国《红楼梦》翻译研讨会"大会总结报告中所说的:"虽然有不少新概念的引入和新方法的使用,但研究方法上还是有一定的束缚和限制。例如定性研究多而定量研究少……"② 虽然有研究的实例,但感悟式的或点评式的研究居多,没有涵盖所有的相关情况,缺乏系统性,而且取样不完整也不够全面,类似本书从语料库包含的海量语言证据中全面抽取有说服力的研究考察尚不多见。

3. 研究模式创新

张美芳指出,"利用语料库进行研究,对一些难以捉摸的和不引人注目的语言习惯进行描述、分析、比较和阐释,能比较令人信服地说明译者的烙印确实存在"③。

本书语料库中的一对多模式,即一个源文本的两个底本分别对应两个译文的模式是一大特色,不仅进行不同翻译方向上跨语际的语言转换对比研究,还进行相同翻译方向上译出文本的类比研究,目前对文学作品领域文本的类似研究模式尚不多见。

4. 研究视角创新

从研究视角来看,前人对霍克斯英译的研究,从传统的归化与异化、直译与意译,开始转向功能对等、目的论和文化研究,即从文化学视角、语言学视角和接受美学的视角来研究。但总体来看,语言层面的阐释多、价值判断多,在价值判断层面上仍然囿于忠实和非忠实的标准;对于霍克斯英译《红楼梦》的效果,前人的研究中都肯定了他作为译者的创造性,也注意到了中西文化及思维的差异,但却鲜有深究译者创造性翻译的动因,更没有深入研究赞助者的意识形态及诗学观对译者的翻译策略的影响。像本书这样涉及译者对社会文化语境、翻译赞助商目的、读者

---

① 刘泽权、田璐:《红楼梦叙事标记语及其英译——基于语料库的对比分析》,《外语学刊》2009年第1期。
② 王宏印:《精诚所至,金石为开——为建立"〈红楼〉译评"的宏伟目标而努力》,载刘士聪、崔永禄等编《红楼译评——〈红楼梦〉翻译研究论文集》,南开大学出版社2004年版,第471—487页。
③ 张美芳:《利用语料库调查译者的文体——贝克研究新法评介》,《解放军外国语学院学报》2002年第10期。

需求等问题的考虑,涉及译者对于作者、译者与读者三者之间地位和自身使命的深刻理解,尤其是文化传播如何借助于翻译手段操作层面得以实现的研究尚不多见。

第一章

霍克斯笔下的林黛玉人物形象

作为《红楼梦》第一女主角，名列"金陵十二钗"正册之首，林黛玉那含露带愁的绝世姿容、超逸灵秀的神女风度、热烈深挚的坚贞情感，渗透着诗情的个性特征，就像一汪清泉永远取之不尽。

作为一个极具美学含义的小说人物，林黛玉已经成为女子多愁善感、多病、爱哭的代名词。"是甚么一种东西，使得我们对于这个好哭的、敏感的、'小性儿'的、孤傲得让人感到有些难于接近的少女，这样的动情和无法忘怀呢？"①

曹雪芹怀着深挚的爱意和悲悯的同情，用历史与未来、现实与理想、哲理与诗情，并饱蘸着血与泪塑造出来的林黛玉，霍克斯怎样显化她的倾城容貌、旷世诗才、聪明灵秀、怯弱多病、清高自傲等形象呢？

第一节 语料采集与基本数据比较

一 林黛玉人物形象翻译对等形式的考察

首先，通过运用 ICTCLAS 对霍底本前八十回（参照语料库）进行分词处理，并运用 WORDSMITH 6.0.0 的 COLLOCATE 的 Word Cloud 功能，显示霍底本中在"黛玉"右侧 R1—R5 位置的语境共现词来观察林黛玉在源文本中的人物形象和活动（见图 1-1）。

---

① 郭豫适：《红楼梦研究文选》，华东师范大学出版社 1988 年版，第 518 页。

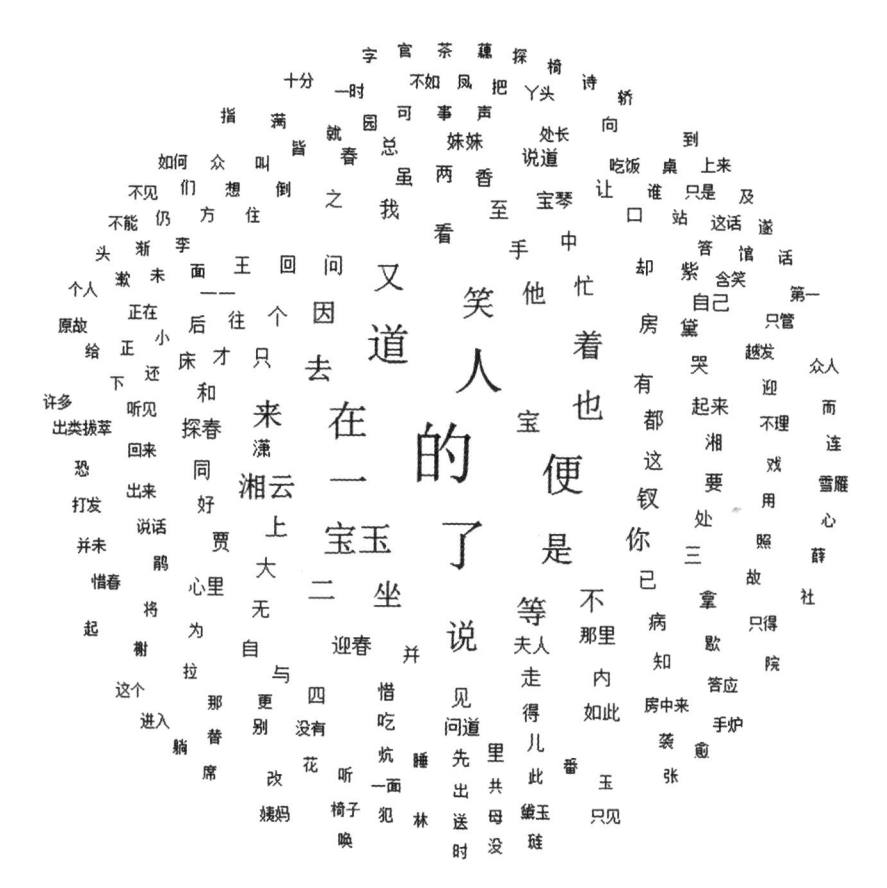

图 1-1 霍底本"黛玉"右侧 R1—R5 位置的语境共现词 Word Cloud

如图 1-1 所示,"的"在"黛玉"右侧出现的次数最多;其次为"人""了""便""道""说""笑"等。经过初步观察,本书拟以"的"及"道"和"说"作为考察节点词,因为:"黛玉的"后续词项及"黛玉道"和"黛玉说"的说话方式很有语义价值,能够展现林黛玉人物形象特征。

陆丙甫认为:"'的'的描写性是其基本意义和初始功能。"[①] 如果考察"黛玉的"后续词项,很容易揭开林黛玉的艺术形象。

另外,众所周知,黛玉语言的突出特点之一是口齿伶俐,有辩才,

---

① 陆丙甫:《"的"的基本功能和派生功能——从描写性到区别性再到指称性》,《世界汉语教学》2003 年第 1 期。

长于辞令。她的语言真诚直率，表里如一，任情任性，是自然天性的尽情流淌，而且她联想快捷、反应机敏，善于暗语映射、泳桑寓柳、设言托意、借题发挥。考察"黛玉"的说话表情方式，也容易揭示林黛玉的艺术形象。

考虑到中英文语序不同，霍底本的中文"黛玉的"有可能翻译成英文为"Dai-yu's"的形式，因此对霍译本在"Dai-yu"右侧 R1 位置的后续词项进行考察。运用 WORDSMITH 6.0.0 的 COLLOCATE 的 Word Cloud 功能，考察霍译本前八十回（考察语料库）中在"Dai-yu"右侧 R1 位置的语境共现词（见图 1-2）。

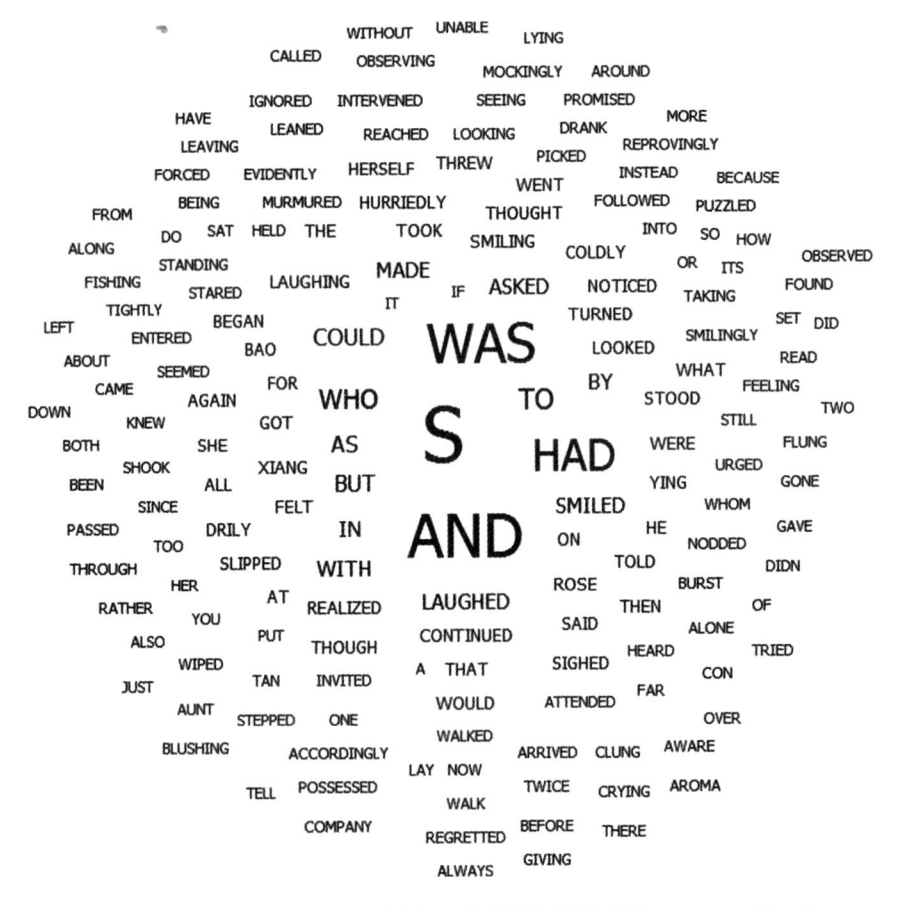

图 1-2 霍译本"Dai-yu"右侧 R1 位置的语境共现词 Word Cloud

第一章　霍克斯笔下的林黛玉人物形象　❋　57

如图 1-2 所示，霍译本中"S"出现的次数最多，而其在"Dai-yu"右侧 R1 位置形成的"Dai-yu's"，与霍底本"黛玉的"正是对等形式。

另外，考虑到中英文语序不同，霍底本中文的"黛玉道"和"黛玉说"有可能翻译成英文为"said Dai-yu"的形式，因此再对"Dai-yu"左侧 L1 位置的语境共现词进行考察。

运用 WORDSMITH 6.0.0 的 COLLOCATE 的 Word Cloud 功能，考察霍译本前八十回（考察语料库）中在"Dai-yu"左侧 L1 位置的语境共现词（见图 1-3）。

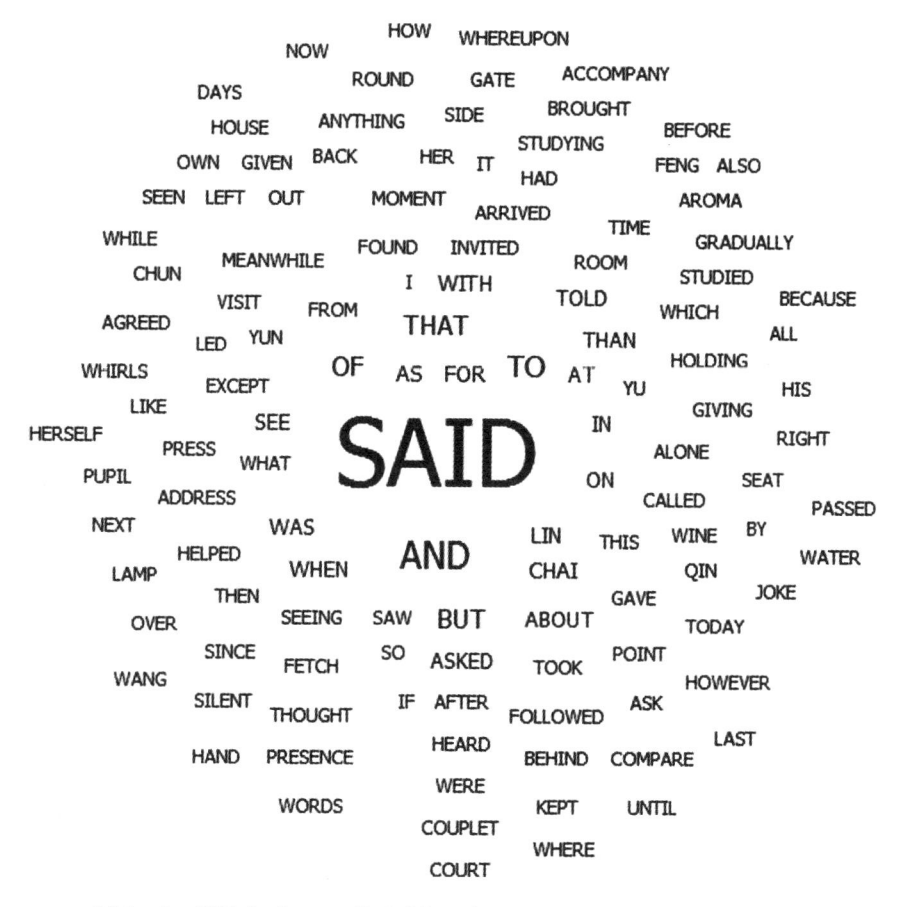

图 1-3　霍译本"Dai-yu"左侧 L1 位置的语境共现词　Word Cloud

如图 1-3 所示，霍译本中，"said"在"Dai-yu"左侧 L1 位置出现的次数最多，而其在"Dai-yu"左侧 L1 位置形成的"said Dai-yu"与霍底本"黛玉道"和"黛玉说"都是对等形式。

以上述对霍译本考察的方法，运用 WORDSMITH 6.0.0 的 COLLOCATE 的 Word Cloud 功能，分别考察杨译本前八十回（对比语料库）中在"Daiyu"右侧 R1 位置和左侧 L1 位置的语境共现词，分别得图 1-4 和图 1-5。

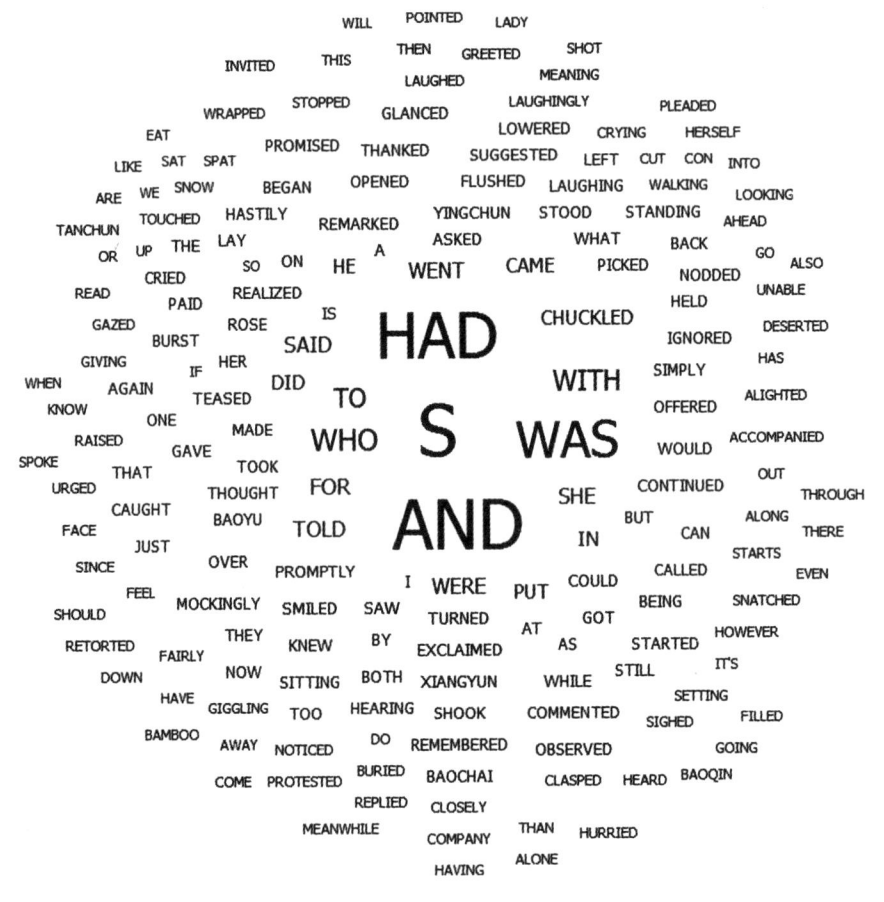

图 1-4 杨译本"Daiyu"右侧 R1 位置的语境共现词 Word Cloud

第一章 霍克斯笔下的林黛玉人物形象 ❋ 59

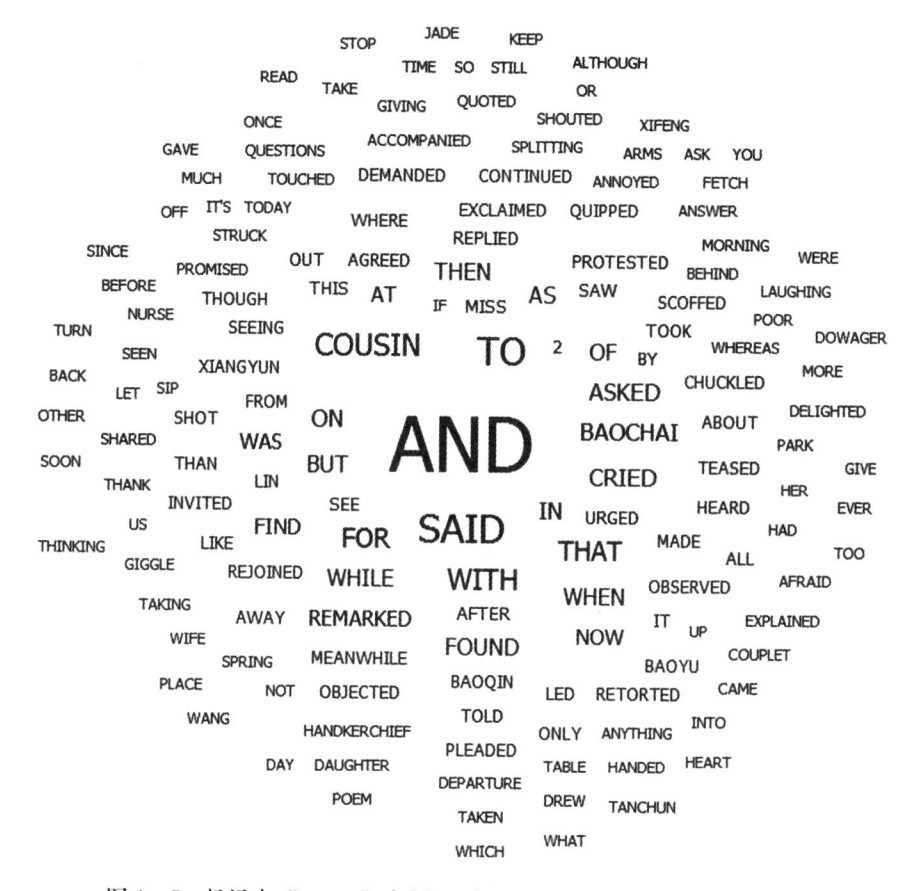

STOP JADE KEEP
READ TIME SO STILL ALTHOUGH
TAKE GIVING QUOTED OR
ONCE ACCOMPANIED SHOUTED XIFENG
GAVE QUESTIONS SPLITTING ARMS ASK YOU
MUCH TOUCHED DEMANDED CONTINUED ANNOYED FETCH
OFF IT'S TODAY EXCLAIMED QUIPPED ANSWER
STRUCK WHERE REPLIED
SINCE PROMISED OUT AGREED THEN PROTESTED MORNING WERE
BEFORE THOUGH THIS AT AS BEHIND LAUGHING
NURSE SEEING IF MISS SAW SCOFFED POOR
TURN SEEN COUSIN TO 2 OF TOOK WHEREAS DOWAGER
BACK XIANGYUN BY MORE
LET SIP FROM ASKED CHUCKLED
OTHER SHOT ON BAOCHAI ABOUT DELIGHTED
SOON SHARED WAS BUT AND PARK
THAN LIN TEASED HER GIVE
THANK INVITED SEE CRIED HEARD EVER
US LIKE FIND FOR SAID IN URGED HAD
THINKING GIGGLE REJOINED WHILE WITH THAT MADE ALL TOO
TAKING AWAY REMARKED AFTER WHEN OBSERVED AFRAID
WIFE SPRING MEANWHILE FOUND NOW IT UP EXPLAINED
PLACE NOT OBJECTED BAOQIN BAOYU COUPLET
WANG HANDKERCHIEF TOLD LED RETORTED CAME
DAY DAUGHTER PLEADED ONLY ANYTHING INTO
POEM DEPARTURE TABLE HANDED HEART
TAKEN DREW TANCHUN
WHICH WHAT

图 1-5 杨译本 "Daiyu" 左侧 L1 位置的语境共现词 Word Cloud

图 1-4 揭示杨译本中 "S" 出现的次数最多，而其在 "Daiyu" 右侧 R1 位置形成的 "Daiyu's" 与霍译本 "Dai-yu's" 正是对等形式；图 1-5 揭示杨译本中，除了功能词 "AND" 外，"SAID" 出现的次数最多，而其在 "Daiyu" 左侧 L1 位置形成的 "said Daiyu" 与霍译本 "said Dai-yu" 乃最为凸显的对等形式。另外，尚有出现频率不十分突出的对等形式 "Daiyu said" "Daiyu told" "remarked Daiyu" "Daiyu remarked" "exclaimed Daiyu" "Daiyu exclaimed" "continued Daiyu" "Daiyu continued" "Daiyu urged" "urged Daiyu" "Daiyu observed" "protested Daiyu" "rejoined Daiyu" 等。

对于本小节的对林黛玉人物形象翻译对等形式的考察结果还需要运用 WORDSMITH 6.0.0 的相关统计功能进行数据对比，该研究将在下节进行。

二 霍底本和霍译本汉英平行语料库的数据比较

运用 WORDSMITH 6.0.0 的 COLLOCATE 的搭配词统计功能，可见前八十回中"黛玉"在霍底本、霍译本[①]中前 20 位的搭配词（按搭配词总频数排列，见表 1-1 和表 1-2）。

表1-1　霍底本中"黛玉"在前八十回中前20位的搭配词（参照语料库）

N	Word	With	Total	Total Left	Total Right	L1	Centre	R1
1	黛玉	黛玉	261	2	2	0	257	0
2	了	黛玉	75	47	28	22	0	0
3	宝玉	黛玉	54	38	16	10	0	4
4	的	黛玉	51	14	37	1	0	22
5	钗	黛玉	41	33	8	19	0	0
6	着	黛玉	41	28	13	19	0	0
7	宝	黛玉	40	31	9	0	0	5
8	说	黛玉	36	22	14	3	0	3
9	便	黛玉	35	14	21	0	0	10
10	人	黛玉	33	7	26	0	0	0
11	又	黛玉	31	18	13	0	0	4
12	一	黛玉	31	12	19	0	0	2
13	是	黛玉	29	14	15	7	0	4
14	在	黛玉	25	5	20	3	0	8
15	来	黛玉	23	11	12	2	0	5
16	因	黛玉	23	14	9	2	0	5
17	见	黛玉	22	16	6	10	0	3
18	去	黛玉	22	10	12	2	0	4
19	道	黛玉	21	0	21	0	0	9
20	也	黛玉	19	4	15	0	0	8

注：N 表示排名；Word 表示所搭配词；With 表示搭配词；Total 表示总频数；Total Left 表示在"黛玉"左边的搭配总频数（含从左边第五个起至左边第一个）；Total Right 表示在"黛玉"右边的搭配总频数（含从右边第五个起至右边第一个）；L1 表示在"黛玉"左边第一个的搭配频数；Centre 表示搭配词居中；R1 表示在"黛玉"右边第一个的搭配频数。

---

① 霍译本为 Dai-yu。

表1-2 霍译本中"黛玉"在前八十回中前20位的搭配词（考察语料库）

N	Word	With	Total	Total Left	Total Right	L1	Centre	R1
1	DAI-YU	Dai-yu	889	0	0	0	889	0
2	AND	Dai-yu	238	98	140	50	0	55
3	TO	Dai-yu	222	104	118	32	0	17
4	THE	Dai-yu	203	93	110	0	0	3
5	SAID	Dai-yu	200	193	7	187	0	4
6	HER	Dai-yu	134	32	102	2	0	2
7	BAO	Dai-yu	121	76	45	0	0	4
8	WAS	Dai-yu	119	34	85	9	0	49
9	S	Dai-yu	107	24	83	0	0	73
10	A	Dai-yu	98	42	56	0	0	2
11	OF	Dai-yu	95	44	51	17	0	1
12	THAT	Dai-yu	91	47	44	19	0	4
13	HAD	Dai-yu	79	20	59	2	0	34
14	IN	Dai-yu	78	39	39	6	0	7
15	YU	Dai-yu	64	42	22	3	0	0
16	CHAI	Dai-yu	57	42	15	13	0	0
17	IT	Dai-yu	56	35	21	1	0	2
18	ON	Dai-yu	55	22	33	8	0	6
19	SHE	Dai-yu	54	25	29	0	0	3
20	AT	Dai-yu	53	22	31	6	0	3

注：N 表示排名；Word 表示所搭配词；With 表示搭配词；Total 表示总频数；Total Left 表示在"Dai-yu"左边的搭配总频数（含从左边第五个起至左边第一个）；Total Right 表示在"Dai-yu"右边的搭配总频数（含从右边第五个起至右边第一个）；L1 表示在"Dai-yu"左边第一个的搭配频数；Centre 表示搭配词居中；R1 表示在"Dai-yu"右边第一个的搭配频数。

如表1-1和表1-2所示，本书的考察语料库霍译本和其对应的原著霍底本在检索节点词"黛玉"的搭配词使用上有明显差别。

首先，最显著的差别是霍底本中与节点词"黛玉"搭配频次序列排第4位的词项"的"在"黛玉"R1位置搭配成"黛玉的"仅为22频次，而"的"的对应形式"'s"在霍译本中虽然与节点词"Dai-yu"搭配频次序列排名降到第9位，但在"Dai-yu"的R1位置搭配成"Dai-yu's"高达

73频次,是霍底本中"黛玉的"3倍之多。

其次,霍底本中"说"和"道"在节点词"黛玉"的 R1 位置与节点词"黛玉"搭配成"黛玉……说"只有 3 频次;另在节点词"黛玉"的 R1 位置与节点词"黛玉"搭配成"黛玉……道"只 9 频次,共达到 12 频次;而"说/道"的对应形式"SAID"在霍译本的 L1 位置搭配成"SAID Dai-yu"的频次高达 187 次,另外,在节点词"黛玉"的 R1 位置搭配成"Dai-yu SAID"还有 4 频次,共达到 191 次,是霍底本中"黛玉……说"和"黛玉……道"出现频次之和的 15 倍左右。另外,如图 1-2 中所示,霍译本中还有"黛玉……说"和"黛玉……道"的其他对应形式,如"Dai-yu said""Dai-yu told""Dai-yu asked""Dai-yu continued"和"Dai-yu murmured",它们出现的次数不多,不在表 1-2 所列的前 20 位搭配词中,但仍需考虑到它们对本书的重要性而并入讨论。

首先,运用 WORDSMITH 6.0.0 的 CONCORD 的语境词共现功能,可显示"黛玉的"在霍底本前八十回中的全部后续词项及"Dai-yu's"在霍译本前八十回中的全部后续词。① 将其中与林黛玉人物形象有关的行分列为表 1-3、表 1-4。

表 1-3　霍底本前八十回中"黛玉的"后续词与林黛玉人物形象有关的行

N	Concordance
1	上,怀里兜的落花撒了一地。试想林黛玉的花颜月貌,将来亦到无
2	提。且说宝玉送了黛玉回来,想着黛玉的孤苦,不免也替他伤感
3	了。三个人又闲话了一回,因提起黛玉的病来,宝钗劝了一回,
4	咱们只管乐咱们的。"那李妈也素知黛玉的为人,说道:"林姐儿,
5	彩的卸了残妆。紫鹃、雪雁素日知道黛玉的情性,无事闷坐,不是

---

① 详见附录一。

表1-4　霍译本前八十回中"Dai-yu's"后续词与林黛玉人物形象有关的行

N	Concordance
1	versation presently turned to the subject of Dai-yu's illness. "When you are out of sorts,
2	r an imitator of Dai-yu, for she had much of Dai-yu's ethereal grace in her looks: the sam
3	Discard Bao-chai's heavenly beauty, destroy Dai-yu's divine intelligence, utterly abolish
4	the Naiad's House. During the past few days Dai-yu's anxiety for Bao-yu had led to a rela
5	i, but there was also something about her of Dai-yu's delicate charm. As he was pondering
6	it helps me forget my troubles." 111 It was Dai-yu's turn to sigh now. A tear rolled down
7	l be able to do it for me." Bao-yu knew what Dai-yu's trouble was as well as Nightingale
8	contained, and because he was uncertain what Dai-yu's feelings would be about his reading
9	d by now wrought a considerable softening on Dai-yu's heart. A sympathetic tear stole dow
10	but on recollection they seem rather stupid. Dai-yu's jokes on the other hand, though the
11	loin them. Now that the weather was warmer, Dai-yu's illness was very much better thoot it
12	urther grounds for tender admiration; and if Dai-yu's divine intelligence is des troyed
13	the best he could, however, in response to Dai-yu's nudge: BAO-YU: The guests on "sca
14	od-humouredly. Bao-chai, long accustomed to Dai-yu's peculiar ways, also ignored them.
15	y it was ever like it was in the beginning." Dai-yu's curiosity got the better of her. she
16	must make our bridal bed." The words, like Dai-yu's languorous line, were from Western C
17	owgoose had long since become habitu¬ated to Dai-yu's moody temperament; they were u
18	unting you and be reborn into another life." Dai-yu's resentment for the gate incident had
19	ly it doesn't count." They had a look at Dai-yu's poem then. It was a Tang-duo-ling. T
20	ing, really. You mustn't be taken in by it." Dai-yu's sobbing had by this time ceased to b
21	oes not concern us. * Bao-yu, believing that Dai-yu's sunstroke was serious and that she m
22	ou died," he said, "I should become a monk." Dai-yu's face darkened immediately: "What
23	ped Dai-yu into bed. As she lay there alone, Dai-yu's thoughts turned to Bao-chai,

续表

N	Concordance
24	recent rapprochement was too familiar with Dai-yu's jealous disposition not to feel
25	Bao-yu came back again. During his absence Dai-yu's sobs seemed to have redoubled
26	ots a flower-patterned fringe BAO-CHAI heard Dai-yu's sarcasm-quite clearly, but her mi
27	eace with her and gradually, very gradually, Dai-yu's equanimity was restored. The Winter
28	ell refuse it. Spring was now at its height. Dai-yu's seasonal cough had returned, and in

为了更加直观，用图1-6和图1-7表示。

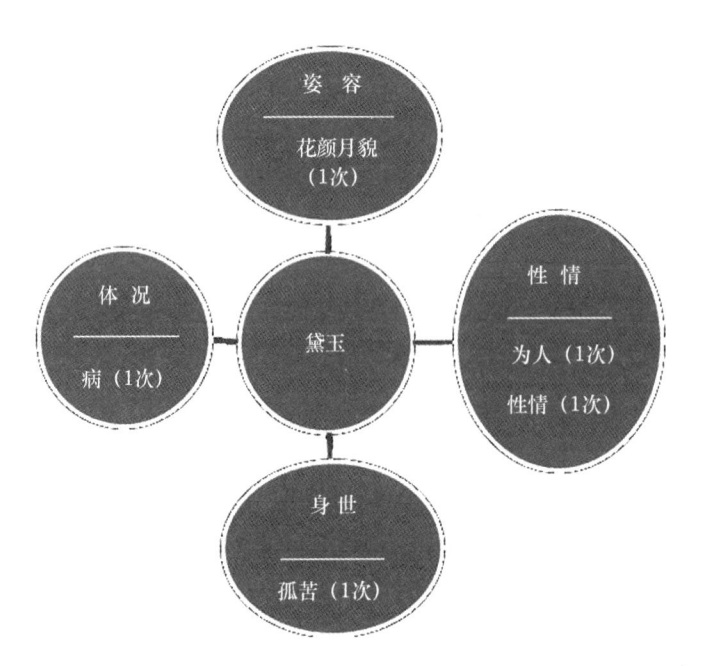

图1-6 霍底本前八十回中"黛玉的"后续词对黛玉人物形象的描述

```
            姿容
    ─────────────
    delicate charm
        (1次)
    ethereal grace
        (1次)
```

```
                        体况
                ─────────────
     性情         illness (2次)
                seasonal cough
        黛玉         (1次)
                sunstroke (1次)
```

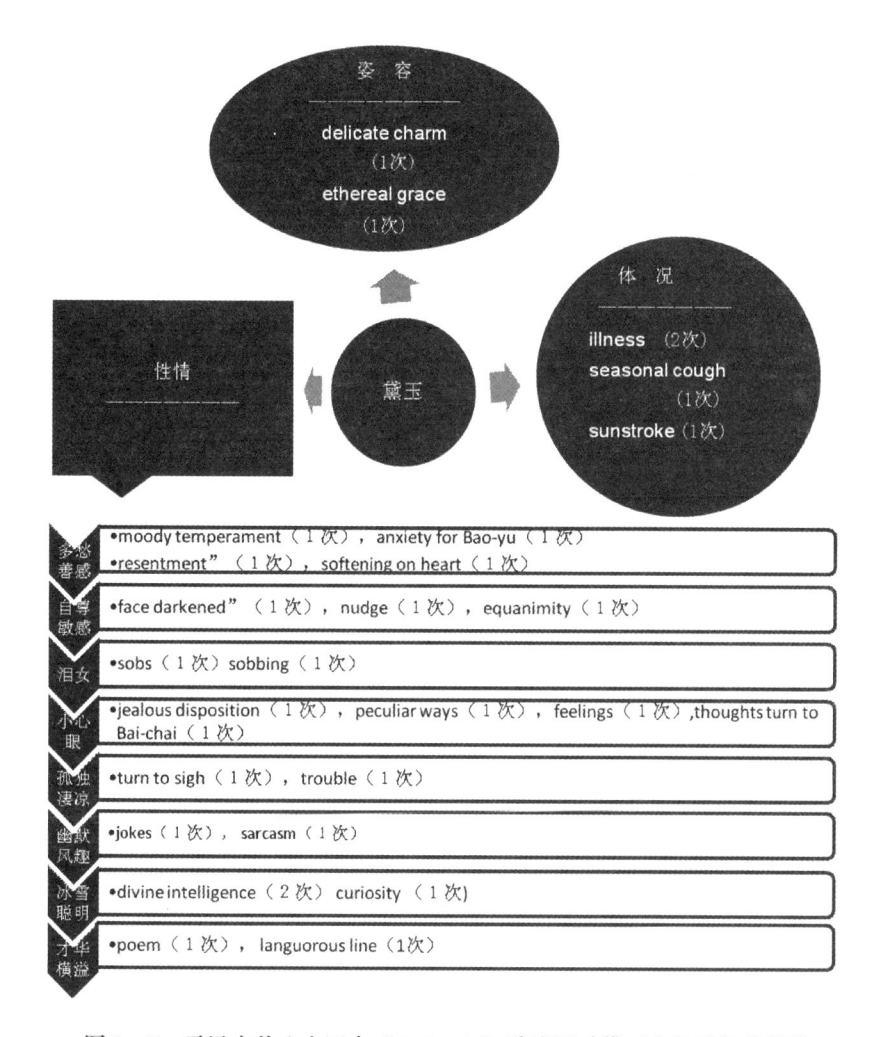

- 多愁善感: moody temperament（1次）, anxiety for Bao-yu（1次）
  resentment"（1次）, softening on heart（1次）
- 自尊敏感: face darkened"（1次）, nudge（1次）, equanimity（1次）
- 泪女: sobs（1次）sobbing（1次）
- 小心眼: jealous disposition（1次）, peculiar ways（1次）, feelings（1次）, thoughts turn to Bai-chai（1次）
- 孤独凄凉: turn to sigh（1次）, trouble（1次）
- 幽默风趣: jokes（1次）, sarcasm（1次）
- 冰雪聪明: divine intelligence（2次）curiosity（1次）
- 才华横溢: poem（1次）, languorous line（1次）

图1-7 霍译本前八十回中"Dai-yu's"后续词对黛玉人物形象的描述

由图1-6和图1-7对比，可见在霍底本前八十回中"黛玉的"后续词提及黛玉"姿容"只有一次，而在霍译本前八十回中"Dai-yu's"后续词两次提及黛玉"姿容"之美；在霍底本前八十回中"黛玉的"后续词提及黛玉"体况"只有一次，而在霍译本前八十回中"Dai-yu's"后续词提及黛玉"体况"多达四次，集中显化她"多病多弱"身；在霍底本前八十回中"黛玉的"后续词提及黛玉"性情"只有两次，且语义模糊，而在霍译本前八十回中"Dai-yu's"后续词提及黛玉"性情"多达28次，多层面、多方位地显化她的性情。

另外，从描写总数上看，在霍译本前八十回"Dai-yu's"后续词与林黛玉人物形象有关的行多达 28 条（见表 1-4），而霍底本前八十回中"黛玉的"后续词与林黛玉人物形象有关的行只有 5 条（见表 1-3）。

可见，从语际显化方向上看，霍译本通过大量增添 Dai-yu's 这一表达形式并在该形式后续词中增添词汇意义描写黛玉，突出原著《红楼梦》林黛玉的人物形象。

接着，运用 WORDSMITH 6.0.0 的 CONCORD 的语境词共现功能，可显示"黛玉"在霍译本、霍底本前八十回中的说话表情方式词。[①] 将其中与林黛玉人物形象有关的后续词分列为表 1-5、表 1-6、表 1-7。

表 1-5　　"黛玉"在霍译本前八十回中的说话表情方式词
（以"said Dai-yu"形式为例）

N	Concordance
1	" "Well, perhaps not quite everything," said Dai-yu wryly. "But she's certainly very obser
2	ou must be very good indeed." "Oh her," said Dai-yu coldly. "I wondered whom you could
3	one in when you get talking!" "Look at her!" said Dai-yu, mockingly. "What a great baby!
4	Who knows whether or not he really lost it?" said Dai-yu scoffingly. "For all we know he
5	wouldn't be worthy of the gold kylin," said Dai-yu huffily, rising from her seat and walk
6	kotow and become my pupil if you like;" said Dai-yu goodnaturedly. "I'm no expert myself,
7	er cup," said Aroma. "Oh, you know me," said Dai-yu smilingly. "I can't drink much
8	! "If you're so anxious to please me," said Dai-yu coldly, "you ought to hire a trour sp
9	hat is all this about?" "Don't ask me!" said Dai-yu coldly. "I don't know. I'm only afign
10	ine you're the only one with a good memory," said Dai-yu haughtily. "I suppose I'm allo
11	re for you, Miss." "I thought as much," said Dai-yu sneeringly. "I get the leavings when e

---

① 详见附录一。

续表

N	Concordance
12	ght of what you have just been saying," said Dai-yu drily, "I'm not at all sure that I ong
13	aithful. "No Reddie at the window seen," said Dai-yu, desperately dredging up a line
14	ld Cousin Xing be pawning her clothes?" said Dai-yu, puzzled. "And why, having pawned
15	ow!" "It would be more romantic still," said Dai-yu drily, "if instead of chanting poems w
16	ion. "I dare say she would be glad to," said Dai-yu drily. "The trouble is that if she sta
17	one! Come in! Come in!" "What is this?" said Dai-yu, joining in the good humour. "A party?
18	"Next thing you'll be catching a cold," said Dai-yu with a sigh, "and then Heaven kno
19	s a large sable tippet. "Look, Monkey!" said Dai-yu, laughing at this furry apparition.
20	ay where you are." "If you were a man," said Dai-yu, laughing, "you could go around like a
21	gers prowled outside in his courtyard," said Dai-yu laughing. "How on earth would she ha
22	room to gether. "Bao-yu," said Dai-yu, addressing him in a heavily mock-serious manner
23	y clever of you to have thought of it," said Dai-yu, smiling, "especially as mimosa does i
24	things to do." "Ah yes, you're busy," said Dai-yu, smiling. "I should have remembered. N
25	was wearing. "Perfume? At this season?" said Dai-yu with a laugh. "I'm not wearing any."
26	snows." "I don't want one, thank you," said Dai-yu laughing. "If I were to wear one of th
27	ould be a bit presumptuous." "But why?" said Dai-yu, smiling. "My window is your win
28	dinary breadth of her knowledge. "Sh!" said Dai-yu, looking round crossly in Bao-yu's dir

表1-6　　　"黛玉"在霍底本前八十回中的说话表情方式词
（以"黛玉……说"形式为例）

1	倒吓了一跳。细看不是别人，却是黛玉，满面含笑，口内说道："好
2	杯来，放在宝玉唇边。宝玉一气饮干，黛玉笑说："多谢。"宝玉替他
3	冒雪而去。李纨命人好好跟着，黛玉忙拦说："不必，有了反
4	手炉儿，黛玉因含笑问他说："谁叫你送来的？难为他费心。那里就
5	来瞧了一瞧，已是子初一刻十分了，黛玉便起身说："我可掌不住了，

表1-7　　　"黛玉"在霍底本前八十回中的说话表情方式词
（以"黛玉……道"形式为例）

N	Concordance
1	炖了肉脯子来吃酒。"众人不解，黛玉笑道："庄子说的'蕉叶
2	席过来，向黛玉笑道："你瞧刘老老的样子。"黛玉笑道："当日圣
3	是心里羡慕，才学这个玩罢了。"探春黛玉都笑道："谁不是玩
4	痴的不成？抬头一看，见是宝玉，黛玉便啐道："呸！我打
5	岂不好看？"宝玉尚未说话，黛玉便先笑道："你看着人家赶蚊
6	他房中嚷起来，大家侧耳听了一听，黛玉先笑道："这是你妈
7	黛玉冷笑道："他在别的上头心还有限，惟有这些人带的东西
8	黛玉旁边冷笑道："也不知是真丢，也不知是给人镶什么戴去
9	黛玉冷笑道："问我呢，我也不知为什么。我原是给你们
10	黛玉冷笑道："我就知道么，别人不挑剩下的也不给我呀。"
11	黛玉听了冷笑道："我当是谁，原来是他。我那里敢挑他
12	黛玉冷笑道："你既这么说，你就特叫一班戏，拣我爱的唱给
13	睡觉呢，等醒来再请罢。"刚说着，黛玉便翻身坐起来，笑道：
14	要着颜色，又要……"刚说到这里，黛玉也自己掌不住，笑道：
15	黛玉笑道："你要是个男人，出去打一个抱不平儿；你又充什
16	黛玉笑道："既要学做诗，你就拜我为师。我虽不通，大略
17	黛玉笑向众人道："我这一社开的又不巧了，偏忘了这两日是
18	黛玉笑道："这时候谁带什么香呢？"宝玉笑道："那
19	黛玉笑道："我不要他。戴上那个，成了画儿上画的和戏上
20	黛玉笑道："你瞧瞧！这么大了，离了姨妈，他就是个最老道
21	黛玉忙笑接道："可是呢，都是他一句话。他是那一门子的老
22	黛玉忙笑道："东西是小，难得你多情如此。宝钗道："这又

如表 1-8 所示，此 3 例"Dai-yu said"不含林黛玉说话表情方式词。

表 1-8   "黛玉"在霍译本前八十回中的说话表情方式词
（以"Dai-yu said"形式为例）

N	Concordance
1	Lotus Pavilion to pay a call on Xi-chun, but Dai-yu said she was going to have a bath, and
2	s because he heard that we were going away." Dai-yu said nothing. After waiting in vain of
3	o-chai and Xi-feng had gone Out of the room, Dai-yu said to Bao-yu. "You see? There are

如表 1-9 所示，此 3 例"Dai-yu told"不含林黛玉说话表情方式词。

表 1-9   "黛玉"在霍译本前八十回中的说话表情方式词
（以"Dai-yu told"形式为例）

N	Concordance
1	with me and study it before I go to bed?" Dai-yu told Nightingale to fetch down the volume to
2	barely read and write." "What's your name?" Dai-yu told him. "What's your school-name?"
3	and then asked Dai-yu about the rose-orris. Dai-yu told Nightingale to wrap some up for her.

如表 1-10 所示，此 7 例"Dai-yu asked"中只有 1 例含林黛玉说话表情方式词。

表 1 – 10　　"黛玉"在霍译本前八十回中的说话表情方式词
（以"Dai-yu asked"形式为例）

N	Concordance
1	many of them do you think you can remember? Dai-yu asked her. "I've been through al the
2	urning on the bed. "Can't you get to sleep?" Dai-yu asked Xiang-yun eventually. "I can new
3	ing noise as the last of the string ran out. Dai-yu asked the others if any of them would
4	s tea made with last year's rain-water too?" Dai-yu asked her. Adamantina looked scornful.
5	rinted." "Is this really true?" Tan-chun and Dai-yu asked incredulously. "If anyone's
6	supper too and were once more in attendance, Dai-yu asked Bao-yu if he was ready to go. H
7	armer for her. "Who told you to bring this?" Dai-yu asked her. "Very kind of them, I amsu

如表 1 – 11 所示，此 6 例"Dai-yu continued"中只有 1 例含林黛玉说话表情方式词。

表 1 – 11　　"黛玉"在霍译本前八十回中的说话表情方式词
（以"Dai-yu continued"形式为例）

N	Concordance
1	fell and birds flew off distressed. As Dai-yu continued weeping there alone, the court
2	or fantasy by losing her handkerchief As Dai-yu continued to crouch there, a prisoner
3	Snowgoose rubbed and pounded her back, Dai-yu continued to retch up wave upon
4	y obtuse!" "You say in your gatha," Dai-yu continued, "…It would be best words un
5	bit too? You can do this cutting later." Dai-yu continued to take no notice. Falling to get
6	omplete. "The others all laughed. Dai-yu continued, laughing so much herself that she

如表 1 – 12 所示，此 2 例"Dai-yu murmured"中均含林黛玉说话表情方式词。

表 1-12　"黛玉"在霍译本前八十回中的说话表情方式词
（以"Dai-yu murmured"形式为例）

N	Concordance
1	ls in the outer room. "Bless His Holy Name!" Dai-yu murmured fervently. Bao-chai la
2	dark shape crosses the cold, bright water - Dai-yu murmured admiringly, but stamp

要之，通过 WORDSMITH 6.0.0 的 CONCORD 的语境词共现功能，可见"黛玉"在霍底本、霍译本前八十回中的全部说话表情方式词（见表 1-13）。

表 1-13　霍底本和霍译本前八十回中"黛玉"的全部说话表情方式词

霍底本"黛玉"说话表情方式词	霍译本"黛玉"说话表情方式词
黛玉（便）啐道（2次）	said Dai-yu scoffingly（1次）
黛玉，满面含笑，口内说道（1次）	said Dai-yu goodnaturedly（1次）
黛玉先笑道（1次）	said Dai-yu smilingly/ Dai-yu smiled at her gratefully（1次）
黛玉便先笑道（1次）	said Dai-yu, smiling,（3次）
黛玉笑道（12次）	said Dai-yu laughing（1次）
探春黛玉都笑道（1次）	said Dai-yu with a laugh（1次）
黛玉因含笑问他说（1次）	said Dai-yu, laughing（2次）
黛玉笑说（1次）	said Dai-yu, laughing at this furry apparition（1次）
黛玉笑向众人道（1次）	said Dai-yu, joining in the good humour（1次）
黛玉忙拦说（1次）	said Dai-yu wryly（1次）
黛玉叹道（3次）	said Dai-yu with a sigh/ Dai-yu sighed（3次）
黛玉冷笑道（6次）	said Dai-yu coldly（3次）
黛玉忙笑接道（1次）	Dai-yu hurriedly corrected herself（1次）
黛玉不解何故，因笑道（1次）	said Dai-yu scornfully（1次）

续表

霍底本"黛玉"说话表情方式词	霍译本"黛玉"说话表情方式词
	said Dai-yu sneeringly（1次）
	said Dai-yu, addressing him in a heavily mock-serious manner（1次）
	said Dai-yu, mockingly（1次）
	said Dai-yu drily（3次）
	said Dai-yu ruefully（1次）
	said Dai-yu huffily/ very frostily（1次）
	said Dai-yu, looking round crossly/she said crossly to herself（1次）
	said Dai-yu haughtily（1次）
	said Dai-yu, puzzled（1次）
	Dai-yu murmured fervently（1次）
	Dai-yu murmured admiringly（1次）
	Dai-yu continued, laughing so much herself（1次）

"黛玉"在霍底本、霍译本前八十回中的说话表情方式词对比如图1-8所示。

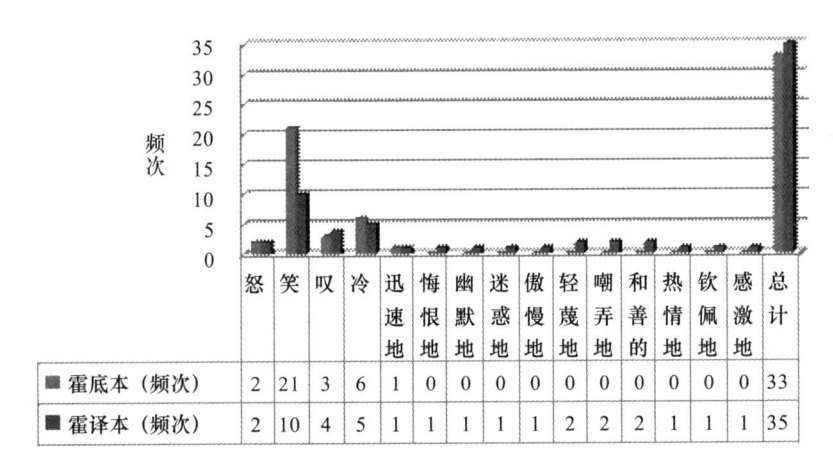

	怒	笑	叹	冷	迅速地	悔恨地	幽默地	迷惑地	傲慢地	轻蔑地	嘲弄地	和善的	热情地	钦佩地	感激地	总计
■霍底本（频次）	2	21	3	6	1	0	0	0	0	0	0	0	0	0	0	33
■霍译本（频次）	2	10	4	5	1	1	1	1	1	2	2	2	1	1	1	35

图1-8 "黛玉"在霍底本、霍译本前八十回中的说话表情方式词对比

图 1-8 显示："黛玉"在霍底本前八十回中的说话表情方式词共出现 33 频次，主要是以"黛玉笑道"的方式出现；"黛玉"在霍译本前八十回中的说话表情方式词共出现 35 频次，高于原著霍底本的 33 频次，而以"黛玉笑道"的方式出现仅仅 10 频次，"笑"的频率低于原著霍底本的 21 频次，但与此同时却出现了原著霍底本中未曾出现的说话表情方式词，霍译本中黛玉的形象更为多样和丰满。可见，从语际显化方向上看，霍译本在形式和意义上均突出了黛玉的形象。

三 霍译本和杨译本英英平行语料库的数据比较

借助 WORDSMITH 6.0.0 的 CONCORD 检索功能，观察对比语料库杨译本中"黛玉"[①]的搭配词特征，检索发现：SAID 在杨译本中与"Daiyu"的搭配频次只到前 21 位，不像霍译本中在前 20 位的范围，如表 1-14 所示。

表 1-14　杨译本前八十回中"黛玉"前 21 位的搭配词（对比语料库）

N	Word	With	Total	Total Left	Total Right	L1	Centre	R1
1	DAIYU	Daiyu	800	4	4	0	792	0
2	AND	Daiyu	234	103	131	60	0	45
3	TO	Daiyu	208	100	108	23	0	11
4	THE	Daiyu	149	53	96	0	0	2
5	HER	Daiyu	121	23	98	1	0	3
6	A	Daiyu	103	28	75	0	0	4
7	WAS	Daiyu	89	29	60	7	0	31
8	HAD	Daiyu	84	21	63	1	0	41
9	BAOYU	Daiyu	77	46	31	2	0	4
10	IN	Daiyu	76	34	42	10	0	5
11	WITH	Daiyu	75	33	42	14	0	12
12	S	Daiyu	75	19	56	0	0	46

---

① 杨译本为 Daiyu。

续表

N	Word	With	Total	Total Left	Total Right	L1	Centre	R1
13	OF	Daiyu	69	40	29	9	0	0
14	BAOCHAI	Daiyu	66	41	25	11	0	2
15	SHE	Daiyu	64	34	30	0	0	6
16	HE	Daiyu	53	29	24	0	0	5
17	THAT	Daiyu	50	27	23	12	0	2
18	AT	Daiyu	47	15	32	7	0	4
19	ON	Daiyu	46	24	22	10	0	4
20	THIS	Daiyu	44	21	23	4	0	1
21	SAID	Daiyu	42	32	10	25	0	7

注：N 表示排名；Word 表示所搭配词；With 表示搭配词；Total 表示总频数；Total Left 表示在"Daiyu"左边的搭配总频数（从左边第五个起至左边第一个）；Total Right 表示在"Daiyu"右边的搭配总频数（从右边第五个起至右边第一个）；L1 表示在"Daiyu"左边第一个的搭配频数；Centre 表示搭配词居中；R1 表示在"Daiyu"右边第一个的搭配频数。

表 1-14 所示的对比语料库杨译本和表 1-2 所示的考察语料库霍译本在检索节点词"黛玉"的搭配词使用上有明显差别。

首先，最显著的差别是霍译本中与节点词"Dai-yu"搭配序列排第 9 位的词项"S"在"Dai-yu"的 R1 位置搭配成"Dai-yu's"高达 73 频次，而在杨译本中"S"与节点词"Daiyu"的搭配序列排名降到第 12 位，且在"Daiyu"的 R1 位置搭配成"Daiyu's"仅 46 频次，几乎只有霍译本对应形式的一半。

其次，霍译本中排名第 5 位的搭配词 SAID 在节点词"Dai-yu"的 L1 位置搭配成"SAID Dai-yu"高达 187 频次，另外，在节点词"Dai-yu"的 R1 位置搭配成"Dai-yu SAID"还有 4 频次，共达到 191 频次。而杨译本中与之对应的词项 SAID 在节点词"Daiyu"的 L1 位置搭配成"SAID Daiyu"只有 25 频次，另外，在节点词"黛玉"的 R1 位置搭配成"Daiyu SAID"还有 7 频次，共只有 32 频次，几乎只有霍译本对应形式的 1/6。

另外，如图 1-4 和图 1-5 所示，杨译本中"Daiyu said""Daiyu told""remarked Daiyu""Daiyu remarked""exclaimed Daiyu""Daiyu exclaimed""continued Daiyu""Daiyu continued""Daiyu urged""urged Daiyu""Daiyu observed""protested Daiyu""rejoined Daiyu"出现的次数不多,不是排名前21位的搭配词,但仍需考虑到它们对本书的重要性,因此我们运用 WORDSMITH 6.0.0 的 CONCORD 的语境词功能,找出了在杨译本前八十回中与这些形式共现的"Daiyu"的说话表情方式词。

首先,运用 WORDSMITH 6.0.0 的 CONCORD 的语境词共现功能,可见"Daiyu's"在杨译本前八十回中的全部后续词,将与林黛玉人物形象有关的后续词行列表如下(见表1-15)。

表1-15　　　杨译本前八十回中"Daiyu's"后续词与
林黛玉人物形象有关的行

N	Concordance
1	tains, then helped her mistress to bed. Daiyu's thoughts turned to Baochai as sh
2	comfort her. All present had been struck by Daiyu's good breeding. For in spite
3	eached Paddy-Sweet Cottage where they showed Daiyu's poem to Li Wan, who
4	to chuckle. And Baochai, aware that this was Daiyu's way, paid no attention eith
5	all my troubles melt away." Tears came into Daiyu's eyes. "She's doing this on
6	wants you." "He's been inquiring after Miss Daiyu's health, and I've been reas
7	shoulders and eyes and eyebrows rather like Daiyu's. She was scolding one o
8	s off well it doesn't count." Then they read Daiyu's poem to the melody Tangduo
9	arrival of concubine Zhao, come to ask after Daiyu's health. Daiyu knew that sh
10	and Xichun. The newcomers having asked after Daiyu's health, they all chatted
11	accommodating ways con trasted strongly with Daiyu's stand-offish reserve an

为了更加直观,用图1-9表示。

```
                        ┌─────────────────────────┐
                        │         姿 容           │
                        │  ─────────────────      │
                        │ shoulders and eys and   │
                        │ eyebrows rather like Daiyu's │
                        │        (1次)            │
                        └─────────────────────────┘
                                  ↑
                               ┌──────┐
                               │ 黛玉 │
                               └──────┘
                              ↙        ↘
                  ┌────────┐              ┌─────────────────────┐
                  │ 性情   │              │       体 况         │
                  └────────┘              │ ─────────────────   │
                                          │ ask after Daiyu's health │
                                          │       (2次)         │
                                          │ inquire after Daiyu's health │
                                          │       (1次)         │
                                          └─────────────────────┘
```

多愁善感	• ways（1次）
自尊敏感	• stand-offish reserve（1次）
泪女	• tears came into Daiyu's eyes（1次）
小心眼	• thoughts turn to Bai-chai（1次）
才华横溢	• poem（2次）
很有教养	• good breeding（1次）

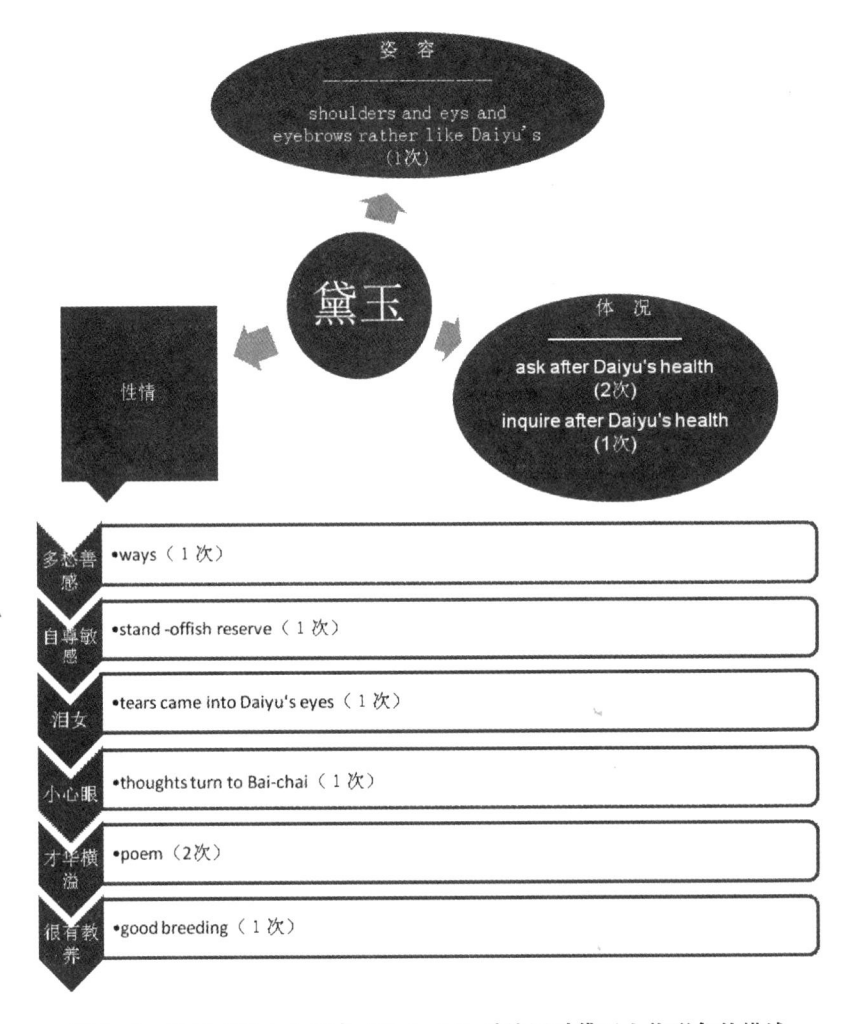

图 1-9　杨译本前八十回中"Daiyu's"后续词对黛玉人物形象的描述

对比图 1-9 和图 1-7，可见在杨译本前八十回中"Daiyu's"后续词中提及黛玉"姿容"只有一次，且并未明确描写"姿容"之美，而在霍译本前八十回中"Dai-yu's"后续词两次提及黛玉"姿容"之美；在杨译本前八十回中"Daiyu's"后续词中提及黛玉"体况"有三次，并未明确描写"体况"之弱，而在霍译本前八十回中"Dai-yu's"后续词提及黛玉"体况"多达四次，且集中显化她"多病多弱"身；在杨译本前八十回中"Daiyu's"的后续词从六个方面提及黛玉"性情"，除了在明确凸显她的"很有教养"时用"good breeding"词项外，其余五个方面都不及霍译本的描写明确,且在霍译本前八十回中"Dai-yu's"后续词还提及林黛玉"孤独凄凉""幽默风趣""冰雪聪明"等方面的形象特征。而从描写总数上的对比更能说明问题,在霍译本前八十回中"Dai-yu's"后续词与林黛玉人物形象有关的多达28行(见表1-4),而杨译本前八十回中"Daiyu's"后续词与林黛玉人物形象有关的只有11行(见表1-15)。

可见,从类比显化方向上看,相比杨译本,霍译本通过大量创设"Dai-yu's"这一表达形式并在该形式后续词中增添信息描写黛玉形象。

其次,运用 WORDSMITH 6.0.0 的 CONCORD 的语境词共现功能,可得"Daiyu"在杨译本前八十回中的说话表情方式词(见表1-16至表1-25)。

表1-16 "Daiyu"在杨译本前八十回中的说话表情方式词
(以"said Daiyu"形式为例)

N	Concordance
1	"In that case you needn't see them either," said Daiyu. Pointing at Baoyu she added, "He's
2	"Fa ilure to answer promptly means defeat," said Daiyu. "And even if he answered it now it
3	done much reading, cousin?" he asked. "No," said Daiyu. "I've only studied for a couple of
4	mall thing, but I appreciate your kindness," said Daiyu gratefully. "It's not worth mentioning
5	ou m stn't forget us." "Speak for yourself," said Daiyu. "Don't drag me in." Turning to Baocha
6	ng, not simply smart." "So much the better," said Daiyu. "This household of ours is too extra
7	this?" he asked the maids. "Whoever it was," said Daiyu, "It's none of Master Bao's busines
8	tudied. "I've just finished the Four Books," said Daiyu. "But I'm very ignorant." Then she
9	y aga in," urged Li Wan. "I'll make a guess," said Daiyu. "Is it 'though good there is no docum
10	n past eleven. "I can't stay up any longer," said Daiyu getting up. "I have to take medicine to

续表

N	Concordance
11	now. A fine fix I'm in." "People are easy," said Daiyu. "But can you paint insects?" "You'r
12	and draw lots to decide which one to play," said Daiyu. This met with general approval and
13	s of her erudition. "Do be quiet and watch," said Daiyu. "Before we've seen The Drunken M
14	k ang minute." "I'd no idea it was so late," said Daiyu. The three girls went to Green Lattice
15	ill x iren comes." "Pay no attention to him," said Daiyu. "First go and get me some water." Zij
16	Thank you very much, aunt, you're too kind," said Daiyu. "Really I shouldn't decline. But it
17	W to bits!" "It's the fault of the bridle," said Daiyu soothingly. "If you adjust it, it'll
18	"If you're set on starting a poetry club," said Daiyu, "we must all be poets. And first, to be
19	art one if you like, but don't count me in," said Daiyu. "I'm not up to it." "If you're not, who
20	been. "With Cousin Baochai." "I thought so," said Daiyu tartly. "Thank goodness there was
21	ttle me." "The lisper loves to rattle away," said Daiyu with a laugh. "Fancy saying ai instead
22	hem quick!" "This is all Xiangyun's doing," said Daiyu. "What did I tell you?" Li Wan hurried
23	red Baochai. "We'll know when we get there," said Daiyu. They went to Paddy-Sweet Cotta
24	yesterday to paint a picture of the Garden," said Daiyu. "She's glad of the excuse to ask for
25	rdly trick." "My kite's gone and I'm tired," said Daiyu, "I'm going back to rest." "Just

上表25例"said Daiyu"中只有4例含林黛玉说话表情方式词。

表1－17　　"Daiyu" 在杨译本前八十回中的说话表情方式词
（以"Daiyu said"形式为例）

N	Concordance
1	in, cousin? Your eyes are red from weeping." Daiyu said nothing. Zijuan, standing to one
2	t to finish. Finding her in such a good mood Daiyu said, "I've never seen you before in s
3	"I'll get you some more." Xiren offered. But Daiyu said, "You know the doctor won't let m
4	ciousness still rankled with Baoyu, and when Daiyu, said this he thought：" I could forgiv
5	her. After the usual exchange of civilities, Daiyu said to Baochai："Your brother must ha
6	d been having. "I've always been like this," Daiyu said with a smile. "I've been taking m
7	whole room laughing. Baochai was also there. Daiyu said nothing but took a seat by th

上表7例"Daiyu said"中只有1例含林黛玉说话内容或表情方式词。

表1－18　　"Daiyu" 在杨译本前八十回中的说话表情方式词
（以"asked...Daiyu/Daiyu...asked"形式为例）

N	Concordance
1	this made with last year's rain-water too?" asked Daiyu. Miaoyu smiled disdainfully. "Can you
2	to the mystification of them all, he asked Daiyu if she had any jade. Imagining that he
3	d Ancestress. I deserve to be caned." Taking Daiyu's hand again, she asked, "How old ar
4	hat's all this crying during the festival?" asked Daiyu mockingly. "Are you fighting for sticky
5	awake. So the two of them tossed and turned. Daiyu asked, "Why aren't you asleep yet?"
6	dark room where the lamps were not yet lit. Daiyu, lying on the bed, asked who it wa
7	Baochai's was more distin¬guished. She then asked Daiyu for her poem. "Have you all finish

续表

N	Concordance
8	ack from their own meal to wait on them, and Daiyu asked Baoyu: "Are you ready to go
9	t the inscription over the lintel. Just then Daiyu came in and he asked her, "Tell me hone
10	by Li Wan and Xifeng. Then her grandmother asked Daiyu what books she had studied. "I've
11	room he told her what had happened. Then he asked Daiyu, who was there, in which part of th
12	oon Baochai stepped into the inner room and asked Daiyu what she was doing, then watched
13	d when it's finished she'll send some more." Daiyu thanked her and asked her to sit down
14	do, I'll really respect you." "Who's that?" Daiyu promptly asked. "Dare you pick fault
15	and Xichun. The newcomers having asked after Daiyu's health, they all chatted for a whil
16	r to his mother's apartment where, on seeing Daiyu, Lady Wang asked: "Has Doctor Bao"
17	you." "Can she be pawning her things?" asked Daiyu. "If so, why send you this ticket?" Rea
18	"How many poems have you memorized?" asked Daiyu. "I've read all those marked with
19	ations sent out that you're here in force?" asked Daiyu jokingly. "I sent you two canisters of
20	go on ahead, leaving him to follow, but now Daiyu asked him: "When will Xiren be back
21	in by his straight face and earnest manner, Daiyu asked to hear about it. Then Baoyu, sup
22	ing away. After they had greeted each other, Daiyu, who was also there, asked Baoyu

上表22例中只有3例含林黛玉说话表情方式词。

表1-19　"Daiyu"在杨译本前八十回中的说话表情方式词
（以"remarked Daiyu/Daiyu remarked"形式为例）

N	Concordance
1	de to think "Yes, this is where we come in," Daiyu remarked, then continued: "One 'ta
2	ere be if every thing is perfect?'" remarked Daiyu. "To my mind this is quite good enou
3	ich the hero sacrifices to his drowned wife, Daiyu remarked to Baochai: "What a fool t
4	l drink with her." As they filled their cups Daiyu remarked to Tanchun, "you're the apri
5	"Their Ladyships are in high spirits today," Daiyu remarked. "This fluting is pleasant a
6	t so observant about other things," remarked Daiyu cuttingly. "But she's most observa
7	good when those two get together," remarked Daiyu. "When ever that happens, ther
8	of them demanded. "Most ingenious," remarked Daiyu with a smile. "Doesn't grass turn
9	"Your third sister's rather smart," remarked Daiyu. "Although she's been put in charge
10	powder for her. "I'm better today," remarked Daiyu. "I mean to go for a stroll. Go back a

上表10例中只有2例含林黛玉说话表情方式词。

表1-20　"Daiyu"在杨译本前八十回中的说话表情方式词
（以"exclaimed Daiyu/Daiyu exclaimed"为例）

N	Concordance
1	e gruel. Before the rest could say anything, Daiyu exclaimed: "Buddha be praised!" Baoc
2	Baochai explained what had happened. Daiyu exclaimed in distress and sympathy,
3	Look, here comes the Monkey King!" exclaimed Daiyu laughing. "She's got a cape too,
4	o try you. "The girl must be mad!" exclaimed Daiyu in amazement. "What am I to be trie
5	tanding heart. "The girl's crazy!" exclaimed Daiyu. "A few days away, and you've sudden
6	A stork's shadow flit across the chilly pool Daiyu exclaimed in admiration again, stamping
7	icine." "How good you always are to others!" Daiyu exclaimed with a sigh. "I'm so touchy

上表 7 例中有 5 例含林黛玉说话表情方式词。

表 1 – 21　　"Daiyu" 在杨译本前八十回中的说话表情方式词
（以 "continued Daiyu/Daiyu continued" 为例）

N	Concordance
1	iff and overloaded." "To my mind," continued Daiyu, "The best line of all is sunset in ch
2	hardly glow. With a giggle Daiyu continued: Daiyu: Snow covers the broom of the mo
3	de to think "Yes, this is where we come in," Daiyu remarked, then continued: "One 'tap
4	upid fellow wants to dabble in metaphysics!" Daiyu continued, "The last two lines of you
5	The sky above is sprinkled with bright stars Daiyu continued: "And everywhere sweet
6	these vulgar words. "To tell you the truth," Daiyu continued, "I'm the one who suggested

上表 6 例中只有 1 例含林黛玉说话表情方式词。

表 1 – 22　　"Daiyu" 在杨译本前八十回中的说话表情方式词
（以 "urged Daiyu/Daiyu…urged" 为例）

N	Concordance
1	t to see her mistress. Xiangling again urged Daiyu to lend her Du Fu's poems, and be
2	ngue." "Go ahead and cut it up," Baoyu urged Daiyu. "I shan't wear it anyway, so it do
3	enjoy watching these three rivals compete. Daiyu urged Xiangyun to go on. "So even
4	ht it, do let us profit by seeing it," urged Daiyu. "They've a whole pile of cases and has
5	d arrived from Li Wan with an invitation for Daiyu, and Baoyu urged her to go with him
6	not be described in detail. The nurses urged Daiyu to sit on the kang, on the edge of
7	clear up the misunderstanding, quick!" urged Daiyu. "That may bring him back to his s

上表 7 例均不含林黛玉说话表情方式词。

表 1-23 "Daiyu" 在杨译本前八十回中的说话表情方式词
（以 "rejoined Daiyu" 形式为例）

N	Concordance
1	gs to do." "I know what keeps you busy," rejoined Daiyu laughingly. "Now that it's turning
2	aid. "Last night there was a fine moon," rejoined Daiyu. "I was meaning to write a poem on
3	nny Liu who started it." "That's right," rejoined Daiyu promptly. "It's all owing to her

上表中有 2 例含林黛玉说话内容或表情方式词。

表 1-24 "Daiyu" 在杨译本前八十回中的说话表情方式词
（以 "protested Daiyu" 形式为例）

N	Concordance
1	rged. "Must you always be hurrying me?" protested Daiyu. "Whether I take it or not is none of y
2	"That really had no classical source," protested Daiyu. "Tomorrow we'll look it up for eve-
3	is head. "Don't be such a spoil-sport," protested Daiyu. "If Uncle sends for you,
4	t once. "You shouldn't have done that," protested Daiyu with a smile. "I've some questions

上表中只有 1 例含林黛玉说话内容或表情方式词。

表 1-25 "Daiyu"在杨译本前八十回中的说话表情方式词
（以"Daiyu observed"形式为例）

N	Concordance
1	right. Very fair." "Mine didn't amount to much," Daiyu observed. "They're rather contrived."
2	to the different apartments to pay her respects. Daiyu observed laughingly, "I picked the wron

上表中只有 1 例含林黛玉说话表情方式词。

要之，通过 WORDSMITH 6.0.0 的 CONCORD 的语境词共现功能，可见"Daiyu"在杨译本前八十回中的全部说话表情方式词（见表1-26）。

表 1-26 杨译本前八十回中"Daiyu"的全部说话表情方式词

said Daiyu gratefully（1次）	rejoined Daiyu promptly（1次）
said Daiyu soothingly（1次）	rejoined Daiyu laughingly（1次）
said Daiyu tartly（1次）	asked Daiyu mockingly（1次）
said Daiyu with a laugh（1次）	asked Daiyu jokingly（1次）
With a giggle Daiyu continued（2次）	Daiyu observed laughingly（1次）
Daiyu said with a smile（1次）	protested Daiyu with a smile（1次）
remarked Daiyu cuttingly（1次）	exclaimed Daiyu in amazement（1次）
remarked Daiyu with a smile（1次）	exclaimed Daiyu laughing（1次）
Daiyu exclaimed in admiration again（1次）	Daiyu exclaimed in distress and sympathy（1次）
Daiyu exclaimed with a sigh（1次）	

"黛玉"在霍译本、杨译本前八十回中的说话表情方式词对比如图 1-10 所示。

第一章　霍克斯笔下的林黛玉人物形象　※　85

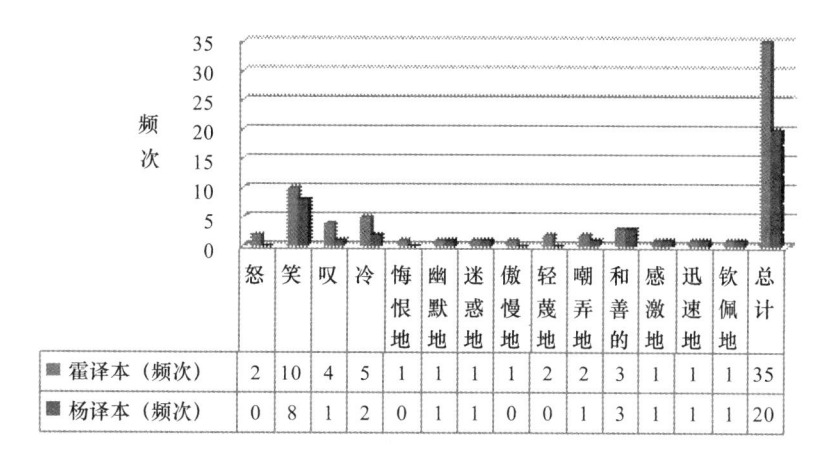

	怒	笑	叹	冷	悔恨地	幽默地	迷惑地	傲慢地	轻蔑地	嘲弄地	和善的	感激地	迅速地	钦佩地	总计
■霍译本（频次）	2	10	4	5	1	1	1	1	2	2	3	1	1	1	35
■杨译本（频次）	0	8	1	2	0	1	1	0	0	1	3	1	1	1	20

图 1-10　霍译本和杨译本前八十回中"黛玉"的说话表情方式词比较

通过图 1-10 可见，在前八十回的"黛玉"说话表情方式词出现频次上，霍译本有 35 次之多，远远高于杨译本的 20 次；另外，虽有部分说话表情方式词重叠，但霍译本中出现了杨译本未曾出现过的黛玉说话表情方式词，黛玉的形象在霍译本中更为多样和丰满。由此，从类比显化方向上看，霍译本在表达形式和意义上均比杨译本突出黛玉的形象。

第二节　分析与讨论

霍克斯在英译中注意到《红楼梦》语言表达上的含蓄特点，根据英汉语言的特点，以一种译者评论的态度，"用更明显的形式表述原著文本的信息，在翻译中增添解释性成分"[①]，通过创设"Dai-yu's"这种极具描写性的语言形式并在其后增添解释性成分的词汇的特点来显化林黛玉形象。另外，通过转词增意塑形象的翻译策略，将林黛玉说话时的态度、性格及品格体现出来，凸显了林黛玉的人物形象。对比原著和杨译本，可以发现霍译的显化翻译方法乃有意识的策略，而非下意识语言选择的结果，即霍克斯对林黛玉人物形象进行了非强制性显化翻译。下面分两

---

① Mark Shuttleworth and Moira Cowie, *Dictionary of Translation Studies*，上海外语教育出版社 1997 年版，第 55 页。

种情况进行讨论。①

第一种：原文中暗含林黛玉某种人物形象或某种说话的表情，但语言表述上不够明确，霍克斯采用增添额外信息的词汇手段等标记方式，将之显示出来，而杨译本中则不显示。

Klaudy 认为"显化不仅仅指原作中不存在而译作中添加的表述，也包括原文中所暗示或只有通过预设才能认识到的信息在译文中加以明示"②。

例 1-1

霍底本：再留神细看，见这女孩子眉蹙春山，眼颦秋水，面薄腰纤，袅袅婷婷，大有<u>黛玉之态</u>。（《红楼梦》第三十回）

霍译本：It was curious that he should have thought her an imitator of Dai-yu, for she had much of <u>Dai-yu's ethereal grace in her looks</u>: the same delicate face and frail, slender body; the same brows like hills in spring, And eyes like autumn's limpid pools; —even the same little frown that had often made him compare Dai-yu with Xi-shi of the legend.

杨底本：再留神细看，只见这女孩子眉蹙春山，眼颦秋水，面薄腰纤，袅袅婷婷，大有<u>林黛玉之态</u>。（《红楼梦》第三十回）

杨译本：With her finely arched eyebrows and limpid eyes, her delicate features, slender waist and graceful movements, she <u>bore a striking resemblance to Daiyu</u>.

分析：翻译"黛玉之态"时，杨译本没有显化林黛玉的姿容特征，而霍译本通过增添额外信息，将之显化为"Dai-yu's ethereal grace in her looks"，凸显了林黛玉"阆苑仙葩"的绝世美丽和超凡气质形象。

---

① 为了防止出现由于杨译本的底本与霍译本的底本不同而导致的译文差异，在分析与讨论中将杨译本的底本呈现出来以论证在相同或相似底本下霍译本与杨译本中林黛玉人物形象的不同。

② Kinga Klaudy, "Back-translation as a Tool for Detecting Explicitation Strategies in Translation", in Kinga Klaudy, José Lambert and Anikó Sohár (ed.), *Translation Studies in Hungary*, Budapest: Scholastica, 1996, pp. 101-102.

例 1-2

霍底本：时届季春，<u>黛玉又犯了咳嗽</u>；湘云又因时气所感，也病卧在蘅芜院，一天医药不断。（《红楼梦》第五十五回）

霍译本：Spring was now at its height. <u>Dai-yu's seasonal cough</u> had returned, and in All-spice Court Shi Xiang-yun lay ill in bed with some epidemic sickness that required constant medical attention.

杨底本：时届孟春，<u>黛玉又犯了</u>嗽症。湘云亦因时气所感，亦卧病于蘅芜院，一天医药不断。（《红楼梦》第五十五回）

杨译本：It was now early spring and <u>Daiyu was coughing again</u>. While Xiangyun too was under the weather, confined to her bed in Alpinia Park, taking medicine day after day.

分析：翻译"黛玉又犯了咳嗽/嗽症"时，杨译本以直译为主，而霍译本通过增添额外信息，将之显化为"Dai-yu's seasonal cough"，凸显了林黛玉"虚弱易病"的形象。

例 1-3

霍底本：紫鹃、雪雁素日知道<u>黛玉的情性</u>，无事闷坐，不是愁眉，便是长叹，且好端端的不知为着什么，常常的便自泪不干的。（《红楼梦》第二十七回）

霍译本：Nightingale and Snowgoose had long since become habituated to <u>Dai-yu's moody temperament</u>; they were used to her unaccountable fits of depression, when she would sit, the picture of misery, in gloomy silence broken only by an occasional gusty sigh, and to her mysterious, perpetual weeping, that was occasioned by no observable cause.

杨底本：紫鹃、雪雁素日知道<u>林黛玉的情性</u>：无事闷坐，不是愁眉，便是长叹；且好端端的不知为什么，常常的便自泪道不干的。（《红楼梦》第二十七回）

杨译本：Zijuan and Xueyan knew <u>their young mistress' ways</u>. She would often sit moodily frowning or sighing over nothing or, for no apparent reason, would give way to tong spells of weeping.

分析：翻译"黛玉的情性"时，杨译本以模糊译模糊，而霍译本通过增添额外信息，将之显化为"Dai-yu's moody temperament"，凸显了林黛玉"多愁善感"的形象。

例 1-4

霍底本：看至此，意趣洋洋，趁着酒兴，不禁提笔续曰：焚花散麝，而闺阁始人含其劝矣。戕钗钦之仙姿，灰黛玉之灵窍，丧天情意，而闺阁之美恶始相类矣。（《红楼梦》第二十一回）

霍译本：The words wonderfully suited his present mood. He read no further. Impulsively picking up a writing-brush, and with the inspiration lent him by his tipsiness, he added the following lines in the margin: Away then with Musk and Aroma, and the female tongue will cease from nagging. Discard Bao-chai's heavenly beauty, destroy Dai-yu's divine intelligence, utterly abolish all tender feelings, and the female heart will cease from envy.

杨底本：看至此段，意趣洋洋，逗着酒兴，不禁提笔续曰：焚花散麝，而闺阁始人含其劝矣；戕宝钗之仙姿，灰黛玉之灵窍，丧减情意，而闺阁之美恶始相类矣。（《红楼梦》第二十一回）

杨译本：Baoyu was so delighted with this passage that, stimulated as he was by wine, he picked up his brush and continued in the same vein: Burn the flower (Xiren), get rid of the musk (Sheyue), and those in the inner apartments will keep their advice to themselves. Spoil the beauty of the precious trinket (Baochai), dull the intelligence of the black jade (Daiyu), do away with affection, and in the inner chambers fair and foul will then be on an equal footing.

分析：翻译"黛玉之灵窍"时，杨译本以直译为主，而霍译本采用了更具描写性的"Dai-yu's"翻译形式，并通过增添额外信息"divine"，凸显了林黛玉作为"仙草化身"的超凡脱俗、得天地精华的聪慧非凡的才智形象。

例 1-5

霍底本："你们细想，颦儿这几句话，虽没什么，回想却有滋味。我

倒笑的动不得了。"(《红楼梦》第四十二回)

霍译本:"Dai-yu's jokes on the other hand, though the words at first appear colourless, are richly humorous to remember. They certainly make me laugh a lot."

杨底本:"你们细想颦儿这几句话,虽淡淡的,回想却有滋味。我倒笑的动不得了。"

杨译本:"but when you consider what she's just said, though there seems nothing to it, It's so funny in retrospect that. I can't move for laughing."(《红楼梦》第四十二回)

分析:翻译"颦儿这几句话"时,杨译本以直译为主,而霍译本采用了更具描写性的"Dai-yu's"翻译形式,并通过增添额外信息"jokes",凸显了林黛玉"灵心慧舌"的幽默形象。

例1-6

霍底本:更可骇者,早有一位仙姬在内,其鲜艳妩媚大似宝钗,袅娜风流又如黛玉。(《红楼梦》第五回)

霍译本:To his intense surprise there was a fairy girl sitting in the middle of it. Her rose-fresh beauty reminded him strongly of Bao-chai, but there was also something about her of Dai-yu's delicate charm.

杨底本:更可骇者,早有一女子在内,其鲜妍妩媚有似宝钗,其袅娜风流则又如黛玉。(《红楼梦》第五回)

杨译本:More amazing still, he saw there a girl whose charm reminded him of Baochai, her grace of Daiyu.

分析:翻译"袅娜风流又如黛玉"时,杨译本以模糊的"grace"来概括,而霍译本采用了更具描写性的"delicate charm",并通过增添额外信息"delicate",凸显了林黛玉"行动如弱柳扶风"的迷离、梦幻、病态、柔弱、动静交融的绝世美丽和超凡气质形象。

例1-7

霍底本:宝玉听这话,知是黛玉借此奚落,也无回复之词,只嘻嘻的笑了一阵罢了。宝钗素知黛玉是如此惯了的,也不理他。(《红楼梦》

第八回)

霍译本：Bao-yu knew perfectly well that these words were really intended for him, but made no reply, beyond laughing good-humouredly. Bao-chai, long accustomed to Dai-yu's peculiar ways, also ignored them.

杨底本：宝玉听这话，知是黛玉借此奚落他，也无回复之词，只嘻嘻的笑两阵罢了。宝钗素知黛玉是如此惯了的，也不去睬他。(《红楼梦》第八回)

杨译本：Although Baoyu knew these remarks were aimed at him, his only reply was to chuckle. And Baochai, aware that this was Daiyu's way, paid no attention either.

分析：翻译"黛玉是如此惯了的"时，杨译本以模糊的"way"来概括，而霍译本采用了更具描写性的"peculiar ways"，并通过增添额外信息"peculiar"，凸显了林黛玉一贯"因爱而讥"的小心眼形象。

例 1-8

霍底本：宝玉听了，笑道："你说说，你这个呢？我也告诉去。"黛玉笑道："你说你会'过目成诵'，难道我就不能'一目十行'了？"(《红楼梦》第二十三回)

霍译本："Well! You can talk!" said Bao-yu laughing. "Listen to you! Now I'm going off to tell on you!" "You needn't imagine you're the only one with a good memory," said Dai-yu haughtily. "I suppose I'm allowed to remember lines too if I like."

杨底本：宝玉听了，笑道："你这个呢？我也告诉去。"林黛玉笑道："你说你会过目成诵，难道我就不能一目十行么？"(《红楼梦》第二十三回)

杨译本：It was Baoyu's turn to laugh. "Now listen to you! I'll tell on you too." "You boast that you can memorize a passage with one reading." "Why can't I 'learn ten lines at a glance'?"

分析：霍译本将"笑道"显化为"said Dai-yu haughtily"，而杨译本不翻译"笑道"，因此不显化林黛玉说话时的表情特征，未能展示林黛玉"自傲"的形象。

例 1-9

霍底本：<u>黛玉笑道</u>："既如此说，连你也可以不必看了。"（《红楼梦》第六十四回）

霍译本："In the light of what you have just been saying," <u>said Dai-yu drily</u>, "I'm not at all sure that I ought to let you look at them either."

杨底本：<u>黛玉笑道</u>："既如此说，连你也可以不必看了。"（《红楼梦》第六十四回）

杨译本："In that case you needn't see them either," <u>said Daiyu</u>.

分析：霍译本将"笑道"显化为"said Dai-yu drily"，而杨译本只译作"said Daiyu"，不显化林黛玉说话时的表情特征，未能展示林黛玉的"诙谐"的形象。

例 1-10

霍底本：<u>黛玉忙问</u>："怎么他也当衣裳不成？既当了，怎么又给你？"（《红楼梦》第五十七回）

霍译本："But why should Cousin Xing be pawning her clothes?" <u>said Dai-yu, puzzled.</u> "And why, having pawned them, should she want you, Chai, to have the ticket?"

杨底本：<u>黛玉忙问</u>："怎么，他也当衣裳不成？既当了，怎么又给你送去？"（《红楼梦》第五十七回）

杨译本："Can she be pawning her things?" <u>asked Daiyu</u>. "If so, why send you this ticket?"

分析：霍译本将"忙问"显化为"said Dai-yu, puzzled"，而杨译本只译作"asked Daiyu"，没有显化林黛玉说话时的表情特征，未能展示林黛玉因对同样寄人篱下的邢岫烟关心而"坦率纯真"的形象。

例 1-11

霍底本：<u>黛玉啐道</u>："呸！你倒来替人派我的不是。"（《红楼梦》第三十回）

霍译本："Poh!" <u>said Dai-yu scornfully</u>. "You are trying to make out that it was my fault because you have taken his side against me."

杨底本：<u>黛玉啐道</u>："你倒来替人派我的不是。"（《红楼梦》第三十回）

杨译本："So you side with the others and blame me," <u>snapped Daiyu</u>.

分析：杨译本将"黛玉啐道"译作"snapped Daiyu"，没有显化林黛玉说话时的表情特征，而且也未能展示林黛玉和紫鹃主仆二人处得如同姐妹一样的亲密关系。而霍译本将"黛玉啐道"显化为"said Dai-yu scornfully"，使林黛玉其实只是对这个为她的终身大事呕心沥血的人——紫鹃"耍小性"的形象呼之欲出。

例 1-12

霍底本：<u>黛玉先笑道</u>："宝玉，我问你：至贵者宝，至坚者玉。尔有何贵？尔有何坚？"（《红楼梦》第二十二回）

霍译本："Bao-yu," <u>said Dai-yu, addressing him in a heavily mock-serious manner</u>, "I wish to propound a question to you：'Bao' is that which is of all things the most precious and 'yu' is that which is of all things the most hard. Wherein lies your preciousness and wherein lies your hardness？"

杨底本：一进来，<u>黛玉便笑道</u>："宝玉，我问你：至贵者是'宝'，至坚者是'玉'。你有何贵？你有何坚？"（《红楼梦》第二十二回）

杨译本：<u>Daiyu opened the attack by saying</u>："Listen, Baoyu. Bao means that which is most precious, and yu that which is most solid. But in what way are you precious？In what way are you solid？"

分析：霍译本将"笑道"显化为"said Dai-yu, addressing him in a heavily mock-serious manner"，而杨译本译作"Daiyu opened the attack by saying"，没有显化林黛玉说话时的表情特征，而且也未能展示林黛玉的"才博"和"诙谐"形象。

第二种：原文中暗含林黛玉人物性格或某种说话的表情，但语言表述上不够明确，霍、杨译本均采用增添额外信息的词汇手段等标记方式，"译者凸显源语文本中隐含的交际参与者之间的关系，语篇中人物的语气和态度即情态意义，语篇中人物的情感、对事物的判断和评价，即评价意义"①，但霍译本显示的形象更丰满和多面。

例 1-13

霍底本：宝玉素昔深知<u>黛玉有些小性儿</u>，尚不知近日黛玉和宝钗之事，正恐贾母疼宝琴，他心中不自在。（《红楼梦》第四十九回）

霍译本：From past experience Bao-yu—who still knew nothing of Dai-yu and Bao-chai's recent rapprochement was too familiar with <u>Dai-yu's jealous disposition</u> not to feel apprehensive that Grandmother Jia's new partiality for Bao-qin might upset her.

杨底本：宝玉素习深知<u>黛玉有些小性儿</u>，然尚不知近日黛玉、宝钗之事，正恐贾母疼宝琴他心中不自在，今见湘云如此说了，宝钗又如此答，再审度黛玉声色亦不似往时，居然与宝钗之说相符，便心中闷一不解。（《红楼梦》第四十九回）

杨译本：Baoyu knew very well <u>how narrow-minded Daiyu could be</u>, and having as yet no idea of what had recently passed between her and Baochai he was really afraid she might resent the Lady Dowager's partiality for Baoqin. Her reactions to Xiangyun's remark and Baochai's answer were not what they would once have been but tallied with what Baochai had said, and this puzzled him.

分析：翻译"黛玉有些小性儿"时，杨译本没有采用"Daiyu's"这种翻译形式，但霍译本采用了更具描写性的"Dai-yu's"翻译形式；此外，在增添额外信息上，霍译本的词汇选择更能够凸显林黛玉为精心守护她的爱而吃醋的"小心眼"的形象。

例 1-14

霍底本：抬头一看，见是宝玉，<u>黛玉便啐道</u>："呸！我打量是谁，原来是这个狠心短命的。"（《红楼梦》第二十八回）

霍译本：But on looking up she saw that it was Bao-yu. "Pshaw!"

---

① 胡开宝：《语料库翻译学概论》，上海交通大学出版社 2011 年版，第 85 页。

she said crossly to herself. "I thought it was another girl, but all the time it was that cruel, hate—"

杨底本：<u>林黛玉看见，便道</u>："啐！我当是谁，原来是这个狠心短命的……"（《红楼梦》第二十八回）

杨译本："So that's who it is." <u>She snorted.</u> "That heartless, wretched…"

分析：霍译本将"黛玉便啐道"显化为"she said crossly to herself"，而杨译本译作"She snorted"，都在显化的是林黛玉"不高兴"，但杨译本显化林黛玉"嗤之以鼻"的不耐烦，轻蔑贾宝玉的形象，而霍译本显化的形象更能显示出林黛玉对贾宝玉"用情至深、自我折磨"的多疑、爱生气形象。

例 1-15

霍底本：<u>黛玉笑道</u>："咱们雪下吟诗，依我说，还不如弄一捆柴火，雪下抽柴，还更有趣儿呢！"（《红楼梦》第三十九回）

霍译本："It would be more romantic still," <u>said Dai-yu drily</u>, "if instead of chanting poems we had a big bundle of firewood and took it in turns to tiptoe through the snow and pull out sticks from it."

杨底本：<u>林黛玉忙笑道</u>："咱们雪下吟诗？依我说，还不如弄一捆柴火，雪下抽柴，还更有趣儿呢。"（《红楼梦》第三十九回）

杨译本："Writing poems in the snow?" <u>put in Daiyu mockingly.</u> "I don't think that would be half as much fun as building a woodpile and having a campfire in the snow."

分析：霍译本将"笑道"显化为"said Dai-yu drily"，而杨译本作"put in Daiyu mockingly"，都显化的是林黛玉说话时的表情特征，但霍译本显化的是林黛玉的"幽默而故作一本正经地雅谑"的形象，而杨译本显化的是林黛玉"形于色的尖酸刻薄地嘲讽"的形象。

例 1-16

霍底本：<u>黛玉笑道</u>："既要学做诗，你就拜我为师。"（《红楼梦》第四十八回）

霍译本:"to write poetry? It would be such a piece of luck for me if you would." "You can make your kotow and become my pupil if you like," said Dai-yu goodnaturedly.

杨底本:黛玉笑道:"既要学作诗,你就拜我为师。"(《红楼梦》第四十八回)

杨译本:"If you want to write poetry you must acknowledge me as your tutor," replied Daiyu teasingly.

分析:霍译本将"笑道"显化为"said Dai-yu goodnaturedly",而杨译本译作"replied Daiyu teasingly",都显化了林黛玉说话时的表情特征,但杨译本显化的是林黛玉"带讽逗笑"的形象,而霍译本显化的是林黛玉的"性敦可亲"的形象。

例 1-17

霍底本:黛玉笑向众人道:"我这一社开的又不巧了,偏忘了这两日是他的生日。"(《红楼梦》第七十回)

霍译本:"My poetry dub seems to have got off to rather a bad start," said Dai-yu ruefully. "I'd forgotten about her birthday. Today and tomorrow will be completely taken up with it."

杨底本:黛玉笑向众人道:"我这一社开的又不巧了,偏忘了这两日是他的生日。"(《红楼梦》第七十回)

杨译本:Daiyu observed laughingly, "I picked the wrong day again to start this club, forgetting that we'd be celebrating her birthday for the next two days."

分析:霍译本将"笑向众人道"显化为"said Dai-yu ruefully",而杨译本译作"Daiyu observed laughingly",显化出的林黛玉形象却是一悲一喜,霍译本显化的是林黛玉的"悔恨"的形象,而杨译本显化的则是林黛玉"开心"的形象。

例 1-18

霍底本:黛玉笑道:"你瞧瞧!这么大了,离了姨妈,他就是个最老道的,见了姨妈他就撒娇儿。"(《红楼梦》第五十七回)

霍译本："Look at her!" said Dai-yu, mockingly. "What a great baby! She's ever so poised and grown-up when you aren't here, Auntie. It's only when she's with you that she puts on this little girl act."

杨底本：黛玉笑道："你瞧，这么大了，离了姨妈他就是个最老道的，见了姨妈他就撒娇儿。"(《红楼梦》第五十七回)

杨译本："Look at her." teased Daiyu. "Such a big girl, and when you're not around, aunt, she looks very dignified; but when she's with you she acts just like a baby."

分析：霍译本将"黛玉笑道"显化为"said Dai-yu, mockingly"，而杨译本译作"teased Daiyu"，都显化了林黛玉"谐"的形象，但杨译本显化林黛玉的"戏弄薛宝钗"的"负面"形象，而霍译本则显化林黛玉"嘲弄薛宝钗"的"幽默"的形象。

例 1-19

霍底本：黛玉先念了一声佛，宝钗笑而不言。(《红楼梦》第二十五回)

霍译本："Bless His Holy Name!" Dai-yu murmured fervently. Bao-chai laughed, but said nothing.

杨底本：闻得吃了米汤，省了人事，别人未开口，林黛玉先就念了一声"阿弥陀佛"。(《红楼梦》第二十五回)

杨译本：when they heard that the patients had come to and eaten some gruel. Before the rest could say anything, Daiyu exclaimed: "Buddha be praised."

分析：霍译本将"黛玉先念了一声佛"显化为"Dai-yu murmured fervently"，而杨译本译作"Daiyu exclaimed"，都显化了林黛玉"挂念贾宝玉"，但霍译本显化的林黛玉形象是一个受封建礼教束缚而不能袒露心迹的、对恋人热切祝愿而不愿为人所知的中国式"恋爱中的女人"形象，而杨译本中显化的是林黛玉"急切而急呼"的形象，似乎过于直白，不符合林黛玉大家闺秀的身份。

例 1-20

霍底本：<u>黛玉笑道</u>："今日齐全，谁下帖子请的？"（《红楼梦》第二十五回）

霍译本："What is this?" <u>said Dai-yu, joining in the good humour.</u> "A party?"

杨底本：<u>林黛玉笑道</u>："今日齐全，谁下帖子请来的？"（《红楼梦》第二十五回）

杨译本："Were invitations sent out that you're here in force?" <u>asked Daiyu jokingly.</u>

分析：霍译本将"笑道"显化为"said Dai-yu, joining in the good humour"，而杨译本译作"asked Daiyu jokingly"，都显化了林黛玉说话时的幽默形象，但霍译本在显化林黛玉"谐"的形象同时显化了林黛玉"亲切敦厚"的形象。

第三节 小结

霍译本为西方读者显化了林黛玉形象。

首先，和原著相比较，从语际显化方向上看，霍译本在形式和意义上均突出原著《红楼梦》人物形象（假设 1）。霍译本创设原著中没有的"Dai-yu's"这种极具描写性的翻译形式，并在其后增添解释性的词汇来显化林黛玉形象；另外，霍译本对林黛玉说话情态方式的种种细致的刻画，很多在原著中是没有的，是糅合了霍克斯对人物形象的理解而增添的。

其次，从类比显化方向上看，霍译本在形式和意义上均比杨译本突出原著《红楼梦》人物形象（假设 2）。霍译本创设比杨译本更多的"Dai-yu's"这种极具描写性的翻译形式，并在其后增添解释性的词汇来显化林黛玉形象。另外，霍译本中林黛玉说话的表情方式词虽有部分和杨译本重叠，但霍译本更多地对林黛玉说话的表情方式进行充分的添加解释和详细的描述，更注意林黛玉说话时形象的体现，黛玉的形象在霍译本中更为多样和丰满，感染力强。

再次，对比原著和杨译本，可以发现霍译本的显化翻译方法乃有意识的策略，而非下意识语言选择的结果（假设3）。例如，霍译本创设"Dai-yu's"高达73频次，是霍底本中"黛玉的"22频次的3倍还多，是对比语料库杨译本的"Daiyu's"46频次的近2倍，霍译本通过在该翻译形式后有意添译与林黛玉人物形象有关的词项，显化翻译了林黛玉的"绝世姿容""弱不禁风""多愁善感""自尊敏感""孤独凄凉""幽默风趣""冰雪聪明""才华横溢"的小心眼泪女形象。另外，霍译本有意识地通过转词增意塑形象的翻译策略，将林黛玉说话时的态度、性格及品格体现出来，凸显了林黛玉说话时既有自傲、敏感、尖刻、多疑的一面，又有谐趣、率直、善良、可爱的一面，使西方读者感受到林黛玉生动鲜活的艺术形象，具有真切感人的审美效果。

笔者曾通过对《红楼梦》霍译本的"Dai-yu's"后面的人物特征名词与原著霍底本进行平行语料库的对比和分析，发现霍译本对"黛玉"的人物特征进行意义显化翻译，[①] 本书的发现进一步印证了这一研究结论。

---

① 姚琴:《基于平行语料库的〈红楼梦〉意义显化考察——以霍译本林黛玉人物特征为例》,《外语教学与研究》2012年第3期。

第 二 章

霍克斯笔下的贾宝玉形象

作为《红楼梦》的第一男主人公，贾宝玉是曹雪芹精心塑造的奇特而光彩的艺术形象，在中国文学中具有永久魅力与深刻意蕴。他聪慧灵秀、才情超远、举止飘逸、风流潇洒，是一个"物性自遂、任性恣情"的情种、富贵乡里的闲人。他玩赏晨夕风露、阶柳庭花，在大观园女儿国中斗草簪花、低吟悄唱，自由自在地生活。他"天分中生成一端痴情"，他把满腔的真情、满腹的同情、满心的体贴都给了这些女儿们，他的情深挚而真切、纯净而丰富，他细腻温柔、体贴入微，因而赢得了警幻仙姑给他的"天下古今第一淫人"的绰号。他"爱博而心劳"[①]，不仅表现在对林黛玉的钟情，还表现在他对一切少女美丽与聪慧的赞赏，对她们不幸命运的深切同情。

曹雪芹满怀理想和激情，倾其心血和才力创造的贾宝玉这一艺术形象，是中国文学史上全新的不朽典型，他丰富又矛盾的思想、"似傻如狂"的行为、"囫囵不可解"的疯话，是"古今未见之一人"，"不独于世上亲见这样的人不曾，即阅古今小说传奇中，也未见这样的文字"[②]。这位自古迄今致为独特的文学人物，霍克斯是怎样显化他的形象的呢？

第一节 语料采集与基本数据比较

一 贾宝玉人物形象翻译对等形式的考察

首先，通过运用 ICTCLAS 对霍底本前八十回（参照语料库）进行分

[①] 鲁迅：《中国小说史略》，人民文学出版社 1973 年版，第 199 页。
[②] 郑红枫、郑庆山：《红楼梦脂评辑校》，国家图书馆出版社 2006 年版。（见第十九回《情切切良宵花解语》批语）

词处理，并运用 WORDSMITH 6.0.0 的 COLLOCATE 的 Word Cloud 功能，显示霍底本中"宝玉"右侧 R1—R5 位置的语境共现词（见图 2-1）。

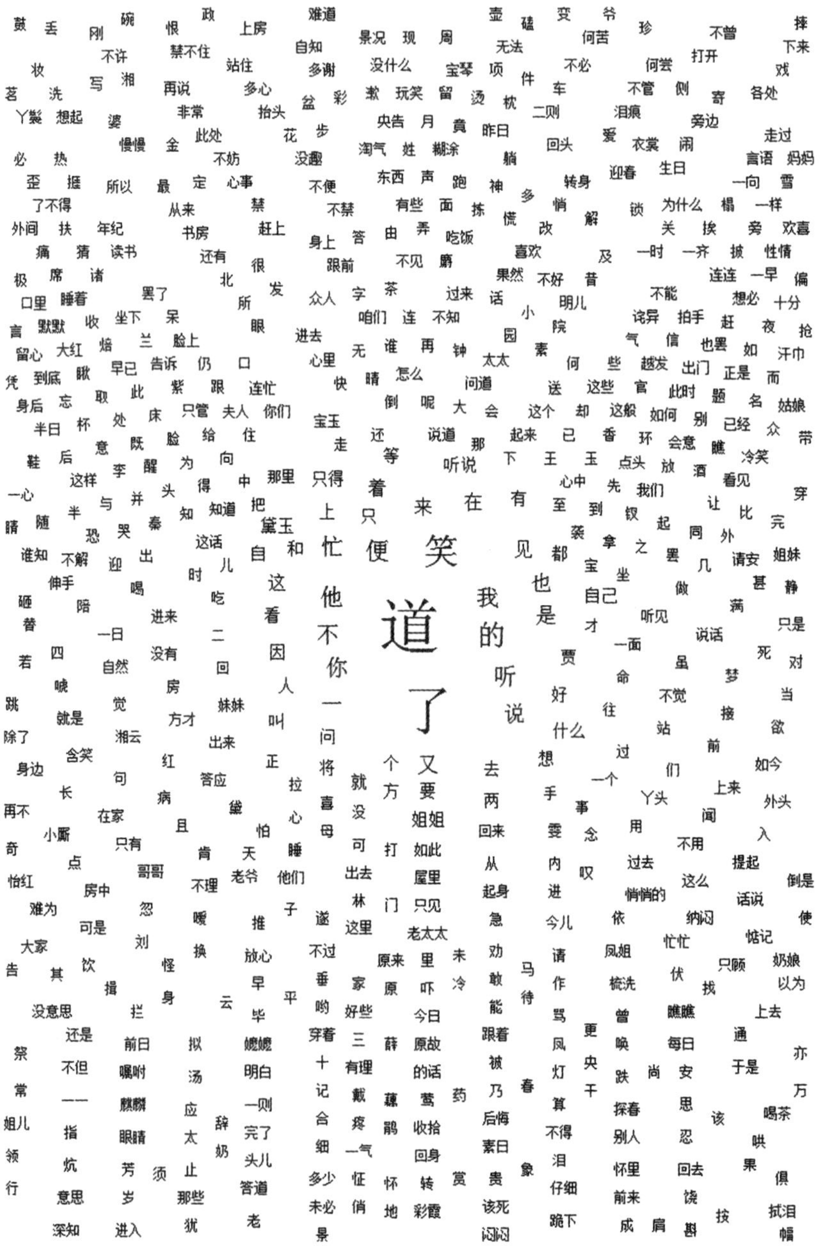

图 2-1 霍底本前八十回中"宝玉"右侧 R1—R5 位置的语境共现词 Word Cloud

如图 2-1 所示，"道"在"宝玉"右侧出现的次数最多；其次为"了""笑""的"等。经过初步观察，本书拟以"道"作为考察节点词，因为"宝玉道"的说话方式很有语义价值，能够展现贾宝玉人物形象特征。

众所周知，宝玉语言的突出特点之一是"似傻如狂"，"囫囵不可解"的疯话、呆话，带着点儿孩子气的可笑的言辞。他的语言真诚直率、任情任性，是自然天性的尽情流淌。考察"宝玉"的说话表情方式，对霍克斯表现贾宝玉说话表情方式的翻译手法进行深入的探究，则容易揭示贾宝玉在霍译本中的艺术形象。

另外，本书也拟以"的"作为考察节点词，因为"'的'的描写性是其基本意义和初始功能"①，考察"宝玉的"后续词的翻译，也很容易揭开贾宝玉在霍译本中的艺术形象。

考虑到中英文语序不同，霍底本中出现的中文构式"宝玉道"有可能翻译成英文为"said Bao-yu"的形式，因此，接着运用 WORDSMITH 6.0.0 的 COLLOCATE 的 Word Cloud 功能，考察霍译本前八十回（考察语料库）中在"Bao-yu"左侧 L1 位置的语境共现词，得到图 2-2。

如图 2-2 所示，霍译本中，"said"在"Bao-yu"左侧 L1 位置出现的次数最多，由此形成的"said Bao-yu"与霍底本"宝玉道"正是对等形式。

另外，考虑到中英文语序不同，霍底本中出现的中文构式"宝玉的"有可能翻译成英文"Bao-yu's"的形式，因此，接着运用 WORDSMITH 6.0.0 的 COLLOCATE 的 Word Cloud 功能，考察霍译本前八十回（考察语料库）中在"Bao-yu"右侧 R1 位置的语境共现词，得到图 2-3。如图 2-3 所示，"S"出现在"Bao-yu"右侧 R1 位置频次最高，而形成的"Bao-yu's"与霍底本"宝玉的"正是对等形式。

其次，以上述对霍译本考察的方法，运用 WORDSMITH 6.0.0 的 COLLOCATE 的 Word Cloud 功能，考察杨译本前八十回（对比语料库）中在"Baoyu"左侧 L1 位置的语境共现词，得到图 2-4。考察后可知，在杨译本中，除了无实际意义的功能词"AND"外，有意义的"SAID"

---

① 陆丙甫：《"的"的基本功能和派生功能——从描写性到区别性再到指称性》，《世界汉语教学》2003 年第 1 期。

出现在"Baoyu"左侧 L1 位置的频次最多。可见，杨译本中"said Baoyu"和霍译本中"said Bao-yu"乃最为凸显的对等形式。

然后，运用 WORDSMITH 6.0.0 的 COLLOCATE 的 Word Cloud 功能，考察杨译本前八十回（对比语料库）中在"Baoyu"右侧 R1 位置的语境共现词，得图 2-5。考察后可知，在杨译本中，除了无实际意义的功能词"AND"和"HAD"外，"S"出现在"Baoyu"右侧 R1 位置频次最高，从而形成的"Baoyu's"和霍译本中"Bao-yu's"乃最为凸显的对等形式。

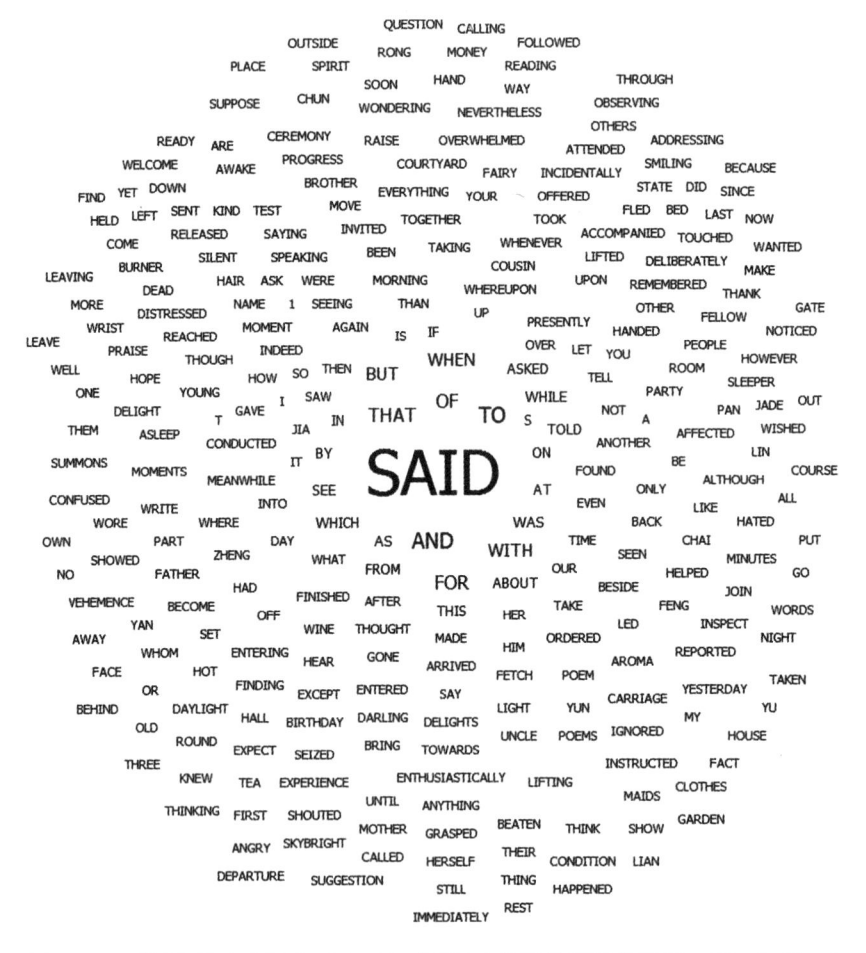

图 2-2 霍译本前八十回中"宝玉"左侧 L1 位置的语境共现词 Word Cloud

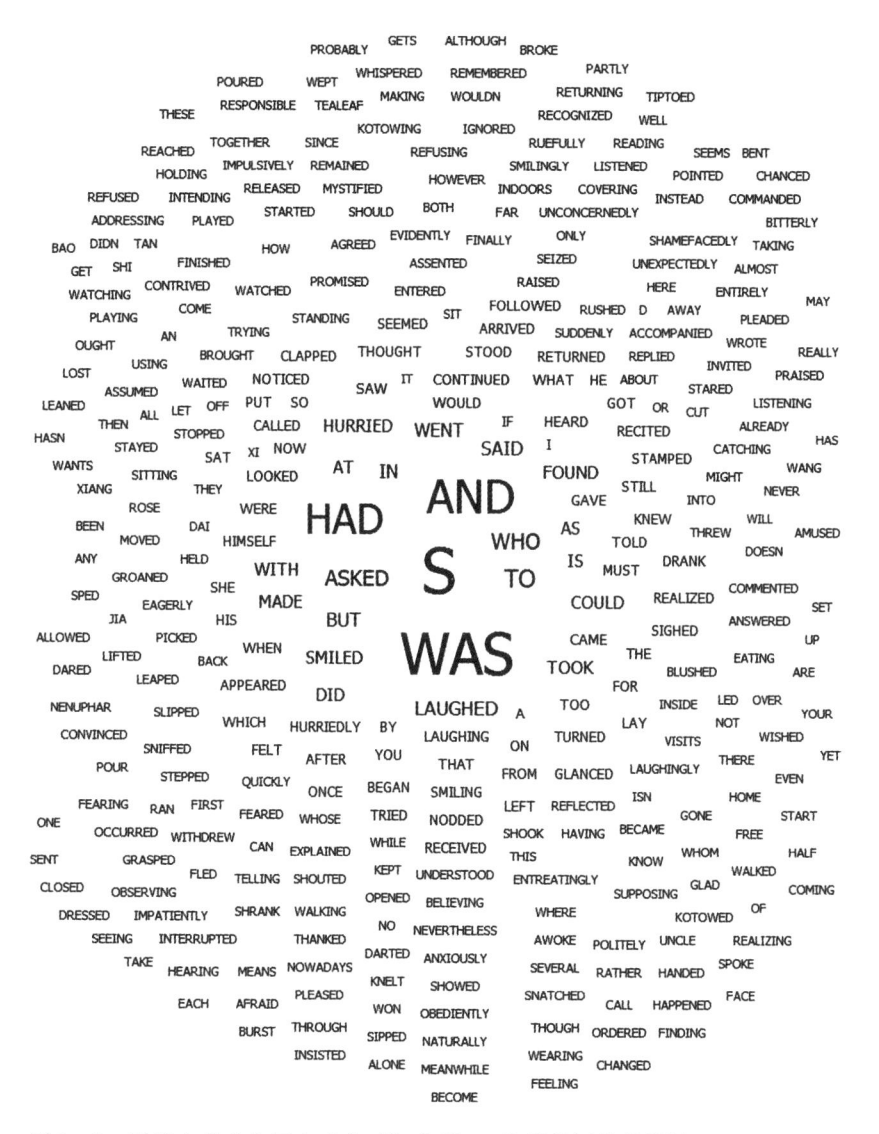

图 2-3　霍译本前八十回中"宝玉"右侧 R1 位置的语境共现词　Word Cloud

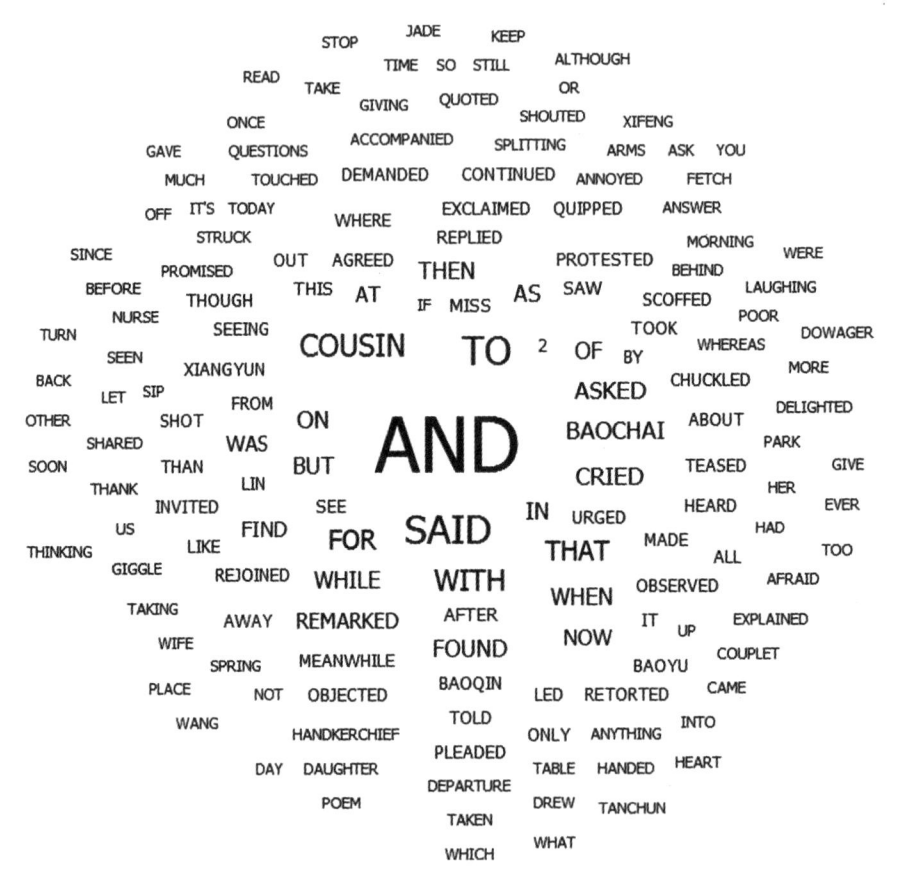

图 2-4　杨译本前八十回中"宝玉"左侧 L1 位置的语境共现词　Word Cloud

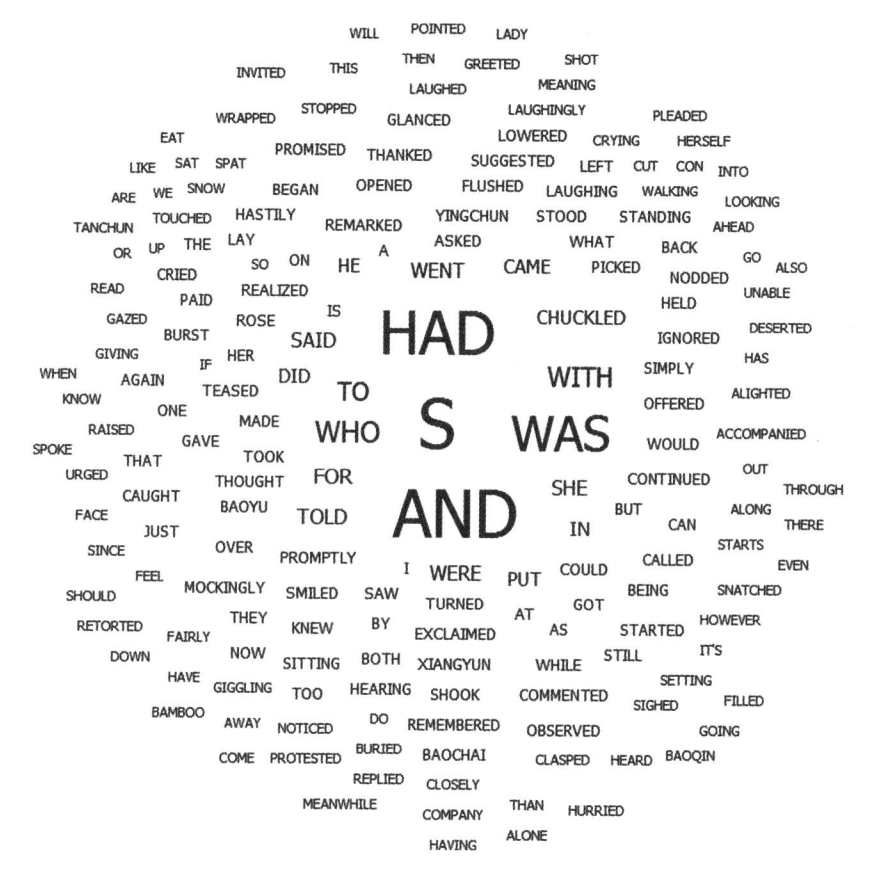

图 2-5　杨译本前八十回中"宝玉"右侧 R1 位置的语境共现词　Word Cloud

对于本小节的对贾宝玉人物形象翻译对等形式的考察结果还需要运用 WORDSMITH 6.0.0 的相关统计功能进行数据对比，该研究将在下节进行。

二　霍底本和霍译本汉英平行语料库的数据比较

运用 WORDSMITH 6.0.0 的 COLLOCATE 的搭配词统计功能，可见"宝玉"在霍底本、霍译本[①]前八十回中的前 10 位搭配词（按搭配词总频数排列，见表 2-1、表 2-2）。

---

①　霍译本为 Bao-yu。

表 2 – 1　　"宝玉"在霍底本前八十回中前 10 位的搭配词（参照语料库）

N	Word	With	Total	Total Left	Total Right	L1	Centre	R1
1	宝玉	宝玉	2643	23	22	8	2598	8
2	了	宝玉	722	167	555	73	0	6
3	道	宝玉	709	30	679	15	0	298
4	笑	宝玉	333	18	315	0	0	222
5	的	宝玉	314	82	232	20	0	52
6	见	宝玉	235	119	116	80	0	74
7	便	宝玉	224	43	181	1	0	68
8	说	宝玉	223	89	134	24	0	20
9	他	宝玉	213	39	174	2	0	2
10	一	宝玉	206	69	137	2	0	24

注：N 表示排名；Word 表示所搭配词；With 表示搭配词；Total 表示总频数；Total Left 表示在"宝玉"左边的搭配总频数（从左边第五个起至左边第一个）；Total Right 表示在"宝玉"右边的搭配总频数（从右边第五个起至右边第一个）；L1 表示在"宝玉"左边第一个的搭配频数；Centre 表示搭配词居中；R1 表示在"宝玉"右边第一个的搭配频数。

表 2 – 2　　"Bao-yu"在霍译本前八十回中前 10 位的搭配词（考察语料库）

N	Word	With	Total	Total Left	Total Right	L1	Centre	R1
1	BAO-YU	Bao-yu	2299	0	0	0	2299	0
2	TO	Bao-yu	586	260	326	78	0	40
3	AND	Bao-yu	544	201	343	84	0	112
4	THE	Bao-yu	528	195	333	0	0	6
5	SAID	Bao-yu	503	464	39	442	0	20
6	WAS	Bao-yu	308	98	210	24	0	146
7	THAT	Bao-yu	267	145	122	54	0	10
8	OF	Bao-yu	254	163	91	55	0	1
9	S	Bao-yu	250	60	190	13	0	163
10	A	Bao-yu	229	83	146	1	0	11

注：N 表示排名；Word 表示所搭配词；With 表示搭配词；Total 表示总频数；Total Left 表示在"Bao-yu"左边的搭配总频数（从左边第五个起至左边第一个）；Total Right 表示在"Bao-yu"右边的搭配总频数（从右边第五个起至右边第一个）；L1 表示在"Bao-yu"左边第一个的搭配频数；Centre 表示搭配词居中；R1 表示在"Bao-yu"右边第一个的搭配频数。

如表 2-1 和表 2-2 所示，本书的考察语料库霍译本和其对应的原著霍底本在检索节点词"宝玉"的搭配词使用上有明显差别。

首先，最显著的差别是霍底本中与节点词"宝玉"搭配频次序列排第 5 位的词"的"在"宝玉"R1 位置搭配成"宝玉的"仅为 52 频次，而"的"的对应形式"S"在霍译本中虽然与节点词"Bao-yu"搭配频次序列排名降到第 9 位，但在"Bao-yu"的 R1 位置搭配成"Bao-yu's"高达 163 频次，是霍底本中"宝玉的"3 倍还多。

其次，霍底本中"道"在节点词"宝玉"的右边位置搭配成"宝玉……道"高达 679 频次，另外，在节点词"宝玉"的右边位置还有"宝玉……说"134 频次，共达 813 频次；而"道"和"说"在霍译本中的对应形式"said"在节点词"Bao-yu"的左边位置搭配成"said Bao-yu"464 频次，另在节点词"Bao-yu"的右边位置搭配成"Bao-yu…said"还有 39 频次，共 503 频次，比霍底本中"宝玉……道/说"频次少。

运用 WORDSMITH 6.0.0 的 CONCORD 的语境词共现功能，可见"宝玉的"在霍底本前八十回中的全部后续词及"Bao-yu's"在霍译本前八十回中的全部后续词①，将其中与贾宝玉人物形象有关的后续词分列如下（见表 2-3、表 2-4）。

表 2-3　　　　霍底本前八十回中"宝玉的"后续词与贾宝玉
人物形象有关的行

N	Concordance
1	几十个原来众客心中，早知贾政要试宝玉的才情，故此只将些俗套敷衍。宝玉
2	故此人以为欢喜时，他反以为悲。那宝玉 的 性情只愿人常聚不散，花常开不
3	叫着了，答应几句话，就散了。至于宝玉的饮食起居，上一层有老奶奶老妈妈们
4	笑。原来黛玉闻得贾政回家，必问宝玉的功课，宝玉一向分心，到临期自然
5	，有丫头来请吃饭，大家方散。从此宝玉的工课，也不敢象先竟撂在脖子
6	的事，竟是姑娘太浮躁了些。别人不知宝玉的脾气，难道咱们也不知道？为那宝

① 详见附录二。

表 2-4　　　霍译本前八十回中 "Bao-yu's" 后续词与
贾宝玉人物形象有关的行

N	Concordance
1	saying "Don't write"; but partly because of Bao-yu's almost girlishly beautiful features,
2	that he was pleased and hastened to commend Bao-yu's remarkable ability. "That's the two
3	into the Garden It may be recalled that when Bao-yu's sickness was at its height, it had b
4	days' onvalescence had ended, not only were Bao-yu's health and strength completely resto
5	a tastes in it were decidedly peculiar. When Bao-yu's poem was praised earlier on, he had
6	early youth Aroma had always been aware that Bao-yu's character was peculiar. His naughtin
7	that?" Aunt Xue urged a less serious view of Bao-yu's derangement: "It's true that he is a
8	a Huan and Jia Lan had come to inquire after Bao-yu's health. "Tell them it's very kind of
9	y' or whatever it was, there was a strain in Bao-yu's own nature which responded to it wit
10	and all felt sorry for them. By this time Bao-yu's hundred days of convalescence had en
11	rief sojourn among them in the early days of Bao-yu's illness, Jia Yun had got by heart th
12	but won't you forgive her for my sake?" Bao-yu's sudden appearance at that moment was
13	she handded her the sheet of paper containing Bao-yu's gatha and the "Clinging Vine" po-em.
14	umiliation in death OUR last chapter told of Bao-yu's delight at seeing the gold kylin aga
15	o was able to guess what the real purpose of Bao-yu's early-morning excursion had been, tu
16	instead and began to walk away. By the time Bao-yu's weeping was over, Dai-yu was no long
17	you know where you are." At these words all Bao-yu's happiness drained away. Slowly he se
18	es, began to sing away for all it was worth. Bao-yu's day-dreaming took another turn. "Tha

续表

N	Concordance
19	ing!" At the same time, Qin Zhong, struck by Bao-yu's rare good looks and princely beating
20	his illness. This, then, was the reason for Bao-yu's unseasonable melancholy—a melancholy

为了直观,用表2-5对比表2-3和表2-4的内容。

表2-5 前八十回中霍底本"宝玉的"及霍译本"Bao-yu's"后续词对宝玉人物形象的描述

搭配词	霍底本"宝玉的"后续词（参照语料库）	霍译本"Bao-yu's"后续词（观察语料库）
肖像描绘	无	Almost girlishly beautiful features, rare good looks and princely beating
体态描绘	无	illness, hundred days of convalescence, sickness, health, Bao-yu's health and strength
动作描绘	饮食起居	early-morning excursion, sudden appearance
性情描绘	性情,脾气	unseasonable melancholy, day-dreaming, soppy nature, peculiar character, derangement, weeping, delight, happiness
才华描绘	才情,功课/工课	remarkable ability, gatha and the "Clinging Vine" poem, poem

为了更加直观,用图2-6和图2-7分别表示霍底本前八十回中"宝玉的"后续词对宝玉人物形象的描述和霍译本前八十回中"Bao-yu's"后续词对宝玉人物形象的描述。

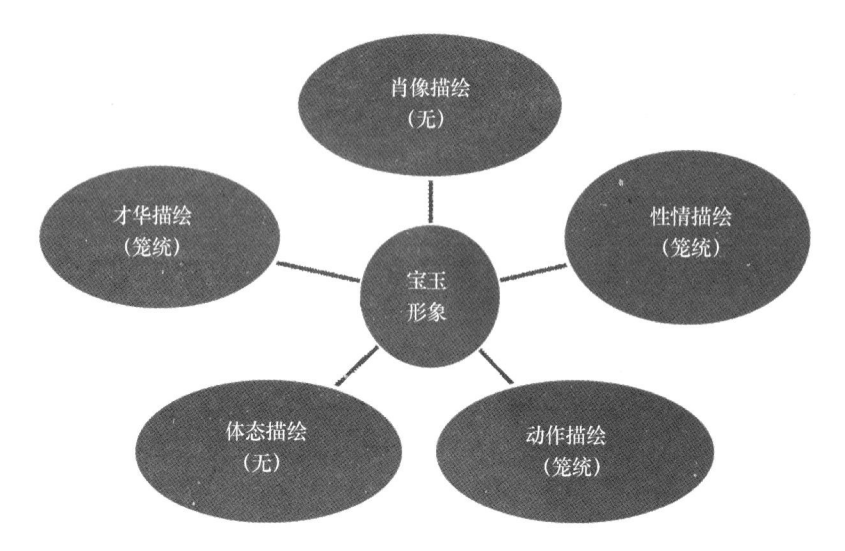

图 2-6 霍底本前八十回中"宝玉的"后续词对宝玉人物形象的描述

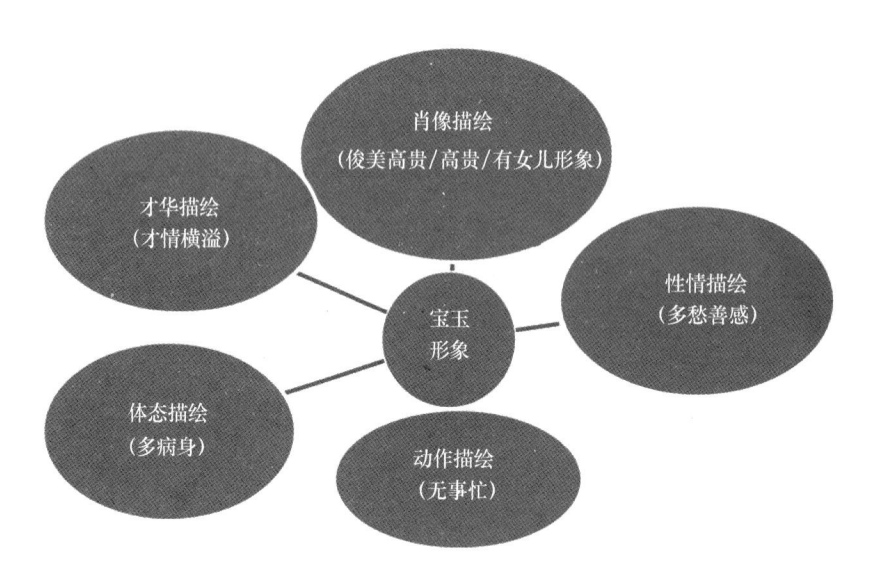

(上图内容：宝玉形象——肖像描绘（无）、性情描绘（笼统）、动作描绘（笼统）、体态描绘（无）、才华描绘（笼统）)

图 2-7 霍译本前八十回中"Bao-yu's"后续词对宝玉人物形象的描述

(下图内容：宝玉形象——肖像描绘（俊美高贵/高贵/有女儿形象）、性情描绘（多愁善感）、动作描绘（无事忙）、体态描绘（多病身）、才华描绘（才情横溢）)

对比图 2-6 和图 2-7，可见在霍底本前八十回中"宝玉的"后续词中没有提及宝玉"肖像"和"体态"，对他的"动作""性情""才华"也仅笼统涉及；而在霍译本前八十回中"Bao-yu's"后续词两次提及宝玉"肖像"之俊美高贵而且有女儿形象，五次提及宝玉"体态"，集中显化他"多病"之身;两次提及宝玉"动作"的异常,显化他"无事忙"的绰号;八次显化宝玉多愁善感的"性情";三次显化宝玉的"才华"。

从描写总数上看,在霍译本前八十回中"Bao-yu's"后续词与贾宝玉人物形象有关的多达 20 行(见表 2-4),而霍底本前八十回中"宝玉的"后续词与贾宝玉人物形象有关的只有 6 行(见表 2-3)。

可见,从语际显化方向上看,霍译本通过大量创设 Bao-yu's 这一表达形式并在该形式后续词上增添信息描写宝玉,突出了原著贾宝玉的人物形象。

接着,运用 WORDSMITH 6.0.0 的 CONCORD 的语境词共现功能,可得"宝玉"在霍译本、霍底本前八十回中的说话表情方式词。①

表 2-6　"宝玉"在霍译本前八十回中的说话表情方式词
（以"said Bao-yu"形式为例）

N	Concordance
1	before I come back again." "Why?" said Bao-yu in some agitation. "That's someth
2	if I had gone away." "Gone away?" said Bao-yu laughingly. "Where would you go t
3	se leave Number Two for me, Chai," said Bao-yu anxiously. "I've already thought
4	s." "I never made the comparison," said Bao-yu hotly, "and I never laughed at yo
5	to give thanks." "Yes, of course," said Bao-yu inattentively, and gave Ripple in
6	no inscription." "Cousin, cousin," said Bao-yu entreatingly, "you've had a look
7	ieve that, do you?" "Indeed I do," said Bao-yu feelingly. "That's precisely what
8	is ex¬ hausted." "Even if it does," said Bao-yu gaily, "I don't suppose you and I
9	ace and red hair!" "Useless dolt!" said Bao-yu angrily. "You can't even do a sim
10	e girl. "Oh, you're a silly girl!" said Bao-yu impatiently. "I'm sure you must h
11	d permanently." "Dearest Grannie," said Bao-yu pleadingly, "I should be perfect l
12	ropes of pearls. "I like it here," said Bao-yu happily. "My room," said Qin-shi
13	t have you got to be angry about?" said Bao-yu, amused. "You just concentrate on
14	t ten year!" "My dear young lady," said Bao-yu pleasantly, "you have all the tim
15	beg of you, don't speak so loud!" said Bao-yu entreatingly. "I shouldn't really
16	er darling grandson." "That doesn't matter," said Bao-yu unconcernedly. "She ought to

---

① 详见附录二。

续表

N	Concordance
17	easonably intelligent." "Tell me," said Bao-yu eagerly, "is there another Bao-yu
18	"You only say that to humour me," said Bao-yu bitterly. "According to you I an
19	them." "That's not spirit money," said Bao-yu hurriedly. "It's waste paper she
20	tears. "Don't be upset, Patience!" said Bao-yu consolingly. "I offer you an apol
21	llow-belly can push us." "Please," said Bao-yu exasperatedly, "don't call her by
22	dy, I don't. quite see the point," said Bao-yu wryly. "In any case, perhaps I'm
23	his concern. "That's no problem!" said Bao-yu encouragingly. "I know just the p
24	e mosquitoes?" "What mosquitoes?" said Bao-yu, mystified. "What are you talking
25	ingale. "Thank the Lord for that!" said Bao-yu fervently. "If only she could sha
26	?" said Oriole. "Never mind that," said Bao-yu airily. "Do me some of every kind
27	people." "When did I ever do such a thing?" said Bao-yu indignantly. "If you're referrin
28	ttle nobody I" "I was only thinking of you," said Bao-yu in great agitation, "yet now
29	, Sunset, I always knew you were," said Bao-yu admiringly, "but there's really n
30	p a moment, there's a good woman," said Bao-yu appealingly, just long enough to
31	you mean, "give and take a bit?" "said Bao-yu in the same lack-lustre voice as
32	t know what you are referring to," said Bao-yu in surprise. "Strike me dead if I
33	those things: to test you." "You?" said Bao-yu in surprise. "What have you got t
34	iquette is that?" "I don't agree," said Bao-yu, smiling. "Adamantina is above et
35	ct, I did." "I don't believe you," said Bao-yu, smiling back at her. "The tone o
36	our mind without much difficulty," said Bao-yu, laughing. "You're afraid that as
37	to talk about Nightingale dying," said Bao-yu, laughing. "You started it," said
38	w did I …?" "I don't know either," said Bao-yu, laughing. "If I had known, I sho
39	"Didn't she call for anyone else?" said Bao-yu, brushing away a tear. "They didn
40	"So that's what was worrying you!" said Bao-yu, smiling. "Well, you are a simple
41	deal with us three later." "You?" said Bao-yu, laughing incredulously. "The fam
42	hat's too great an honour for me!" said Bao-yu, laughing. Aroma nevertheless bro
43	ld!" "you're absolutely mistaken," said Bao-yu, laughing. "We're planning to roa
44	"So you have an inscription, too?" said Bao-yu pricking up his ears. "I must hew
45	ve come just at the right moment," said Bao-yu, smiling at her. "Here, sweep the
46	he had been asking for you." "No," said Bao-yu, smiling at her concern. "Whoever

续表

N	Concordance
47	are the sort of things you want," said Bao-yu laughing, "it's very simple. Just
48	big ones against one little one," said Bao-yu, laughing. "I shall have to see a
49	such great shakes after all then," said Bao-yu, smiling. "I said plasters couldn
50	atter to you?" "You're right," said Bao-yu, laughing. "If you were to go for
51	now." "There's something in that," said Bao-yu laughing, and handed it to her. H
52	unterfeit!" "Well! You can talk!" said Bao-yu laughing. "Listen to you! Now I'm
53	! Isn't that stretching it a bit?" said Bao-yu with a laugh. "For eight bearers
54	ou shouldn't be too long, either," said Bao-yu with a smile. "I've got something
55	t on with at all." "You go along I." said Bao-yu with a smile. "We shall be all ri
56	ood-looking since I saw you last," said Bao-yu with a grin. "You could almost be
57	" "What's a Cold Fragrance Pill ?" said Bao-yu with a laugh. "Won't you give me
58	d to pass through. "Here's Sappy," said Bao-yu with a meaningful smile. "Well w
59	fast asleep. "Just look at that!" said Bao-yu with a laugh. "It's a bit early f
60	rse. "Thank you for your trouble," said Bao-yu with a winning smile as he rode i

运用 WORDSMITH 6.0.0 的 CONCORD 语境词共现功能，可见"Bao-yu…said"在霍译本前八十回中的说话共现语境词如下。

表 2-7　　"宝玉"在霍译本前八十回中的说话表情方式词
（以"Bao-yu…said"形式为例）

N	Concordance
1	say good-bye to your cousin Bao-chai?" Bao-yu smiled but said nothing and went stra
2	a bit of money to keep up my reputation!" Bao-yu smiled and said a few words to com
3	again. "Where did that stuff come from?" Bao-yu blushed furiously and said nothing.

另外，虽然之前的图 2-1 和图 2-2 揭示了霍译本中"said Bao-yu"与霍底本"宝玉……道"乃最为凸显的对等形式，但通过表 2-1 可知霍底本中"宝玉……说"还有多例。故又运用 WORDSMITH 6.0.0 的 CONCORD 语境词共现功能，分别查看"宝玉……道"和"宝玉……说"在霍底本前八十回中的说话共现语境词（见表 2-8、表 2-9）。

表 2-8　　"宝玉"在霍底本前八十回中的说话表情方式词
（以"宝玉……道"形式为例）

N	Concordance
1	！怕也不中用，跟我快走罢！"宝玉忙道："他并没烧纸，原是林姑娘
2	说道："我也乏了！明儿再撕罢。"宝玉笑道："古人云'千金难买一笑'
3	道："不干你事，快念书去罢。"宝玉笑道："姐姐们且站一站，我有
4	、朵儿、霜儿、雪儿替我炮制。我有的是那些俗香罢了！"宝玉笑道："凡我说一句，你就拉上这些。不给你个利
5	："老爷不在书房里，天天锁着，爷可以不用下来罢了。"宝玉笑道："虽锁着，也要下来的。"钱升、李贵都笑
6	，仍将前番自己常日吃茶的那只绿玉斗来斟与宝玉。宝玉笑道："常言'世法平等'，他两个就用那样古玩奇
7	就将路上所有之事，一概告诉了宝玉。宝玉笑道："大喜，大喜！难得这个标致
8	个个都好，怎么写的这样好了！明儿也替我写个匾。"宝玉笑道："你又哄我了。"说着又问："袭人姐姐呢？
9	呢！倘或再砸了盘子，更不得了了。"宝玉笑道："你爱砸就砸。这些东西，
10	怕死，你长命百岁的活着，好不好？"宝玉笑道："要象只管这么闹，我还怕
11	那熏笼上又暖和，比不得那屋里炕凉，今儿可以不用。"宝玉笑道："你们两个都在那上头睡了，我这外边没个人
12	的意思不叫我安生，我就离了你。"说着往外就走。宝玉笑道："你到那里我跟到那里。"一面仍拿着荷包来
13	嫂子的好鹅掌。薛姨妈连忙把自己糟的取了来给他尝。宝玉笑道："这个就酒才好！"薛姨妈便命人灌了上等
14	你不信尝一尝就知道了。"玉钏儿果真赌气尝了一尝。宝玉笑道："这可好吃了！"玉钏儿听说，方解过他的
15	这么'跑解马'的打扮儿，伶伶俐俐的出去了不成？"宝玉笑道："可不就是这么出去了。"麝月道："你死不
16	而是这个。明日倘或把印也丢了，难道也就罢了不成？"宝玉笑道："倒是丢了印平常，若丢了这个，我就该死了
17	不披衣，只穿着小袄便蹑手蹑脚的下了熏笼，随后出来。宝玉劝道："罢呀，冻着不是玩的！"晴雯只摆手，随
18	"倒是你们这里热闹，大清早起就咕咕呱呱的玩成一处。"宝玉笑道："你们那里人也不少，怎么不玩？"碧月道："

续表

N	Concordance
19	是宝公也在坐，见其娇而且闻其香？不然何体贴至此。"<u>宝玉笑道</u>："闺阁习武，任其勇悍，怎似男人？不问而可
20	？"紫鹃道："身上病好了，只是心里气还不大好。"<u>宝玉笑道</u>："我知道了，有什么气呢。"一面说着，一面
21	了个念头，写了几个帖儿试一试，谁知一招皆到。"<u>宝玉笑道</u>："可惜迟了，早该起个社的。"黛玉说道：
22	你。我们这起东西，可是'白玷辱了好名好姓'的！"<u>宝玉笑道</u>："你今儿还记着呢？"袭人道："一百年还记
23	也太婆婆妈妈的了。这样的话，怎么是你读书的人说的？"<u>宝玉叹道</u>："你们那里知道，不但草木，凡天下有情有理的东
24	几天戏来。宝姑娘一定要还席的。"<u>宝玉冷笑道</u>："他还不还，与我什么相
25	？我知道你心里的缘故。想是说，他那里配穿红的？"<u>宝玉笑道</u>："不是不是。那样的人不配穿红的，谁还敢穿
26	是托他两个的福，独你来了，我是不能给你吃的。"<u>宝玉笑道</u>："我深知道，我也不领你的情，只谢他二人
27	又道："坐一坐就回去罢，这个地方儿不是你来的。"<u>宝玉笑道</u>："你就家去才好呢，我还替你留着好东西呢
28	手炉，笑道："我击了，若鼓绝不成，又要罚的。"<u>宝玉笑道</u>："我已有了。"黛玉提起笔来，笑道："你
29	笑道："好哥哥，你只别嚷，你要念么着都使的。"<u>宝玉笑道</u>："这会子也不用说，等一会儿睡下咱们再慢慢儿
30	退了几步，说道："你又要死了！又这么动手动脚的。"<u>宝玉笑道</u>："说话忘了情，不觉的动了手，也就顾不得死活
31	道："原来'上'字从'依依'两个字上化出来的。"<u>宝玉大笑道</u>："你已得了。不用再讲，要再讲，倒学离
32	不早来听古记儿，这会子来了，自惊自怪的。"<u>宝玉笑道</u>："咱们明儿下一社又有了题目了，就咏水仙、
33	宝琴笑道："你猜是谁做的？"<u>宝玉笑道</u>："自然是潇湘子的稿子了。"
34	跑出去了，晴雯因赶芳官，将杯内的子儿撒了一地。<u>宝玉笑道</u>："如此长天，我不在家里，正怕你们寂寞，吃了
35	"怨不得都说你空长了个好胎子，真真是个傻东西。"<u>宝玉笑道</u>："人事难定，谁死谁活？倘或我在今日明日、

续表

N	Concordance
36	？"探春笑道："只怕又是杜撰。"宝玉笑道："除了'四书'，杜撰的也
37	。"湘莲笑道："原是我自己一时忘情，好歹别多心。"宝玉笑道："何必再提，这倒似有心了。"湘莲作揖
38	来问宝玉："那是一两的星儿？"宝玉笑道："你问的我有趣儿，你倒
39	里就唬死了他了？偏惯会这么蝎蝎螫螫老婆子的样儿。"宝玉笑道："倒不是怕唬坏了他。头一件你冻着也不好
40	，连他也不认得？他是廊下住的五嫂子的儿子芸儿。"宝玉笑道："是了，我怎么就忘了。"因问他："你母
41	，拣我爱的唱给我听，这会子犯不上借着光儿问儿。"宝玉笑道："这有什么难的，明儿就叫一班子，也叫他们
42	起来。麝月道："这是怎么说，拿我的东西开心儿！"宝玉笑道："你打开扇子匣子拣去，什么好东西！"麝月道
43	我，别理他。他虽腼腆，却脾气拐孤，不大随和儿。"宝玉笑道："你去罢，我知道了。"秦氏又嘱咐了他兄弟
44	珀。等要戏去了。见麝月一人在外间屋里灯下抹骨牌。宝玉笑道："你怎么不和他们去？"麝月道"没有钱。"
45	完就好了。"王夫人道："放屁！什么药就这么贵！"宝玉笑道："当真的呢。我这个方子比别的不同，那个药名儿
46	过的。"贾母笑道："又胡说了，你何曾见过？"宝玉笑道："虽没见过，却看着面善，心里倒象是远别重
47	："这可罢了，不但说没有方子，就是听也没有听见过。"宝玉笑道："这样还算不得什么！"王一贴又忙道："这
48	。且说那秦钟宝玉二人正在殿上玩耍，因见智能儿过来，宝玉笑道："能儿来了。"秦钟说："理他作什么？"
49	之处，嘴乖的也有一宗可嫌的，倒不如不说的好。"宝玉笑道："这就是了。我说大嫂子不大说话呢，老太太也
50	们这些奴才白陪着挨打受骂的。从此也可怜见些才好！"宝玉笑道："好哥哥，你别委屈，我明儿请你。"李贵道
51	玉钏儿道："我从不会喂人东西，等他们来了再喝。"宝玉笑道："我不是要你喂我，我因为走不动，你递给
52	的笑着下地说："我怎么……"却说不出下半句来。宝玉笑道："我竟也不知道了。若知道，给你脸上抹些墨

续表

N	Concordance
53	回去商议着邀一社，又还了席，也请老太太赏菊何如？"<u>宝玉笑道</u>："老太太说了，还要摆酒还史妹妹的席，叫咱们
54	过活，也并没有哥儿弟兄。可惜他竟一门尽绝了后。"<u>宝玉忙道</u>："咱们也别管他绝后不绝后，只是这姑娘可好？
55	子什么勾当？"贾芸指贾琏道："找二叔说句话。"<u>宝玉笑道</u>："你倒比先越发出挑了，倒象我的儿子。
56	。"宝玉道："你本姓什么？"莺儿道："姓黄。"<u>宝玉笑道</u>："这个姓名倒对了，果然是'黄莺儿'。"
57	了一回，复又要了热螃蟹，就在大圆桌上吃了一回。<u>宝玉笑道</u>："今日持螯赏桂，亦不可无诗，我已吟成，
58	絮为题，限各色小调。"又都看了湘云，称赏了一回。<u>宝玉笑道</u>："这词上我倒平常，少不得也要胡诌了。"于是
59	惦记着黛玉，并不理论这事。此刻忽见<u>宝玉笑道</u>："宝姐姐，我瞧瞧你的那香
60	"偏这小狗攘知道，有这些蛆嚼！"<u>宝玉冷笑道</u>："我只当是谁亲戚，原来
61	出的多，进的少，如今若不省俭，必致后手不接。"<u>宝玉笑道</u>："凭他怎么后手不接，也不短了咱们两个人的
62	榧子吃呢！我都听见了。"二人正说话，只见紫鹃进来，<u>宝玉笑道</u>："紫鹃，把你们的好茶沏碗我喝。"紫鹃道
63	那婆子又恨又气，只得忍耐下去了。芳官吹了几口，<u>宝玉笑道</u>："你尝尝，好了没有？"芳官当是玩话，只是
64	便击了一下，笑道："一鼓绝。"<u>宝玉笑道</u>："有了，你写罢。"众人
65	回头见是宝玉，便勉强笑道："好好的，我何曾哭来。"<u>宝玉笑道</u>："你瞧瞧，眼睛上的泪珠儿没干，还撒谎呢。
66	，让我洗澡去。"袭人、麝月都洗了，我叫他们来。"<u>宝玉笑道</u>："我才喝了好些酒，还得洗洗。你既没洗，
67	又说让我，我那里禁当的起？所以特给二爷来磕头。"<u>宝玉笑道</u>："我也禁当不起。"袭人早在门旁安了座让
68	忘了？想是还有别的事，等完了再发放我们也未可知。"<u>宝玉笑道</u>："你是头一个出了名的至善至贤的人，他两
69	们再往后找找去罢，只怕还找出两个人来，也未可知。"<u>宝玉笑道</u>："这可再没有了。"鸳鸯已知这话俱被宝玉

续表

N	Concordance
70	柜子里头的香气熏染的，也未可知。"宝玉摇头道："未必。这香的气味奇怪，
71	一面想，一面顺步早到了一所院内。宝玉诧异道："除了怡红院，也竟还有这
72	有'红绽雨肥梅'、'水荇牵风翠带长'等语。"宝玉笑道："固然如此，但我知道姐姐断不许妹妹有此伤悼
73	大好了，你就去罢。"紫鹃听说，方打叠铺盖妆奁之类。宝玉笑道："我看见你文具儿里头有两三面镜子，你把那面
74	酒来，少不得也睡了。一宿无语。次日天明方醒，只见宝玉笑道："夜里失了盗也不知道，你瞧瞧裤子上。"袭
75	人了，我要走，连你也不必告诉，只回了太太就走。"宝玉笑道："就算我不好，你回了太太去了，叫别人听见说
76	雯道："这话也是，只是疑他为什么忽然又瞒起我来？"宝玉笑道："等我从后门出去，到那窗户根下听说些什么，
77	"薛蟠听说，笑道："不值一坛，再唱好的来。"宝玉笑道："听我说罢，这么滥饮，易醉而无味。我先
78	，罚一回，没的怪臊的。"说着，便两手握起脸来。宝玉笑道："何苦来，又打起我做什么，我还不怕臊呢，
79	道："今儿奇怪，刚才太太打发人给我送了两碗菜来。"宝玉笑道："必定是今儿菜多，送给你们大家吃的。"袭人
80	肩上担着花锄，花锄上挂着纱囊，手内拿着花帚。宝玉笑道："来的正好，你把这些花瓣儿都扫起来，撂在那
81	李纨又问宝玉："你可有了？"宝玉忙道："我倒有了，才一看见这
82	新写的三个字。一时黛玉来了，宝玉笑道："好妹妹，你别撒谎，你看
83	闹起来，把我的新裙子也糟蹋了。"宝玉笑道："你有夫妻蕙，我这里倒有
84	笑，说道："云姑娘，你如今大了，越发心直嘴快了。"宝玉笑道："我说你们这几个人难说话，果然不错。"史湘云
85	却还一气，只是宝玉又落了第了。"宝玉笑道："我原不会联句，只好担待
86	要吃酒，给我两碗酒吃就是了。"宝玉笑道："你也爱吃酒？等着咱们
87	"说晴雯出去了，我怎么没见。一定是要唬我去了。"宝玉笑道："这不是他？在这里渥着呢。我若不嚷的快
88	不能兼，不想你兼有了，就叫你'富贵闲人'也罢了。"宝玉笑道："当不起，当不起！倒是随你混叫去罢。

续表

N	Concordance
89	把咱们熏臭了。"说着一径去了。<u>宝玉纳闷道</u>："从来没有人如此荼毒我，
90	的可好些？"紫鹃道："好些了。"<u>宝玉笑道</u>："阿弥陀佛！宁可好了罢。"
91	他来，都笑说："又来了一个！没了你的坐处了。"<u>宝玉笑道</u>："好一幅'冬闺集艳图'，可惜我迟来了。
92	："老太太有了这个好孙女儿，就忘了你这孙子了。"<u>宝玉笑道</u>："这倒不妨，原该多疼女孩儿些是正理。明儿
93	李纨道："你还是你的旧号'绛洞花主'就是了。"<u>宝玉笑道</u>："小时候干的营生，还提他做什么。"宝钗道
94	了，忙起来夺在手内，灯上烧了。<u>宝玉笑道</u>："我已记熟了。"黛玉道
95	还怕腻烦了呢。"说的大家都笑了。<u>宝玉笑道</u>："这场我又落第了。难道
96	人连忙拉住，坐了一坐，便去了。<u>宝玉笑道</u>："走乏了！"便歪在床上
97	，大家别走。纵有了事，也就赖不着这边的人了。"<u>宝玉笑道</u>："原来姐姐也知道我们那边近日丢了东西？"宝钗
98	探春也笑着进来找宝玉，因说："咱们诗社可兴旺了。"<u>宝玉笑道</u>："正是呢。这是一高兴起诗社，鬼使神差来了这些
99	点风儿他也是乱响。你偏要比他，你也太下流了。"<u>宝玉笑道</u>："松柏不敢比。连孔夫子都说：'岁寒然后知
100	一日送一两燕窝来呢？这就是了。"<u>宝玉笑道</u>："这要天天吃惯了，吃上
101	着，只见宝钗走进来，笑道："偏了我们新鲜东西了。"<u>宝玉笑道</u>："姐姐家的东西，自然先偏了我们了。"宝钗
102	身上好？我整整的三天没见你了。"<u>宝玉笑道</u>："妹妹身上好？我前儿还在
103	面上，闻个不住。黛玉夺了手道："这可该去了。"<u>宝玉笑道</u>："要去不能。咱们斯斯文文的躺着说话儿。"说
104	客，自然先沏了茶来再舀水去。"说着，倒茶去了。<u>宝玉笑道</u>："好丫头！'若共你多情小姐同鸳帐，怎舍得
105	着又要伸手。黛玉忙笑道："好哥哥，我可不敢了。"<u>宝玉笑道</u>："饶你不难，只把袖子我闻一闻。"说着便
106	。你要果然都依了，就拿八人轿也抬不出我去了。"<u>宝玉笑道</u>："你这里长远了，不怕没八人轿你坐。"袭人
107	不的。谁知他们都爱上了，都当宝贝儿似的抢了去了。"<u>宝玉笑道</u>："原来要这个。这不值什么，拿几吊钱出去给

续表

N	Concordance
108	至墙上把头一个《忆菊》勾了，底下又赘一个"蘅"字。<u>宝玉忙道</u>："好姐姐，第二个我已有了四句了，你让我
109	定又是风流悲感，不同此等的了。"<u>宝玉笑道</u>："这个题目似不称近体，须
110	头晕，今儿不留你们吃饭了。"贾环等等应着便出去了。<u>宝玉笑道</u>："可是姐姐们都过来了，怎么不见？"邢夫人道
111	咽了气：正三刻上，就有人来叫我们，说你来了。"<u>宝玉忙道</u>："你不认得字，所以不知道，这原是有的。不但
112	'哥哥的。回来赶围棋儿，又该你闹'么爱三'了。"<u>宝玉笑道</u>："你学惯了，明儿连你还咬起来呢。"湘云道
113	便冷笑道："哦！交杯盏儿还没吃，就上了头了！"<u>宝玉笑道</u>："你来，我也替你蓖蓖。"晴雯道："我没
114	，就闭了眼住了口，事世不知，只有倒气的分儿了。"<u>宝玉忙道</u>："一夜叫的是谁？"小丫头道："一夜叫的
115	："好妹妹，替我梳梳呢。"湘云道："这可不能了。"<u>宝玉笑道</u>："好妹妹，你先时候儿怎么替我梳了呢？"湘
116	你大五六岁呢，就给你作儿子了？"<u>宝玉笑道</u>："你今年十几岁？"贾芸道
117	了，认了儿子，不是好开交的。"说着笑着进去了。<u>宝玉笑道</u>："明儿你闲了，只管来找我，别和他们鬼鬼祟祟
118	喜喜欢欢的，你又怎么这个样儿了？"<u>宝玉冷笑道</u>："他们娘儿们姐儿们喜欢不喜
119	来了。白哭一会子，也无益了。"<u>宝玉冷笑道</u>："原是想他自幼娇生惯养的
120	你才那些诗比众人都强，今儿得了彩头，该赏我们了。"<u>宝玉笑道</u>："每人一吊。"众人道："谁没见那一吊钱
121	很。我也巴不得早些过来，又添了一个做诗的人了。"<u>宝玉冷笑道</u>："虽如此说，但只我倒替你担心虑后呢。"
122	当宝二爷再不上我们的门了，谁知道这会子又来了。"<u>宝玉笑道</u>："你们把极小的事情倒说大了，好好的为什么不
123	就来。"茗烟道："就近地方谁家可去？这却难了。"<u>宝玉笑道</u>："依我的主意，咱们竟找花大姐姐去，瞧他在家
124	兄弟侄儿照样，就惹人笑话这家子的人眼里没有长辈了。"<u>宝玉笑道</u>："妈妈说的是。我不过是一时半刻偶然叫一句
125	说，就完了。"说毕，即转身走了。<u>宝玉笑道</u>："可不是我疯了？往虎口里

续表

N	Concordance
126	笑道："你死了，别人不知怎么样，我先就哭死了。"宝玉笑道："你死了，我做和尚去。"袭人道："你老实
127	阵雨来。宝玉看那女孩子头上往下滴水，把衣裳登时湿了。宝玉想道："这是下雨了，他这个身子，如何禁得骤雨一激
128	虑后呢。"香菱道："这是什么话？我倒不懂了。"宝玉笑道："这有什么不懂？只怕再有个人来，薛大哥
129	袭人晴雯等忙问："又怎么了？谁又有了不是了？"宝玉指道："砚台下是什么？一定又是那位的样子，忘记收
130	："可是你没的说了。好好的，我多早晚又伤心了？"宝玉笑道："妹妹脸上现有泪痕，如何还哄我呢？只是我想
131	。忙跑出来迎着宝玉，一把拉着问："你怎么来了？"宝玉笑道："我怪闷的，来瞧瞧你作什么呢。"袭人听
132	"王夫人道："扯你娘的臊！又欠你老子捶你了。"宝玉笑道："我老子再不为这个捶我。"王夫人又道：
133	冒撞冲犯了你？明儿赌气花几两银子买进他们来就是了。"宝玉笑道："你说的话怎么叫人答言呢？我不过是赞他好
134	太来了混输了，他气的睡去了。"宝玉笑道："你们别和他一般见识，由他
135	看见，又该说我们躲懒，连你穿带的东西都不经心了。"宝玉笑道："这真难为你想的到。只是也不可过于赶，热
136	"贾母听如此说，方命人接下了。宝玉笑道："老太太，张爷爷既这么说，
137	人多，你那里禁的住那些气味？不想恰好你倒来了。"宝玉笑道："多谢姐姐惦记。我也因今日没事，又见姐姐这
138	了饭。贾母因问道："跟着你娘吃了什么好的了？"宝玉笑道："也没什么好的，我倒多吃了一碗饭。"因
139	，人也没了，庙也烂了，那泥胎儿可就成了精咧。"宝玉忙道："不是成精，规矩这样人是不死的。"刘姥姥
140	困了睡，再过几年，不过是这样，一点后事也不虑。"宝玉笑道："我能够和姊妹们过一日，是一日，死了就完了
141	来，都湃在那水晶缸里呢。叫他们打发你吃不好吗？"宝玉笑道："既这么着，你不洗，就洗洗手给我拿果子来吃
142	："既这么说，就把扇子搬出来，让他尽力撕不好吗？"宝玉笑道："你就搬去。"麝月道："我可不造这样孽

续表

N	Concordance
143	石榴树下。探春因说道:"这几天,老爷没叫你吗?"宝玉笑道:"没有叫。"探春道:"昨儿我恍惚听见说,
144	我们回来了。"王夫人忙问:"今日可丢了丑了没有?"宝玉笑道:"不但不丢丑,拐了许多东西来。"接着就有老
145	摸索着宝玉的脖项说道:"前儿的丸药都吃完了没有?"宝玉答应道:"还有一丸。"王夫人道:"明儿再取十丸
146	只问着我!"王夫人也道:"宝玉很会欺负你妹妹。"宝玉笑道:"太太不知道这个原故。宝姐姐先在家里住着,
147	亲自爬高上梯,贴了半天,这会子还冻的手僵着呢。"宝玉笑道:"我忘了,你手冷,我替你握着。"便伸手
148	也记得这么清楚?"众人听了,都笑道:"果然明白。"宝玉笑道:"还是这么会说话,不让人。"黛玉听了,冷
149	呆了一天,做了一首又不好,自然这会子另做呢。"宝玉笑道:"这正是'地灵人杰',老天生人,再不虚赋情
150	"众人笑道:"你要脱,你脱,我们还轮流安席呢。"宝玉笑道:"这一安席,就要到五更天了。知道我最怕这
151	去呢。你二姐姐已有人家求准了,所以叫你们过去呢。"宝玉忙道:"何必如此忙?我身上也不大好,明儿还未必能
152	吗?"湘云道:"怎么匡人看见孔子,只当是阳货呢?"宝玉笑道:"孔子阳货虽同貌,却不同名;蔺与司马虽同
153	云道:"怎么列国有个蔺相如,汉朝又有个司马相如呢?"宝玉笑道:"这也罢了,偏又模样儿也一样,这也是有的
154	二件。到那里纵然你有了书,你的字写的在那里呢?"宝玉笑道:"我时常也有写了的好些,难道都没收着?"
155	潇湘子的稿子了。"宝琴笑道:"现在是我做的呢。"宝玉笑道:"我不信。这声调口气,迎乎不象。"宝琴笑
156	要走的动,叫哥儿明儿过去散散心,太太着实惦记着呢。"宝玉忙道:"要走得了,必定过来请太太的安去。疼的比
157	我说狂话,只怕你家里未必找的出这么一个俗器来呢!"宝玉笑道:"俗语说:'随乡入乡',到了你这里,自然
158	拿今日天气比,分明冷些,怎么你倒脱了青肷披风呢?"宝玉笑道:"何尝没穿?见你一恼,我一暴燥,就脱了

续表

N	Concordance
159	，合别人说笑一会子啊？"黛玉道："你管我呢！"<u>宝玉笑道</u>："我自然不敢管你，只是你自己糟塌坏了身子
160	道："好几处都有，都称赞的了不得，还和我们寻呢！"<u>宝玉笑道</u>："不值什么，你们说给我的小么儿们就是了。
161	上回的鞋做一双你穿，比那双还加工夫，如何呢？"<u>宝玉笑道</u>："你提起鞋来，我想起故事来了。一回穿着，
162	就是他了。我们村庄上的人商量着还要拿榔头砸他呢。"<u>宝玉忙道</u>："快别如此。要平了庙，罪过不小！"刘姥姥
163	要瞧瞧笼着何物。黛玉笑道："这时候谁带什么香呢？"<u>宝玉笑道</u>："那么着，这香是那里来的？"黛玉笑道："
164	这些话你怎么怨得老爷不气，不时时刻刻的要打你呢？"<u>宝玉笑道</u>："再不说了。那是我小时候儿不知天多高地多厚
165	"一夜叫的是谁？"小丫头道："一夜叫的是娘。"<u>宝玉拭泪道</u>："还叫谁？"小丫头："没有听见叫别人了
166	改罢。一年大，二年小，……"一面说话一面咳嗽起来。<u>宝玉忙道</u>："这里风冷，咱们只顾站着，凉着呢可不是玩的
167	我疑惑，故说出这谎话来问你，谁知你就傻闹起来！"<u>宝玉笑道</u>："原来是你愁这个，所以你是傻子！从此后再别
168	探春道："昨儿我恍惚听见说，老爷叫你出去来着。"<u>宝玉笑道</u>："那想是别人听错了，并没叫我。"探春又
169	笑道："你往那里去呢？"黛玉道："我回家去。"<u>宝玉笑道</u>："我跟了去。"黛玉道："我死了呢？"
170	他看也没有什么，但只我嫌他是不是的写给人看去。"<u>宝玉忙道</u>："我多早晚给人看来？昨日那把扇子，原是我
171	你个巧方儿，你往东小院儿里头拿环哥儿和彩云去。"<u>宝玉笑道</u>："谁管他的事呢！咱们只说咱们的。"只见
172	惊，忙问："谁家去？"紫鹃道："妹妹回苏州去。"<u>宝玉笑道</u>："你又说白话。苏州虽是原籍，因没了姑母，
173	说话去。今见他回来，又说还要些玫瑰露给柳五儿吃去，<u>宝玉忙道</u>："有着呢，我又不大吃，你都给他吃去罢。
174	，说："我该死，胡说。你好歹告诉我，他品行如何？"<u>宝玉笑道</u>："你既深知，又来问我做甚么？连我也未必干

续表

N	Concordance
175	中榻上，默默盘算，不觉昏昏睡去，竟到一座花园之内。宝玉诧异道："除了我们大观园，竟又有这一个园子？"正疑
176	众丫鬟忙已接过，插入瓶内。众人都道："来赏玩！"宝玉笑道："你们如今赏罢，也不知费了我多少精神呢。"
177	宝玉因不见黛玉，便到他房中来寻，只见黛玉歪在炕上。宝玉笑道："起来吃饭去。就开戏了，你爱听那一出？
178	点，点了一点头就走。麝月等忙胡乱掷了盒盖跟上来。宝玉笑道："这两个女人倒和气，会说话。他们天天乏了，
179	笑道："你才说什么？"黛玉道："我没说什么。"宝玉笑道："给你个榧子吃呢！我都听见了。"二人正
180	铺床？"黛玉登时急了，撂下脸来说道："你说什么？"宝玉笑道："我何尝说什么？"黛玉便哭道："如今新兴
181	玉笑道："能儿来了。"秦钟说："理他作什么？"宝玉笑道："你别弄鬼儿，那一日在老太太屋里，一个人没有
182	。"正说着，宝玉和探春来了，都入座听他讲诗。宝玉笑道："既是这样，也不用看诗，'会心处不在远'
183	了线？咱们拿下他来。"宝玉等听了，也都出来看时，宝玉笑道："我认得这风筝，这是大老爷那院里嫣红姑娘放
184	玉。二人相会，如鱼得水。湘莲因问贾琏偷娶二房之事。宝玉笑道："我听见焙茗说，我却未见。我也不敢多管
185	拿来我瞧瞧罢！没那福气穿就罢了，这会子又着急。"宝玉笑道："这话倒说的是。"说着，便递给晴雯，又
186	知道，给你脸上抹些墨。"说着，丫头进来，伺候梳洗。宝玉笑道："昨日有扰，今日晚上我还席。"袭人笑道：
187	晴雯向里间炕上努嘴儿。宝玉看时，见袭人和衣睡着。宝玉笑道："好啊！这么早就睡了。"又问晴雯道："
188	，待要不理他，听他说只说一句话，便道："请说。"宝玉笑道："两句话，说了你听不听呢？"黛玉听说，
189	惟有他的令比人唠叨！倒也有些意思。"便催宝玉快说。宝玉笑道："谁说过这个，也等想一想儿。"黛玉便道：
190	人，余香满口。一面看了，只管出神，心内还默默记诵。宝玉笑道："妹妹，你说好不好？"黛玉笑着点头儿。宝

续表

N	Concordance
191	。"王夫人又问:"你想什么吃?回来好给你送来。"<u>宝玉笑道</u>:"也倒不想什么吃。倒是那一回做的那小荷叶
192	我就听见老太太说要定了琴姑娘呢,不然,那么疼他?"<u>宝玉笑道</u>:"人人只说我傻,你比我更傻!不过是句玩
193	半新不旧的两条绢子?他又要恼了,说你打趣他。"<u>宝玉笑道</u>:"你放心,他自然知道。"晴雯听了,只得
194	公婆跟前就不献好儿。凤儿嘴乖,怎么怨得人疼他。"<u>宝玉笑道</u>:"要这么说,不大说话的就不疼了?"贾母道:
195	诉我听。"莺儿道:"我告诉你,你可不许告诉他。"<u>宝玉笑道</u>:"这个自然。"正说着,只听见外头说道:"
196	不如你抬了去,这花儿倒清净了,没什么杂味来搅他。"<u>宝玉笑道</u>:"我屋里今儿也有个病人煎药呢。你怎么知道的
197	一面咻的一声又笑了,端过汤来。<u>宝玉笑道</u>:"好姐姐你要生气,只管
198	又如此?这是力量不加,故又弄出这些堆砌货来搪塞。"<u>宝玉笑道</u>:"长歌也须得要些词藻点缀点缀,不然便觉萧索
199	在院子里,你和他说,烦他们莺儿来打上几根绦子。"<u>宝玉笑道</u>:"亏了你提起来。"说着,便仰头向窗外道:
200	宝玉道:"松花色配什么?"莺儿道:"松花配桃红。"<u>宝玉笑道</u>:"这才娇艳。再要雅淡之中带些娇艳。"莺儿
201	如何?"晴雯笑道:"果然通快些。只是太阳还疼。"<u>宝玉笑道</u>:"越发尽用西洋药治一治,只怕就好了。"说
202	了,摇头笑道:"起的平平。"湘云又道:"快着。"<u>宝玉笑道</u>:"寻春问腊到蓬莱。"黛玉、湘云都点头笑道:"
203	晴雯因方才一冷,如今又一暖,不觉打了两个嚏喷。<u>宝玉叹道</u>:"如何?到底伤了风了。"麝月笑道:"他
204	爷写的斗方儿,越发好了,多早晚赏我们几张帖帖。"<u>宝玉笑道</u>:"在那里看见了?"众人道:"好几处都有,
205	以想到这里,自己伤起心来了。"紫鹃也便挨他坐着。<u>宝玉笑道</u>:"方才对面说话,你还走开,这会子怎么又来挨
206	玉听了,便知有文章,因笑道:"你念出来我听听。"<u>宝玉笑道</u>:"那《闹简》上有一句说的最好:'是几时

续表

N	Concordance
207	宝玉笑道:"妹妹,你说好不好?"黛玉笑着点头儿。<u>宝玉笑道</u>:"我就是个'多愁多病的身',你就是那'
208	是宝玉。袭人先笑道:"叫我好找,你在那里来着?"<u>宝玉笑道</u>:"我打四妹妹那里出来,迎头看见你走了来,我
209	么,叫人看见什么样儿呢!我这个身子本不配坐在这里。"<u>宝玉笑道</u>:"你既知道不配,为什么躺着呢?"晴雯没的
210	拍手笑道:"这还了得,要这样,十年也打不完了。"<u>宝玉笑道</u>:"好姑娘,你闲着也没事,都替我打了罢。
211	我错怪了你娘,你怎么也不提我,看着你娘受委屈。"<u>宝玉笑道</u>:"我偏着母亲说大爷大娘不成?通共一个不是,
212	说了名。宝玉又道:"表字?"黛玉道:"无字。"<u>宝玉笑道</u>:"我送妹妹一字:莫若'颦颦'二字极妙。"
213	姨妈忙扶他睡下,又问他:"想什么,只管告诉我。"<u>宝玉笑道</u>:"我想起来,自然和姨娘要去。"王夫人又问
214	"黛玉道:"我不依。你们是一气的,都来戏弄我。"<u>宝玉劝道</u>:"罢哟,谁敢戏弄你?你不打趣他,他就敢
215	。"晴雯听说,就上来掖了一掖,伸手进去渥一渥。<u>宝玉笑道</u>:"好冷手,我说看冻着。"一面又见晴雯两
216	你带,好不好?"黛玉将头一扭道:"我不稀罕。"<u>宝玉笑道</u>:"你既不稀罕,我可就拿着了。"说着,又
217	袭人。袭人忙赶了来,才夺下来。<u>宝玉冷笑道</u>:"我是砸我的东西,与你
218	两个赔个不是罢。"平儿笑道:"与你什么相干?"<u>宝玉笑道</u>:"我们弟兄姐妹都一样。他们得罪了人,我替他
219	了想,说:"是了,是我早起吃了冷香丸的香气。"<u>宝玉笑道</u>:"什么'冷香丸',这么好闻?好姐姐,给我
220	换衣服,不防又把扇子失了手掉在地下,将骨子跌折。<u>宝玉叹道</u>:"蠢才,蠢才,将来怎么样!明日你自己当家立业
221	公主于含章殿下卧的宝榻,悬的是同昌公主制的连珠帐。<u>宝玉含笑道</u>:"这里好,这里好!"秦氏笑道:"我这屋
222	就是才受祭的阴魂儿也不安嘔。二爷想我这话怎么样?"<u>宝玉笑道</u>:"你的意思我猜着了。你想着只你一个跟了
223	芳官便忙递给宝玉瞧,又说:"是擦春癣的蔷薇硝。"<u>宝玉笑道</u>:"难为他想的到。"贾环听了,便伸着头瞧

续表

N	Concordance
224	是你跟了去了。"莺儿抿嘴一笑。宝玉笑道："我常常和你花大姐姐说，
225	，倒有当归、陈皮、白芍等药，那分两较先也减了些，宝玉喜道："这才是女孩儿们的药。虽疏散，也不可太过
226	道："你也念起佛来，真是新闻。"宝玉笑道："所谓'病急乱投医'了。
227	这鞋袜于是不怕的？也倒干净些呀。"宝玉笑道："我这一套是全的。一双
228	的有些动人心处，在那里羞的脸红耳赤，低首无言。宝玉跺脚道："还不快跑！"一语提醒，那丫头飞跑去了。
229	"你既这么说，为什么我去了，你不叫丫头开门呢！"宝玉诧异道："这话从那里说起？我要是这么着，立刻就死
230	陌路，尚然'肥马轻裘，敝之无憾'，何况咱们？"宝玉笑道："论交道，不在'肥马轻裘'，即黄金白璧
231	个小小的白玉盒子，里面盛着一盒，如玫瑰膏子一样。宝玉笑道："铺子里卖的胭脂不干净，颜色也薄，这是上
232	'在望'！又暗合'杏花村'意思。"宝玉冷笑道："村若用'杏花'二字
233	忙。黛玉笑道："这样的诗，一时要一百首也有。"宝玉笑道："你这会子才力已尽，不说不能作了，还褒贬

表2-9　　"宝玉"在霍底本前八十回中的说话表情方式词
（以"宝玉……说"形式为例）

N	Concordance
1	有理，忙将宝玉抱下车来，送上马去。宝玉笑说："倒难为你了。"于是仍进
2	这里宝钗只刚做了两三个花瓣，忽见宝玉在梦中喊骂，说："和尚道士的话如
3	灯向地下一照，只见一口鲜血在地。宝玉慌了，只说："了不得！"袭人见
4	自己送他的。芳官便又告诉了宝玉，宝玉也慌了，说："露虽有了，若勾
5	口，平儿也打扮的花枝招展的来了。宝玉忙迎出来，笑说："我方才到凤姐
6	哭，一行将方才莺儿等事都说出来。宝玉越发急起来，说："你只在这里闹
7	正为劝你这些个，更说的狠了！"宝玉忙说道："再不说这话了。"袭人道
8	"在南京收着呢，此时那里去取？"宝玉听了，大失所望，便说："没福得
9	半。接着又听"嗤""嗤"几声。宝玉在旁笑着说："撕的好！再撕响
10	不信只问他！"说毕，指着宝玉。宝玉没好意思起来，说："薛大哥，你该
11	了两三声，方见两三个老婆子走进来。宝玉见了，连忙摇手说："罢罢，不用了

续表

N	Concordance
12	炕上又并了一张桌子，方坐开了。宝玉忙说："林妹妹怕冷，过这边靠板
13	把海棠社改作桃花社，岂不大妙呢？"宝玉听着点头，说："很好。"且忙
14	早说出来，我们也少受些辛苦，岂不念公子之德呢！"宝玉连说："实在不知。恐是讹传也未见得。"那长府官冷笑
15	伴，宝姑娘坐了一坐的话，告诉宝玉。宝玉听了，忙说："不该，我怎么睡着
16	湘云、宝琴、岫烟、惜春也都来了。宝玉忙迎出来，笑说："不敢起动。快
17	湘云说着笑着跑出来，怕黛玉赶上。宝玉在后忙说："绊倒了！那里就赶上
18	，人倒疑惑起来，索性再等一等。"宝玉点头，因说："我出去走走。四儿
19	仗利害，留神天上吊下火纸来烧着。"宝玉笑回说："不往远去，只出去就
20	干人？"只见那些丫鬟笑道："宝玉怎么跑到这里来？"宝玉只当是说他，忙来陪笑说道："因我偶步到此，不
21	将门锁上，把钥匙要了，自己拿着。宝玉忙说："这一道门何必关？又没多

要之，运用 WORDSMITH 6.0.0 的 CONCORD 的语境词共现功能，可知"宝玉"在霍译本、霍底本前八十回中含有"说话"表情方式词。[①] 总结如表 2-10。

表 2-10　霍底本前八十回中"宝玉"的"说话"的表情方式词

宝玉笑道（204 次）	宝玉听说，喜的拍手道（1 次）
宝玉又笑道（2 次）	宝玉喜道（1 次）
宝玉含笑道（1 次）	宝玉喜的忙道（1 次）
宝玉大笑道（1 次）	宝玉陪笑道（1 次）
宝玉便笑央道（1 次）	宝玉含羞央告道（1 次）
宝玉赶上去笑道（1 次）	宝玉央及道（1 次）
宝玉听了，笑道（1 次）	宝玉冷笑道（7 次）
宝玉方悄悄的笑道（1 次）	宝玉发狠道（1 次）
宝玉悄笑道（1 次）	宝玉还骂道（1 次）
宝玉听说，忙笑道（1 次）	宝玉叹道（3 次）

① 详见附录二。

续表

宝玉忙笑道（8次）	宝玉跺脚道（1次）
宝玉便上来笑道（1次）	宝玉乃叹道（1次）
宝玉便笑道（2次）	宝玉点头叹道（2次）
宝玉笑着道（1次）	宝玉见了叹道（1次）
宝玉笑回道（1次）	宝玉跌脚叹道（1次）
宝玉笑央道（1次）	宝玉在身后面叹道（1次）
宝玉笑了半日道（1次）	宝玉忙道（13次）
宝玉在窗外笑道（1次）	宝玉听了，忙道（1次）
宝玉笑着道（1次）	宝玉忙劝道（4次）
宝玉听了，拍手笑道（1次）	宝玉忙叫道（1次）
宝玉听了，忙笑道（2次）	宝玉一把拉住道（1次）
宝玉听了，点头笑道（1次）	宝玉忙接道（1次）
宝玉笑向莺儿道（1次）	宝玉又赶出去叫道（1次）
宝玉、薛蟠都笑道（1次）	宝玉忙上前拉住道（1次）
宝玉红了脸，笑道（1次）	宝玉听了，忙说（1次）
宝玉拍手笑道（1次）	宝玉在后忙说（1次）
宝玉，便拍手笑道（1次）	宝玉忙说（1次）
宝玉见问，便笑道（1次）	宝玉越发急起来，说（1次）
宝玉忙按他，笑道（1次）	宝玉见了，连忙摇手说（1次）
宝玉因笑道（1次）	宝玉慌了，只说（1次）
宝玉听了笑道（1次）	宝玉忙说道（1次）
宝玉走进来，笑道（1次）	宝玉忙说（1次）
宝玉一面拭泪，笑道（1次）	宝玉忙站起来答应道（1次）
宝玉喜的笑道（1次）	宝玉诧异道（3次）
宝玉一旁笑劝道（1次）	宝玉又诧异道（1次）
宝玉在马上笑道（1次）	宝玉纳闷道（1次）
宝玉擎茶笑道（1次）	宝玉听说，心下猜疑道（1次）
宝玉看罢，笑道（1次）	宝玉推他道（2次）
宝玉听了笑道（1次）	宝玉听了，拍手道（1次）
只见宝玉来了，笑道（1次）	宝玉听了，因点头道（1次）
宝玉听了，笑道（1次）	宝玉点头道（1次）
宝玉连忙带笑拦住，道（1次）	宝玉听着点头，说（1次）

宝玉推他笑道（1次）	宝玉点头，因说（1次）
宝玉会意，忙笑道（1次）	宝玉摇头道（1次）
宝玉见说，携着他的手笑道（1次）	宝玉拭泪道（1次）
宝玉笑回说（1次）	宝玉满面泪痕哭道（1次）
宝玉忙迎出来，笑说（1次）	忽见宝玉在梦中喊骂，说（1次）
宝玉听了，笑说（1次）	宝玉又叫道（1次）
宝玉忙笑说（1次）	宝玉乜斜倦眼道（1次）
宝玉笑说（1次）	宝玉跟跄着回头道（1次）
宝玉在旁笑着说（1次）	宝玉见宝钗如说，便拭汗说道（1次）
宝玉指道（1次）	宝玉便推他出去说（1次）
宝玉唱道（1次）	宝玉一面道谢，说（1次）
宝玉听了，大失所望，便说（1次）	宝玉也慌了，说（1次）
宝玉也慌了，说（1次）	宝玉没好意思起来，说（1次）

表2-11　霍译本前八十回中"宝玉"的"说话"表情方式词

said Bao-yu with a smile（2次）	said Bao-yu in surprise（2次）
said Bao-yu, smiling back at her（1次）	said Bao-yu exasperatedly（1次）
said Bao-yu, smiling at her（1次）	said Bao-yu angrily（1次）
said Bao-yu with a winning smile（1次）	said Bao-yu indignantly（1次）
said Bao-yu, smiling（3次）	said Bao-yu reproachfully（1次）
said Bao-yu, smiling at her concern（1次）	said Bao-yu, removing one of the cups for himself（1次）
said Bao-yu with a meaningful smile（1次）	said Bao-yu anxiously（1次）
said Bao-yu, returning her smile（1次）	said Bao-yu eagerly（1次）
said Bao-yu laughingly（1次）	said Bao-yu ruefully（1次）
said Bao-yu, laughing（11次）	said Bao-yu, mystified（1次）
said Bao-yu with a laugh（3次）	said Bao-yu inattentively（1次）
said Bao-yu, laughing incredulously（1次）	said Bao-yu unconcernedly（1次）
said Bao-yu with a grin（1次）	said Bao-yu fervently（1次）
said Bao-yu gaily（1次）	said Bao-yu hotly（1次）

续表

said Bao-yu happily（1次）	said Bao-yu in the same lack-lustre voice（1次）
said Bao-yu pleasantly（1次）	said Bao-yu feelingly（1次）
said Bao-yu, pleased but a little concerned（1次）	said Bao-yu bitterly（1次）
said Bao-yu, amused（1次）	said Bao-yu wryly（1次）
said Bao-yu, brushing away a tear（1次）	said Bao-yu admiringly（1次）
said Bao-yu, his face streaming with tears and sobbing hysterically（1次）	said Bao-yu encouragingly（1次）
said Bao-yu pricking up his ears（1次）	said Bao-yu hurriedly（1次）
said Bao-yu over his shoulder, swaying slightly（1次）	said Bao-yu impatiently（1次）
said Bao-yu, misquoting slightly（1次）	said Bao-yu, a trifle pettishly（1次）
said Bao-yu consolingly（1次）	said Bao-yu airily（1次）
said Bao-yu genially（1次）	said Bao-yu pleadingly（1次）
said Bao-yu scornfully（1次）	said Bao-yu appealingly（1次）
said Bao-yu in answer to the question（1次）	said Bao-yu entreatingly（2次）
said Bao-yu, chipping in（1次）	said Bao-yu, covering her mouth with his hand（1次）
said Bao-yu, restraining her（1次）	said Bao-yu, mopping the perspiration（1次）
said Bao-yu, taking up the purse and beginning to fasten it on again（1次）	said Bao-yu in some agitation（1次）
said Bao-yu in great agitation（1次）	Bao-yu smiled and said a few words to comfort（1次）
Bao-yu blushed furiously and said nothing（1次）	Bao-yu smiled but said nothing（1次）

"宝玉"在霍译本、霍底本前八十回中的说话表情方式词对比如图2-8所示。

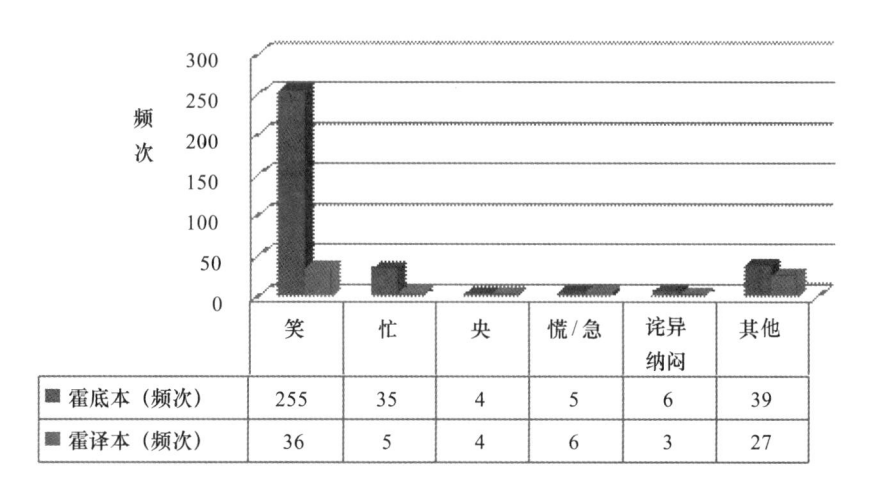

	笑	忙	央	慌/急	诧异纳闷	其他
霍底本（频次）	255	35	4	5	6	39
霍译本（频次）	36	5	4	6	3	27

图 2-8 前八十回中霍底本和霍译本"宝玉"的"说话"表情方式词比较

图 2-8 显示，"宝玉"在霍译本前八十回的"说话"表情方式词频次明显低于原著霍底本，除了在"宝玉央（告）/急道"的形象词上频次趋同外，在其他说话表情方式所体现的人物形象词上频次差异很大。尤其是霍底本前八十回中主要是以"宝玉笑道/说"的形象出现，共出现 255 频次，而在霍译本前八十回中，以"宝玉笑道"的形象出现仅仅 36 频次，明显低于原著霍底本，这个现象有待进一步分析讨论。

三 霍译本和杨译本英英平行语料库的数据比较

借助 WORDSMITH 6.0.0 的 CONCORD 检索功能，观察对比语料库杨译本中"宝玉"[①]的搭配词特征，检索发现，SAID 在杨译本中与"Baoyu"的搭配频次已经下降到了前 22 位，而非霍译本中在前 10 位的范围（见表 2-12）。

---

① 杨译本为 Baoyu。

表 2-12 "宝玉"在杨译本前八十回中前 22 位的搭配词（对比语料库）

N	Word	With	Total	Total Left	Total Right	L1	Centre	R1
1	BAOYU	Baoyu	1850	2	2	0	1846	0
2	TO	Baoyu	523	209	314	69	0	46
3	AND	Baoyu	430	183	247	77	0	76
4	THE	Baoyu	381	164	217	0	0	11
5	WAS	Baoyu	204	41	163	8	0	109
6	HIS	Baoyu	185	28	157	0	0	2
7	A	Baoyu	184	64	120	1	0	3
8	HAD	Baoyu	184	52	132	3	0	86
9	IN	Baoyu	183	75	108	21	0	24
10	OF	Baoyu	172	89	83	32	0	3
11	S	Baoyu	163	42	121	5	0	98
12	THAT	Baoyu	152	93	59	42	0	6
13	SHE	Baoyu	148	92	56	0	0	20
14	HER	Baoyu	143	40	103	1	0	1
15	AS	Baoyu	135	71	64	34	0	8
16	WITH	Baoyu	130	53	77	29	0	14
17	THIS	Baoyu	120	60	60	9	0	2
18	HE	Baoyu	117	28	89	0	0	12
19	FOR	Baoyu	113	57	56	29	0	4
20	ON	Baoyu	111	42	69	17	0	9
21	AT	Baoyu	88	53	35	17	0	5
22	SAID	Baoyu	85	65	20	58	0	13

注：N 表示排名；Word 表示所搭配词；With 表示搭配词；Total 表示总频数；Total Left 表示在"Baoyu"左边的搭配总频数（从左边第五个起至左边第一个）；Total Right 表示在"Baoyu"右边的搭配总频数（从右边第五个起至右边第一个）；L1 表示在"Baoyu"左边第一个的搭配频数；Centre 表示搭配词居中；R1 表示在"Baoyu"右边第一个的搭配频数。

表 2-12 所示的对比语料库杨译本和表 2-2 所示的考察语料库霍译本在检索节点词"宝玉"的搭配词使用上有明显差别。

首先，最显著的差别是在霍译本中与节点词"Bao-yu"搭配序列排第9位的词"S"在"Bao-yu"的R1位置搭配成"Bao-yu's"高达163频次,而其对应词"S"在杨译本中与节点词"Baoyu"的搭配序列排名降到第11位,且在"Baoyu"的R1位置搭配成"Baoyu's"仅98频次,几乎只有霍译本对应形式的一半。

其次,在霍译本中处于第5位的搭配词"SAID"在节点词"Bao-yu"的左边位置搭配成"SAID Bao-yu"高达464频次,在节点词"Bao-yu"的右边位置搭配成"Bao-yu SAID"还有39频次,共达到503频次。而杨译本中与之对应的词SAID在节点词"Baoyu"的左边搭配成"SAID Baoyu"只有65频次,在节点词"Baoyu"的右边位置搭配成"Baoyu SAID"有20频次,共只达到85频次,不到霍译本对应形式的1/6。

接着,运用WORDSMITH 6.0.0的CONCORD的语境词共现功能,可得"Bao-yu's"在杨译本前八十回中的全部后续词①,将与贾宝玉人物形象后续词有关的行呈列如下。

表2-13　杨译本前八十回中"Baoyu's"后续词与贾宝玉人物形象有关的行

N	Concordance
1	m the last chapter in which Jia Zheng tested Baoyu's literary talent, you may wonder to fi
2	nk are a nathema to me." In Qin Zhong's eyes, Baoyu's striking appearance and ingenuous beh
3	e and went back to Bamboo Lodge. The news of Baoyu's disorder had made Daiyu suffer a rela
4	re they were going. The stewards wives knew Baoyu's quirky ways and did not want him to p
5	hey were much inferior. Besides, they lacked Baoyu's literary brilliance and poetic flair.
6	s frustrated, and slept. Now some time after Baoyu's abrupt departure Daiyu came, o

---

① 详见附录二。

续表

N	Concordance
7	criptions in order to test him. And although Baoyu's childish efforts were far from inspir
8	rs. Hua and her son did not press the point. Baoyu's unexpected visit and the apparent int
9	rs. eager to please him, hastened to commend Baoyu's remarkable talent. "The selection of

为了直观，用表 2-14 对比表 2-13 和表 2-4 的内容。

表 2-14　杨译本 "Baoyu's" 及霍译本 "Bao-yu's" 后续词对宝玉人物形象的描述

搭配词	杨译本 Baoyu's 后续词（对比语料库）	霍译本 Bao-yu's 后续词（观察语料库）
肖像描绘	striking appearance	Almost girlishly beautiful features, rare good looks and princely beating
体态描绘	disorder	illness, hundred days of convalescence, sickness, health, Bao-yu's health and strength
动作描绘	unexpected visit, abrupt departure	early-morning excursion, sudden appearance
性情描绘	quirky ways	unseasonable melancholy, day-dreaming, soppy nature, peculiar character, derangement, weeping, delight, happiness
才华描绘	literary talent, literary brilliance and poetic flair, remarkable talent	remarkable ability, gatha and the "Clinging Vine" poem, poem

为了更加直观，参见图 2-9。

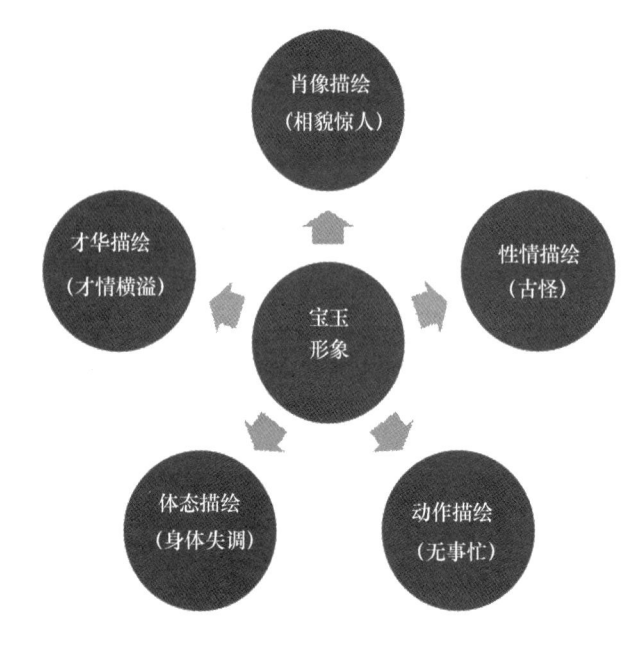

图 2-9 杨译本前八十回中"Baoyu's"后续词对宝玉人物形象的描述

由图 2-9 和图 2-7 对比，可知杨、霍译本前八十回中都凸显了贾宝玉的"才情横溢"和"无事忙"形象；而在"肖像""性情""体态"等方面杨译本不及霍译本醒目：在杨译本前八十回中"Baoyu's"后续词笼统描绘宝玉"肖像"只有一次，且并未如霍译本那样凸显"高贵"和"有女儿形象"；在杨译本前八十回中"Baoyu's"后续词仅有一次提及宝玉"有病"，未如霍译本那样多次凸显他"多病身"；在杨译本前八十回中"Baoyu's"后续词仅一次笼统提及宝玉"性情古怪"，未如霍译本那样多次凸显他"多愁善感"形象。

另外，从描写总数上对比更能说明问题，在霍译本前八十回中"Bao-yu's"后续词与贾宝玉人物形象有关的多达 20 行（见表 2-4），而杨译本前八十回中"Baoyu's"后续词与贾宝玉人物形象有关的只有 9 行（见表 2-13）。

可见，从类比显化方向上看，霍译本通过大量创设"Bao-yu's"这一表达形式并在该形式后续词上添加信息，由此比杨译本更加凸显贾宝玉的形象。

接着，运用 WORDSMITH 6.0.0 的 CONCORD 的语境词共现功能，查看"said…Baoyu"在杨译本前八十回中的说话共现语境，所得如表 2-15 所示。

表 2-15　　"宝玉"在杨译本前八十回中的说话表情方式词
　　　　　　　（以"said...Baoyu"形式为例）

N	Concordance
1	sed whenever people snub me," said Baoyu. "Well, now that you've stopp
2	all the name." "I can guess," said Baoyu. "Just ginseng tonic pills."
3	ed to be having a good chat," said Baoyu to Xiren. "Why did Cousin Bao
4	pair it." "That explains it," said Baoyu. "Last month when the lotus se
5	e you're in." "you're right," said Baoyu, smiling. He handed the cape
6	that be fine?" "Don't worry," said Baoyu. "Let's go and tell your brot
7	ilence until Xiren, forcing a smile, said Baoyu: "Just because of the tassel on your ja
8	died out." "Never mind that," said Baoyu. "What's the girl like? How d
9	surprise. "That's all right," said Baoyu. "It's a horn lantern, and it
10	d to fly into such a temper," said Baoyu to Qingwen. "I know what's on
11	f it. "I must have lost it out riding," said Baoyu. But when he went to bed and she saw th
12	i Gui. "So that's who he is!" said Baoyu scornfully. "Cousin Jia Huang
13	g came in. "Look who's here," said Baoyu with a smile. "What about it?
14	hing." "Don't be too modest," said Baoyu. "The other day, when I was di
15	d pouches, or sashes?" "Yes," said Baoyu. "One for a sash would be nic
16	ngs are no use to me, madam," said Baoyu, "why not let my pages carry
17	to look. "I know this kite," said Baoyu. "It belongs to Yanhong in th
18	sh?" asked Yinger. "Scarlet," said Baoyu. "A black or slate-blue net w
19	Cousin Daiyu feels the cold," said Baoyu. "Come and sit by the partit
20	inted out. "Don't be afraid," said Baoyu. "My Third Sister likes drink
21	'll eat here with you, madam," said Baoyu. "No, no," objected Lady Wang.
22	hat's what I intended to do," said Baoyu, "but when I got there I foun
23	ace is swarming with people," said Baoyu. "Take any of them you like.
24	n't show." "That's splendid," said Baoyu. "Where would we find a Russi
25	ne." "You don't know, madam," said Baoyu, "Cousin Lin suffers from an
26	men should be treated alike," said Baoyu with a grin. "Why give me thi
27	that day? "Oh, nothing much," said Baoyu. "It simply occurred to me th
28	several times. "That'll do," said Baoyu. "Don't tire yourself. Taste
29	itality. "I've a suggestion," said Baoyu. "As we're not inviting outsi
30	is no time for snivelling," said Baoyu. "If you don't like it here,

续表

N	Concordance
31	to romantic trash." Then he said sternly to Baoyu: "What are you standing there for, yo
32	d Shenyue. "Oh yes, she did," said Baoyu. "You deserve to catch your d
33	aper. "I'm glad you've come," said Baoyu. "I'd quite forgotten, I meant
34	no good, that's quite fair," said Baoyu with a smile. "But you should
35	"The moon's bright tonight," said Baoyu, clearing his throat. "We'll
36	e of Baoyu. "I can't go out," said Baoyu. "Whatever happens, don't let
37	tion. "Go ahead and enjoy it," said Baoyu. "You don't know the trouble
38	hink of a name. "Never mind," said Baoyu. "Names don't matter, just tel
39	pirits." "There's some here," said Baoyu promptly. He told the maids t
40	tting her." "that's all right," said Baoyu. "I shall ask my grandmother
41	write verses about this too," said Baoyu presently. "I've already made
42	ou astray?" "Leave it to me," said Baoyu. Then Mingyan brought round h
43	musk, moon or islands here," said Baoyu. "If you want allusive couple
44	s much as you, third sister," said Baoyu. "I'm always urging you not t
45	f Beijing's favourite concubines died," said Baoyu. "I went to offer condolences. He was
46	l laughter. "I'm last again," said Baoyu cheerfully. "But surely my 'W
47	e. "If you're free tomorrow," said Baoyu to Yun, "lust drop in and see
48	en' was given by some poet," said Baoyu, "because this flower is as r
49	yself." "Sit down, sit down," said Baoyu. "Why stand on ceremony with
50	shan't be drinking any wine," said Baoyu. "Why not put a plate or two
51	we accuse her?" "Never mind," said Baoyu. "I'll take the blame for tha
52	rop in any time you're free," said Baoyu, before telling Zhuier to see
53	uld bear with her." "I know," said Baoyu, and dashed off. Back in his
54	ared at this point. "Zijuan," said Baoyu, "Pour a cup of that good tea
55	misses!" "Go and have lunch," said Baoyu, "and come back as soon as yo
56	money in¬ stead?" "All right," said Baoyu. "We'll keep them and distrib
57	u accept it." "That's right," said Baoyu. "It seems that you can't be
58	" "I suppose you won't stop," said Baoyu, "till you've knocked out you
59	d better keep out of his way. "I see," said Baoyu after a thoughtful pause. "Well, you
60	ery decent of Sister Caiyun," said Baoyu. "But there's no need for you

上表 65 例 "said...Baoyu" 中只有 8 例含贾宝玉说话表情方式词。

表 2 - 16　　"宝玉" 在杨译本前八十回中的说话表情方式词
（以 "Baoyu...said" 形式为例）

N	Concordance
1	red plum-blossom." "That would do nicely," Baoyu said. At the same time he asked Xire
2	o forget it. After holding out for some time Baoyu said, "All right, I won't tell if un
3	more stylish and poignant than the others." Baoyu said with a smile, "This subject see
4	than before. Much impressed by this account Baoyu said with delight, "No wonder y
5	he Taoist's officiousness still rankled with Baoyu, and when Daiyu, said this he thought:
6	to enjoy her drink. As soon as she had gone Baoyu said, "Don't bother to heat it. I prefe
7	er. Any more argument will be penalized." So Baoyu said no more. "I've decided that fro
8	nd then Xiangyun's poem, which they praised. Baoyu said: "I'm no good at irregular metr
9	At least that's my idea. Do think it over." Baoyu agreed with all she said. "I've packed
10	n too busy till today to call to see her and Baoyu," said Aunt Xue. "And now I find both
11	of poems for him. Asked if he had finished, Baoyu said, "I've only done three. All left
12	and Daiyu returned to her own rooms to rest. Baoyu followed her there and said with a s
13	t this a firecracker?" asked Jia Zheng. When Baoyu said that was right, his father read
14	up from the warm pot. After sipping some tea Baoyu said with an apologetic smile, "I
15	ould I know? Better ask yourself." This took Baoyu so aback that he said nothing. Then,
16	se was nearly burnt up. The others laughed. "Baoyu's lost again," said Li Wan. "you'd
17	o keep Yingchun company and cheer her up. To Baoyu she said, "Mind you don't breathe
18	n of burn¬ing sacrificial paper; but luckily Baoyu said he'd asked her to do it, and that
19	r." At this point Qianxue brought in tea and Baoyu said, "Do have some tea, Cousin Lin."
20	"Who asked your opinion?" roared his father. Baoyu stepped back nervously and said no more.

上表20例"Baoyu…said"中只有4例含贾宝玉说话表情方式词。

要之,运用WORDSMITH 6.0.0的CONCORD的语境词共现功能,可将"宝玉"在杨译本前八十回中的说话表情方式词总结如下(见表2-17)。

表2-17   "宝玉"在杨译本前八十回中的说话表情方式词

said Baoyu, smiling(1次)	said Baoyu, clearing his throat(1次)
said Baoyu with a smile(2次)	said Baoyu presently(1次)
said Baoyu with a grin(1次)	Baoyu said with a smile(2次)
said Baoyu cheerfully(1次)	Baoyu said with delight(1次)
said Baoyu promptly(1次)	Baoyu stepped back nervously and said no(1次)
said Baoyu scornfully(1次)	Baoyu said with an apologetic smile(1次)
said Baoyu after a thoughtful pause(1次)	

"宝玉"在霍译本、杨译本前八十回的说话表情方式词对比如图2-10所示。

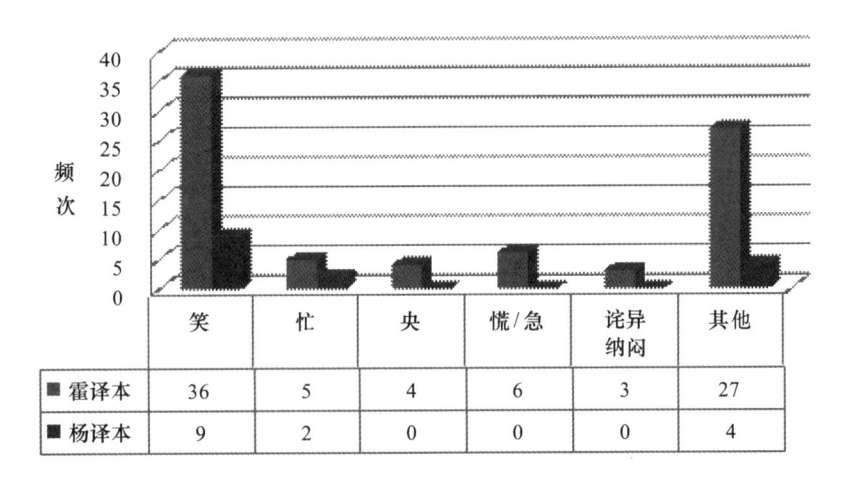

频次	笑	忙	央	慌/急	诧异纳闷	其他
霍译本	36	5	4	6	3	27
杨译本	9	2	0	0	0	4

图2-10 霍译本和杨译本前八十回中"宝玉"的说话表情方式词比较

图2-10显示,总体来说,在前八十回的"宝玉"说话表情方式词

出现频次上，霍译本远远高于杨译本；另外，霍译本出现了杨译本未曾出现的说话表情方式词，宝玉的形象在霍译本中更为多样和丰满。

第二节 分析与讨论

霍克斯在英译中注意到《红楼梦》语言表达上的含蓄特点，根据英汉语言的特点，以一种译者评论的态度，"在译文中增添有助于译文读者理解的显化表达，或者说将原文隐含的信息显化于译文中，使意思更明确，逻辑更清楚"①。通过创设"Bao-yu's"这种极具描写性的语言形式并在其后增添解释性成分的词汇的特点来显化贾宝玉形象，另外通过转词增意塑形象的翻译策略，将贾宝玉说话时的态度、性格及品格体现出来，彰显了贾宝玉的人物形象。对比原著和杨译本，可以发现霍译本的显化翻译乃有意识的策略，而非下意识语言选择的结果，即霍克斯对贾宝玉人物形象进行了非强制性显化翻译。下面分两种情况进行讨论。②

第一种情况，霍克斯"以更明显的形式表述原著文本的信息，在翻译中增添解释性成分"③来显化贾宝玉形象。20世纪初，鲁迅先生把"移情""益智""异国情调"等美学思想移植到翻译理论中，认为"凡是翻译，必须兼顾两面，一面当然力求其易解，一面则保存着原作的风姿"④。译者的任务是要努力再现源文本人物形象，成功的译者须追踪源文本人物形象描写，将所拥有的艺术形象创造的自由度显化到译本中去。

例 2-1

霍底本：一则宝玉脸面俊秀；二则花叶繁茂，上下俱被枝叶隐住，刚露着半边脸儿；那女孩子只当也是个丫头，再不想是宝玉，因笑道："多谢姐姐提醒了我。"（《红楼梦》第三十回）

霍译本：but partly because of Bao-yu's almost girlishly beautiful fea-

---

① 柯飞：《翻译中的隐和显》，《外语教学与研究》2005 年第 4 期。
② 为了防止由于杨译本的底本与霍译本的底本不同而导致的译文差异，在分析与讨论中将杨译本的底本呈现出来以论证在相同或相似底本下霍译与杨译贾宝玉人物形象的不同。
③ Mark Shuttleworth, Moira Cowie, *Dictionary of Translation Studies*, 上海外语教育出版社 1997 年版，第 55 页。
④ 陈福康：《中国译学理论史稿》，上海外语教育出版社 1992 年版，第 174 页。

tures, and partly because she could in any case only see about half of his face, everything above and below being hidden by flowers and foliage, she took him for a maid; so instead of rushing from his presence as she would have done if she had known that it was Bao-yu, she smiled up at him gratefully: "Thank you for reminding me."

杨底本：一则<u>宝玉脸面俊秀</u>；二则花叶繁茂，上下俱被枝叶隐住，刚露着半边脸，那女孩子只当是个丫头，再不想是宝玉，因笑道："多谢姐姐提醒了我。"（《红楼梦》第三十回）

杨译：As Baoyu was <u>finely-featured</u> and as the thick foliage screened all but the top of his face, she took him for a maid. "Thanks, <u>sister</u>," she said with a smile.

例 2-1 中，霍译本通过创设"Bao-yu's"这种极具描写性的语言形式并在其后增添"almost girlishly"显化贾宝玉的"女性化"肖像特征，与源文本遥相呼应。

通过索引底本的相关语境我们可以找到霍译本这样显化翻译贾宝玉女性化肖像特征的根据：宝玉刚一出场，曹雪芹就紧紧抓住他的"女性化"肖像特征，并反复强调、烘托和渲染。小说第三回，曹雪芹通过林黛玉的眼睛，两次浓墨重彩地描绘过这个怡红公子的"秀色"：当黛玉正在疑惑宝玉"不知是怎生个惫懒人物"时，写宝玉已经走了进来："面若中秋之月，色如春晓之花，鬓若刀裁，眉如墨画，面如桃瓣，目若秋波……"不一会儿，当宝玉"换了冠带"后，小说又写他："面如敷粉，唇若施脂；转盼多情，语言若笑；天然一段风韵，全在眉梢；平身万种情思，悉堆眼角。"而后，又通过北静王的眼睛，写宝玉："面若春花，目如点漆。"通过秦钟的眼睛写他："形容出众，举止不浮，更兼金冠绣服，骄婢侈童。"通过其父贾政的眼睛写他："神采飘逸，秀色夺人。"老祖宗在"眼越发花"时，竟指着他问："这是那个女孩儿？"

另外，宝玉所居之地怡红院室内的布置和室外的景致也形象地体现了宝玉女性化的心理要求：怡红院室内摆设精美雅致，色彩浓艳明丽，所以刘姥姥醉卧宝玉房间，醒来后问："这是那个小姐的绣房，这样精致？"室外景观艳丽缤纷："绕着碧桃花，穿过竹篱花障编就的月洞门，俄见粉垣环护，绿柳周垂……院中点衬几块山石，一边种几株芭蕉，那一边是西府海棠,其势若伞,丝垂金缕,葩吐丹砂。"

再有,宝玉平常所密切交往的男性朋友,也大都具有女性化的特点:秦钟"怯怯羞羞,有女儿之态",北静王水溶"形容秀美,性情谦和",戏子棋官"妩媚温柔"。

所以,霍译本把贾宝玉的肖像显化为"almost girlishly",与源文本所暗示预设的信息遥相呼应;但杨译本译作"finely-featured",因为没有凸显贾宝玉的女性化肖像特征,所以后文中龄官对说贾宝玉"Thanks, sister"就可能让读者莫名其妙。

例 2-2

霍底本:秦钟本自怯弱,又带病未痊受了笞杖,今见老父气死,悔痛无及,又添了许多病症。因此,<u>宝玉心中怅怅不乐</u>。(《红楼梦》第十六回)

霍译本:Qin Zhong had always been of a weak and nervous disposition and had still not fully recovered from his sickness when these events occurred. The severe beating followed by the overwhelming grief and remorse attendant on the death of his father from anger which he had himself provoked led to serious complications in his illness. This, then, was the reason for <u>Bao-yu's unseasonable melancholy.</u>

杨底本:秦钟本自怯弱,又带病未愈,受了笞杖,今见老父气死了,此时痛悔无及,更又添了许多征候。因此<u>宝玉心中,怅然如有所失</u>。(《红楼梦》第十六回)

杨译本:Qin Zhong had never been strong nor had he fully recovered from his illness when he received this beating. His father's death filled him with such remorse that his condition was now serious. All <u>this was preying so much on Baoyu's mind.</u>

例 2-2 画线处,虽然霍、杨底本文字不尽相同,但表述意思相近,在翻译时,霍译本通过创设"Bao-yu's"这种极具描写性的语言形式并在其后增添"unseasonable"来显化贾宝玉的"无故寻愁觅恨"性情特征,与源文本所暗示预设的信息遥相呼应。

通过索引底本的相关语境我们可以找到源文本所暗示预设的信息:

宝玉刚一出场，曹雪芹就通过《西江月》说他"无故寻愁觅恨"；小说第三十五回写贾宝玉"时常没人在跟前，就自哭自笑"，他"看见燕子就和燕子说话，看见了鱼儿就和鱼儿说话，见了星星月亮，他便不是长吁短叹的，就是咕咕哝哝的"。"多愁善感"成了贾宝玉的生活常态，他听到林黛玉哭诵"侬今葬花人笑痴，他年葬侬知是谁？试看春残花渐落，便是红颜老死时，一朝春尽红颜老，花落人亡两不知"等句，"不觉恸倒在山坡之上，心碎肠断"。他望见杏子满枝，便联想到邢岫烟出嫁后日渐衰老的悲凉："不过两年，便也要'绿叶成荫子满枝'了。再过几日，这杏树子落枝空，再几年，岫烟未免乌发如银，红颜似槁了，因此不免伤心，只管对杏流泪叹息。"可见，霍译本这样显化翻译贾宝玉"多愁善感"的性情是有源文本作为依据的。

相比之下，杨译本用"this was preying so much on Baoyu's mind"，没有显化出贾宝玉"多愁善感"的人物形象。

原著中宝玉形象的构建集中地体现了他"转盼多情，语言常笑"，"虽怒时而若笑，即嗔时而有情"，以255频次对"宝玉笑道/说"加以重复渲染，使其温柔多情之风韵跃然而出。对于贾宝玉独特的"笑"的说话表情特征的多次重复，霍译本根据实际的语境，大多采用省译"笑"的方式，只翻译了其中36次（后面分两种情况分析），而杨译本中只有9次，因为杨译本中往往将"笑"和"道"一并省译，只译对话内容，让读者通过阅读宝玉的说话内容推断宝玉的说话表情方式，如图2-11所示。

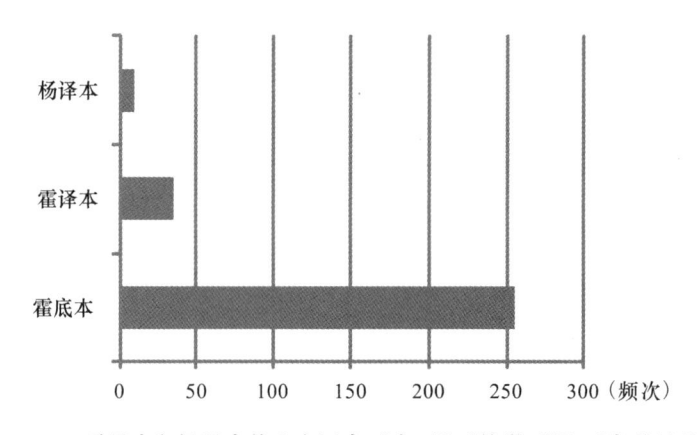

图2-11　霍译本和杨译本前八十回中"宝玉""笑道/说"形象统计比较

第二章　霍克斯笔下的贾宝玉形象　　145

下面举 10 例此类省译情况。

例 2-3

霍底本：宝玉笑道："虽没见过，却看着面善，心里倒象是远别重逢的一般。"（《红楼梦》第三回）

霍译本："Well, perhaps not," said Bao-yu, "but her face seems so familiar that I have the impression of meeting her again after a long separation."

杨底本：宝玉笑道："虽然未曾见过他，然我看着面善，心里就算是旧相识，今日只作远别重逢，亦未为不可。"（《红楼梦》第三回）

杨译本："Well, even if I haven't, her face looks familiar. I feel we're old friends meeting again after a long separation."

例 2-4

霍底本：宝玉笑道："你学惯了，明儿连你还咬起来呢。"湘云道："他再不放人一点儿，专会挑人。"（《红楼梦》第二十回）

霍译本："You'd better not imitate her," said Bao-yu. "It'll get to be a habit. You'll be lisping yourself before you know where you are." "How you do pick on one!" said Xiang-yun. "Always finding fault."

杨底本：宝玉笑道："你学惯了他，明儿连你还咬起来呢。"史湘云道："他再不放人一点儿，专挑人的不好。"（《红楼梦》第二十回）

杨译本："If you copy her long enough, you'll soon be talking the same way," Baoyu teased. "How you do pick on one!" cried Xiangyun. "Always finding fault."

例 2-5

霍底本：宝玉笑道："你死了，我做和尚去。"（《红楼梦》第三十一回）

霍译本："I should become a monk," said Bao-Hu.

杨底本：宝玉道："你死了，我做和尚！"（《红楼梦》第三十回）

杨译本："I'd become a monk."

例 2-6

霍底本：宝玉笑道："听我说罢，这么滥饮，易醉而无味。"（《红楼梦》第二十八回）

霍译本："Now just a minute," said Bao-yu. "Just guzzling like this will make us drunk in no time without giving us any real enjoyment. I've got a good new drinking-game for you."

杨底本：宝玉笑道："听我说来：如此滥饮，易醉而无味。"（《红楼梦》第二十八回）

杨译本："Listen," put in Baoyu. "If you drink so fast, you'll soon be drunk and we shan't have any fun."

例 2-7

霍底本：宝玉笑道："你们两个都在那上头睡了，我这外边没个人，我怪怕的，一夜也睡不着。"（《红楼梦》第五十一回）

霍译本："You're not both going to sleep on the clothes-warmer, are you?" said Bao-yu. "I shall be scared, all on my own in the closet-bed with nobody near me. I shan't be able to sleep."

杨底本：宝玉笑道："这个话，你们两个都在那上头睡了，我这外边没个人，怪怕的，一夜也睡不着。"（《红楼梦》第五十一回）

杨译本："If you both sleep on that clothes-warmer, I'll be all alone out here." objected Baoyu. "I'd be too scared to get a wink of sleep."

例 2-8

霍底本：宝玉笑道："还是这么会说话，不让人。"（《红楼梦》第三十一回）

霍译本："you're always so eloquent," said Bao-yu. "No one else gets a chance."

杨底本：宝玉笑道："还是这么会说话，不让人。"（《红楼梦》第三

十一回)

杨译本:"Still such a talker!" cried Baoyu.

例 2-9

霍底本:宝玉笑道:"人事难定,谁死谁活?"(《红楼梦》第七十一回)

霍译本:"Man's life is uncertain," said Bao-yu. "Which of us knows when his time will come?"

杨底本:宝玉笑道:"人事莫定,知道谁死谁活?"(《红楼梦》第七十一回)

杨译本:"A man's fate is uncertain," Baoyu quipped. "Who knows when he will die?"

例 2-10

霍底本:宝玉笑道:"俗语说:'随乡入乡',到了你这里,自然把这金珠玉宝一概贬为俗器了。"(《红楼梦》第四十一回)

霍译本:"In the world's eyes, yes," said Bao-yu. "But 'other countries, other ways', you know. When I enter your domain, I naturally adopt your standards and look on gold, jewels and jade as common, vulgar things."

杨底本:宝玉笑道:"俗说'随乡入乡'到了你这里,自然把那金玉珠宝一概贬为俗器了。"(《红楼梦》第四十一回)

杨译本:"As people say, 'Other countries, other ways'." Here with a person like you, gold, pearls, jade and jewels must all count as vulgar."

例 2-11

霍底本:宝玉笑道:"论交道,不在'肥马轻裘',即黄金白璧亦不当锱铢较量。"(《红楼梦》第七十九回)

霍译本: "I agree with you that one ought to share with one's friends," said Bao-yu, "and not only furs and horses, but even more precious things if one has them."

杨底本：宝玉笑道："论交之道，不在肥马轻裘，即黄金白璧，亦不当锱铢较量。"（《红楼梦》第七十九回）

杨译本："Among friends one shouldn't be stingy even with gold and jade, to say nothing of horses and furs," he agreed.

例 2-12

霍底本：因笑道："我说呢，正纳闷'是几时孟光接了梁鸿案'，原来是从'小孩儿家口没遮拦'上就接了案了。"（《红楼梦》第四十九回）

霍译本："I see," said Bao-yu. "I needn't have been so puzzled then. It seems that the question 'Since when did Meng Guang accept Liang Hong's tray?' could have been answered with another line from the same act of the same play. It was since you spoke Like a child whose unbridled tongue knows no concealment!"

杨底本：宝玉方知缘故，因笑道："我说呢，正纳闷'是几时孟光接了梁鸿案'原来是从'小孩儿家口没遮拦'上就接了案了。"（《红楼梦》第四十九回）

杨译本：This explained matters to Baoyu. "I was wondering since when 'Liang Hong and Meng Guang started to hit it off so well," he said. "So it all came of her 'being young and talking too freely."

另外，对原著中一部分"宝玉笑道"，霍译本采用两种有意识的策略显化"宝玉笑道"的真实形象，即增词塑形象、转词塑形象。

第一种：霍译本翻译"宝玉笑道"时，在翻译"笑"形象的同时增添信息塑造宝玉形象。

例 2-13

霍底本：探春道："昨儿我恍惚听见说，老爷叫你出去来着。"宝玉笑道："那想是别人听错了，并没叫我。"（《红楼梦》第二十七回）

霍译本："I thought I heard someone say yesterday that he had been asking for you." "No," said Bao-yu, smiling at her concern. "Whoever it was mistaken. He certainly hasn't asked for me."

杨底本：探春说："昨儿我恍惚听见说老爷叫你出去的。"宝玉<u>笑道</u>："那想是别人听错了，并没叫的。"（《红楼梦》第二十七回）

杨译本："Has father sent for you these last few days?" asked Tan-chun. Baoyu <u>smiled</u>. "No, he hasn't."

例 2 – 14

霍底本：宝玉<u>笑道</u>："你是头一个出了名的至善至贤的人，他两个又是你陶冶教育的，焉得有什么该罚之处？"（《红楼梦》第七十七回）

霍译本："You?" said Bao-yu, <u>laughing incredulously</u>. "The famous paragon of all the virtues? There's little danger of her finding fault with you. Or with those other two, whom you trained and moulded in your own image."

杨底本：宝玉<u>笑道</u>："你是头一个出了名的至善至贤之人，他两个又是你陶冶教育的，焉能还有孟浪该罚之处！"（《红楼梦》第七十七回）

杨译本："You're known as a paragon of virtue," he <u>retorted</u>. "And those two are influenced by you. So how could you slip up so as to deserve punishment?"

例 2 – 15

霍底本：宝琴笑道："现在是我做的呢。"宝玉<u>笑道</u>："我不信。这声调口气，迥乎不象。"（《红楼梦》第七十回）

霍译本："Really?" said Bao-qin. "Well, as a matter of fact, I did." "I don't believe you," <u>said</u> Bao-yu, <u>smiling back at her</u>. "The tone of voice is entirely different from yours."

杨底本：宝琴笑道："现是我作的呢。"宝玉笑道："我不信。这声调口气，迥乎不像蘅芜之体，所以不信。"（《红楼梦》第七十回）

杨译本："No, she didn't," giggled Baoqin. "I did." "I don't believe it. The style and spirit are definitely not yours."

例 2 - 16

霍底本：一面让他进来，一面笑着说道："我只当宝二爷再不上我们的门了，谁知道这会子又来了。"宝玉笑道："你们把极小的事情倒说大了，好好的为什么不来？"（《红楼梦》第三十回）

霍译本：She unfastened the gate and welcomed him in with a friendly smile. "Master Bao! I was beginning to think you weren't coming to see us any more, I certainly didn't expect to see you here again so soon." "Oh, you've been making a mountain out of a molehill," said Bao-yu, returning her smile. "Why ever shouldn't I come?"

杨底本：一面让他进来，一面笑着说道："我只当是宝二爷再不上我们这门了，谁知这会子又来了。"宝玉笑道："你们把极小的事倒说大了。"（《红楼梦》第三十回）

杨译本："I thought you'd never cross this threshold of ours again," she remarked. "But here you are." "You take things far too seriously." He chuckled.

以上四例中，霍译本均在"笑"的基础上增词，在形式和意义上均比杨译本突出宝玉对女孩子们不同一般的温柔体贴，不管是对小姐或对丫鬟都尊重体贴、百般逢迎，尽心尽力来赢得她们的欢心。

第二种：霍译本翻译"宝玉笑道"时，转译笼统的"笑"字来塑造宝玉说话时真实的形象。

例 2 - 17

霍底本：湘莲自惭失言，连忙作揖，说："我该死，胡说。你好歹告诉我，他品行如何？"宝玉笑道："你既深知，又来问我做甚么？连我也未必干净了。"（《红楼梦》第六十六回）

霍译本：and Xiang-lian, realizing that he had gone too far, began pumping his bands apologetically. "I'm sorry, I shouldn't have said that. But surely you can tell me something about her character?" "Since you appear to know already, I don't quite see the point," said Bao-yu wryly. "In any case, perhaps I'm none too clean myself."

杨底本：湘莲自惭失言，连忙作揖说："我该死胡说。你好歹告诉我，他品行如何？"宝玉<u>笑道</u>："你既深知，又来问我作什么？连我也未必干净了。"（《红楼梦》第六十六回）

杨译本：And Xianglian, regretting his tactlessness, made haste to bow. "I deserve death for talking such nonsense. But do at any rate tell me what her character's like." "If you know so much already, why ask me? may not be clean myself either."

分析：杨译本不翻译"笑道"，没有显化贾宝玉说话时的表情特征，而霍译本将宝玉"笑"转译为"wryly"，显化贾宝玉因为柳湘莲否定贾府而难堪的"尴尬"形象。

例 2-18

霍底本：莺儿也嘻嘻的笑道："我听这两句话，倒象和姑娘项圈上的两句话是一对儿。"宝玉听了，<u>忙笑道</u>："原来姐姐那项圈上也有字？我也赏鉴赏鉴。"宝钗道："你别听他的话，没有什么字。"（《红楼梦》第八回）

霍译本：Oriole laughed. "Because those words sounded like a perfect match to the ones on your necklace." "So you have an inscription, too?" said Bao-yu <u>pricking up his ears</u>. "I must have a look." "Don't take any notice of her!" said ao-chai. "There is no inscription."

杨底本：莺儿嘻嘻笑道："我听这两句话，倒像和姑娘的项圈上的两句话是一对儿。"宝玉听了，<u>笑说道</u>："原来姐姐那项圈上也有八个字，我也赏鉴赏鉴。"宝钗道："你别听他的话，没有什么字。"（《红楼梦》第八回）

杨译本：Yinger answered with a giggle, "Those two lines seem to match the words on your locket, miss." "Why, cousin," <u>cried</u> Baoyu <u>eagerly</u>, "Does that locket of yours have an inscription too? Do let me see it." "Don't listen to her," replied Baochai. "There aren't any characters on it."

分析：杨译本显化贾宝玉想看项圈的热切心情，而霍译本将"笑"

的形象转化为"竖起耳朵"的机智警觉的形象。

例 2-19

霍底本：宝玉听说，笑道："这有何难，我荐一个人与你，权理这一个月的事，管保妥当。"（《红楼梦》第十三回）

霍译本："That's no problem!" said Bao-yu encouragingly. "I know just the person for this. Put her in temporary control here for a month, and I guarantee that you will have nothing further to worry about."

杨底本：宝玉听说，笑道："这有何难，我荐一个人与你，权理这一个月的事，管必妥当。"（《红楼梦》第十三回）

杨译本：When told the reason, he said cheerfully, "That's no problem. I'll recommend someone to take charge for you. Let her see to things this month and I guarantee that everything will go smoothly."

分析：杨译本将宝玉"笑道"译为"said cheerfully"，基本为直译，而霍译本将宝玉"笑道"转译为"said Bao-yu encouragingly"，既呼应上文贾珍的忧虑，又显化他对王熙凤很"有信心"的形象。

例 2-20

霍底本：宝玉笑道："这场我又落第了。难道'谁家种'，'何处秋'，'蜡屐远来'，'冷吟不尽'，那都不是访不成？'昨夜雨'，'今朝霜'，都不是种不成？"（《红楼梦》第三十八回）

霍译本："I seem to be bottom again," said Bao-yu ruefully. "Though I must say I should have thought that '… to go on an excursion—Some garden where. was planted' 'The glory of autumn being our destination' and so forth was a perfectly satisfactory exposition of 'seeking the chrysanthemums'; and that 'A shower last night the wilting leaves revived', 'Opening the morning-buds all silver-hoar' dealt with the theme of transplanting chrysanthemums rather successfully."

杨底本：宝玉笑道："我又落第。难道'谁家种'，'何处秋'，'蜡屐远来'，'冷吟不尽'，都不是访？'昨夜雨'，'今朝霜'都不是种不成？"（《红楼梦》第三十八回）

杨译本："I'm last again," said Baoyu cheerfully. "But surely my 'Who has planted this flower?' 'Whence springs this autumn glory?' 'waxed sandals come from far away,' and 'chants endless poems' describe visiting the chrysanthemum all right? And don't 'rain last night' and 'this morning's frost' describe the planting?"

分析：杨译本将宝玉"笑道"译为"said Baoyu cheerfully"，基本为直译。而霍译本将宝玉"笑道"转译为"said Bao-yu ruefully"，呼应下文"我又落第"的难堪，霍译本显化了的宝玉"悲伤"形象更加符合语境。

例 2-21

霍底本：宝玉笑道："姐姐们且站一站，我有道理。"周瑞家的便道："太太吩咐不许少捱时刻。又有什么道理？"（《红楼梦》第七十七回）

霍译本："Just stop a moment, there's a good woman," said Bao-yu appealingly, "just long enough to hear what I've got to say." "Her Ladyship told us we were under no circumstances to delay," said Zhou-rui's wife. "There's nothing to be said."

杨底本：宝玉笑道："好姐姐们，且站一站，我有道理。"周瑞家的便道："太太吩咐不许少捱一刻，又有什么道理。"（《红楼梦》第七十七回）

杨译本："Good sisters, please wait a moment," he begged. "I have something to say." "The mistress ordered us not to lose any time. And what can you have to say?"

分析：此例中，对于强拉司棋出园子的"周瑞家的"和几个已婚妇人，杨译本将"笑道"转译为"恳求"，但霍译本将宝玉"笑"转译为"appealingly"，更加从脸部表情上显化贾宝玉的"哀求"的形象。

例 2-22

霍底本：又笑道："老太太有了这个好孙女儿，就忘了你这孙子了。"宝玉笑道："这倒不妨，原该多疼女孩儿些是正理。"（《红楼梦》第四十九回）

霍译本：There was a glint of mischief in her eye："Now that she's got such a beautiful granddaughter, she'll probably lose interest in her darling grandson."

"That doesn't matter," said Bao-yu <u>unconcernedly</u>. "She ought to give preference to girls. that's as it should be."

杨底本：又<u>笑道</u>："有了这个好孙女儿，就忘了你这孙子了。"宝玉<u>笑道</u>："这倒不妨，原该多疼女儿些才是正理。"（《红楼梦》第四十九回）

杨译本："Now that the old lady has this good grand-daughter she'll forget you, her grandson." "I don't mind. It's only right to love girls more."

分析：杨译本省译了宝玉"笑道"的说话表情方式，但霍译本将宝玉"笑"转译为"unconcernedly"，引人注目地显化了贾宝玉对于女孩子有着特殊亲爱和尊重的形象。

以上六例中，霍译本均将"笑"转译，在形式和意义上比原著更突显宝玉真挚多情、天真率直、有关爱之心等充满人性美的形象。

第二种情况，霍译本对原著中的"宝玉道/说"中暗含贾宝玉某种说话的表情，但并没有明确表明的说话方式，也"在译文中增添有助于译文读者理解的显化表达，或者说将原文隐含的信息显化于译文中"[①]，增添的方式既有单方向的，也有先减后加双向的。

第一种：霍译本对"宝玉道"增添说话方式词塑造宝玉形象。

例 2 - 23

霍底本：小丫头道："一夜叫的是娘。"宝玉拭泪道："还叫谁？"小丫头说："没有听见叫别人了。"宝玉道："你糊涂。想必没有听真。"（《红楼梦》第七十八回）

霍译本："Her mother," said the girl. "They said she just went on calling 'Mamma'! All night long." "Didn't she call for anyone else?" said Bao-yu, brushing away a tear. "They didn't mention anyone else,"

---

① 柯飞：《翻译中的隐和显》，《外语教学与研究》2005 年第 4 期。

said the girl. "Oh, you're a silly girl!" said Bao-yu <u>impatiently</u>. "I'm sure you must have misheard."

杨底本：小丫头子道："一夜叫的是娘。"宝玉拭泪道："还叫谁？"小丫头子道："没有听见别人了。"宝玉道："你糊涂，想必没有听真。"（《红楼梦》第七十八回）

杨译本："Her mother." Baoyu wiped his tears. "Who else?" "Nobody else." "You silly thing, you can't have heard her clearly."

分析：杨译本省译了"宝玉道"，但霍译本将"宝玉道"翻译出来，同时增译"impatiently"，将宝玉对晴雯的爱和想知道晴雯是否爱他、是否在临死前呼唤他的急切心情凸显出来，显化了贾宝玉对晴雯的牵挂。

例 2-24

霍底本：老太太说了：明儿叫你一个五更天进去谢恩呢。宝玉<u>道</u>："自然要走一趟。"（《红楼梦》第二十八回）

霍译本：Her Old Ladyship says she wants you to go to Court at four o'clock tomorrow morning to give thanks. "Yes, of course," said Bao-yu <u>inattentively</u>.

杨底本："老太太说了，明儿叫你一个五更天进去谢恩呢。"宝玉<u>道</u>："自然要走一趟。"（《红楼梦》第二十八回）

杨译本："she said you must go to the Palace at the fifth watch tomorrow to express your thanks." "Yes, of course."

分析：杨译本省译了"宝玉道"，但霍克斯将"宝玉道"翻译出来，并增译"inattentively"，将贾宝玉对姐姐的"轻慢态度"凸显出来，显化了贾宝玉对于姐姐的这次赏赐是很不满意的，因为在给所有人的赏赐中，唯独他和薛宝钗的是一样的，也从侧面显化了宝玉对黛玉的感情。

第二种：霍译本对"宝玉道/说"的表情方式减词兼增词，双管齐下塑造宝玉形象。

例 2-25

霍底本：宝玉听了，喜的<u>忙</u>说："他们是那里的钱？"晴雯道："他们

没钱,难道我们是有钱的?这原是各人的心。"(《红楼梦》第六十三回)

霍译本:"How did the younger ones manage to give so much?" said Bao-yu, pleased but a little concerned. "What about us then?" said Skybright. "We're not exactly rich. This is something they wanted to do for you."

杨底本:宝玉听了,喜的忙说:"他们是那里的钱,不该叫他们出才是。"晴雯道:"他们没钱,难道我们是有钱的!这原是各人的心。"(《红楼梦》第六十三回)

杨译本:Baoyu was delighted but demurred, "How can they afford it? You shouldn't have made them chip in." Qingwen demanded, "Do we have money and not they? All of us are just showing our feeling."

分析:此例中,霍、杨译本均将宝玉"喜的忙说"中的"忙"减译,与此同时,分别增加"担心"和"反对",这样减增之间,一个"体贴"丫鬟的宝玉形象已深入人心。

例 2-26

霍底本:宝玉冷笑道:"他们娘儿们姐儿们喜欢不喜欢,也与我无干。"袭人笑道:"大家随和儿,你随和点儿不好?"宝玉道:"什么'大家彼此',他们有'大家彼此',我只是赤条条无牵挂的!"(《红楼梦》第二十二回)

霍译本:"Whether their ladyships and the young ladies are enjoying themselves or not," said Bao-yu, "what concern is it of mine?" Aroma laughed. "Seeing that they're all doing their best to be agreeable, couldn't you try to do likewise?" "Surely It's much better ail round if everyone will give and take a bit?" "What do you mean, 'give and take a bit'?" said Bao-yu in the same lack-lustre voice as before. "They can give and take a bit if they like. My destiny is a different one: naked and friendless through the world to roam."

杨底本:宝玉冷笑道:"他们娘儿们、姊妹们欢喜不欢喜,也与我无干。"袭人笑道:"他们既随和,你也随和,岂不大家彼此有趣。"宝玉道:"什么是'大家彼此'!他们有'大家彼此',我是'赤条条来去无

牵挂'。"(《红楼梦》第二十二回)

杨译本:"I don't care whether they're enjoying themselves or not." "If they are so obliging to each other, shouldn't you be obliging too?" "Wouldn't that be pleasanter for everyone?" "For everyone?" "Let them oblige each other while 'naked I go without impediment.'"

分析:此例中,杨译本省译了"宝玉冷笑道"和"宝玉道",但霍译本将"宝玉冷笑道"中的"冷"字减译,与此同时,将"宝玉道"增译为"in the same lack-lustre voice as before",非但将之前减译的"冷"的意味补出,而且将宝玉说这番话的整个心态表情凸显得极为醒目。这样减增之间,一个"赌气"的宝玉形象呼之欲出。

第三节 小结

霍译本为《红楼梦》的西方读者显化了贾宝玉形象。

首先,和原著霍底本相比较,从语际显化方向上看,霍译本在形式和意义上均突出原著《红楼梦》人物形象(假设1)。霍译本创设了原著中没有的"Bao-yu's"这种极具描写性的翻译形式并在其后增添信息来显化贾宝玉形象。

另外,霍译本对"宝玉道/说"采用增词或增减转化的策略凸显宝玉说话的情感、态度,而将255次"宝玉笑道/说"形式中的"笑"的形象大部分省译,这一点与本书的假设1(即从语际显化方向上看,霍译本在形式和意义上均突出原著《红楼梦》人物形象)看似不符,但霍克斯在翻译其中一部分"笑"的形象时,将"笑"增译或转译成为其他符合上下文语境的形象,又与该假设相符,这是一组矛盾现象,但与 Shlesinger[①]及 Toury[②] 的研究结论相吻合。他们的研究均发现:对于源文的重复表达,译文要么省译(omitting them)要么转译(rewording them)。

---

① M. Shlesinger, "Interpreter Latitude Vs. Due Process: Simultaneous and Consecutive Interpretation in Multilingual Trials", in S. Tirkkonen-Condit (ed.), *Empirical Research in Translation and Intercultural Studies*, Tübingen: Gunter Narr Verlag, 1991.

② G. Toury, "What are Descriptive Studies into Translation Likely to Yield Apart from Isolated Descriptions", in K. M. Van Leuven-Zwart & T. Naaijkens (ed.), *Translation Studies: State of the Art*, Amsterdam: Rodopi, 1991.

其次，从类比显化方向上看，霍译本在形式和意义上均比杨译本突出原著《红楼梦》人物形象（假设2）。霍译本创设比杨译本更多的"Bao-yu's"这种极具描写性的翻译形式并在其后增添信息来显化贾宝玉形象。另外，霍译本在翻译"宝玉道/说"时，往往在形式和意义上显化宝玉说话时的态度和性格形象，而杨译本在绝大多数情况下省译了宝玉"道"的翻译，让读者自己通过阅读宝玉的说话内容推断宝玉的说话表情方式，故杨译本中宝玉说话时的形象特征没有霍译本中多样和丰满。

对比原著和杨译本，可以发现霍译本的显化翻译乃有意识的策略，而非下意识语言选择的结果（假设3）。例如，霍克斯创设"Bao-yu's"高达163频次，是原著霍底本中"宝玉的"52频次的3倍还多，是对比语料库杨译本的"Baoyu's"98频次的近2倍。霍克斯通过在该翻译形式后有意添译与贾宝玉人物形象有关的词，显化翻译了"俊美高贵""多愁善感""才情横溢""无事忙"且"多病身"的女性化贾宝玉形象。另外，虽然霍克斯在翻译"宝玉笑道/说"形式中的"笑"的形象时，省译其中大部分"笑"的形象，但在翻译其中一部分"笑"的形象时，有意识地用了两种方法显化翻译宝玉的说话表情态度，展示贾宝玉的真实说话形象，即"笑"后增词塑形象和转"笑"显真形象。另外，霍克斯对原著中"宝玉道"增添说话表情态度词塑造其形象，有时对原著中"宝玉道/说"的表情方式减原词兼增新词，双管齐下塑造其形象。

第 三 章

霍克斯笔下的薛宝钗形象

《红楼梦》金陵十二钗形象中，尤以"艳冠群芳"的薛宝钗为突出。"在《红楼梦》人物群像中，薛宝钗是与宝玉、黛玉鼎足而三的重要人物……其独特的艺术魅力吸引了一代又一代学人的瞩目、垂青。"① 这个艺术典型之所以如此撩动千万红迷的心弦，缘于她"温柔敦厚的贤淑风范、雍容大方的高贵气质、艳冠群芳的美貌、广博出众的才学和才干。她随分从时、谙熟世故；体贴周全、绵里藏针；心性随和、谨小慎微；既顾全大局，又善于笼络人心，将荣府上下的关系处理得游刃有余……"②

曹雪芹满怀深情塑造的"温柔敦厚""庄重典雅""任是无情也动人"的薛宝钗，霍克斯怎样显化她的艺术形象呢？

第一节 语料采集与基本数据比较

一 薛宝钗人物形象翻译对等形式的考察

首先，通过运用 ICTCLAS 对霍底本前八十回（参照语料库）进行分词处理，并运用 WORDSMITH 6.0.0 的 COLLOCATE 的 Word Cloud 功能，显示霍底本中在"宝钗"右侧 R1—R5 位置的语境共现词如图 3-1。

如图 3-1 所示，"道"在"宝钗"右侧出现次数最多，其次为"笑"。但本书不拟以"道"或"笑"作为考察节点词，因为众所周知，薛宝钗不喜欢争风头，不喜涉及是非，她总是"罕言寡语，人谓藏愚，

---

① 张娅丽：《近十年薛宝钗研究述评》，《龙岩学院学报》2012 年第 1 期。
② 李希凡、李萌：《"可叹停机德"——薛宝钗论》，《红楼梦学刊》2005 年第 2 期。

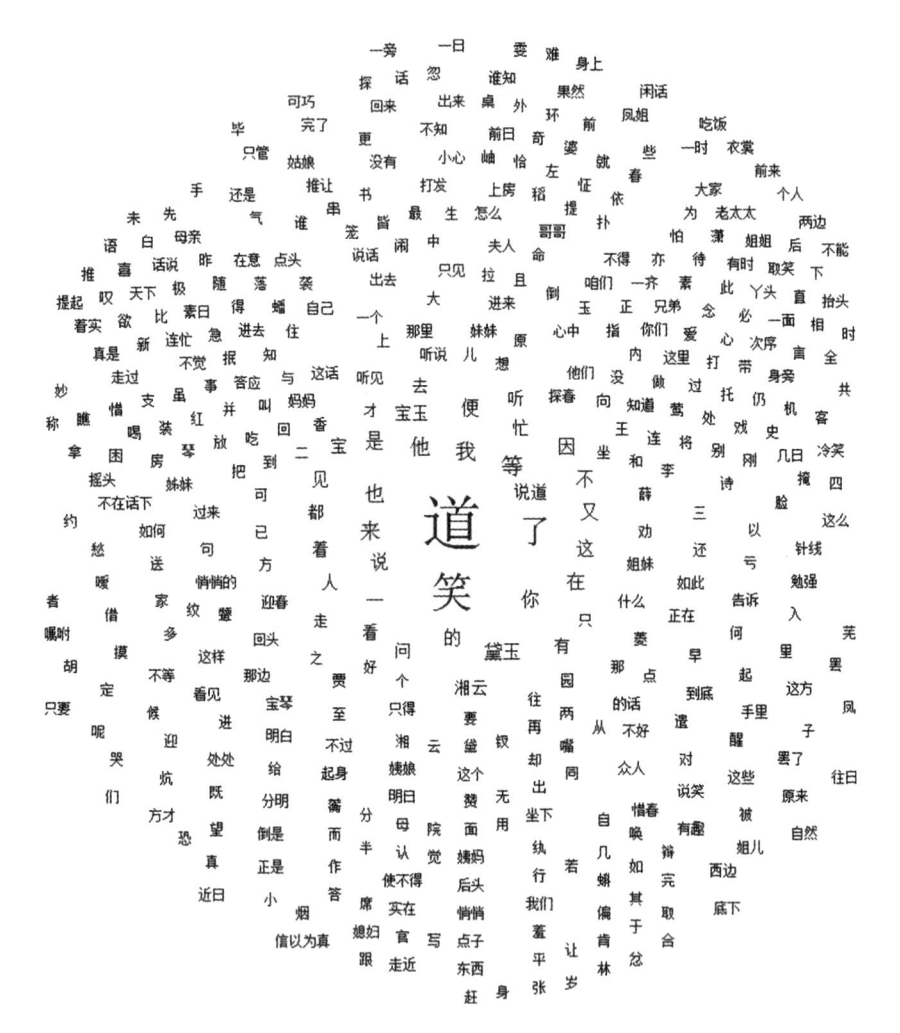

图 3-1 霍底本前八十回中"宝钗"右侧 R1—R5 位置的语境共现词 Word Cloud

安分随时，自云守拙"。她满腹才学，却从不张扬；处世为人方面，总是以理克情，严格审视自己的一言一行，谦恭、退后，而不高高在上、盛气凌人、以势压人。正如脂评所说："待人接物不亲不疏，不远不近，可厌之人未见冷淡之态，形诸声色；可喜之人亦未见醴密之情，形诸声色。"如果考察"宝钗道"或"宝钗笑"的表情方式，并不容易揭开薛宝钗的艺术形象。

因此，本书拟以在"宝钗"右侧出现次数不是最多的"的"作为考察节点词,因为"'的'的描写性是其基本意义和初始功能"[①],如果考察"宝钗的"后续词的翻译,则很容易揭开薛宝钗在霍译本中的艺术形象。

接着,考虑到霍底本中的"宝钗的"有可能翻译成"Bao-chai's"形式,因此对霍译本在"Bao-chai"右侧 R1 位置的后续词进行考察。

运用 WORDSMITH 6.0.0 的 COLLOCATE 的 Word Cloud 功能,考察霍译本前八十回(考察语料库)中在"Bao-chai"右侧 R1 位置的语境共现词(见图 3-2)。

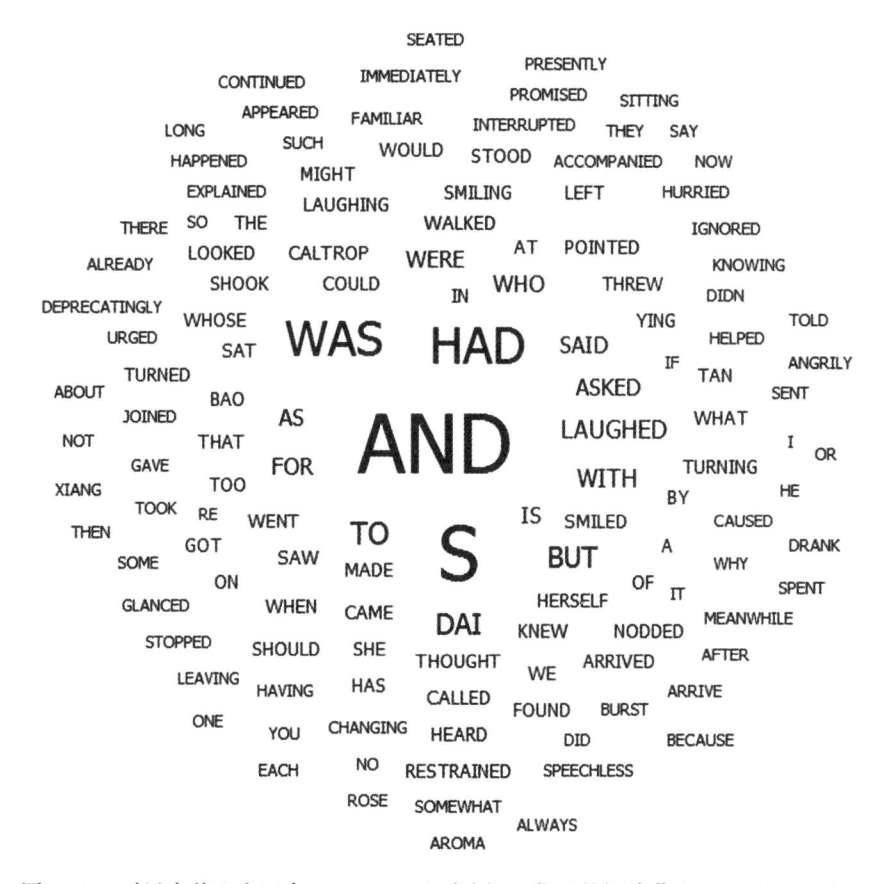

图 3-2 霍译本前八十回中"Bao-chai"右侧 R1 位置的语境共现词 Word Cloud

---

① 陆丙甫:《"的"的基本功能和派生功能——从描写性到区别性再到指称性》,《世界汉语教学》2003 年第 1 期。

如图 3-2 所示，霍译本中，除了"AND"外，"S"在"Bao-chai"右侧 R1 位置出现的次数最多，而形成的"Bao-chai's"与霍底本"宝钗的"正是对等形式。

另外，以上述对霍译本考察的方法，运用 WORDSMITH 6.0.0 的 COLLOCATE 的 Word Cloud 功能，考察杨译本前八十回（对比语料库）中在"Baochai"右侧 R1 位置的语境共现词（如图 3-3），可发现在杨译本中，除了"AND"外，"S"在"Baochai"右侧 R1 位置出现的次数最多，由此形成的"Baochai's"和霍译本中"Bao-chai's"乃对等形式。

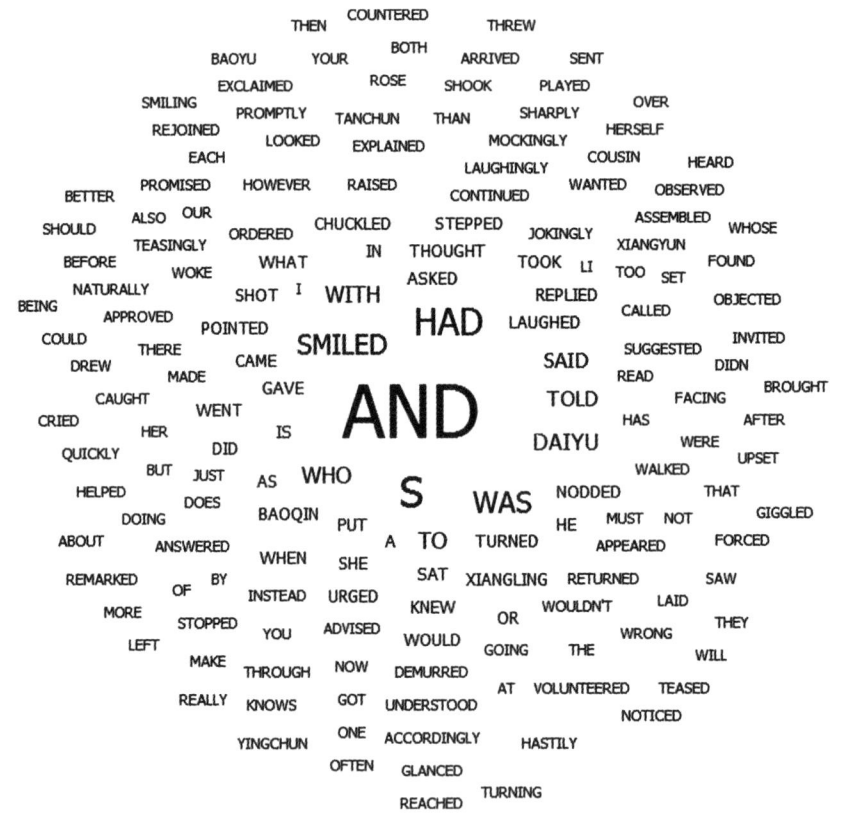

图 3-3　杨译本前八十回中"Baochai"右侧 R1 位置的
语境共现词　Word Cloud

对薛宝钗人物形象翻译对等形式的考察结果还需要运用 WORDSMITH 6.0.0 的相关统计功能进行数据对比，本书将在下节进行。

二 霍底本和霍译本汉英平行语料库的数据比较

运用 WORDSMITH 6.0.0 的 COLLOCATE 的搭配词统计功能，可得"宝钗"在霍底本前八十回中前 15 位、霍译本①前八十回中前 10 位的搭配词（按搭配词总频数排列，见表 3-1、表 3-2）。

表 3-1　霍底本前八十回中"宝钗"的前 15 位搭配词（参照语料库）

N	Word	With	Total	Total Left	Total Right	L1	Centre	R1
1	宝钗	宝钗	666	0	0	0	666	0
2	道	宝钗	236	0	236	0	0	87
3	笑	宝钗	151	4	147	0	0	100
4	了	宝钗	137	43	94	16	0	0
5	说	宝钗	70	29	41	4	0	5
6	来	宝钗	58	16	42	3	0	11
7	等	宝钗	55	4	51	0	0	28
8	便	宝钗	54	16	38	0	0	17
9	一	宝钗	54	20	34	1	0	7
10	他	宝钗	52	5	47	0	0	0
11	也	宝钗	48	2	46	0	0	12
12	是	宝钗	48	13	35	7	0	1
13	我	宝钗	47	0	47	0	0	0
14	着	宝钗	46	26	20	14	0	0
15	的	宝钗	46	12	34	4	0	4

注：N 表示排名；Word 表示所搭配词；With 表示搭配词；Total 表示总频数；Total Left 表示在"宝钗"左边的搭配总频数（含从左边第五个起至左边第一个）；Total Right 表示在"宝钗"右边的搭配总频数（含从右边第五个起至右边第一个）；L1 表示在"宝钗"左边第一个的搭配频数；Centre 表示搭配词居中；R1 表示在"宝钗"右边第一个的搭配频数。

---

① 霍译本为"Bao-chai"。

表 3-2　　霍译本前八十回中"Bao-chai"的前 10 位搭配词（考察语料库）

N	Word	With	Total	Total Left	Total Right	L1	Centre	R1
1	BAO-CHAI	Bao-chai	689	0	0	0	689	0
2	AND	Bao-chai	200	75	125	41	0	59
3	SAID	Bao-chai	177	164	13	158	0	7
4	TO	Bao-chai	158	72	86	25	0	13
5	THE	Bao-chai	157	73	84	0	0	2
6	HER	Bao-chai	107	33	74	1	0	0
7	A	Bao-chai	80	21	59	1	0	2
8	OF	Bao-chai	79	52	27	13	0	2
9	S	Bao-chai	78	16	62	1	0	51
10	YU	Bao-chai	75	28	47	2	0	0

注：N 表示排名；Word 表示所搭配词；With 表示搭配词；Total 表示总频数；Total Left 表示在"Bao-chai"左边的搭配总频数（含从左边第五个起至左边第一个）；Total Right 表示在"Bao-chai"右边的搭配总频数（从右边第五个起至右边第一个）；L1 表示在"Bao-chai"左边第一个的搭配频数；Centre 表示搭配词居中；R1 表示在"Bao-chai"右边第一个的搭配频数。

如表 3-1 和表 3-2 所示，本书的考察语料库霍译本和其对应的原著霍底本在检索节点词"宝钗"的搭配词使用上有明显差别，最显著的差别是霍底本中第 15 位搭配词"的"在节点词"宝钗"的右侧 R1 位置搭配成"宝钗的"只有 4 频次，而霍译本中与之对应的词"S"在节点词"Bao-chai"的右边 R1 位置搭配成"Bao-chai's"多达 51 频次，下面将对此差别进行研究。

先运用 WORDSMITH 6.0.0 的 CONCORD 的语境词共现功能，可得"宝钗的"在霍底本前八十回中的全部后续词行（如表 3-3）。

表 3-3　　霍底本前八十回中"宝钗的"后续词行（全部）

N	Concordance
1	趁早知会他们去。"说着便起身走了。接着宝 钗 的 饭至，平儿忙进来伏侍。那时赵姨娘
2	我咏黄昏。大家看了，称赏一回，又看宝 钗 的 道：珍重芳姿昼掩门，自携手瓮灌苔盆

续表

N	Concordance
3	琥珀、珍珠，黛玉的丫头紫鹃、雪雁、鹦哥，宝钗的丫头莺儿、文杏，迎春的丫头司棋、绣
4	是宝玉做的？"贾政就不言语。往下再看宝钗的，道是：有眼无珠腹内空，荷花出水喜

接着，运用 WORDSMITH 6.0.0 的 CONCORD 的语境词共现功能，可得"Bao-chai's"在霍译本前八十回中的全部后续词，① 其中与薛宝钗人物形象有关的后续词示例如表3-4。

表3-4　霍译本前八十回中"Bao-chai's"后续词与薛宝钗人物形象有关的行（示例）

N	Concordance
1	wife Jin-gui reacted to Caltrop's defence of Bao-chai's intelligence with a toss of the h
2	had finished reading it. Then they looked at Bao-chai's: Guard the sweet scent behind clo
3	rather fear of quarrels and estrangements; if Bao-chai's heavenly beauty is discarded there
4	courtyard, her heart full of gratitude for Bao-chai's kindness. Reentering Bao-yu's roo

为了直观，用表3-5对比霍底本前八十回中"宝钗的"后续词和霍译本前八十回中"Bao-chai's"在R1位置的后续词与薛宝钗人物形象有关的内容。

表3-5　前八十回中霍底本"宝钗的"和霍译本"Bao-chai's"R1位置后续词对薛宝钗人物形象描写

特征	霍底本"宝钗的"后续词	霍译本"Bao-chai's"后续词
容颜	无	Bao-chai's eye, Bao-chai's face, Bao-chai's lips, Bao-chai's heavenly beauty（2次）
体态	无	Bao-chai's hand（2次），Bao-chai's shoulder, Bao-chai's lap

① 详见附录三。

续表

特征	霍底本"宝钗的"后续词	霍译本"Bao-chai's"后续词
言语	无	Bao-chai's strictures, Bao-chai's rejoinder, Bao-chai's objection
动作	无	Bao-chai's first arrival, Bao-chai's arrival（3次）, Bao-chai's company（2次）
性情	无	Bao-chai's kindness, her placid and dependable disposition
才情	宝钗的（诗）	Bao-chai's（poem）、Bao-chai's intelligence

由表 3-5 可知，在霍底本前八十回中"宝钗的"R1 位置全部 4 项后续词中除了一次模糊地提及宝钗的"才情"外，对宝钗的其他人物形象特征未曾谈及，而在霍译本前八十回中"Bao-chai's"后续 R1 位置的人物特征词项凸显了薛宝钗五官中的"eye""face"和"lips"，使译语读者联想到她"唇不点而红，眉不画而翠，脸若银盆，眼如水杏"的"任是无情也动人""冠艳群芳"之美；并两次凸显了薛宝钗具有"heavenly beauty"。还有，霍译本在"宝钗"后续 R1 位置对薛宝钗的体态描写较立体：上至"shoulder"，下到"lap"，并且黛玉和平儿都拉住她的"hand"说话，凸显她"生得肌肤丰泽"，与"行动处似弱柳扶风"的林黛玉有明显区别。霍译本凸显薛宝钗的"随分从时"的言语智慧：博得老祖宗的欢心；恰当而巧妙地化解黛玉的敌意；直言不讳规劝宝玉和亲兄薛蟠，等等。另外，霍译本在"宝钗的"后续 R1 位置多次提及薛宝钗的动作，如三次提及"Bao-chai's arrival"，显示薛宝钗多次去怡红院，凸显宝钗对宝玉的深情，无怪乎晴雯说薛宝钗"有事没事跑了来坐着，叫我们三更半夜的不得睡觉"。霍译本在"宝钗"后续 R1 位置凸显薛宝钗的性情，用词如"kindness""placid and dependable"，符合贾母夸她"稳重和平"。霍译本在"宝钗的"后续 R1 位置除了提及"Bao-chai's"（poem）以外，还明晰地评价她具有"intelligence"，使译语读者联想到她的诗词、画论、品戏、参禅、理家等广博出众的才学和才干。可见，霍译本前八十回中"Bao-chai's"的后续词多层面、多方位地显化了她的形象。

为了更加直观，用图 3-4 表示。

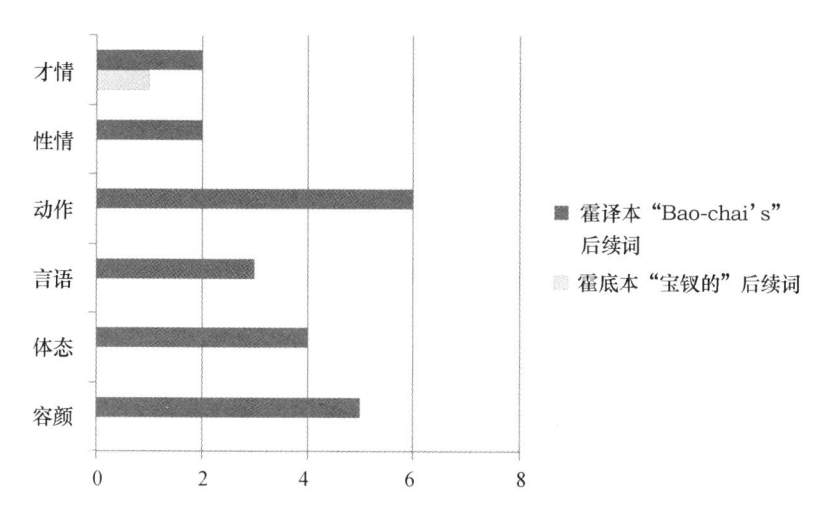

图 4　前八十回中霍底本"宝钗的"和霍译本"Bao-chai's"后续词在 R1 位置对薛宝钗人物形象描写的统计

由图 3-4 可知，从描写总数上看，在霍译本前八十回中"Bao-chai's" R1 位置后续词与薛宝钗人物形象有关的多达 22 频次，而霍底本前八十回中"黛玉的" R1 位置后续词与林黛玉人物形象有关的只有 1 频次。

可见，从语际显化方向上看，霍译本通过大量增添"Bao-chai's"这一表达形式并在该形式后续词上增添词汇意义描写宝钗，凸显原著薛宝钗的人物形象。

三　霍译本和杨译本英英平行语料库的数据比较

借助 WORDSMITH 6.0.0 的 CONCORD 检索功能，观察对比语料库杨译本中"Baochai"[①]的搭配词特征，检索发现："S"在杨译本中与"Bao-chai"的搭配频次已经到了前 7 位，比霍译本中排名更靠前，如表 3-6 所示。

---

① 杨译本为"Baochai"。

表3-6　"Baochai"在杨译本前八十回中前10位的搭配词（对比语料库）

N	Word	With	Total	Total Left	Total Right	L1	Centre	R1
1	BAOCHAI	Baochai	693	3	3	0	687	0
2	AND	Baochai	242	97	145	50	0	73
3	TO	Baochai	168	77	91	26	0	13
4	THE	Baochai	149	57	92	0	0	2
5	HER	Baochai	103	24	79	0	0	2
6	A	Baochai	90	35	55	0	0	5
7	S	Baochai	75	24	51	2	0	36
8	DAIYU	Baochai	66	25	41	2	0	11
9	WITH	Baochai	63	23	40	9	0	13
10	HAD	Baochai	62	13	49	0	0	27

注：N 表示排名；Word 表示所搭配词；With 表示搭配词；Total 表示总频数；Total Left 表示在"Baochai"左边的搭配总频数（从左边第五个起至左边第一个）；Total Right 表示在"Baochai"右边的搭配总频数（从右边第五个起至右边第一个）；L1 表示在"Baochai"左边第一个的搭配频数；Centre 表示搭配词居中；R1 表示在"Baochai"右边第一个的搭配频数。

表3-6所示的对比语料库杨译本和表3-2所示的考察语料库霍译本在检索节点词的搭配词使用上有明显差别：霍译本中与节点词"Bao-chai"搭配排第9位的词"S"在"Bao-chai"的R1位置搭配成"Bao-chai's"高达51频次，而在杨译本中与节点词"Baochai"的搭配排名虽然上升到第7位，但在"Baochai"的R1位置搭配成"Baochai's"仅36频次，几乎只有霍译本对应形式的一半。

接着，运用 WORDSMITH 6.0.0 的 CONCORD 的语境词共现功能，可得"Baochai's"在杨译本前八十回中的全部后续词，[①] 将与薛宝钗人物形象有关的后续词行列表如下（见表3-7）。

[①] 详见附录三。

表 3-7　杨译本前八十回中"Baochai's"后续词与薛宝钗人物形象有关的行（示例）

N	Concordance
1	ing. You always insist that nobody can rival Baochai's looks but you should just see her
2	verses, then remarked with a smile, "Cousin Baochai's and Cousin Daiyu's are specially go
3	praise of Baochai. "Everyone speaks of Miss Baochai's good manners and generosity," she g
4	emperament. Besides, Baochai's generous, tactful, and accommodatinting ways contrasted st

为了直观，用表 3-8 对比杨译本前八十回中"Baochai's"后续词和霍译本前八十回中"Bao-chai's"后续词与薛宝钗人物形象有关的内容。

表 3-8　前八十回中杨译本"Baochai's"和霍译本"Bao-chai's" R1 位置后续词对薛宝钗人物形象的描写

特征	杨译本"Baochai's"后续词	霍译本"Bao-chai's"后续词
容颜	Baochai's looks	Bao-chai's eye, Bao-chai's face, Bao-chai's lips, Bao-chai's heavenly beauty（2 次）
体态	Baochai's lap, Baochai's arm, Baochai's recent indisposition	Bao-chai's hand（2 次）, Bao-chai's shoulder, Bao-chai's lap
言语	Baochai's repeated reminders	Bao-chai's strictures, Bao-chai's rejoinder, Bao-chai's objection
动作	Baochai's arrival, Baochai's leaving	Bao-chai's first arrival, Bao-chai's arrival（3 次）, Bao-chai's company（2 次）
性情	Baochai's generous, tactful, and accommodating ways; Baochai's good manners and generosity	Bao-chai's kindness, her placid and dependable disposition
才情	Baochai's（verses）	Bao-chai's（poem）, Bao-chai's intelligence

由表 3-8 对比，可知在"容颜"上，霍译本两次凸显了薛宝钗具有 "heavenly beauty"，而杨译本后续 R1 位置的人物特征词仅一次提到薛宝钗的"looks"，且模糊不清，未明示她容颜如何；在"体态"上，霍译本

在"宝钗"后续 R1 位置对薛宝钗的体态描写较杨译本健康;在"言语"上,霍译本比杨译本在后续 R1 位置更多地提及薛宝钗的言语,凸显薛宝钗的"随分从时"的言语智慧;在"动作"上,霍译本比杨译本在后续 R1 位置更多地提及薛宝钗到怡红院,凸显宝钗对宝玉的深情;在"性情"上,与杨译本相比,霍译本在"宝钗"后续 R1 位置对薛宝钗的性情描写偏褒,用词如"kindness""placid and dependable",更符合贾母夸她"稳重和平";在"才情"上,与杨译本相比,霍译本在"宝钗"后续 R1 位置除了提及"Bao-chai's(poem)"以外,还明晰地评价她具有聪慧天资"intelligence"。

为了更加直观,用图 3-5 表示。

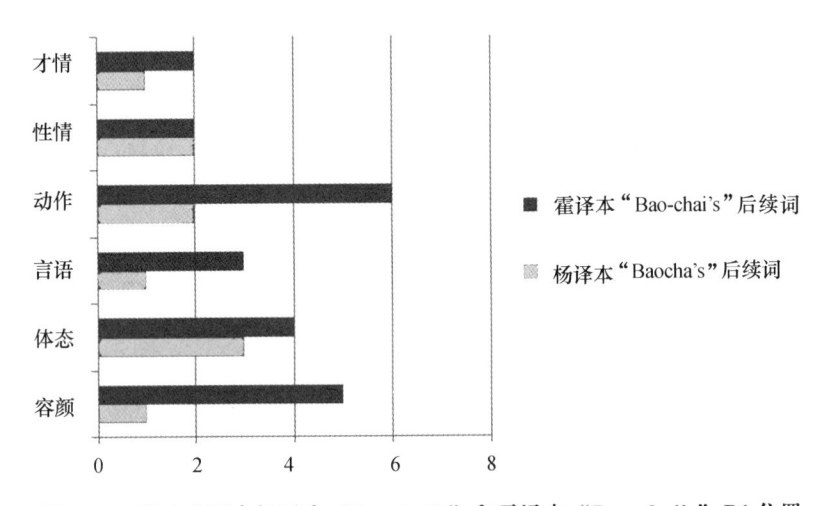

图 3-5　前八十回中杨译本"Baochai's"和霍译本"Bao-chai's"R1 位置后续词对薛宝钗人物形象的描写统计

由图 3-5 可知,从描写总数上看,在霍译本前八十回中"Bao-chai's"后续词与薛宝钗人物形象有关的多达 22 频次,而杨译本前八十回中"Baochai's"后续词与薛宝钗人物形象有关的只有 10 频次。

可见,从类比显化方向上看,霍译本通过大量增添"Bao-chai's"这一表达形式和在该形式后续词上描写宝钗特征而比杨译本更加突出原著中薛宝钗的形象。

第二节 分析与讨论

霍克斯在英译中注意到《红楼梦》语言表达上的含蓄特点,根据英汉语言的特点,以一种译者评论的态度,"在译文中增添有助于译文读者理解的显化表达,或者说将原文隐含的信息显化于译文中,使意思更明确,逻辑更清楚"①。通过创设"Bao-chai's"这种极具描写性的语言形式并在其后增添解释性成分词汇的特点来显化薛宝钗形象,对比原著和杨译,可以发现霍译的显化翻译乃有意识的策略,而非下意识语言选择的结果,即霍克斯对薛宝钗人物形象进行了非强制性显化翻译。下面分三种情况进行讨论。②

第一种:霍译本明晰含糊讯息,凸显薛宝钗人物特征。

霍克斯"在翻译时,当原著文本中表意不清时,往往在翻译时对此加以详细解释"③。

例 3-1

霍底本:彼含其劝,则无参商之虞矣。戒其仙姿,无恋爱之心矣。灰其灵窍,无才思之情矣。(《红楼梦》第二十一回)

霍译本:If the female tongue ceases from nagging there will be no further fear of quarrels and estrangements; if Bao-chai's heavenly beauty is discarded there will be no further grounds for tender admiration; and if Dai-yu's divine intelligence is destroyed there will be no further cause for romantic imaginings.

杨底本:彼含其劝,则无参商之虞矣;戒其仙姿,无恋爱之心矣;灰其灵窍,无才思之情矣。(《红楼梦》第二十一回)

杨译本:Advice kept to oneself does away with the danger of discord;

---

① 柯飞:《翻译中的隐和显》,《外语教学与研究》2005年第4期。
② 为了防止由于杨译本的底本与霍译本的底本不同而导致的译文差异,在分析与讨论中将杨译本的底本呈现出来以论证在相同或相似底本下霍译与杨译薛宝钗人物形象的不同。
③ M. Baker, "Corpus-based Translation Studies: The Challenges That Lie Ahead", in H. Somers (ed.), *Terminology, LSP and Translation*, Amsterdam: John Benjamins, 1996, p.180.

beauty marred obviates affection; intelligence dulled cuts out admiration for talents.

分析：对于"戒其仙姿"的翻译，杨译本没有将含糊讯息"其"明晰为"宝钗"，而霍译本非但明晰"其"为"宝钗"，而且比杨译本增加了"heavenly"。

此例中，霍克斯通过明晰地创设"Bao-chai's"及增添"heavenly"，将薛宝钗的美凸显得非常醒目，向译语读者传递了源文本中薛宝钗那"艳冠群芳"的美女形象。

通过底本的相关语境我们可以找到霍克斯增添"heavenly"显化翻译薛宝钗貌若天仙的根据。宝钗容貌美丽："眉唇不点而红，不画而翠"，"脸若银盆，眼如水杏"，"任是无情也动人"；她肌骨莹润，举止娴雅；她肌肤白皙，宝玉有次见了好雪白的一段酥臂，也不觉动了艳羡之心，想"摸一摸"。

第二种：霍译本在"宝钗"后续 R1 位置增补压缩讯息，凸显薛宝钗人物特征。"在源语文本生成过程中，作者常常隐去与读者共享的或读者已知的语言信息和文化信息，或采用替代、省略等手段避免重复上下文中不言自明的信息。但是，由于源语和目的语语言文化间的差异，这些信息对于目的语文本读者而言不再是已知信息或具体语境中已经明确交代的信息。为了方便目的语读者的理解，译者常常运用不同方法将这些信息明朗化。"[①]

例 3－2

背景：一日金桂无事，因和香菱闲谈，问香菱家乡父母。香菱皆答忘记，金桂便不悦，说有意欺瞒了他。回问他"香菱"二字是谁起的名字，香菱便答："姑娘起的。"金桂冷笑道："人人都说姑娘通，只这一个名字就不通。"香菱忙笑道："嗳哟，奶奶不知道，我们姑娘的学问连我们姨老爷时常还夸呢。"欲明后事，且见下回。（《红楼梦》第七十九回）

霍底本：话说金桂听了，将脖项一扭，嘴唇一撇，鼻孔里哧哧两声，

---

① 胡开宝、朱一凡：《基于语料库的莎剧〈哈姆雷特〉汉译文本中显化现象及其动因研究》，《外语研究》2008 年第 2 期。

冷笑道："菱角花开，谁见香来？可是不通之极！"（《红楼梦》第八十回）

霍译本：Jin-gui reacted to Caltrop's defence of Bao-chai's intelligence with a toss of the head, a scornful curl of the lip and a couple of loud, contemptuous sniffs. "The flowers that girls are named after are supposed to be beautiful, sweet-smelling ones. What is there beautiful or sweet-smelling about a caltrop-flower? It's a ridiculous choice for a name."（《红楼梦》第八十回）

杨底本：话说香菱言还未尽，金桂将脖项一扭，嘴唇一撇，鼻孔里"哧"了两声，拍着手冷笑道："菱角花谁闻见香来着？"

杨译本：Jingui turned away her head, pursed her lips and snorted. Striking the palms of both hands together she sneered: "What scent has the caltrop, pray? This name is certainly senseless!"（《红楼梦》第八十回）

分析：霍底本中，夏金桂听了"谁的话"，采用省略手段避免重复，没有明说，但霍克斯增补这句话出自香菱"Caltrop's"之口，非但如此，霍译本还在翻译时增补上文出现过而此处被压缩的讯息"我们姑娘的学问"，但却将"学问"转译成更高的赞誉："Bao-chai's intelligence"。而杨底本中虽然明说了夏金桂是听了"香菱"的话，杨译本中却省译了"她"，更没有增补"宝钗的学问"。

此例中，霍译本通过明晰地创设"Bao-chai's"及增补"intelligence"凸显薛宝钗的博学多才、聪明颖慧，将源文本所暗示的薛宝钗形象予以明示，向译语读者传递了源文本中薛宝钗那"行止见识皆出于人之上"的才女形象。

通过底本的相关语境我们可以找到霍克斯增补"学问"并将之转译成更高的赞誉"intelligence"的根据：薛宝钗对文学、艺术、历史、医学以至诸子百家、佛学经典都有广泛的涉猎，连以"杂学旁收"著称的贾宝玉也远非所及。如元春省亲归来，要求姐妹们各作诗一首，当宝钗看到宝玉将芭蕉比拟为"绿玉"时，提醒他：元春因不喜"绿玉"，把匾额都改了，再用这二字岂不是让她不高兴？不如改成"绿蜡"，并讲典故

"冷烛无烟绿蜡干",被宝玉称为一字之师;再如薛宝钗品戏,凸显出她对戏文信手拈来般的熟悉;三位男女主人公相互驳难"参禅",薛宝钗对南禅之祖弘忍向六祖慧能传衣钵的故事如数家珍,显示出她佛学知识的渊博,比黛玉更胜一筹;再如,宝钗所讲工笔画的要求、布局的构思以至画具、色料、用纸的开列,都是学问;至于诗词方面的文学造诣,确如贵妃贾元春所说:"终是薛林二妹之作与众不同,非愚姐妹所同列者",如她的《讽和螃蟹咏》,被众诗人赞为"食螃蟹绝唱",她的代表作《咏絮诗》,更展示出她超群的才情和襟怀,被"众人拍案叫绝,都说'果然翻得好气力,自然是这首为尊'"。

第三种:霍译本在"宝钗"后续 R1 位置增添评价性阐释,凸显薛宝钗人物特征。Klaudy 认为"显化不仅仅指原作中不存在而译作中添加的表述,也包括原文中所暗示或只有通过预设才能认识到的信息在译文中加以明示"①。

例 3 – 3

霍底本:宝钗回头笑道:"这有什么的,只劝他好生养着,别胡思乱想就好了。要想什么吃的玩的,悄悄的往我那里只管取去,不必惊动老太太、太太众人。倘或吹到老爷耳朵里,虽然彼时不怎么样,将来对景,终是要吃亏的。"说着去了。袭人抽身回来,心内着实感激宝钗。(《红楼梦》第三十四回)

霍译本:"It's nothing at all," said Bao-chai, turning back to her with a smile. "Do tell him to rest properly, though, and not to brood. And if there's anything at all he wants, just quietly come round to my place for it. don't go bothering Lady Jia or Lady Wang or any of the others, in case my uncle gets to hear of it. It probably wouldn't matter at the time, but it might do later on, next time there is any trouble." With that she left. and Aroma turned back into the courtyard, her heart full of gratitude for Bao-chai's kindness.

---

① Kinga Klaudy, "Back-translation as a Tool for Detecting Explicitation Strategies in Translation", in Kinga Klaudy, José Lambert and Anikó Sohár (ed.), *Translation Studies in Hungary*, Budapest: Scholastica, 1996.

杨底本：宝钗回头笑道："有什么谢处？你只劝他好生静养，别胡思乱想的就好了。不必惊动老太太、太太众人，倘或吹到老爷耳朵里，虽然彼时不怎么样，将来对景，终是要吃亏的。"说着，一面去了。袭人抽身回来，心内着实感激宝钗。（《红楼梦》第三十四回）

杨译本：Baochai turned and smiled. "There's nothing to thank me for. Just persuade him to rest properly and not let his imagination run away with him. We don't want the old lady and the mistress and everyone disturbed. For if word of it reached the master's ears, even if he did nothing for the time being, there'd be trouble later on." So saying, she went off. With a warm sense of gratitude to her, Xiren returned to Baoyu.

分析：对于袭人"心内着实感激宝钗"的翻译，杨译本没有增添信息，而霍译本增译为"Bao-chai's kindness"。

此例中，霍克斯通过明晰地创设"Bao-chai's"及增添"kindness"，将薛宝钗的宽容大度凸显得非常醒目。袭人告薛蟠的状，薛宝钗非但没有生气，反而处处为宝玉着想，这样的增添信息，更能体现袭人为什么感激宝钗，同时也向译语读者传递了源文本中薛宝钗那"温柔敦厚"的淑女形象。

通过底本的相关语境我们可以找到霍克斯增添"kindness"显化翻译薛宝钗特征的根据，如送燕窝给病中的黛玉、救济邢岫烟、暗自帮助湘云等种种，即使对大观园的下人，她也能体贴他们起早睡晚、终年辛苦的处境，为他们筹划一点额外的进益。贾母夸她"稳重和平"，说"所有姐妹，都比不上宝丫头"；从不称赞别人的赵姨娘也说她"真是大户的姑娘，又展样，又大方，怎么叫人不敬重"；史湘云曾说："要是宝姐姐是我的亲姐姐该多好"；黛玉曾叹道："你素日待人，固然是极好的；然我最是个多心的人，只当你藏奸。从前日你说看杂书不好，又劝我那些好话，竟大感激你。往日竟是我错了，实在误到如今……"

第三节　小结

霍译本为《红楼梦》译本的西方读者显化了薛宝钗形象。

首先，和原著霍底本相比较，从语际显化方向上看，霍译本在形式和意义上均突出原著《红楼梦》的人物形象（假设1）。霍译本创设了更多原著中没有的"Bao-chai's"这种极具描写性的翻译形式并在其后增添解释性的词汇来显化薛宝钗形象。

其次，从类比显化方向上看，霍译本在形式和意义上均比杨译本突出原著《红楼梦》的人物形象（假设2）。霍译本创设比杨译本更多的"Bao-chai's"这种极具描写性的翻译形式，并在其后增添更多的解释性词汇来显化薛宝钗形象，薛宝钗的形象特征在霍译本中更加凸显。

对比原著和杨译本，可以发现霍译本的显化翻译乃有意识的策略，而非下意识语言选择的结果（假设3）。例如，霍译本创设"Bao-chai's"高达51频次，是原著霍底本中"宝钗的"4频次的十几倍，是对比语料库杨译本的"Baochai"36频次的近2倍，霍译本通过在该翻译形式后有意添译与薛宝钗人物形象有关的词，显化翻译了薛宝钗"容貌美丽""品格端庄""才华出众""学识渊博"且"关心人、体贴人、帮助人"的形象。

第 四 章

霍克斯显化翻译红楼主人公形象的多维动因

对比霍克斯与杨宪益夫妇英译的《红楼梦》前八十回主人公形象，一个很突出的事实就是：霍克斯在显化翻译《红楼梦》的主人公形象。霍克斯为什么要进行显化翻译，其中隐含着译者什么样的考量呢？本章将尝试探讨霍克斯采用这种特定译法的内在原因。

> 他（霍克斯）正视差异，尊重差异，将文本所含的原作者的视界与译者在不同历史文化背景中形成的视界融合在一起，达到了一个全新的视界，使原作获得了再生。……起关键、中介作用的是译者的文化意识、文化差异感和主观能动性。[①]

霍克斯对《红楼梦》的英译，在充分把握源文内涵的基础上，调动各种显化手段，以确保不仅仅译出原文的字面意思，而且把字里行间的含义也充分地表达出来，其翻译效果得到了一致的肯定。

那么，霍克斯为什么会采取显化的翻译策略呢？

第一节　翻译活动所受制的特定社会文化背景

翻译是语言之间的转换，不同语言所承载的文化和思维内容不同，

[①] 陈可培：《译者的文化意识与译作的再生》，载刘士聪、崔永禄等编《红楼译评——〈红楼梦〉翻译研究论文集》，南开大学出版社 2004 年版，第 363—374 页。

因此表现出不同的特点。Casagrande 提出了"译者事实上不是在翻译语言,而是在翻译文化"①的观点。每个民族和语言之间的系统组成存在差别,即读者在阅读译文之前存有着固有的语言知识和百科知识体系,英语读者在阅读《红楼梦》时,已经具备了自己的世界观、百科知识及语言知识,即阅读前"预先有的文化习惯""预先有的概念系统"以及"预先已有的假设",但对中国古典小说中涉及的文化内容和文本建构方式缺乏相关认知背景。"译者择书而译时,一边是外域文化,一边是本土文化。他在两种文化间比较沟通,是文化的联系人。译者动手翻译时,左边是原文,右边是译文。他在两种语言间选词炼句,是语言的转换人。这就是翻译。它在语言和文化中周旋。"②"翻译涉及的两种语言在社会和文化上的差距越大,可能越需要解释性的'显化'。"③"因为源语和目的语语言文化规范毕竟存在差异。译者需要根据目的语语言文化规范,重新确定具体语言文化信息是明示还是隐含,必要时就要明示原文隐含的一些信息,以保证翻译这一特殊语言交际活动的成功。"④ 因为异质文化的接受者总是按照自身文化的思维模式和习惯去观照另一种文化,译者的任务就是通过改变或增加读者预先有的文化背景和概念系统,使读者理解并欣赏《红楼梦》的人物形象。

一 源语与目标语语言符号系统的规则性差异

翻译是两种语言之间的转换,而语言是文化的核心组成部分,是文化的载体,故此,文化的差异必然反映在语言上。

语言符号系统的规则性和功能性是所有人类语言的共性,同时也是导致每一种语言都有自己的个性或区别于其他语言的特点的原因。不同语言社团的人在认知与描述、交流与沟通时,要依照所使用的语言符号系统的规则,而且由于传承的关系,文化会使其认知与描述、交流与沟通都带上特有的色彩。这些规则上的差异和表述上的色彩就成了翻译的

---

① J. B. Casagrande, "The Ends of Translation", *International Journal of American Linguistics*, Vol. 20, 1954, p. 338.
② 王克非:《翻译:在语言文化间周旋》,《中国外语》2010 年第 5 期。
③ 柯飞:《翻译中的隐和显》,《外语教学与研究》2005 年第 4 期。
④ 胡开宝、朱一凡:《基于语料库的莎剧〈哈姆雷特〉汉译文本中显化现象及其动因研究》,《外语研究》2008 年第 2 期。

障碍。

汉语是音形义兼具的符号系统,它"除了具有理性意义之外,还唤起人脑的表象活动"①,在形态、动态、色彩和声音方面容易产生形象感,产生如见其人、如闻其声、如临其境的生动性的艺术效果,使得作品文采飞扬又添许多真实感。《红楼梦》描述语言的生动性给读者展现了一幕幕形象鲜活的图画。在汉语对人物形象的描写方面,具有可以"看"、可以"听"的优势,那么,又如何将这种生动的、如闻其声的人物形象在英语中再现呢?英语也有音与义,但与"形"却没有必然结合,霍克斯要如何再现这种生动形象的艺术效果呢?霍克斯斟词酌句,注意英、汉两种语言在表达方式上的差异,准确表达人物复杂而曲折的心理,尽量通过显化等补偿方式增加人物形象的直观性,从而生动地展现人物形象。

二 源语与目标语语义及其内涵、外延上的差异

语言还有一个很重要的功能,即记载和传承。它能使人类的经验得以超越时代、跨越地域。同时,由于这一传承,语言沉淀了更丰厚的文化内涵。这就使得一种语言不仅在结构上、规则上与其他语言相区别,更在语义及其内涵、外延上形成了自己的独特性,使语言之间的转换即翻译平添许多困难。傅雷先生曾指出,中英文……民族的 mentahty(精神面貌)相差太远。外文都是分析的、散文的,中文却是综合的、诗的。这两个不同的美学原则使双方的词汇不容易融合。② 中西方思维明显地呈现不同的倾向。中国先贤的哲学思想沿着政治、道德和伦理的方向发展,这种政治伦理型的思维方式重伦理道德、重修身养性、重稳定安邦,明显带有主体意向性,因此中国传统思维重直觉感悟和整体综合,也使思维带有模糊性。西方哲学思想却沿着追求自然科学、认知的方向发展,科学上追求科学的理性,力图求真,重逻辑思辨,擅长用分析和实证的方法来建立新的知识体系。由于东西方思维方式的差异,中国人重综合、归纳,在表达上就较为含蓄,强调"点到为止"。而西方人重分析、演绎,在表达上力求准确、明晰,而且细微曲折,挖掘唯恐不深,描写唯

---

① 吴篮玲:《言外意、弦外音、境外味——简析〈红楼梦〉语言的橄榄美》,《修辞学习》1997 年第 7 期。

② 陈福康:《中国译学理论史稿》,上海外语教育出版社 1992 年版,第 321 页。

恐不周。

英语读者缺乏源语文本中的文学知识和语言知识，很难理解含蓄蕴美的原著人物形象。冯庆华说："中国人所认定的'部分'并不总是会在英语读者的脑海中勾勒出与中国读者脑海中一模一样的'整体'画面；而这两幅'整体'画面之间的差异很可能进一步导致对原著的理解上的差异。"① 正如霍克斯在第二卷的序中所言，"……对西方读者来说，由于缺乏曹雪芹认定他的同时代人能够理解的文学背景，常常会感到困惑或不可理解"②，译者首先必须意识到这种源语与目标语语义及其内涵、外延上的差异以及由此带来的翻译上的障碍，尽量通过显化等补偿方式增加人物形象的直观性，从而生动地展现人物形象。

三 《红楼梦》对人物描写的"隐现"手法

含蓄是中华民族的语言特色，也是中国文学作品的风格。中国文学中"隐现"的手法，在《红楼梦》中使用较多。"隐"即隐藏，含而不露，若隐若现；"现"即显现。曹雪芹在运用含蓄表现的手段上有很多独创性，他用多种含蓄的语言表达《红楼梦》的人物形象，关于这一点，《脂砚斋重评石头记》的脂砚斋批语评价十分全面：

> 事则实事，然亦叙得有间架，有曲折，有顺逆，有映带，有隐有现，有正有间，以至草蛇灰线，空谷传声，一击两鸣，明修栈道，暗渡陈仓，云龙雾（雨）豹，两山对峙，烘云托月，背面傅粉，千皴万染诸奇。书中之秘法，亦不复少……颊上三毫，追魂摄魄，横云断岭……③

《红楼梦》的人物形象是需要读者反复回味、反复理解的。"若隐若现"的结构特点是《红楼梦》既让人费解又魅力无穷的地方。而西方人

---

① 冯庆华：《红译艺坛——〈红楼梦〉翻译艺术研究》，上海外语教育出版社2006年版，第161页。
② 范圣宇：《〈红楼梦〉管窥》，中国社会科学出版社2004年版，第343页。
③ 《脂砚斋重评石头记》（庚辰本），文学古籍刊行社1955年朱墨套印本；周振甫：《小说例话》，江苏教育出版社2005年版，第144页。

的精密性思维与中国文学作品语言的含蓄模糊就存在着差异，对"隐现"的手法不理解就不能完成对人物的理解，更达不到对人物形象欣赏的层次。

《红楼梦》的人物形象建构和创作方式上的波澜曲折、含蓄韵味都是翻译中的难点所在。"的确，翻译转换是需要精通两种语言、熟悉两种文化的译者来执行的。译者不仅是两种语言文化之间的联系人、搭桥人，他本身就处于两种语言文化的交叉部分，他产生的译作因而也处于两种语言文化的交叉部分，形成交互部分。"①

译者首先必须意识到这种"隐现"手法以及由此带来的翻译上的障碍，尽量通过显化翻译明示原著人物形象建构中的语义表达和呈现方式，使译文读者获得与原文读者同样的人物形象审美愉悦。

第二节 翻译活动的赞助人

"翻译的目的由翻译行为的发起者或委托人确定"②，以勒菲韦尔（Lefevere）为代表的"改写"理论强调社会文化语境对翻译的制约，同时提出赞助者通过意识形态及诗学观操控翻译的学说。赞助者的意识形态及诗学观对翻译活动的操控往往与市场、读者期待及教育机构的需求相结合。译者与发起者或委托人即赞助人达成协议后，生产出满足翻译要求、实现翻译目的的文本。

一 符合市场需求是企鹅书局的一贯原则

"翻译绝不是在真空中产生，也绝不是在真空中被接受"（Bassnett & Lefevere），"目的语文本的意向读者乃确定翻译目的最重要的因素之一"。

企鹅书局由埃伦·雷恩（Alan Lane）爵士于1935年创建，目前已成为世界上最著名的英语图书出版商之一。创办人雷恩的理念是以"低廉的价格、高雅的内容及优质的印刷和大众营销来打造企鹅书局的品牌独

---

① 王克非：《翻译：在语言文化间周旋》，《中国外语》2010年第5期。
② Christiane Nord, *Translating as a Purposeful Activity-Functionalist Approaches Explained*, Shanghai: Shanghai Foreign Language Education Press, 2001, p.12.

特性"①。企鹅书局始终遵行的是雷恩创办书局时就坚守的一条原则："公众会欢迎以一个可接受的价格出售的高质量的书籍，甚至是平装本。"②

二　企鹅古典丛书主编的效果对等原则

企鹅古典丛书首任主编为里欧（E. V. Rieu，1887—1972），英国皇家文学社（Royal Society of Literature）的副主席，他本人曾翻译过《奥德赛》（*Odyssey*）和《伊利亚特》（*Iliad*）。有学者这样评价："读E. V. Rieu 的翻译，也觉得他的行文，像一江流水，浩浩荡荡，奔腾而去，没有板滞之处。他以诗的语言绘出壮阔的画面，传达出了荷马的高贵气质。"③

里欧把数学上的"等值"概念引入了翻译领域，坚持"译者艺术的北极星"（the lodestar of the translator's art, I call it）是"效果对等原则"（the same effect），指译本能够对现代读者产生原作带给其第一批读者的同样效果，最为接近原作效果的译本就是最好的译本。④ 他说："……大声朗读译文（to read my translation aloud）。自己大声朗读完一遍后，再让那些称职的批评家手里拿着笔和本子坐在你的旁边听你读并为你提意见。"⑤ "对译者他只提出了两个字的要求：Write English! 这是以'顺'为主的翻译原则，但是这个'顺'必须用现代地道英语表现出来，Rieu 自己就以荷马史诗的新译实践了这个主张。"⑥

里欧作为翻译活动的赞助商——企鹅书局的翻译丛书主编，他的翻译理念与霍克斯的《红楼梦》翻译理念有着惊人的契合，"英国企鹅翻译

---

① Jonathan Rose & Patricia J. Anderson (eds.), *Dictionary of Literary Biography*, London: Gale Research Inc., 1991, p. 252. 原文如下："Lane's idea was to combine quality—both in production and in literary content – with low prices and mass marketing."

② Ibid., p. 261.

③ 曹鸿昭：《伊利亚特》（西方正典），吉林出版集团有限责任公司2010年版，"译者序"第1页。

④ Rev. E. H. Robertson (ed.), "Translating the Gospels: A Discussion Between Dr. E. V. Rieu and the Rev, J. B. Phillips", *The Bible Translator*, Vol. 6, No. 4, October 1955, p. 153.

⑤ Ibid., p. l55.

⑥ 王佐良：《英语文体学论文集》，外语教学与研究出版社1980年版。

丛书主编 E. V. Rieu 和别的译界权威都重视译文的通畅"①，故而1970年他与企鹅出版社签订了翻译的合同后，辞去牛津大学汉学教授的职务，专心致力于《红楼梦》的翻译。

霍克斯通过显化等补偿翻译方式增加人物形象的直观性，从而让"公众能够通畅地将译文读懂"，也是效果对等原则的体现。

第三节　译者的主体性

译者主体性指"作为翻译主体的译者在尊重翻译对象的前提下，为实现翻译目的而在翻译活动中表现出的主观能动性，其基本特征是翻译主体自觉的文化意识、人文品格和文化、审美创造性"②，或是"译者在翻译活动中创造性地发挥自己的主体意识，在翻译策略和翻译方法上凸显译者的独特性的过程"③。因为翻译是在对原作品体验和认知的基础上用另一种语言来表达的，必然存在着译者对原作品的识解以及语言的再创造，译者的主体作用是显然的。冯庆华指出："译者不同的时代背景、教育背景、生活背景、个人经历以及意向中的读者群（intended readers）和读者的能力预计和要求，都将直接影响译者在翻译活动中的思维模式和对文化成分处理的方式。"④

一　译者认识到《红楼梦》的伟大及对节译的不满

许钧认为，译者主体性体现在其"对翻译活动起着直接而重要的影响"的"个性、气质、心理禀赋、知识面、语言运用能力、立场、道德"⑤等方面。

霍克斯明确肯定了《红楼梦》的伟大及其全译的必要。他对《红楼梦》有极高评价："这是一部真正伟大的中国小说，目前已有的两部英译

---

① 思果：《翻译新究》，中国对外翻译出版公司2001年版，第1页。
② 查明建、田雨：《论译者主体性——从译者文化地位的边缘化谈起》，《中国翻译》2003年第3期。
③ 刘军平：《从跨学科角度看译者主体性的四个维度及其特点》，《外语与外语教学》2008年第8期。
④ 冯庆华：《母语文化下的译者风格》，上海外语教育出版社2008年版，第2页。
⑤ 许钧：《文学翻译的理论与实践——翻译对话录》，译林出版社2001年版，第22页。

本虽然不错,但在为英语读者提供鲜活的译文方面仍做得相当不够"①,《红楼梦》是"一部从某种意义上说可以象征中国整个文化的作品,当大多数中国人被要求说出其文学中最伟大的作品时均会指向此部作品,它在中国被一遍遍地阅读,犹如我们不断重读莎士比亚"②,"如果英语读者不相信此部小说的伟大,那是因为至今还没有可供使用的英语全译本出现"③。

霍克斯对王际真1958年节译本的评价:"是最出色的,但节译使原作由令人愉悦的漫步变成了令人上气不接下气的慢跑,破坏了后半部不紧不慢、慢条斯理的节奏。只会使(读了节译本的)英语读者琢磨中国人对这部小说的赞美是否真的恰如其分。"④

1998年霍克斯在访谈中又谈到了他的全译本之前的另外两个译本:库恩译本和王际真译本。霍克斯评价库恩"译本比译者所宣称的要删节得厉害"⑤,而对王际真译本,他说:"王际真本我喜欢,我喜欢读它,我阅读时很享受。但我的印象是开头还是全文翻译,后来大约是累了(笑),就开始飞跑——因此最后一部分就压缩得很厉害。因此我觉得这部小说真的值得好好翻译,有人应该来完成这项全译工作。"⑥

由此可见,《红楼梦》的伟大及对现有译文的不满促成霍克斯下决心

---

① David Hawkes, "From the Chinese", in John Minford & Siu-kit Wong (ed.), *Classical, Modern and Human: Essays in Chinese Literature*, Hong Kong: The Chinese University Press, 1989, p. 246. 原文如下:"the one really great Chinese novel, which two competent translations published during the past few years have still not quite brought to life for the English reader."

② Ibid., p. 268. 原文如下:"Most Chinese will point to it unhesitatingly as the greatest work in their literature, a book that in some sense epitomizes their whole culture. It is read and reread as we read and reread Shakespeare."

③ Ibid.. 原文如下:"If the English reader has to take the novel's greatness on trust, it is because the complete text of it has never yet become available in an English version."

④ Ibid.. 原文如下:"But abridgment removes the delectable meanderings of the original and turns the slow, remorseless pace of the second half into a breathless canter. The English reader is left wondering whether Chinese superlatives about the novel can be justified."

⑤ Connie Chan, "Appendix: Interview with David Hawkes", *The Story of the Stone's Journey to the West: a Study in Chinese-English Translation History*, Conducted at 6 Addison Crescent, Oxford, 7th December, 1998, p. 323.

⑥ Connie Chan, "Appendix: Interview with David Hawkes", *The Story of the Stone's Journey to the West: A Study in Chinese-English Translation History*, Conducted at 6 Addison Crescent, Oxford, 7th December, 1998, p. 323.

翻译《红楼梦》的全译本并且要出一个具有高度可读性的本子。

在霍克斯 1959—1971 年任牛津汉学教授期间，他一直兼任牛津东亚文学丛书（Oxford Library of East Asian Literatures）的主编。在这套东亚文学全译系列的必译书单（a list of desiderata）中已纳入他翻译《红楼梦》的计划。可见，早在 20 世纪 60 年代霍克斯就已做出了全译中国古典名著《红楼梦》的决定。

二 译者预期的读者群及有意识的翻译"策略"

"译者需调动其在对所选文本的接受过程及理解—阐释过程中所获得的理解和审美感悟以及其译语语言文化素养，根据译本的潜在读者的期待视野采取相应翻译策略，以实现其翻译目的"①，"翻译行为所要达到的目的决定整个翻译行为的过程"②。

"所有《红楼梦》译者首先是被原著的魅力所迷，然后才着手翻译的，译者祈望能将他们所感受到的小说魅力传达一些给别人。"③ 霍克斯在翻译中始终想把《红楼梦》作为生动的故事讲给西方读者听，他希望通过自己的翻译"能够让英国读者也能体会到我阅读时所感受到的哪怕一丝快乐，那我就没有虚度此生"④。

威尔斯指出："要较为客观地评价译者，翻译评论者需了解译者的翻译目的和各种决策。"⑤

在霍克斯看来，"译者处理原作大致有两种方式，一种是译者选择他所认为的最佳版本然后一直遵从它；另一种是创造一个译者自己的折中的版本，即在不同的版本间选择以构成一个生动的故事（make the best

---

① 刘迎姣：《〈红楼梦〉英全译本译者主体性对比研究》，《外国语文》2012 年第 1 期。
② Christiane Nord, *Translating as a Purposeful Activity-Functionalist Approaches Explained*, Shanghai: Shanghai Foreign Language Education Press, 2001, p. 124.
③ David Hawkes, "Letter from David Hawkes"，载刘士聪编《红楼译评——〈红楼梦〉翻译研究论文集》，南开大学出版社 2004 年版，第 7—8 页。
④ David Hawkes, "Introduction", in David Hawkes (trans.), *The Story of the Stone*, Harmondsworth: Penguin Books, Vol. 1, 1973, p. 46.
⑤ Wolfram Wilss, *The Science of Translation: Problems and Methods*, Tübingen: Gunter Narr, 1982, p. 221.

story)"①。他指出:"对于文本问题我没有以符合学术规范的方式来处理……我只是折中,旨在讲述一个生动的故事(make a good story)。"②

他认为,凡是书里有的,都有它的作用,所以总要设法表达出来。他在《石头记》卷一"导言"中明确提到翻译过程中其恪守的一条原则为"译出一切,甚至双关"③,也就是说霍克斯不仅要求自己译出原作的所有文字,还要求自己译出原作的写作技巧,再现原作的文学魅力。霍克斯充分考虑到了中西文化和语言的差异,正是因为他对中国文化和《红楼梦》研究的深入,才使他有着强烈的文化差异意识。在双语文化和思维的差异下,霍克斯如何能够做到他所说的悟守"要把一切都译出来"的原则,有效而不失忠实地传播中国文化,让读者易于接受中国文化中的人物形象,一个很突出的事实就是,对比霍克斯与杨宪益夫妇英译的《红楼梦》,霍克斯英译中对人物形象的显化翻译现象特别多。

霍克斯1973年发表于《石头记》第一卷翻译刚结束之时的书评,又进一步表达了他的翻译思想。他说:"当然,当把汉语翻译成英文时,无论是何种文体,都无法在形式上做到与原作相像……译者只能选择或创造某种形式,并借助这种形式把原作带给他的感受(feeling)最佳地表达出来。译文是否成功与原作、译作间形式上有多少相似之处没有多大关系。"④ 这篇书评清晰地传达了霍克斯翻译《红楼梦》的主导思想:选择或创造某种形式向读者传达原作带给译者的感受。

霍克斯在翻译《红楼梦》的过程中努力对差异和碰撞做出弥补,这从他的《红楼梦英译笔记》⑤ 中可以略见一斑:《红楼梦英译笔记》中除了对版本的核实之外,主要记录了他对中国文化和语言的难点所进行

---

① David Hawkes, "The Translator, the Mirror and the Dream – Some Observations on a New Theory", in John Minford & Siu-kit Wong (ed.), *Classic, Modern and Humane Essays in Chinese Literature*, Hong Kong: The Chinese University Press, 1989, p. 159.

② Connie Chan, "Appendix: Interview with David Hawkes", *The Story of the Stone's Journey to the West: A Study in Chinese-English Translation History*, Conducted at 6 Addison Crescent, Oxford, 7th December, 1998, pp. 327 – 328.

③ David Hawkes (trans.), *The Story of the Stone* (Volume I-III), London: The Penguin Books Ltd., 1973, p. 46.

④ David Hawkes, "(Untitled Review) Chinese Rhyme-prose by Burton Watson", *Reviews of Books. Asia Major*, Vol. 18, 1973, p. 253.

⑤ 霍克斯:《红楼梦英译笔记》,香港岭南大学文学与翻译研究中心2000年版。

的查阅和解释,包括对诗词典故出处的说明,对建筑物方位以及结构用图画形式的标注,对医药原理的说明,对中医药材的成分以及功效的查实,对风俗习惯的来源以及祭祀的用品的说明,对诗词的韵律以及词牌名的记录以及对词语意思的解释,等等。霍克斯不断地弥补这种语言的背景知识,因为激活译本读者的认知要求译者首先具备对源语有一定的语言和文化知识。只有译者自己有了明晰概念以后,才可能真正翻译出来。

基于对读者认知基础的考虑和正确判断,霍克斯考虑到了《红楼梦》人物形象翻译成英文给西方读者带来的阅读的困难。为了让读者产生与他一样的审美愉悦,彰显作品人物形象内涵,激发英语读者的审美兴趣,霍克斯采用显化人物形象的翻译策略来补偿读者有关文化方面的内容和文本构建方式命题的知识,显现出霍克斯的良苦用心和高超的艺术手法。

> 他在可允许的范围之内,这里补充一下,那里修润一下,使语言更见具体,情景更见真切,整个描述笔酣墨饱。这纯粹是因为中英文体以及习惯用法的不同,并不是由于他手痒难熬,认为可以把原作修改得更好。[①]

香港岭南大学翻译系主任孙艺风曾说:"翻译行为是一种阐释模式,译作就是阐释的结果。字面翻译,表面上看很忠实,实际上是一种懒惰而不负责任的做法,它很少或几乎不涉及阐释,没有任何风险。"[②]

霍克斯在翻译过程中,充分发挥译者的主体性,以他对译语文化和语言的精通,从西方读者的立场出发,全面而又准确地判断了读者的认知世界,在翻译过程中不断采用显化翻译来激活文本中的隐含信息,调动他们的识解能力,通过"增义补形"的翻译策略填补西方读者对《红楼梦》人物形象的认知空白,让读者产生具体化的审美愉悦,让作品人

---

① 林以亮:《红楼梦 西游记——细评红楼梦新英译》,台湾联经出版事业公司1976年版,第118—119页。
② 孙艺风:《视角、阐释、文化:文学翻译与翻译理论》,清华大学出版社2004年版,第83页。

物为读者所认识、接受和审美。

正如《红楼梦》全本的另一英译者杨宪益对他的评价:"霍克斯译《红楼梦》译得像英国小说,我则较忠实于原作。"①

---

① 杨宪益:《银翘集》,(香港)天地图书有限公司1995年版,第126页。

结　　语

在前几章，笔者首先在微观层面对《红楼梦》人物形象翻译的概貌及翻译情况进行了定量性质的描述分析，追溯和厘定了霍译本和杨译本的底本并建立了两组平行语料库，然后，在显化翻译学的宏观框架下，结合语料库的工具，考察了霍克斯对《红楼梦》主人公林黛玉、贾宝玉和薛宝钗的人物形象显化翻译的特点，分析了霍译本与原著及杨译本对这些人物形象呈现方式的差异，并指出霍克斯采用显化翻译的多维动因。通过前几章的研究，笔者发现：

（1）从语际显化方向上看，霍译本在形式和意义上均突出原著《红楼梦》主人公林黛玉、贾宝玉和薛宝钗的人物形象。霍克斯创设更多原著中没有的"人物+'s"这种极具描写性的翻译形式并在其后增添解释性的词汇来显化林黛玉、贾宝玉和薛宝钗的人物形象；另外，霍译本对原著中林黛玉和贾宝玉的说话情态方式进行种种细致的刻画，通过增词和转词凸显他们的说话态度、品格和形象。本书的第一个假设基本得到了证实。

但是，笔者也发现了一个与第一个假设不完全相符的现象：霍克斯在翻译原著中"宝玉笑道/说"这个形式时，对其中大部分的"笑"不是采用比原著更加显化的翻译，反而采用省译"笑"的形象的翻译策略，这一点与本书的第一个假设不尽吻合。对此，笔者认为有两个可能的原因：其一，方梦之认为"省略（法）"——"与'增词（法）'相对，指原文有些词不必译出，因为译文中虽无其词已有其意；或者在译文中是不言而喻的"[①]。从原著宝玉的人物形象上看，他天生就是一个情种，"转

[①] 方梦之主编：《中国译学大辞典》，上海外语教育出版社2011年版，第116页。

盼多情，语言常笑"，"虽怒时而若笑，即瞋视而有情" 是他的一贯作风，他爱他周围生活环境里的所有女孩子，对她们"昵而敬之，恐拂其意"，所以"宝玉笑道/说"在原著里出现极为频繁，对于这种笼统的"笑"的形象，每次都翻译，不仅没有必要，而且太过单一，因为"译者对纯属冗赘的文本完全具有酌情权加以浓缩处理。'啰嗦'的行文误事害人，纯属低档次的非逻辑化"①，故此，霍克斯往往将此形象省译，这一点也与Shlesinger 及 Toury 的研究结论相吻合。他们的研究均发现：对于源文的重复表达，译文要么省译（omitting them）要么转译（rewording them）②。其二，Baker 指出译者有在目标语文本中对源语文本中的某些"语言/信息下意识地简单化"处理的倾向。③ 王宏印认为"省译""和增补是相辅相成的两种翻译技巧"④。柯飞也指出："翻译中的显与隐是共存的，翻译中的隐、显现象及其程度可能与语言的形式化程度和翻译方向相关，同时还会受到译者、社会文化和文本因素的影响。"⑤ 几位学者都提到了在翻译中译者"简化"或省译现象的存在，这也是一种可能的解释。关于省译或隐译或简化翻译的深层机制，因为不是本书的主要目的，不宜在此赘述。

（2）从类比显化方向上看，霍译本在形式和意义上均比杨译本突出原著《红楼梦》主人公林黛玉、贾宝玉和薛宝钗的人物形象。首先，霍译本添加比杨译本更多的"人物+'s"这种极具描写性的翻译形式并在其后增添解释性的词汇来显化林黛玉、贾宝玉和薛宝钗的人物形象。另外，霍译本中林黛玉和贾宝玉的说话表情方式词虽有部分和杨译本重叠，但霍译本比杨译本更高频次地对林黛玉和贾宝玉的说话表情方式进行添加信息和转化信息的描述，使林黛玉和贾宝玉的说话形象在霍译本中比在

---

① 刘宓庆：《翻译与语言哲学》，中国对外翻译出版公司 2004 年版，第 464 页。
② M. Shlesinger, "Interpreter Latitude vs. Due Process: Simultaneous and Consecutive Interpretation in Multilingual Trials", in S. Tirkkonen-Condit (ed.), *Empirical Research in Translation and Intercultural Studies*, Tübingen: Gunter Narr Verlag, 1991; G. Toury, "What are Descriptive Studies into Translation Likely to Yield Apart from Isolated Descriptions", in K. M. Van Leuven-Zwart & T. Naaijkens (ed.), *Translation Studies: State of the Art*, Amsterdam: Rodopi, 1991.
③ M. Baker, "Corpus-based Translation Studies: The Challenges that Lie Ahead", in H. Somers (ed.), *Terminology, LSP and Translation*, Amsterdam: John Benjamins, 1996, p. 176.
④ 王宏印：《英汉翻译综合教程》，辽宁师范大学出版社 2002 年版，第 30 页。
⑤ 柯飞：《翻译中的隐和显》，《外语教学与研究》2005 年第 4 期。

杨译本中更为具体和丰满。本书的第二个假设得到了证实。

（3）对比原著和杨译本，可以发现霍译本对原著《红楼梦》主人公林黛玉、贾宝玉和薛宝钗的显化翻译乃有意识的策略，而非下意识语言选择的结果。例如，霍译本创设的"人物 + 's"这种翻译形式往往是原著"人物 + 的"的好几倍频次，也比杨译本"人物 + 's"的形式多出近一倍的频次，霍译本通过在该翻译形式后有意添加与人物外貌、品质、本性等特征有关的片言文字来显化该人物形象。另外，相较于原著和杨译本，霍译本有意识地通过转词增意塑形象的翻译策略，在"SAID + 人物"后进行情状方式文字的增益或转化，显化说话者真实的表情、态度、性格、品质等特征。本书的第三个假设也得到了证实。

（4）霍克斯在翻译主人公林黛玉、贾宝玉和薛宝钗时，文字的增益和转化都不是凭空捏造的，都是根据原著内容和上下文语境糅合而来的。

（5）除了译者主体性的内因外，一些语言外的因素，如特定的社会文化背景差异、翻译活动赞助人的意识形态也是霍克斯显化翻译《红楼梦》主人公的原因所在。

本书理论意义主要见于如下三点：其一，提出了人物形象翻译的显化概念并着重探讨了《红楼梦》主人公形象的显化翻译；其二，拓宽了《红楼梦》英译的人物形象领域探索范围；其三，促进我国的显化翻译研究国际化。此外，本书尚不乏充分的实际应用价值，基于语料库的《红楼梦》人物形象系统研究在一定程度上将对"红学"研究和文化翻译以及中国古典白话小说的英译产生积极的可借鉴作用。

本书最为突出的理论贡献是基于翻译共性概念，尝试提出"人物形象显化翻译"概念。简言之，"人物形象显化翻译"指的是中华文化典籍英译中增义塑形的翻译现象和策略方法。具体来说，霍克斯在翻译《红楼梦》主人公形象时，创设"人物 + 's"的翻译形式，并在其后有意增添与人物外貌、品质、本性等特征有关的片言文字来显化该人物形象；或在"SAID + 人物"后进行情状方式文字的增益或转化，显化说话者真实的表情、态度、性格、品质等特征。

自杨、霍译本诞生以来，《红楼梦》英译研究领域不断扩大，但是在人物形象领域英译研究依然是一个相对薄弱的探究空间。本书以霍、杨译本为例，在前人零星研究的基础上对其中最为著名的主人公人物形象英译现象进行了基于语料库的定性定量分析考察，较之先前研究，研究对象覆盖面有一定程度扩大，改善了《红楼梦》人物形象英译研究的零散局面，在增强人物形象研究的系统性方面做出了有益尝试，从而在一定程度上拓展了《红楼梦》人物形象领域的英译研究。

目前国际上对于包含显化在内的翻译共性的实证研究更多地还停留在对少数（印欧语系）语言对之间"文学译本的比较"①，而我国的显化翻译研究无论是数量还是程度上都还处于起步阶段。本书将作为中国传统文化缩影的《红楼梦》置于全球化语境下，多视角、多维度地研究人物文化形象翻译活动，有望丰富我们对显化翻译人物形象规律的认识。

本书创建《红楼梦》两组汉英平行语料库，目的是增强语料选取客观性。从人物形象英译研究来说，分别创建两组语料库的方法也许在一定程度上优于仅仅参照一个《红楼梦》汉语版本的做法。但是，由于霍、杨译本参照底本的模糊性，平行语料库中汉语版本的择取本身也存在无法避免的局限性。另外，限于篇幅，在涵盖面和系统性上还有待进一步扩大，同时也为后续研究课题留下一定探讨空间，譬如：

（1）除了"人名"的后续词和人物说话的语气情态之外，"人物形象显化翻译"还出现在哪些内容的翻译中？有哪些体现方式？

（2）原著语言人物美学观和价值观背景与目的语文化背景在"人物形象显化翻译"中充当什么样角色？

此外，在《红楼梦》英文全译本出现之前存在相当数量的节译本。其中有些节译本对于原著人物形象特征非常重视，在译本中有一定程度保留（例如《红楼梦》王际真译本），这就为节译本人物形象显化翻译英译探究提供了一定的研究条件和研究必要性。这种研究着重解决如下一些问题：节译本中显化了哪些人物形象特征，如何显化，节译本中仅存的一些人物形象是否能够体现原著人物特色，等等。

人物形象显化翻译研究不仅局限于《红楼梦》，还可以扩展到《红楼梦》以外的古典白话小说，尤其是我国四大名著中的《西游记》《三国演义》和《水浒传》。研究内容可以包括横向和纵向两部分。横向来说，可以对比诸如四大名著人物形象英译异同点，并结合译者身份和目标读者

---

① Donna Williams, *Recurret Features of Translation Features in Canada: A Corpus-based Study*, Ottawa: School of Translation and Interpretation, University of Ottawa, 2005, p. 36.

等背景探讨其理据。纵向来说，可以按照年代特征，着重研究其中某一部古典白话小说人物形象英译在不同历史时期的嬗变，并探寻其中缘由。同时，在研究条件许可的情况下，还可以考虑结合多个语种，如日语、法语和德语等进行人物形象翻译对比。这些都是与"人物形象显化翻译"相关且具有相当探讨价值的后续研究课题。

经典文化外译已成为中国文化输出的重要战略之一。19世纪上半叶开始的我国古典白话小说西渐，由于译者、译入语读者以及翻译目的等因素的制约，我国古典白话小说英译主要以变译为主，焦点在于故事情节的传输和描述，[①] 对于原著鲜明的人物形象特色则关注甚少，而能使异域文化群体领悟到我国经典文化中深邃广博的世界观、人生哲学、人格美学形态和内涵的翻译更是凤毛麟角。

中国典籍的独特人物文化形象充分体现了中国文化既抽象又现实生动的生命形态和诗性化人文哲学形态。如何在翻译过程中弘扬民族文化人物形象，彰显中国传统文化意象，确保典籍文化在输出的同时不变形、不失真，使中国典籍中的人物以原有的文化艺术形象和文化内涵在世界范围内传播，已成为译者的重要使命。霍克斯在英译《红楼梦》人物形象的过程中采取显化翻译策略，充分和有效地传播了中国文化。

杨义在《中国古典小说史论》导言中郑重提出，在全球多元文化交流的碰撞中，需要"文化原我"意识的全面觉醒："在当今全球文化大交流、大对话中，我们首先面临的是拿什么样的具有原创性文化专利权的思想方式和话语表达，去平等而积极地参与这场各显智慧多样性之优势的交流和对话。……这就使我们在中外文化的沟通中，获得了一个对自身文化特质及其现代价值的自我和认定的历史契机。"[②]

正是在此时代背景下，本书借助语料库进行人物形象显化翻译策略研究具有鲜明时代感和现实意义，为21世纪我国典籍人物形象英译提供了一定参考和借鉴。

[①] 陈琳：《〈红楼梦〉"看官"英译与中国古典白话小说西渐》，《红楼梦学刊》2011年第1期。

[②] 杨义：《中国古典小说史论》，中国社会科学出版社2004年版，第1页。

附录一

林黛玉人物形象语料库数据

霍底本"黛玉的"后续共现语境词

N	Concordance
1	老祖宗了,该打,该打!"又忙拉着黛玉的手问道:"妹妹几岁了?
2	礼,以"嫂"呼之。这熙凤携着黛玉的手,上下细细打量一回,
3	忙接银子进来,一共两封,连宝钗、黛玉的都有了。尤氏问:"还
4	贾母的丫头鸳鸯、鹦鹉、琥珀、珍珠,黛玉的丫头紫鹃、雪雁、鹦哥,
5	了。纵然好,也算不得。"说着,看黛玉的,是一阕《唐多令》:
6	上,怀里兜的落花撒了一地。试想林黛玉的花颜月貌,将来亦到无
7	胎填白盖碗。那妙玉便把宝钗、黛玉的衣襟一拉,二人随他出
8	内,至仪门前方下了车。邢夫人挽着黛玉的手进入院中,黛玉度其
9	回家去坐着罢。"一面说,一面拉着黛玉的手,回潇湘馆来,果
10	不得见面,怎不伤心!"说着,携了黛玉的手又哭起来。众人都忙
11	提。且说宝玉送了黛玉回来,想着黛玉的孤苦,不免也替他伤感
12	,和李纨笑着去了。这里宝玉拉了黛玉的手,只是笑,又不说
13	了。三个人又闲话了一回,因提起黛玉的病来,宝钗劝了一回,
14	!"雪雁听了,只当是他又受了黛玉的委屈,只得回至屋里。黛
15	咱们只管乐咱们的。"那李妈也素知黛玉的为人,说道:"林姐儿,
16	这里淘气的可厌。"一面说,一面便将黛玉的匙箸用了一块洋巾包
17	,小名红玉,因"玉"字犯了宝玉、黛玉的名,便改唤他做"小
18	。宝玉才走上来,要扳他的身子,只见黛玉的奶娘并两个婆子却跟进
19	出去问时,原来是薛姨妈打发人来了接黛玉的。众人因问:"几更了
20	春道:"是。"贾政再往下看,是黛玉的,道:"朝罢谁携两袖烟?
21	彩的卸了残妆。紫鹃、雪雁素日知道黛玉的情性,无事闷坐,不是
22	闻之令人醉魂酥骨。宝玉一把便将黛玉的衣袖拉住,要瞧瞧笼着

霍底本"黛玉……道"共现语境词

N	Concordance
1	我一暴燥,就脱了。"黛玉叹道:"回来伤了风,又该讹着吵吃的
2	痴的不成?"抬头一看,见是宝玉,黛玉便啐道:"呸!我打
3	黛玉冷笑道:"他在别的上头心还有限,惟有这些人戴的东西
4	黛玉旁边冷笑道:"也不知是真丢,也不知是给人镶什么戴去
5	黛玉冷笑道:"问我呢,我也不知为什么。我原是给你们
6	黛玉冷笑道:"我就知道么,别人不挑剩下的也不给我呀。"
7	黛玉听了冷笑道:"我当是谁,原来是他。我那里敢挑他
8	黛玉冷笑道:"你既这么说,你就特叫一班戏,拣我爱的唱给
9	睡觉呢,等醒来再请罢。"刚说着,黛玉便翻身坐起来,笑道:
10	要着颜色,又要……"刚说到这里,黛玉也自己掌不住,笑道:
11	他房中嚷起来,大家侧耳听了一听,黛玉先笑道:"这是你妈
12	岂不好看?"宝玉尚未说话,黛玉便先笑道:"你看着人家赶蚊
13	炖了肉脯子来吃酒。"众人不解,黛玉笑道:"庄子说的'蕉叶
14	黛玉笑道:"你知道我这病,大夫不许多吃茶,这半钟尽够了,
15	是心里羡慕,才学这个玩罢了。"探春黛玉都笑道:"谁不是玩
16	黛玉笑道:"你要是个男人,出去打一个抱不平儿;你又充什
17	黛玉笑道:"既要学做诗,你就拜我为师。我虽不通,大略
18	黛玉笑向众人道:"我这一社开的又不巧了,偏忘了这两日是
19	黛玉笑道:"这时候谁带什么香呢?"宝玉笑道:"那
20	黛玉笑道:"我不要他。戴上那个,成了画儿上画的和戏上
21	黛玉笑道:"你瞧瞧!这么大了,离了姨妈,他就是个最老道
22	黛玉忙笑接道:"可是呢,都是他一句话。他是那一门子的老
23	黛玉忙笑道:"东西是小,难得你多情如此。"宝钗道:"这又
24	席过来,向黛玉笑道:"你瞧刘老老的样子。"黛玉笑道:"当日圣

霍底本"黛玉……说"共现语境词

N	Concordance
1	来瞧了一瞧,已是子初一刻十分了,黛玉便起身说:"我可掌不住了
2	事,都笑了。湘云笑指那自行船给黛玉看,又说:"快坐上那船
3	中,宝钗要约着黛玉往藕香榭去,黛玉因说还要洗澡,便各自散了

续表

N	Concordance
4	宝玉也乐为，答应着就要走。湘云、黛玉一起说着："外头冷得很，
5	有荣府打发轿子并拉行李车辆伺候。这黛玉尝听得母亲说，他外祖母
6	要是别人跟前断不能动这肝火，只是黛玉说了这话，倒又比往日别
7	玉的丫头雪雁走来给黛玉送小手炉儿，黛玉因含笑问他说："谁叫你
8	二姐姐也跟着我撒谎不成？"脸望着黛玉说，却拿眼睛瞟着宝钗。
9	笼，二人又去。果然宝钗说夜深了，黛玉说身上不好。他二人再三央
10	去，必从梦中惊醒，不是哭了，说黛玉已去，便是说有人来接。
11	倒吓了一跳。细看不是别人，却是黛玉，满面含笑，口内说道："好
12	冒雪而去。李纨命人好好跟着，黛玉忙拦说："不必，有了反
14	杯来，放在宝玉唇边。宝玉一气饮干，黛玉笑说："多谢。"宝玉替他

霍译本"Dai-yu's"后续共现语境词

N	Concordance
1	and Bao-chai wereall the same age as Aroma; Dai-yu's birthday was on the same day "but t
2	versation presently turned to the subject of Dai-yu's illness. "When you are out of sorts,
3	r an imitator of Dai-yu, for she had much of Dai-yu's ethereal grace in her looks; the sam
4	Discard Bao-chai's heavenly beauty, destroy Dai-yu's divine intelligence, utterly abolish
5	ugh he too was distres8ed at the prospect of Dai-yu's leaving him, could scarcely seek to
6	, and he too now embarked in the capacity of Dai-yu's escort. In due course they arrived i
7	e, and partly from the fear that to do so in Dai-yu's presence might seem pre¬sumptuous. T
8	sly and the old women got out. The places of Dai-yu's bearers were taken by four handsom
9	served each diner with tea on a little tray. Dai-yu's parents had brought their daughter u
10	ct of a jest We have shown how Bao-yu was in Dai-yu's room telling her the story of the ma
11	the Naiad's House. During the past few days Dai-yu's anxiety for Bao-yu had led to a rela
12	sheet of paper sticking out from underneath Dai-yu's inkstone. The temptation to reach ou
13	i, but there was also something about her of Dai-yu's delicate charm. As he was pondering
14	ve her off our hands for a bit!" She got out Dai-yu's spoon and chopsticks, wrapped them l
15	e. "Poor child! She has no one." She stroked Dai-yu's hair and tried to comfort her. "Don'
16	it helps me forget my troubles." It was Dai-yu's turn to sigh now. A tear rolled down
17	ood fretting about it now. I'll go and enjoy Dai-yu's company for a while; and after that,
18	l be able to do it for me." Bao-yu knew what Dai-yu's trouble was as well as night in gale,

续表

N	Concordance
19	contained, and because he was uncertain what Dai-yu's feelings would be about his reading
20	d by now wrought a considerable softening on Dai-yu's heart. A sym¬ pathetic tear stole dow
21	id Tan-chun The next riddle he looked at was Dai-yu's: At court levée my smoke is in your
22	but on recollection they seem rather stupid. Dai-yu's jokes on the other hand, though the
23	loin them. Now that the weather was warmer, Dai-yu's illness was very much better than it
24	e puzzled when he studied the expression on Dai-yu's face and found that, far from show in
25	watching. Bao-chai had observed the smirk on Dai-yu's face and knew very well that Bao-yu
26	urther grounds for tender admiration; and if Dai-yu's divine intelligence is detroyed
27	ps out and gestured towards the table behind Dai-yu's bed. His eyes followed her gesture t
28	hun's further self-justification in reply to Dai-yu's comment was cut short by the arrival
29	t is!" said Zhou Rui's wife, and moved on to Dai-yu's room. Dai-yu was not in her own room
30	the best he could, however, in response to Dai-yu's nudge: BAO-YU: The guests on "sca
31	od – humouredly. Bao-chai, long accustomed to Dai-yu's peculiar ways, also ignored them.
32	y it was ever like it was in the beginning." Dai-yu's curiosity got the better of her. She
33	to call in at Dai-yu's on the way back; but Dai-yu's maids told him that their mistress w
34	for Bao-chai," said Li Wan. "Not regal, like Dai-yu's, but aristocratic, at any rate. What
35	, must make our bridal bed." The words, like Dai-yu's languorous line, were from Western C
36	ful, Parrot, Amber and Pearl; after them Lin Dai-yu's maids, Nightingale, Snowgoose and D
37	was able to give her undivided attention to Dai-yu's welfare-to seeing that she had goo
38	owgoose had long since become habituated to Dai-yu's moody temperament; they were u
39	unting you and be reborn into another life." Dai-yu's resentment for the gate incident had
40	t was an unhappy one-mote unhappy even than Dai-yu's! At this point in his reflections he
41	ontribution for Bao-chai, and one, including Dai-yu's contribution, from Lady Xing. "Who d
42	distasteful to him. He decided to call in at Dai-yu's on the way back; but Dai-yu's maids
43	of her, slipped from his seat to whisper in Dai-yu's ear. "Look at the old grannie!" "It
44	or them and set off, one in the direction of Dai-yu's place and one in the direction of Ba
45	ther Jia chanced to notice that the gauze in Dai-yu's windows was faded, and drew Lady W
46	ly it doesn't count." They had a look at Dai-yu's poem then. It was a Tang-duo-ling. T

续表

N	Concordance
47	pleased her. The smiling answer she gave to Dai-yu's question was therefore not without a
48	turn her back again, but just at that moment Dai-yu's old wet-nurse came hurrying in with
49	ing, really. You mustn't be taken in by it." Dai-yu's sobbing had by this time ceased to b
50	can't help being upset!" And holding fast to Dai-yu's hand, she once more burst into tears
51	oes not concern us. Bao-yu, believing that Dai-yu's sunstroke was serious and that she m
52	ou died," he said, "I should become a monk." Dai-yu's face darkened immediately. "What an
53	mind at rest." As she said this, she seized Dai-yu's hand and began marching off with he
54	he other maids rushed off excitedly to fetch Dai-yu's kite. It was the kind called a "pret
55	ed after the new arrivals had inquired about Dai-yu's health, but of a general, unserious
56	(albeit a remote one) of Jia Lian and also Dai-yu's former teacher, it had been resolved
57	y conversation that followed it banished all Dai-yu's desire to sleep and enabled him to l
58	smans and their matching inscriptions, which Dai-yu's remark had reminded him of. He look
59	ped Dai-yu into bed. As she lay there alone, Dai-yu's thoughts turned to Bao-chai, at fir
60	we digress. During the last few days, since Dai-yu's return to her father had deprived hi
61	s was beauty of quite a different order from Dai-yu's. Fascinated by it, he continued to
62	recent rapprochement was too familiar with Dai-yu's jealous disposition not to feel appr
63	or Five Fair Women"; and without waiting for Dai-yu's approval, he picked up her writing-b
64	but of course be didn't say it. On her side Dai-yu's thoughts were somewhat as follows: "
65	, Bao-yu came back again. During his absence Dai-yu's sobs seemed to have redoubled in i
66	ade quilts, satin coverlets and the like for Dai-yu's bedding. Dai-yu had brought only two
67	hed this comfortable conclusion, he accepted Dai-yu's condition with a laugh. "Who wants t
68	ots a flower-patterned fringe BAO-CHAI heard Dai-yu's sarcasm-quite clearly, but her mind
69	hai could not suppress a giggle. She pinched Dai-yu's cheek playfully. "Really, Miss Frown
70	was sent to look after Dai-yu in her place. Dai-yu's other maid, Snowgoose, was kept busy
71	touched". But then there was Jia Lian's and Dai-yu's homecoming to look forward to. The a
72	eace with her and gradually, very gradually, Dai-yu's equanimity was restored. The Winter
73	ell refuse it. Spring was now at its height. Dai-yu's seasonal cough had returned, and in

霍译本 "said Dai-yu" 共现语境词

N	Concordance
1	it?" "Failure to answer means defeat," said Dai-yu. "In any case, if he were to answer no
2	concealing it. "Don't try to fool me!" said Dai-yu. "You would have done much better to l
3	e of Lin. "That's false, for a start," said Dai-yu. "I've never heard of a mountain of th
4	rather wounded. "Oh, Leave him alone!" said Dai-yu. "He will be all right presently." Gra
5	ld Cousin Xing be pawning her clothes?" said Dai-yu, puzzled. "And why, having pawned
6	Dai!" "Whatever you come here about," said Dai-yu, "You always seem to end up by nosi
7	ago." "Well I don't think it's a pity," said Dai-yu. Do, by all means, have a poetry club
8	ir and brilliant morn feed my despair," said Dai-yu. Bao-chai, recognizing the quotation,
9	"How thoroughly disagreeable you are!" said Dai-yu. "What do I care whether you go to s
10	den my experience." "Don't be a tease!" said Dai-yu, giving Bao-qin a tug. "You didn't lea
11	this evening and talk to me for a bit," said Dai-yu. Bao-chai promised to do so and depart
12	be original." "you've hit it exactly I." said Dai-yu. "As a matter of fact even the languag
13	on. "Don't spoil everyone's enjoyment," said Dai-yu. "Even if Uncle does call for you, you
14	rn out that sort of poem by the dozen," said Dai-yu. "You've used up all your inspiration,
15	one! Come in! Come in!" "What is this?" said Dai-yu, joining in the good humour. "A party?
16	ou're the only one with a good memory," said Dai-yu haughtily. "I suppose I'm allowed to r
17	if I ever did any such thing!" "Hush!" said Dai-yu. "Talking about death at this time of
18	e now I know she's a very good person," said Dai-yu. "Before I used to think she was two-
19	"Next thing you'll be catching a cold," said Dai-yu with a sigh, "and then Heaven knows wh
20	to me that I thought nothing of them," said Dai-yu. "Now, after all these years, they hav
21	ought in my gold-gestating day-lilies," said Dai-yu. "And as regards my second line, I sho
22	Aroma to come." "Never mind about him!" said Dai-yu. "First go and get me some water!"
23	e things." "I wasn't thinking of that," said Dai-yu. "Between cousins there is no need for
24	p over and break it." "Which is worse," said Dai-yu, "A broken lamp or a broken leg? You'r
25	s a large sable tippet. "Look, Monkey!" said Dai-yu, laughing at this furry apparition.
26	on a previous occasion. "What a girl!" said Dai-yu. "These are exactly the same as the on
27	ou look like a party of down-and-outs," said Dai-yu. "Oh dear, oh dear! Poor Snowy Rush
28	aid Bao-yu, laughing. "You started it," said Dai-yu. "I know what," said Bao-yu. "I've got
29	to share yours." "Don't be ridiculous!" said Dai-yu. "Look at all those pillows in the nex
30	e in mind of the allusion." "Allusion?" said Dai-yu. "You vilify someone else and then cal

续表

N	Concordance
31	a good idea to tip them in the water," said Dai-yu. "The water you see here is clean, but
32	detached". "I'm very glad to hear it," said Dai-yu. "We are all much too extravagant. Alt
33	say such things to me." "Only a maid?" said Dai-yu. "I always think of you as my sister-in
34	n't seem to make very much difference," said Dai-yu. "Grandmother has put me back on
35	ith a smile. "Do you call that a joke?" said Dai-yu. "It was a silly, idle remark, and ver
36	t them." "That sounds very perceptive," said Dai-yu. "What about giving an example or two
37	them with." "Don't be so stuffy, Chai!" said Dai-yu. "Talk about 'gluing the bridges of th
38	do with me." "She wasn't my maid," said Dai-yu. "It doesn't make sense. Besides,
39	he startled mallard across the water," said Dai-yu. "Two." A wild goose passes, lamentin
40	ithful. "No Reddie at the window seen," said Dai-yu, desperately dredging up a line this t
41	tired. I think I shall go in and rest," said Dai-yu. "Just wait until we've released ours,
42	I can't imagine why you should say so," said Dai-yu. "I am perfectly all right." "How can
43	ai. "There's no comparison between us," said Dai-yu. "You've got your mother and your br
44	a beginner, of course, it's very good," said Dai-yu. "But it isn't really right yet. It's
45	tion," said Bao-chai flatly. "But why?" said Dai-yu. Bao-chai smiled mischievously. "Tell
46	ght of what you have just been saying," said Dai-yu drily, "I'm not at all sure that I oug
47	ery good looking boy." "That's nothing," said Dai-yu. "What about that time last year when
48	wasting time." "That's all very well," said Dai-yu, "but I don't like your other line eit
49	orized it." "I want to, go to bed now," said Dai-yu. "Please go now. Come again tomorrow."
50	ink now." "What's the matter with you?" said Dai-yu. "Always fussing! What does it matter
51	re for you, Miss." "I thought as much," said Dai-yu sneeringly. "I get the leavings when e
52	s-making?" "Whoever told her to do it." said Dai-yu, it has nothing whatever to do with M
53	to be ironed again. "Leave it alone!" said Dai-yu, laying down her shears. "It will be a
54	or you, miss." "Oh, but it's charming!" said Dai-yu, taking it. "No wonder they're always
55	adies could do with a good talking-to," said Dai-yu, "Though it's not really for me to sa

续表

N	Concordance
56	ly a year wouldn't be at all too long," said Dai-yu. "If it took a whole year to build the
57	tart. It was Caltrop. "You silly girl!" said Dai-yu. "You gave me quite a shock, creeping
58	h like that couplet of Cloud Maiden's," said Dai-yu. "On frosty nights I'll dream you bac
59	and fetch his winter cape. "You see!" said Dai-yu. "When I come, he has to go!" "Who sai
60	gers prowled outside in his courtyard," said Dai-yu laughing. "How on earth would she ha
61	room together. "Bao-yu," said Dai-yu, addressing him in a heavily mock-serious manner
62	eel better." "I am sure you are right," said Dai-yu. "I have in fact come to the same conc
63	she's got to have Old Mother Locust," said Dai-yu. "Without her the painting would be in
64	hat is all this about?" "Don't ask me!" said Dai-yu coldly. "I don't know. I'm only a figu
65	er cup," said Aroma. "Oh, you know me," said Dai-yu smilingly. "I can't drink much tea bec
66	more civil?" "Of course you must go." said Dai-yu, before he had time to reply. "Surely
67	ay where you are. "If you were a man," said Dai-yu, laughing, "You could go around like a
68	"Do you study books yet, cousin?" "No," said Dai-yu. "I have only been taking lessons for
69	kotow and become my pupil if you like," said Dai-yu goodnaturedly. "I'm no expert myself,
70	to have got off to rather a bad start," said Dai-yu ruefully. "I'd forgotten about her bir
71	y clever of you to have thought of it," said Dai-yu, smiling, "Especially as mimosa does i
72	verses for us by himself. "Good ideal." said Dai-yu. "And I've got another idea. Several p
73	dead. It would be a relief." "Exactly!" said Dai-yu. "If I were to die, it would be a reli
74	inst, how else could I keep my end up?" said Dai-yu. "Because I put so much into that last
75	things to do." "Ah yes, you're busy," said Dai-yu, smiling. "I should have remembered. N
76	h to go there tomorrow." "How typical!" said Dai-yu. "I should try to grow out of these ch
77	ou must be very good indeed." "Oh her," said Dai-yu coldly. "I wondered whom you could
78	to be about?" "All right, let it pass," said Dai-yu. "We'll have another look at it tomorr
79	tching their bad luck?" "You're right," said Dai-yu. "We don't know whose bad luck it mig
80	I have finished my story. "Carry on," said Dai-yu. "Now in the Cave of Lin there lived a
81	was wearing. "Perfume? At this season?" said Dai-yu with a laugh. "I'm not wearing any."
82	snows." "I don't want one, thank you," said Dai-yu laughing. "If I were to wear one of th
83	et through that lot." "Drink the wine," said Dai-yu. I'll do the rest for you." Bao-yu dr

续表

N	Concordance
84	better. "I have always been like this," said Dai-yu. "I have been taking medicine ever sin
85	now?" "What an extraordinary question!" said Dai-yu. "I know nothing about it. How should
86	back again. Strange!" "Now praised be!" said Dai-yu. "I have a nice, kind cousin to stick
87	t for her. "No, let me pour it myself," said Dai-yu. "That is half the fun. You get on wit
88	nows whether or not he really lost it?" said Dai-yu scoffingly. "For all we know he may ha
89	oks she was studying. "The Four Books," said Dai-yu, and inquired in turn what books her
90	this way indefinitely." "It's no good," said Dai-yu. "This illness will never go away comp
91	animals dancing to the music of Shun," said Dai-yu. "Only in this case it's just one old
92	Perhaps you can tell me." "Certainly," said Dai-yu. "Discussion is what I was hoping for.
93	iously detached person your sister is!" said Dai-yu. "She has been actually invited to tak
94	" "I've been in the room all the time," said Dai-yu. "I just this moment went to have a lo
95	had at least one good cry in it!" "No," said Dai-yu as she wiped her eyes. "I feel very lo
96	h." "There's no need for you to swear," said Dai-yu. "I know very well that Cousin Dai has
97	end you some more." "That's very kind," said Dai-yu. "Won't you sit outside with the girls
98	an have it all." "Thank you very much," said Dai-yu. "I'll send someone round to fetch it.
99	ct them." "Where is the original text?" said Dai-yu. "I should need to have a careful look
100	ow!" "It would be more romantic still," said Dai-yu drily, "If instead of chanting poems w
101	d Bao-chai. "Let me have a look." "Oh," said Dai-yu, "As soon as I went outside he flew aw
102	ay. "Aiyo!" he said. "My head!" "Good!" said Dai-yu. "It serves you right!" Then Bao-yu le
103	aid Xi-feng, "But you were out." "Yes," said Dai-yu. "I'm sorry. I forgot to thank you."
104	It's not witchcraft, it's generalship," said Dai-yu. "Don't you remember what it says in
105	ai. "Try again," said Li Wan. "I know," said Dai-yu. "Isn't it ... though good, yet havin
106	"I'm much better at night than I was," said Dai-yu. "Last night I only coughed twice. But
107	t got a medicine-skillet on the stove," said Dai-yu. "I seem practically to live on medici
108	flowering tree. "Where are you going?" said Dai-yu. "To my mother's." She answered wit
109	me." "That shows you don't read much," said Dai-yu. "It's a perfectly good allusion. Ther
110	looking at some lives of famous women," said Dai-yu, "All of them women who are famou

续表

N	Concordance
111	meeting today?" "I don't see why not," said Dai-yu. She told the servants to prepare som
112	"You say you love me as much as Chai," said Dai-yu. "Let me be your god-daughter then
113	wouldn't be worthy of the gold kylin," said Dai-yu huffily, rising from her seat and walk
114	es quietly, as we were doing just now," said Dai-yu, "Instead of all this prancing about?"
115	up, for Cousin Bao's sake. "I won't!" said Dai-yu. "You're all in league against me. You
116	suppose because your brother is away," said Dai-yu, "Or perhaps their horoscopes are in
117	them." "Yun is at the bottom of this," said Dai-yu. "Mark my words!" Li Wan hurried off t
118	a reasonably good memory." "All right," said Dai-yu. "I'll start with something very prosy
119	n by your Chief Steward Lai Da's wife," said Dai-yu. "Two pots of narcissi and two of wint
120	of absence." "I can guess why that is," said Dai-yu. "It's because of what Grandmother sai
121	ould be a bit presumptuous." "But why?" said Dai-yu, smiling. "My window is your window.
122	s." "All right, you wait for him then," said Dai-yu. "I'm going on ahead. And off she wen
123	ryone's approval. "I'll tell you what," said Dai-yu. "Why not write the names of different
124	ught to be going back now in any case," said Dai-yu. "It's time I went to bed. We'll see
125	rison; you would like to have laughed," said Dai-yu. " to me your way of no: comparing and
126	ly." "Whatever it was you said to him," said Dai-yu, "You'd better go over there straight
127	is is all Frowner's doing." "Nonsense!" said Dai-yu. "The Sage tells us that we should be
128	t, notwithstanding. "Why don't you go?" said Dai-yu. "There's a tiger in this room. You mi
129	two should never be allowed together," said Dai-yu. "As soon as ever they get together t
130	"Now that really is a bogus allusion," said Dai-yu. "We'll look both our allusions up tom
131	don't know myself where it comes from," said Dai-yu. "I suppose it might have come from
132	"To use with the ginger and soy sauce," said Dai-yu. "Then she'll be able to cook the colo
133	lly, although you won't know this yet," said Dai-yu, "That 'smoke-thread climbs' line you
134	an by that?" "What do I mean by that?" said Dai-yu. "I mean that if I only come when he d
135	th me. 'there's nothing in it really," said Dai-yu. "There's really hardly anything to lea
136	have a look and satisfy our curiosity," said Dai-yu. "She's got such a great pile of stuff
137	n. "We could use a number for a rhyme," said Dai-yu. "Let's count the uprights in the rail
138	mess." "Human figures are no problem," said Dai-yu. "It's the insect-painting that's goin
139	mustn't go reading that sort of stuff!" said Dai-yu. "It's only because of your lack of ex

续表

N	Concordance
140	gged an amnesty for Xiang-yun. "Never!" said Dai-yu, endeavouring to tug one of his han
141	on whether I feel in the mood or not," said Dai-yu. Chatting together they went out of th
142	and what you mean about not worrying," said Dai-yu. Bao-yu sighed again and shook his
143	ide a minute if you want us to get up," said Dai-yu. Bao-yu went into the outer room. Dai-
144	can't abide the poems of Li Shang-yin," said Dai-yu, "But there is just one line of his th
145	Last night there was a very fine moon," said Dai-yu. "I've been thinking of writing a poem
146	roofs and courts below. "Well capped!" said Dai-yu. "But then in your next line you wande
147	ve managed to get round to us at last!" said Dai-yu. Or hunt for rhymes, propped
148	n when you get talking!" "Look at her!" said Dai-yu, mockingly. "What a great baby! She's
149	Lotus Pavilion. "So that's who it was!" said Dai-yu. "I wasn't expecting him to be there.
150	arted making fun of me." "Tell me now," said Dai-yu, taking Xi-chun's hand in her own, "Is
151	fterwards which of us had done better," said Dai-yu, "But unfortunately we haven't got any
152	ink every day." "Oh, I quite liked it," said Dai-yu. "Your palates must be more sensitive
153	tter let me do it myself." "Come here!" said Dai-yu standing on the edge of the kang. "I'l
154	of you?" "You don't understand, Aunt," said Dai-yu. "It doesn't matter here, with you; bu
155	to people's rooms when they're asleep?" said Dai-yu, smiling up at Bao-yu as she sat on t
156	raid mine aren't really all that good," said Dai-yu. "They are a bit too contrived." "Ther
157	" "Well, perhaps not quite everything," said Dai-yu wryly. "But she's certainly very obser
158	efinitely going to have a poetry club," said Dai-yu, "Then as members of the club we are a
159	ang are obviously enjoying themselves," said Dai-yu, smiling. The flute is a very happy to
160	ion. "I dare say she would be glad to," said Dai-yu drily. "The trouble is that if she sta
161	lled to him to come inside. "Sit down," said Dai-yu. Bao-yu noticed that she had been cry
162	"That capping line is not good," said Dai-yu. "It merely repeats what my line said
163	trict order. "Ah, that's a good line!" said Dai-yu. She thought a bit before capping it.
164	etty well protected against the rain," said Dai-yu, "But what about the bottom part? Stil
165	u say things like that any more?" "No," said Dai-yu, laughing weakly, "I promise." she pro
166	hinking about my head." "No, I forgot," said Dai-yu. "Losing your head is nothing, is it?

续表

N	Concordance
167	h of you fancies. "No, that won't do," said Dai-yu. "As you live in the House of Green De
168	ead of night' read 'on a stone bench'," said Dai-yu. The others laughed, remembering Xi
169	ou produce some good lines later then," said Dai-yu. "Otherwise you are going to look pre
170	dly mind your own business, would you?" said Dai-yu. Bao-yu glanced inside and saw t
171	!"If you're so anxious to please me," said Dai-yu coldly, "You ought to hire a troupe sp
172	hai. "We shall soon find out if we go," said Dai-yu. So off she went, and Bao-chai with he
173	coloured haze diaphene in our windows," said Dai-yu. "Instead of 'the young man in his cr
174	"You finished the couplet very well," said Dai-yu, "But that second line is a bit weak,
175	dinary breadth of her knowledge. "Sh!" said Dai-yu, looking round crossly in Bao-yu's dir
176	gether. "He's not eating lunch today," said Dai-yu. "Come on, let's go!" Whether he's ea
177	e past on account of that jade!" "Poh!" said Dai-yu scornfully. "You are trying to make Ou
178	re I came in?" "I didn't say anything," said Dai-yu. Bao-yu laughed and snapped his finger
179	e've got the lantern ready. "Lantern?" said Dai-yu. "In this weather?" "The rain makes no
180	d those words in a work of literature," said Dai-yu. "Jiang Yan uses them in his prose-poe
181	and I'll give you a hand." "What book?" said Dai-yu. "Oh... The Doctrine of the Mean and
182	g." "This girl's gone out of her mind," said Dai-yu. "Just these few days away and she's
183	ologize." "I forbid you to let him in," said Dai-yu. "There you go again!" said Nightingal
184	irst." "It's fun to see them fly away," said Dai-yu, "And yet it seems rather a pity." "Bu
185	ting harder all the time now to rhyme," said Dai-yu. Leaving a moonscape hush
186	ho seeks perfection must abandon joy," said Dai-yu. "If you ask me, I think we are very w
187	you a wonder if you do. "Who's that?" said Dai-yu. "If you can find any shortcomings in C
188	one in when you get talking!" "Look at her!" said Dai-yu, mockingly. "What a great baby!
189	Who knows whether or not he really lost it?" said Dai-yu scoffingly. "For all we know he

霍译本"Dai-yu said"共现语境词

N	Concordance
1	Lotus Pavilion to pay a call on Xi-chun, but Dai-yu said she was going to have a bath, and
2	s because he heard that we were going away." Dai-yu said nothing. After waiting in vain fo
3	o-chai and Xi-feng had gone Out of the room, Dai-yu said to Bao-yu. "You see? There are

霍译本"Dai-yu…saying"共现语境词

N	Concordance
1	ng to worry about as far as I'm concerned." Dai-yu, without saying a word, quietly reliev
2	o the recording of outward appearances. When Dai-yu, far from saying something nice

霍译本"Dai-yu murmured"共现语境词

N	Concordance
1	ls in the outer room. "Bless His Holy Name!" Dai-yu murmured fervently. Bao-chai la
2	dark shape crosses the cold, bright water. Dai-yu murmured admiringly, but stamp

霍译本"Dai-yu asked"共现语境词

N	Concordance
1	supper too and were once more in attendance, Dai-yu asked Bao-yu if he was ready to go. H
2	ing noise as the last of the string ran out. Dai-yu asked the others if any of them would
3	urning on the bed. "Can't you get to sleep?" Dai-yu asked Xiang-yun eventually. "I can nev
4	s tea made with last year's rain-water too?" Dai-yu asked her. Adamantina looked scornful.
5	many of them do you think you can remember?" Dai-yu asked her. "I've been through all the
6	armer for her. "Who told you to bring this?" Dai-yu asked her. "Very kind of them, I am su
7	rinted." "Is this really true?" Tan-chun and Dai-yu asked incredulously. "If anyone's

霍译本"Dai-yu told"共现语境词

N	Concordance
1	with me and study it before I go to bed?" Dai-yu told Nightingale to fetch down the volume o
2	and then asked Dai-yu about the rose-orris. Dai-yu told Nightingale to wrap some up for her. "
3	barely read and write." "What's your name?" Dai-yu told him. "What's your school-name?" "I ha

霍译本"Dai-yu continued"共现语境词

N	Concordance
1	fell and birds flew off distressed. As Dai-yu continued weeping there alone, the court
2	omplete." The others all laughed. Dai-yu continued, laughing so much herself that she

续表

N	Concordance
3	bit too? You can do this cutting later. " Dai-yu continued to take no notice. Falling to get
4	Snowgoose rubbed and pounded her back, Dai-yu continued to retch up wave upon
5	y obtuse!" "You say in your gatha," Dai-yu continued, "... It would be best Words un
6	or fantasy by losing her handkerchief As Dai-yu continued to crouch there, a prisoner

杨译本"said Daiyu"共现语境词

N	Concordance
1	"In that case you needn't see them either," said Daiyu. Pointing at Baoyu she added, "He's
2	"Failure to answer promptly means defeat," said Daiyu. "And even if he answered it now it
3	done much reading, cousin?" he asked. "No," said Daiyu. "I've only studied for a couple of
4	mall thing, but I appreciate your kindness," said Daiyu gratefully. "It's not worth mentioning.
5	ou mustn't forget us.' Speak for yourself," said Daiyu. "Don't drag me in." Turning to Baocha
6	ng, not simply smart." "So much the better," said Daiyu. "This household of ours is too extra
7	this?" he asked the maids. "Whoever it was," said Daiyu, "It's none of Master Bao's busines
8	tudied. "I've just finished the Four Books," said Daiyu. "But I'm very ignorant." Then she
9	y again," urged Li Wan. "I'll make a guess," said Daiyu. "Is it 'though good there is no docum
10	n past eleven. "I can't stay up any longer," said Daiyu getting up. "I have to take medicine to
11	now. A fine fix I'm in." "People are easy," said Daiyu. "But can you paint insects?" "You're
12	and draw lots to decide which one to play," said Daiyu. This met with general approval and
13	s of her erudition. "Do be quiet and watch," said Daiyu. "Before we've seen The Drunken M
14	k any minute." "I'd no idea it was so late," said Daiyu. The three girls went to Green Lattice
15	ill Xiren comes." "Pay no attention to him," said Daiyu. "First go and get me some water." Zij
16	Thank you very much, aunt, you're too kind," said Daiyu. "Really I shouldn't decline. But it
17	ou to bits!" "It's the fault of the bridle," said Daiyu soothingly. "If you adjust it, it'll

续表

N	Concordance
18	"If you're set on starting a poetry club," said Daiyu, "We must all be poets. And first, to be
19	art one if you like, but don't count me in," said Daiyu. "I'm not up to it." "If you're not, who
20	been. "With Cousin Baochai." "I thought so," said Daiyu tartly. "Thank goodness there was
21	ttle me." "The lisper loves to rattle away," said Daiyu with a laugh. "Fancy saying ai instead
22	hem, quick!" "This is all Xiangyun's doing," said Daiyu. "What did I tell you?" Li Wan hurried
23	red Baochai. "We'll know when we get there," said Daiyu. They went to Paddy-Sweet Cotta
24	yesterday to paint a picture of the Garden," said Daiyu. "She's glad of the excuse to ask for
25	rdly trick." "My kite's gone and I'm tired," said Daiyu, "I'm going back to rest." "Just

杨译本"Daiyu said"共现语境词

N	Concordance
1	in, cousin? Your eyes are red from weeping." Daiyu said nothing. Zijuan, standing to on
2	t to finish. Finding her in such a good mood Daiyu said, "I've never seen you before in s
3	"I'll get you some more." Xiren offered. But Daiyu said, "You know the doctor won't let m
4	ciousness still rankled with Baoyu, and when Daiyu, said this he thought. "I could forgiv
5	her. After the usual exchange of civilities, Daiyu said to Baochai. "Your brother must ha
6	d been having. "I've always been like this," Daiyu said with a smile. "I've been taking m
7	whole room laughing. Baochai was also there. Daiyu said nothing but took a seat by th

杨译本"Daiyu told"共现语境词

N	Concordance
1	e really. There's hardly anything to learn," Daiyu told her. "In regulated verse it's jus
2	How is it I didn't notice them yesterday?" Daiyu told him, "The wife of your chief stewa
3	m. "But there you go using pet names again." Daiyu told Xiangyun, "He has somethin
4	more by selecting Liu Er Pawns His Clothes. Daiyu, told to choose next, deferred to A
5	Wang. "Don't trouble to pour any more." Then Daiyu told a maid to fetch her favourite
6	with me, and I'll read a few poems tonight." Daiyu told Zijuan to fetch Wang Wei's Reg

杨译本"remarked Daiyu"共现语境词

N	Concordance
1	ere be if everything is perfect?" remarked Daiyu. "To my mind this is quite good enou
2	t so observant about other things," remarked Daiyu cuttingly. "But she's most observa
3	powder for her. "I'm better today," remarked Daiyu. "I mean to go for a stroll. Go back a
4	good when those two get together," remarked Daiyu. "Whenever that happens, ther
5	of them demanded. "Most ingenious," remarked Daiyu with a smile. "Doesn't grass turn
6	"Your third sister's rather smart," remarked Daiyu. "Although she's been put in charge

杨译本"Daiyu remarked"共现语境词

N	Concordance
1	l drink with her." As they filled their cups Daiyu remarked to Tanchun, "You're the apri
2	de to think. "Yes, this is where we come in," Daiyu remarked, then continued: "One 'ta
3	ich the hero sacrifices to his drowned wife, Daiyu remarked to Baochai: "What a fool t
4	"Their Ladyships are in high spirits today," Daiyu remarked. "This fluting is pleasant a

杨译本"urged Daiyu"共现语境词

N	Concordance
1	ngue." "Go ahead and cut it up," Baoyu urged Daiyu. "I shan't wear it anyway, so it do
2	t to see her mistress. Xiangling again urged Daiyu to lend her Du Fu's poems, and be
3	not be described in detail. The nurses urged Daiyu to sit on the kang, on the edge of
4	ht it, do let us profit by seeing it," urged Daiyu. "They've a whole pile of cases and bas
5	clear up the misunderstanding, quick!" urged Daiyu. "That may bring him back to his s

杨译本"Daiyu urged"共现语境词

N	Concordance
1	enjoy watching these three rivals compete. Daiyu urged Xiangyun to go on. "So even

杨译本"exclaimed Daiyu"共现语境词

N	Concordance
1	o try you. "The girl must be mad!" exclaimed Daiyu in amazement. "What am I to be trie
2	tanding heart. "The girl's crazy!" exclaimed Daiyu. "A few days away, and you've sudden
3	Look, here comes the Monkey King!" exclaimed Daiyu laughing. "She's got a cape too,

杨译本"Daiyu exclaimed"共现语境词

N	Concordance
1	e gruel. Before the rest could say anything, Daiyu exclaimed: "Buddha be praised!" Baoc
2	Baochai explained what had happened. Daiyu exclaimed in distress and sympathy,
3	icine." "How good you always are to others!" Daiyu exclaimed with a sigh. "I'm so touchy
4	A stork's shadow flit across the chilly pool Daiyu exclaimed in admiration again, stamping

杨译本"Daiyu continued"共现语境词

N	Concordance
1	these vulgar words. "To tell you the truth," Daiyu continued, "I'm the one who suggested
2	arm the wine will hardly glow. With a giggle Daiyu continued: "Snow covers the
3	upid fellow wants to dabble in metaphysics!" Daiyu continued, "The last two lines of yow
4	The sky above is sprinkled with bright stars Daiyu continued: "And everywhere sweet
5	iff and overloaded." "To my mind," continued Daiyu, "The best line of all is sunset in ch
6	de to think. "Yes, this is where we come in," Daiyu remarked, then continued: "One 'tap
7	The sky above is sprinkled with bright stars Daiyu continued: "And everywhere sweet
8	these vulgar words. "To tell you the truth," Daiyu continued, "I'm the one who suggested

杨译本"asked Daiyu"共现语境词

N	Concordance
1	hat's all this crying during the festival?" asked Daiyu mockingly. "Are you fighting for sticky
2	ations sent out that you're here in force?" asked Daiyu jokingly. "I sent you two canisters of
3	Verse. "How many poems have you memorized?" asked Daiyu. "I've read all those marked wit

续表

N	Concordance
4	show you." "Can she be pawning her things?" asked Daiyu. "If so, why send you this ticket?"
5	this made with last year's rain-water too?" asked Daiyu. Miaoyu smiled disdainfully. "Can you

杨译本"Daiyu observed"共现语境词

N	Concordance
1	to the different apartments to pay her respects. Daiyu observed laughingly, "I picked the wron
2	right. Very fair." "Mine didn't amount to much," Daiyu observed. "They're rather contrived."

杨译本"protested Daiyu"共现语境词

N	Concordance
1	is head. "Don't be such a spoil-sport," protested Daiyu. "If Uncle sends for you, cousin, we
2	"That really had no classical source," protested Daiyu. "Tomorrow we'll look it up for everyone
3	t once. "You shouldn't have done that," protested Daiyu with a smile. "I've some questions
4	rged. "Must you always be hurrying me?" protested Daiyu. "Whether I take it or not is none of y

杨译本"rejoined Daiyu"共现语境词

N	Concordance
1	nny Liu who started it." "That's right," rejoined Daiyu promptly. "It's all owing to her.
2	aid. "Last night there was a fine moon," rejoined Daiyu. "I was meaning to write a poem on it
3	gs to do." "I know what keeps you busy," rejoined Daiyu laughingly. "Now that it's turning

附录二

贾宝玉人物形象语料库数据

霍底本"宝玉的"共现语境词

N	Concordance
1	老的携了宝玉出去。贾政因问:"跟宝玉的是谁?"只听见外面答应了一声
2	出来了。又令人好生招呼着。忽想起跟宝玉的人来,遂问众人:"李奶子怎么
3	只道在里边去了,也不理论。至于跟宝玉的小厮们,那年纪大些的,知宝玉
4	径往宝钗院内来,刚至沁芳亭畔,只见宝玉的奶娘李嬷嬷从那边来。小红立住,
5	的人做的。"史湘云听了,便知是宝玉的鞋,因笑道:"既这么说,我
6	成?"这个四儿见王夫人说着他素日和宝玉的私话,不禁红了脸,低头垂泪。
7	瞒列位,就是荣国公的孙子,小名儿叫宝玉的。"那判官听了,先就唬的慌张
8	"叫了几十声。黛玉心里原是再不理宝玉的,这会子听见宝玉说"别叫人知
9	们从小儿在一处混了几年,这自然是宝玉的旧东西。况且这符儿合扇子,都
10	说毕饮干,将杯放下。袭人又来接宝玉的。宝玉因问:"这半日不见芳官
11	又值他今儿输了钱,迁怒于人,排揎宝玉的丫头。便连忙走过来拉了李嬷嬷,
12	忿,我明日偏抬举他。"袭人忙拉了宝玉的手道:"他一个糊涂人,你和他
13	:"回什么?"秋纹道:"问一问宝玉的月钱、我们的月钱,多早晚才领?
14	的造化。竟不劳你费心!既是老太太给宝玉的,我明儿回了老太太再撑你!"
15	因他多日未见宝玉,忙上来打千儿请宝玉的安,宝玉含笑伸手叫他起来。众人
16	叫门。紫鹃听了听,笑道:"这是宝玉的声音,想必是来赔不是来了。"黛
17	么就忘了你两三个月!"贾芸听见是宝玉的声音,连忙进入房内,抬头一看,
18	叫着了,答应几句话,就散了。至于宝玉的饮食起居,上一层有老奶奶老妈妈们
19	两根葱管一般的指甲齐根咬下,拉了宝玉的手,将指甲搁在他手里。又回手
20	是丫头们睡觉。转过十锦槅子,来至宝玉的房内,宝玉在床上睡着了,袭人
21	老祖宗放心,只管交给我就是了。"因向宝玉的奶娘丫鬟等道:"嬷嬷、姐姐们,
22	来请,便都往前头去了。袭人回明宝玉的事,贾母不乐,便命人接去。

续表

N	Concordance
23	你拣,你怎么不拣?"黛玉昨日所恼宝玉的心事,早又丢开,只顾今日的事了
24	碎,难保不有口角之事。即如此刻,宝玉的心内想的是:"别人不知我的心
25	已宽衣卧下之时,悄向黛玉笑道:"宝玉的心倒实,听见咱们去,就这么病
26	样男人物件,都是小孩子的东西,想是宝玉的旧物,没甚关系的。"凤姐听了
27	:"到底是蘅芜君!"说着,又看宝玉的道:秋容浅淡映重门,七节攒
28	能,果觉自形污秽不堪。警幻忙携住宝玉的手向众仙姬笑道:"你等不知原委
29	宝钗也放起个一连七个大雁来。独有宝玉的美人儿,再放不起来。宝玉说丫头
30	笑。原来黛玉闻得贾政回家,必问宝玉的功课,宝玉一向分心,到临期自然
31	二则又可以完了静虚的事,三则顺了宝玉的心。因此便向宝玉道:"我的事
32	纸片、笔、砚等物撒了一桌,又把宝玉的一碗茶也砸得碗碎茶流。那贾
33	的事,竟是姑娘太浮躁了些。别人不知宝玉的脾气,难道咱们也不知道?为那玉
34	上浇油,那板子越下去的又狠又快。按宝玉的两个小厮忙松手走开,宝玉早已动弹
35	是怎么样了,一步步行来。见宝钗进宝玉的园内去了,自己也随后走了来。
36	扶得起?好容易欠起半身,晴雯伸手把宝玉的袄儿往自己身上拉。宝玉连忙给他
37	屋里月钱之内。环哥的是姨娘领二两;宝玉的,老太太屋里袭人领二两;兰哥儿
38	的丫头分例上领。如今说因为袭人是宝玉的人,裁了这一两银子,断乎使不得
39	两个哭的悲痛,也心酸起来。又摸着宝玉的手冰凉,要劝宝玉不哭罢,一则
40	几十个。原来众客心中,早知贾政要试宝玉的才情,故此只将些俗套敷衍。宝玉
41	了黛玉一眼。黛玉自悔失言,原是打趣宝玉的,就忘了村了彩云了,自悔不及
42	我何曾说要去,不过拿来预备着。"宝玉的奶母李嬷嬷便说道:"天又下雪
43	秦钟正骑着马随他父亲的轿,忽见宝玉的小厮跑来请他去打尖。秦钟远看
44	。他姊弟三人依旧坐下。王夫人摸索着宝玉的脖项说道:"前儿的丸药都吃完
45	几个"是"。老嬷嬷跟至厅上,只见宝玉的奶兄李贵、王荣和张若锦、赵
46	。我闲着还要做老太太屋里的针线,所以宝玉的事竟不曾留心。太太既怪,从此后
47	咱们且去上香。"说着,便起身扶着宝玉的肩,带领众人齐往园中来。当
48	,有丫头来请吃饭,大家方散。从此宝玉的工课,也不敢象先竟摆在脖子
49	的人,忙上去请了贾母的安,拿了宝玉的手,诊了一回。那紫鹃少不得低
50	你倒不象跟二爷的人,这些话倒象是宝玉的人。"尤二姐才要又问,忽见
51	强笑道:"好好儿的,觉怎么样呢!"宝玉的意思即刻便要叫人烫黄酒,要山羊
52	故此人以为欢喜时,他反以为悲。那宝玉的性情只愿人常聚不散,花常开不

霍底本"宝玉……道"共现语境词

N	Concordance
1	月二十八日去的,前儿也就回来了。"宝玉道:"怪道前儿初三四儿我在沈
2	你大五六岁呢,就给你作儿子了?"宝玉笑道:"你今年十几岁?"贾芸道
3	怕死,你长命百岁的活着,好不好?"宝玉笑道:"要象只管这么闹,我还怕
4	身上好?我整整的三天没见你了。"宝玉笑道:"妹妹身上好?我前儿还在
5	本姓什么?"莺儿道:"姓黄。"宝玉笑道:"这个姓名倒对了,果然是
6	"你想什么吃?回来好给你送来。"宝玉笑道:"也倒不想什么吃。倒是那
7	呢!倘或再砸了盘子,更了不得了。"宝玉笑道:"你爱砸就砸。这些东西,
8	二人正在殿上玩耍,因见智能儿过来,宝玉笑道:"能儿来了。"秦钟说:
9	花儿倒清净了,没什么杂味来搅他。"宝玉笑道:"我屋里今儿也有个病人煎
10	谎话来问你,谁知你就傻闹起来!"宝玉笑道:"原来是你愁这个,所以你
11	就将路上所有之事,一概告诉了宝玉。宝玉笑道:"大喜,大喜!难得这个标致
12	。"又都看了湘云,称赏了一回。宝玉笑道:"这词上我倒平常,少不得
13	了,忙起来夺在手内,灯上烧了。宝玉笑道:"我已记熟了。"黛玉道
14	:"这是什么话?我倒不懂了。"宝玉笑道:"这有什么不懂的?只怕再
15	,别人不知怎么样,我先就哭死了。"宝玉笑道:"你死了,我做和尚去。
16	了事,也就赖不着这边的人了。"宝玉笑道:"原来姐姐也知道我们那边近日
17	了。"正说着,只见贾蓉进来请安。宝玉因道:"大哥哥今儿不在家么?"
18	了,就叫你"富贵闲人"也罢了。"宝玉笑道:"当不起,当不起!倒是
19	了热螃蟹,就在大圆桌上吃了一回。宝玉笑道:"今日持螯赏桂,亦不可无
20	,手里拿着一幅花笺,送与他看。宝玉因道:"可是我忘了,才要瞧瞧三
21	人都道:"好个'崇光泛彩'!"宝玉也道:"妙。"又说:"只是可惜
22	强,今儿得了彩头,该赏我们了。"宝玉笑道:"每人一吊。"众人道:"
23	的事,等完了再发放我们也未可知。"宝玉笑道:"你是头一个出了名的至
24	穿,比那双还加工夫,如何呢?"宝玉笑道:"你提起鞋来,我想起故事
25	说,烦他们莺儿来打上几根绦子。"宝玉笑道:"亏了你提起来。"说着,
26	走。麝月等忙胡乱掷了盒盖跟上来。宝玉笑道:"这两个女人倒和气,会说
27	忙笑道:"好哥哥,我可不敢了。"宝玉笑道:"饶你不难,只把袖子我闻
28	加,故又弄出这些堆砌货来搪塞。"宝玉笑道:"长歌也须得要些词藻点缀
29	只得忍耐下去了。芳官吹了几口,宝玉笑道:"你尝尝,好了没有?"芳
30	"我怎么……"却说不出下半句来。宝玉笑道:"我竟也不知道了。若知道
31	便击了一下,笑道:"一鼓绝。"宝玉笑道:"有了,你写罢。"众人

续表

N	Concordance
32	禁当的起？所以特给二爷来磕头。"宝玉笑道："我也禁当不起。"袭人
33	羞的。"说着，便两手握起脸来。宝玉笑道："何苦来，又打起我做什么
34	黛玉夺了手道："这可该去了。"宝玉笑道："要去不能。咱们斯斯文文的
35	又来了一个！没了你的坐处了。"宝玉笑道："好一幅'冬闺集艳图'
36	见麝月一人在外间屋里灯下抹骨牌。宝玉笑道："你怎么不和他们去？"麝
37	比不得那屋里炕凉，今儿可以不用。宝玉笑道："你们两个都在那上头睡了
38	，大清早起就咭咭呱呱的玩成一处。"宝玉笑道："你们那里人也不少，怎么不
39	芸指贾琏道："找二叔说句话。"宝玉笑道："你倒比我越发出挑了，
40	："又胡说了，你何曾见过？"宝玉笑道："虽没见过，却看着面善
41	些墨。"说着，丫头进来，伺候梳洗。宝玉笑道："昨日有扰，今日晚上我还
42	说没有方子，就是听也没有听见过。"宝玉笑道："这样还算不得什么！"王一
43	有一宗可嫌的，倒不如不说的好。"宝玉笑道："这就是了。我说大嫂子不
44	夫人道："放屁！什么药就这么贵！"宝玉笑道："当真的呢。我这个方子比
45	。贾母听如此说，方命人接下了。宝玉笑道："老太太，张爷爷既这么说，
46	猜是道士的，也有猜是偶戏人的。宝玉笑了半日道："都不是。我猜着
47	"秦钟笑道："这可是没有的话。"宝玉道："有没有也不管你，你只叫他
48	："谁这会子叫门？没人开去。"宝玉道："是我。"麝月道："是宝
49	宝二爷又来怄气了。到底是怎么样？"宝玉一面拭泪，笑道："谁敢怄妹妹了
50	擦的胭脂，和那个爱红的毛病儿了。"宝玉道："都改！都改！再有什么快
51	的可好些？"紫鹃道："好些了。"宝玉笑道："阿弥陀佛！宁可好了罢。"
52	、湘云都点头笑道："有些意思了。"宝玉又道：不求大士瓶中露，为乞嫦
53	说我引着二爷胡走，要打我呢。"宝玉道："有我呢！"茗烟听说，拉
54	趟，他心里正不自在呢。何苦来？"宝玉道："理他呢，过一会子就好了
55	"是个玉顶儿，还会衔旗串戏。"宝玉道："多少钱买的？"贾蔷道：
56	，你又说粗陋不妥。你且说你的。"宝玉道："用'泻玉'二字，则不若
57	大道。出去了冷清清，没有什么玩的。"宝玉听说，点头道："正要冷清清的地方。
58	"又怎么了？谁又有了不是了？"宝玉指道："砚台下是什么？一定又是
59	我记得是一样的，怎么少了一颗？"宝玉道："丢了一颗。"湘云道："必
60	。若看完了还不交卷，是必罚的。"宝玉道："稻香老农虽不善作，却善看
61	笑道："横竖是给你放晦气罢了。"宝玉道："再把大螃蟹拿来罢。"丫头
62	了一声，眼中泪直流下来，回身便走。宝玉忙上前拉住道："好妹妹，且略站

续表

N	Concordance
63	：“你林妹妹可在咱们家住长了。”宝玉道：“了不得，想来这几日他不知哭
64	不然就用'秦人旧舍'四字也罢。"宝玉道："越发背谬了。'秦人旧舍'
65	、十六这两日，是必往我那里去。"宝玉道："到底要起个社名才是。"
66	他底下的。"贾政道："姑存之。"宝玉又道：遂教美女习骑射。歌艳舞不
67	我天诛地灭？"黛玉一时解不过这话来。宝玉又："昨儿还为这个起了誓呢
68	还怕腻烦了呢。"说的大家都笑了。宝玉笑道："这场我又落第了。难道
69	人连忙拉住，坐了一坐，便去了。宝玉笑道："走乏了！"便歪在床上
70	一日送一两燕窝来呢？这就是了。宝玉笑道："这要天天吃惯了，吃上
71	要吃酒，给我两碗酒吃就是了。"宝玉笑道："你也爱吃酒？等着咱们
72	却还一气，只是宝玉又落了第了。宝玉笑道："我原不会联句，只好担待
73	惦记着黛玉，并不理论这事。此刻忽见宝玉笑道："宝姐姐，我瞧瞧你的那香
74	，只是疑他为什么忽然又瞒起我来？"宝玉笑道："等我从后门出去，到那窗
75	强笑道："好好的，我何曾哭来。"宝玉笑道："你瞧瞧，眼睛上的泪珠儿
76	字？"王夫人见贾政不喜欢了，便替宝玉掩饰道："是老太太起的。"贾政道
77	，如今若不省俭，必致后手不接。"宝玉笑道："凭他怎么后手不接，也不
78	了。好好的，我多早晚又伤心了？"宝玉笑道："妹妹脸上现有泪痕，如何还
79	一句，宝玉念一句佛。凤姐说完了，宝玉又道："太太打量怎么着？这不过也
80	柜子里头的香气熏染的，也未可知。"宝玉摇头道："未必。这香的气味奇怪，
81	笑道："依你说，都没王法了！"宝玉因道："怎么咱们家没人来牌子支
82	交杯盏儿还没吃，就上了头了！"宝玉笑道："你来，我也替你篦篦。
83	个好孙女儿，就忘了你这孙子了。"宝玉笑道："这倒不妨，原该多疼女
84	说，就完了。"说毕，即转身走了。宝玉笑道："可不是我疯了？往虎口里
85	定又是风流悲感，不同此等的了。"宝玉笑道："这个题目似不称近体，须
86	太来为混输了，他气的睡去了。"宝玉笑道："你们别和他一般见识，由他
87	养荣丸。"王夫人道："不是。"宝玉又道："八珍益母丸？左归，右
88	政道："太多了，底下只怕累赘呢。"宝玉又道：恒王得意数谁行？将军林四
89	有了书，你的字写的在那里呢？"宝玉笑道："我时常也有写了的好些，
90	打扮儿，伶伶俐俐的出去了不成？"宝玉笑道："可不就是这么出去了。"麝
91	把印也丢了，难道也就罢了不成？"宝玉笑道："倒是丢了印平常，若丢了
92	来问宝玉："那是一两的星儿？"宝玉笑道："你问的我有趣儿，你倒
93	回去罢，这个地方儿不是你来的。"宝玉笑道："你就家去才好呢，我还

续表

N	Concordance
94	”宝琴笑道：“你猜是谁做的？”宝玉笑道：“自然是潇湘子的稿子了。
95	麝月对镜，二人在镜内相视而笑。宝玉笑着道：“满屋里就只是他磨牙。
96	那里就丢了他？一时不见就这样找。”宝玉笑着道：“不是怕丢了他。因我
97	你只别嚷，你要念么着都使的。”宝玉笑道：“这会子也不用说，等一会儿
98	两大海。那冯紫英站着，一气而尽。宝玉道：“你到底把这个'不幸之幸'
99	手里打着，一面答话：“十五岁了。”宝玉道：“你本姓什么？”莺儿道：
100	劝劝。”正说着，晴雯进来了，因问宝玉道：“你回来了，你又要叫劝谁
101	的这样好了！明儿也替我写个匾。”宝玉笑道：“你又哄我了。”说着又
102	日吃茶的那只绿玉斗来斟与宝玉。宝玉笑道：“常言'世法平等'，他两
103	：“果然通快些。只是太阳还疼。”宝玉笑道：“越发尽用西洋药治一治，
104	道：“不干你事，快念书去罢。”宝玉笑道：“姐姐们且站一站，我有
105	说道：“我也乏了！明儿再撕罢。”宝玉笑道：“古人云'千金难买一笑'
106	葱绿。”莺儿道：“什么花样呢？”宝玉道：“也有几样花样？”莺儿道
107	偏惯会这么蝎蝎螫螫老婆子的样儿。”宝玉笑道：“倒不是怕唬坏了他。头
108	闹起来，把我的新裙子也遭塌了。”宝玉笑道：“你有夫妻蕙，我这里倒有
109	道了。”玉钏儿果真赌气尝了一尝。宝玉笑道：“这可好吃了！”玉钏儿
110	身上病好了，只是心里气还不大好。”宝玉笑道：“我知道了，有什么气呢。
111	个帖儿试一试，谁知一招皆到。”宝玉笑道：“可惜迟了，早该起个社
112	？”探春笑道：“只怕又是杜撰。”宝玉笑道：“除了《四书》，杜撰的也
113	道：“你也念起佛来，真是新闻。”宝玉笑道：“所谓'病急乱投医'了
114	李纨又问宝玉：“你可有了？”宝玉忙道：“我倒有了，才一看见这
115	儿明儿过去散散心，太太着实惦记着呢。"宝玉忙道："要走得了，必定过来请太
116	，世事不知，只有倒气的分儿。”宝玉忙道：“一夜叫的是谁？”小丫
117	你的旧号'绛洞花主'就是了。”宝玉笑道：“小时候干的营生，还提他
118	孩子头上往下滴水，把衣裳登时湿了。宝玉想道：“这是下雨了，他这个身
119	，又说：“是擦春癣的蔷薇硝。”宝玉笑道：“难为他想的到。”贾环
120	原是我自己一时忘情，好歹别多心。”宝玉笑道：“何必再提，这倒似有心了
121	虽腼腆，却脾气拐孤，不大随和儿。”宝玉笑道：“你去罢，我知道了。”
122	姨妈连忙把自己糟的取了来给他尝。宝玉笑道：“这个就酒才好！”薛姨妈
123	他是廊下住的五嫂子的儿子芸儿。”宝玉笑道：“是了，我怎么就忘。
124	，又说还要些玫瑰露给柳五儿吃去，宝玉忙道：“有着呢，我又不大吃，你

续表

N	Concordance
125	是你跟了去了。"莺儿抿嘴一笑。宝玉笑道："我常常和你花大姐姐说，
126	这鞋袜于是不怕的？也倒干净些呀。"宝玉笑道："我这一套是全的。一双
127	盆""魂""痕""昏"四块来。宝玉道："这'盆''门'两个字不
128	上，就有人来叫我们，说你来了。"宝玉忙道："你不认得字，所以不知道
129	但只我嫌他是不是的写给人看去。"宝玉忙道："我多早晚给人看来？昨日
130	烂了，那泥胎儿可就成了精咧。"宝玉忙道："不是成精，规矩这样人是
131	上的人商量着还要拿榔头砸他呢。"宝玉忙道："快别如此。要平了庙，
132	！一怕也不中用，跟我快走罢！"宝玉忙道："他并没烧纸，原是林姑娘
133	有人家求准了，所以叫你们过去呢。"宝玉忙道："何必如此忙？我身上也不
134	找着琏二奶奶，说完了正经话再来。"宝玉道："什么正经话，这般忙？"香菱
135	才太太打发人给我送了两碗菜来。"宝玉笑道："必定是今儿菜多，送给你们
136	衣裳，他们就不问你往那里去吗？"宝玉道："原是珍大爷请过去看戏换的
137	的也太不公些，小的也太可恶些。"宝玉道："怨不得芳官。自古说：'物
138	没了，便问他："往那里去了？"宝玉道："马上丢了。"袭人也不理论
139	我恍惚听见说，老爷叫你出去来着。"宝玉笑道："那想是别人听错了，并
140	阅人。暂且说不到后文，如今且说宝玉，只道王夫人不过来搜检搜检，无
141	，咱们在一处吧？"金钏儿不答。宝玉又道："等太太醒了，我就说。
142	好打点齐备了，省的明儿早起费手。"宝玉道："什么顺手就是什么罢了。一年
143	听不听呢？"黛玉听说，回头就走。宝玉在身后面叹道："既有今日，何必当
144	说道："别动这个，我另拿些来。"宝玉会意，忙笑道："且包上拿去。
145	冷些，怎么你倒脱了青肷披风呢？"宝玉笑道："何尝没穿？见你一恼，
146	'"黛玉听了，翻身爬起来，按着宝玉笑道："我把你这个烂了嘴的！
147	的门了，谁知道这会子又来了。"宝玉笑道："你们把极小的事情倒说大
148	花锄上挂着纱囊，手内拿着花帚。宝玉笑道："来的正好，你把这些花瓣儿
149	起的平平。"湘云又道："快着。"宝玉笑道：寻春问腊到蓬莱。黛玉、
150	，一面哧的一声又笑了，端过汤来。宝玉笑道："好姐姐你要生气，只管在
151	打受骂的。从此也可怜些才好！"宝玉笑道："好哥哥，你别委屈，我明
152	女，男不男'，成个什么理数。"宝玉听说，忙笑道："姐姐不知道，他
153	'、'水荇牵风翠带长'等语。"宝玉笑道："固然如此，但我知道姐姐断
154	个蔺相如，汉朝又有个司马相如呢？"宝玉笑道："这也罢了，偏又模样儿也
155	说，连你也可以不必看了。"又指着宝玉笑道："他早已抢了去了。"

续表

N	Concordance
156	怎么也不提我，看着你娘受委屈。"宝玉笑道："我偏着母亲说大爷大娘不
157	你也不必告诉，只回了太太就走。"宝玉笑道："就算我不好，你回了太太
158	。一宿无语。次日天明方醒，只见宝玉笑道："夜里失了盗也不知道，你
159	新写的三个字。一时黛玉来了，宝玉笑道："好妹妹，你别撒谎，你看
160	糊的向凤姐请安问好。凤姐喜的先推宝玉笑道："比下去了！"便探身一
161	什么？"莺儿道："松花配桃红。"宝玉笑道："这才娇艳。再要雅淡之中
162	，天天锁着，爷可以不用下来罢了。"宝玉笑道："虽锁着，也要下来的。
163	了半天，这会子还冻的手僵着呢。"宝玉笑道："我忘了，你手冷，我替
164	，这会子来了，自惊自怪的。"宝玉笑道："咱们明儿下一社又有了题
165	么匡人看见孔子，只当是阳货呢？"宝玉笑道："孔子阳货虽同貌，却不同
166	黛玉将头一扭道："我不稀罕。"宝玉笑道："你既不稀罕，我可就拿
167	踢在肋上。袭人"嗳哟"了一声。宝玉还骂道："下流东西们，我素日担待
168	的'玉'字改作'蜡'字就是了。"宝玉道："'绿蜡'可有出处？"宝
169	："妹妹尊名？"黛玉便说了名。宝玉又道："表字？"黛玉道："无
170	道："若不如此，也没个了局。"宝玉又道："我还有一句话要和你商量，
171	上了一年学，些须认得几个字。"宝玉又道："妹妹尊名？"黛玉便说
172	张若锦、赵亦华在两边，紧贴宝玉身后。宝玉在马上笑道："周哥，钱哥，咱们
173	上来披了一披，伸手进去就渥一渥。宝玉笑道："好冷手，我说你冻着。
174	，凤姐倚着门和平儿说话呢。一见了宝玉，笑道："你回来了么？我才盼咐
175	我怎么没见。一定是要唬我去了。"宝玉笑道："这不是他？在这里渥着呢
176	空黑黄。看到这里，众人不禁叫绝。宝玉道："骂得痛快！我的诗也该烧
177	又问他："想什么，只管告诉我。"宝玉笑道："我想起来，自然和姨娘要
178	凤姐听了笑道："嗳哟！你原来是宝玉屋里的，怪道呢。也罢了，等他问
179	了得，要这样，十年也打不完了。"宝玉笑道："好姑娘，你闲着也没事，
180	。"紫鹃听说，方打叠铺盖妆奁之类。宝玉笑道："我看见你文具儿里头有两三
181	儿呢！我这个身子本不配坐在这里。"宝玉笑道："你既知道不配，为什么躺着
182	梳梳呢。"湘云道："这可不能了。"宝玉笑道："好妹妹，你先时候儿怎么
183	"这样的诗，一时要一百首也有。"宝玉笑道："你这会子才力已尽，不
184	做工夫，怎么今儿个就发起汕来了？"宝玉红了脸，笑道："姐姐撒开手
185	了，我就说。"金钏儿睁开眼，将宝玉一推，笑道："你忙什么？'金簪
186	静王又将腕上一串念珠卸下来，递与宝玉道："今日初会，仓卒无敬贺之物

续表

N	Concordance
187	的妈妈都还没来呢，且略等等儿。"宝玉道："我们倒等着他们！有丫头们
188	粉线，黛玉弯着腰拿剪子裁什么呢。宝玉走进来，笑道："哦！这是做什么
189	告诉我，明日回去，拦住他们就是了。"宝玉道："我们老太太、太太都是善人，
190	，你说好不好？"黛玉笑着点头儿。宝玉笑道："我就是个'多愁多病的
191	越发好了，多早晚赏我们几张帖帖。"宝玉笑道："在那里看见了？"众人道
192	入作《簪菊》？让我作。"又指着宝玉笑道："才宣过：总不许带出闺阁
193	"宝琴笑道："现在是我做的呢。"宝玉笑道："我不信。这声调口气，迎
194	："表字？"黛玉道："无字。"宝玉笑道："我送妹妹一字：莫若'颦
195	，都称赞的了不得，还和我们寻呢！"宝玉笑道："不值什么，你们说给我的
196	道："叫我好找，你在那里来着？"宝玉笑道："我打四妹妹那里出来，迎头
197	了。"二人正说话，只见紫鹃进来，宝玉笑道："紫鹃，把你们的好茶沏
198	棋儿，又该你闹'么爱三'了。"宝玉笑道："你学惯了，明儿连你还
199	只怕还找出两个人来，也未可知。"宝玉笑道："这可再没有了。"鸳鸯
200	人、麝月都洗了，我叫他们来。"宝玉笑道："我才喝了好些酒，还得
201	了，我再如此说，还不算迟呢。"宝玉听了笑道："这是何苦，又咒他
202	极妙。"探春便道："何处出典？"宝玉道："《古今人物通考》上说：'
203	'字花样，所以他的名字叫做万儿。"宝玉听了笑道："想必他将来有些造化。
204	其娇而且闻其香？不然何体贴至此。宝玉笑道："闺阁习武，任其勇悍，怎
205	章，因笑道："你念出来我听听。"宝玉笑道："那《闹简》上有一句说
206	雨声。'偏你们又不留着残荷了。"宝玉道："果然好句，以后咱们别叫拔
207	跟着，"我们送了这些东西去再来。"宝玉道："好姐姐，等一等我再去。
208	告诉宝玉方才的诗题，又催宝玉快做。宝玉道："好姐姐好妹妹们，让我自己
209	给他们收拾房屋，另作一番安置罢。"宝玉道："好祖宗，我就在碧纱厨外
210	。"湘云笑道："袭人姐姐好？"宝玉道："好，多谢你想着。"湘云道
211	"袭人在那边早已听见，忙赶过来，向宝玉道："好好儿的，又怎么了？可是我
212	笑道："好长腿子，快上来罢。"宝玉道："我们偏了。"凤姐道："
213	起心来了。"紫鹃也便挨他坐着。宝玉笑道："方才对面说话，你还走开，
214	，天天逛不了，那里肯在家一日呢？"宝玉道："姐姐可大安了？"薛姨妈道
215	正值袭人端了两碗菜走进来，告诉宝玉道："今儿奇怪，刚才太太打发人给
216	撂在被外，上面明显着两个金镯子。宝玉见了叹道："睡觉还是不老实！回来
217	马轻裘，敝之无憾'，何况咱们？"宝玉笑道："论交道，不在'肥马轻

续表

N	Concordance
218	去呢?"黛玉道:"我回家去。"宝玉笑道:"我跟了去。"黛玉道:
219	儿也不安哪。二爷想我这话怎么样?"宝玉笑道:"你的意思我猜着了。你
220	要脱,你脱,我们还轮流安席呢。"宝玉笑道:"这一安席,就要到五更天
221	子啊?"黛玉道:"你管我呢!"宝玉笑道:"我自然不敢管你,只是你
222	,我就离了你。"说着往外就走。宝玉笑道:"你到那里我跟到那里。"
223	尽乐了,要不吃东西,断使不得。"宝玉道:"戏酒不吃,这随便的吃些
224	日必来,三五日头里就拿香熏了。"宝玉道:"可是呢,天天只听见说你的
225	了。"连叫了两三声,秦钟不睬。宝玉又叫道:"宝玉来了。"那秦钟早
226	牙,看着十个小厮们挪花盆呢。见宝玉来了,笑道:"你来的好,进来
227	"这就扯谎,自来也没听见这山。"宝玉道:"天下山水多着呢,你那里都知
228	凤姐儿走了。赵周两人也都出去了。宝玉道:"我不能出去,你们好歹别叫舅
229	排穗褂。贾母道:"下雪呢么?"宝玉道:"天阴着,还没下呢。"贾
230	一阵风来,把个老婆子撮了去了。"宝玉点头叹道:"这个不知是那里的账,
231	站在一处,只怕那一个还高些呢。"宝玉道:"我怎么没有见过他?你带他
232	下这一分,省的到了跟前扎煞手。"宝玉:"我也正为这个,要打发焙茗
233	,我先走了。"说着,便出去了。宝玉道:"我今儿还跟着太太吃罢。"
234	,就拿八人轿也抬不出我去了。"宝玉笑道:"你这里长远了,不怕没八
235	,进门就声顿脚。麝月忙问原故,宝玉道:"今儿老太太喜喜欢欢的给了这
236	。你偏要比他,你也太下流了。"宝玉笑道:"松柏不敢比。连孔夫子都
237	"就近地方谁家可去?这却难了。"宝玉笑道:"依我的主意,咱们竟找花
238	玉笑道:"这时候谁带什么香呢?"宝玉笑道:"那么着,这香是那里来的
239	口微微的疼,须得热热的吃口烧酒。"宝玉忙接道:"有烧酒。"便命将那
240	钟面如白蜡,合目呼吸,展转枕上。宝玉忙叫道:"鲸哥!宝玉来了。"
241	了。"麝月也笑了,又要去问人。宝玉道:"拣那大的给他一块就是了。
242	是了。"妙玉便命人拿来递给宝玉。宝玉接了,又道:"等我们出去了,我
243	"在这边外头吃的,还是那边吃的?"宝玉道:"同那些浑人吃什么!还是那边
244	"宝玉因要茶吃。袭人倒了茶来,宝玉乃叹道:"我近来叫惯了他,却
245	一件正经事去回,岂不叫太太犯疑?"宝玉道:"太太必不犯疑,我只明说是
246	议定了再去。如今且说拿什么画?"宝玉道:"家里有雪浪纸,又大,又
247	好。他也问的好,你也问的好。"宝玉道:"先时你只疑我,如今你也
248	老糊涂了,倒要让他一步儿的是。"宝玉道:"我知道了。"说毕走来。

续表

N	Concordance
249	梳洗去。再迟了，就赶不上了。"宝玉道："我过那里去？"袭人冷笑道
250	道："他祭的就是死了的药官儿。"宝玉道："他们两个也算朋友，也是应
251	道："我真不明白放心不放心的话。"宝玉点头叹道："好妹妹，你别哄我。
252	之声，一面数落着，哭的好不伤心。宝玉心下想道："这不知是那屋里的丫
253	原是个好的，我们那里比得上他？"宝玉道："太太屋里的彩霞，是个老实人
254	，别提小名儿了。"刚说着，只见宝玉来了，笑道："云妹妹来了！怎么
255	"是这个名儿。如今我也糊涂了。"宝玉道："太太倒不糊涂，都是叫'金
256	明儿来拜寿，打算送什么新鲜物儿？"宝玉道："我没有什么送。若论银钱
257	，这时候又跑了来？"小鹊连忙悄向宝玉道："我来告诉你个信儿，方才我
258	。老太太还叫我吃王大夫的药呢。"宝玉："太太不知道：林妹妹是内症
259	菊》、《画菊》、《忆菊》次之。"宝玉听说，喜的拍手道："极是！极公
260	一条，我做了一条，今儿才上身。"宝玉跌脚叹道："若你们家，一日遭塌
261	去，还怕他不倒？何用我说呢！"宝玉道："我叫他倒的是无情意的，
262	画，或轻巧玩意儿，替我带些来。"宝玉道："我这么逛去，城里城外大廊
263	么誓呢？谁管你什么金什么玉的！"宝玉道："我心里的事也难对你说，
264	在那潮地下做什么？"黛玉也不理。宝玉道："我可顾不得你了，管他好歹
265	那里知道这出戏，排场词藻都好呢。"宝玉道："我从来怕这些热闹戏。"宝
266	去，也到底打发个人来给个信儿！"宝玉道："我何尝不要送信儿，因冯世兄
267	，隐着一道曲栏，比别处幽静些。"宝玉听了，拍手笑道："合了我的主意
268	，走过来一瞧，果然一件没有，因向宝玉道："我给你的那个荷包也给他们
269	黛玉因问宝玉道："你走不走？"宝玉乜斜倦眼道："你要走我和你同
270	一个人在这里，怎么是个了手呢？"宝玉道："我不叫你去也难哪！"袭
271	，笑道："晴雯姑娘昨儿放走了。"宝玉道："我还没放一遭儿呢。"探
272	，明日顺了手，只管打起别人来。"宝玉道："我才也不是安心。"袭人道
273	这个又比那个亮，正是雨里点的。"宝玉道："我也有这么一个，怕他们失
274	风散毒。其效如神，贴过便知。"宝玉道："我不信一张膏药就治这些病
275	说着，只见宝钗约着他们往后头去。宝玉道："我就来。"等他二人去远
276	，变着法儿打发我去也不能够的。"宝玉道："我何曾经过这样吵闹？一定是
277	道："花大姐姐还不知搁在那里呢？"宝玉道："我常见着在那小螺甸柜里
278	问："二爷为何不看这样的好戏？"宝玉道："看了半日，怪烦的，出来逛
279	我没告诉，不知芳官可说了没有。"宝玉道："我却没告诉过他。也罢，等

续表

N	Concordance
280	再问，只说："二爷明说了罢。"宝玉道："我问你，可有贴女人的炉
281	子。"莺儿道："装什么的络子？"宝玉见问，便笑道："不管装什么的，
282	，闲着做什么？所以演习演习骑射。"宝玉道："磕了牙，那时候儿才不演
283	说了个丸药的名子，我也忘了。"宝玉道："我知道那些丸药，不过叫他吃
284	胭脂一般，用手摸一摸，也觉冰冷。宝玉道："快进被来渥渥罢。"一语
285	那边去老老实实的坐着，咱们说话儿。"宝玉道："我也歪着。"黛玉道："
286	什么人了呢？我为的是我的心！"宝玉道："我也为的是我的心。你难
287	笑道："我就是'秋爽居士'罢"宝玉道："''居士''主人'，到底不
288	水仙庵的，如何今儿又这样喜欢了？"宝玉道："我素日最恨俗人不知原故混
289	玉道："我正忘了，多谢想着。"宝玉道："我尝了不好，也不知别人说
290	上了，都当宝贝儿似的抢了去了。"宝玉笑道："原来要这个。这不值什么
291	来再舀水去。"说着，倒茶去了。宝玉笑道："好丫头！'若共你多情小
292	你娘的臊！又欠你老子捶你了。"宝玉笑道："我老子再不为这个捶我。
293	医，只是慢些儿，不能立刻见效的。"宝玉道："什么汤？怎样吃法？"王一
294	"说着，拿出绢子来，挽着一个搭。宝玉道："又是什么好物儿？你倒不如
295	宝玉，因说："咱们诗社可兴旺了。"宝玉笑道："正是呢。这是一高兴起诗
296	懒，连你穿带的东西都不经心了。"宝玉笑道："这真难为你想的到。只是
297	道："跟着你娘吃了什么好的了？"宝玉笑道："也没什么好的，我倒多吃
298	头乱闹呢！这是尺寸地方儿。"指着宝玉道："连我们的爷还守规矩呢，你
299	，笑道："偏了我们新鲜东西了。"宝玉笑道："姐姐家的东西，自然先偏
300	住那些气味？不想恰好你倒来了。"宝玉笑道："多谢姐姐惦记。我也因今日
301	。贾政笑道："且放着，再续。"宝玉道："使得，我便一气连下去了；
302	就有，没有就没有，起什么誓呢！"宝玉道："实在没有见你去，就是宝姐姐
303	"莺儿道："是'攒心梅花'。"宝玉道："就是那样好。"一面说，一面
304	明儿我再替你挑一个，可使得么？"宝玉道："我屋里的人也多的很，姐姐
305	他的心。你若要，我转送你如何？"宝玉道："我屋里却有两盆，只是不及
306	岁了？"茗烟道："不过十六七了。"宝玉道："连他的岁数也不问问，就作
307	的我又跑出来了，活象真的似的！"宝玉喜的笑道："他能变化人了，自然
308	："大家随和儿，你随和点儿不好？"宝玉道："什么'大家彼此'他们有'大
309	了这一个，你可吃的了这一海？"宝玉喜的忙道："吃的了。"妙玉笑
310	都说你有情有义儿的。"便一手拉了宝玉进里间来，笑："你要不叫我

续表

N	Concordance
311	气不理,他后来不知赔多少不是呢。"宝玉道:"林姑娘从来说过这些混账话吗
312	,二姐姐又病了,终是七上八下的。"宝玉道:"二姐姐又不大做诗,没有他
313	。袭人笑推宝玉:"你再作揖。"宝玉道:"已经完了,怎么又作揖?"
314	、荆芥等药,后面又有权实、麻黄。宝玉道:"该死该死,他拿着女孩儿们
315	袭人道:"这是头一件要改的。"宝玉道:"改了,再说你就拧嘴!还有
316	,仍旧回来,命将残席收拾了另摆。宝玉道:"也不用摆,咱们且做诗。把
317	旁时,另取出一件中衣与宝玉换上。宝玉含羞央告道:"好姐姐,千万别告诉
318	臊的!"说着"嗤"的一声笑了。宝玉道:"好妹妹,明儿另替我做个香
319	跑!"一语提醒,那丫头飞跑去了。宝玉又赶出去叫道:"你别怕,我不
320	殊不知这里说不出来的烦难,更利害!宝玉道:"谁都象三妹妹多心多事?我
321	又不说了?还要等人请教你不成?"宝玉听了回道:"此处并没有什么'兰
322	听了别人的闲言,在气头上罢了。"宝玉道:"我究竟不知晴雯犯了什么迷
323	了的,还不快作主意撕拔开了罢!"宝玉道:"撕拔什么?我必要回去的!
324	我今儿吃斋,你正经吃你的去罢。"宝玉道:"我也跟着吃斋。"说着,便
325	?"探春道:"这个封号极好。"宝玉道:"我呢?你们也替我想一个。
326	有知道的,一一告诉了名色并其用处。宝玉听了,因点头道:"怪道古人诗上
327	和姑娘项圈上的两句话是一对儿。"宝玉听了,忙笑道:"原来姐姐那项圈
328	'蟾宫折桂'了!我不能送你了。"宝玉道:"好妹妹,等我下学再吃晚饭
329	也不敢亲近二爷,权当我去了。"宝玉听了笑道:"你往那里去呢?"
330	好看,或是石青的,才压得住颜色。"宝玉道:"松花色配什么?"莺儿道:
331	咧,弄的这屋里药气,如何使得?"宝玉道:"药气比一切的花香还香呢。
332	贾政道:"薜藤萝那得有此异香?"宝玉道:"果然不是。这众草中也有
333	一两银子,才是我们这样门户的礼。"宝玉道:"王大夫来了,给他多少?"
334	,晴雯果觉有些鼻塞重,懒怠动弹。宝玉道:"快别声张.太太知道了,又
335	晴雯笑道:"外头有个鬼等着呢。"宝玉道:"外头自然有大月亮的。我们说
336	:"怡红公子是压尾,你服不服?"宝玉道:"我的那首原不好,这评的
337	,拿着我比戏子,给众人取笑儿!"宝玉道:"我并没有比你,也并没有笑
338	些真正上等洋烟。晴雯只顾看画儿,宝玉道:"闻些,走了气就不好了。
339	的说了!"一面说,一面拉起他来。宝玉道:"可往那里去呢?怪腻腻烦烦
340	这个还不好吃,也不知什么好吃呢!"宝玉道:"一点味儿也没有,你不信尝
341	又可以得朋友之乐,岂不是美事?"宝玉道:"放心,放心!咱们回来告诉你
342	,不过是扇子,香坠儿,汗巾子。"宝玉道:"汗巾子就好。"莺儿道:

续表

N	Concordance
343	一夜，今儿还没歇过来，浑身酸疼。"宝玉道："酸疼事小，睡出来的病大，
344	嬷嬷上来道："姨太太，酒倒罢了。"宝玉笑央道："好妈妈，我只喝一钟
345	这句更不通了。"说着，便要斟酒。宝玉道："押韵就好。"薛蟠道："
346	姐道："你回来，我还有一句话呢。"宝玉道："老太太叫我呢，有话等回来
347	"越往前越冷了，老太太未必高兴。"宝玉道："老太太又喜欢下雨下雪的，咱们
348	不足取。"贾政道："依你如何？"宝玉道："依我，题'红香绿玉'四
349	；你如今好好的咒他，就该了？"宝玉道："我不是妄口咒人，今年春天
350	听，这会子犯不上借着光儿问儿。"宝玉笑道："这有什么难的，明儿就叫
351	"湘云又把不限韵的缘故说了一番，宝玉道："这才是正理。我也最不喜
352	，赶着换了也就好了，过后再说。"宝玉道："你快休动，只站着方好，
353	麝月忙起来，单穿着红绸小棉袄儿。宝玉道："披了我的皮袄再去，仔细冷
354	"我从后院子里去罢，回来再来。"宝玉一把拉住道："这又奇了，好好
355	宝钗点，宝钗点了一出《山门》。宝玉道："你只好点这些戏。"宝钗道
356	自悔莽撞剪了香袋，低着头一言不发。宝玉道："你也不用铰，我知你是懒
357	不妥。"贾政冷笑道："怎么不妥？"宝玉道："这是第一处行幸之所，必须
358	你姐儿几个？"芸香道："四个。"宝玉道："你第几个？"蕙香道："
359	："好，好！如猜镜子，妙极！"宝玉笑回道："是。"贾政道："这
360	围，在铁网山叫兔鹘梢了一翅膀。"宝玉道："几时的话？"紫英道："三
361	钟暗拉宝玉道："此卿大有意趣。"宝玉推他道："再胡说，我就打了！
362	了莺儿过来问宝玉："打什么绦子？"宝玉笑向莺儿道："才只顾说话，就忘
363	俱被宝玉听了，只伏在石头上装睡。宝玉推他笑道："这石头上冷，咱们回
364	，反叫你们三个管起我来了。"宝玉道："既这样，咱们就往稻香村去
365	在地下站着，那个大两岁清秀些的，宝玉问他道："你不是叫什么'香'
366	："你别听他的话，没有什么字。"宝玉央及道："好姐姐，你怎么瞧我的
367	的人么？"那丫头笑应道："是。"宝玉："既是这屋里的，我怎么不认
368	歇歇儿，你且别处去闹会子再来。"宝玉推他道："我往那里去呢，见了
369	替我炮制。我有的是那些俗香罢了！"宝玉笑道："凡我说一句，你就拉上
370	洗了手，换了衣服，问他换不换，宝玉道："不换。"也就罢了。仆妇们
371	知说什么。必是说我病了不出去。"宝玉道："平儿不是那样人。况且他并
372	着却好，不知你们的脾胃是怎样的。"宝玉道："你说好，把我的都拿了吃

续表

N	Concordance
373	。"黛玉笑道："这个天点灯笼?"宝玉道："不相干,是羊角的,不怕雨。
374	"说着,便又委屈,禁不住泪流下来。宝玉忙劝道："好姐姐,别伤心,我替
375	意。贾政听了,便回头命宝玉拟来。宝玉道："尝听见古人说:'编新不如
376	"为你哥哥娶嫂子的话,所以要紧。"宝玉道："正是说的是那一家的好? 只
377	来。再看时,只见黛玉在床上伸懒腰。宝玉在窗外笑道："为什么'每日家情思
378	虽如此说,只是这气如何忍得住!"宝玉道："这有什么气的,你只养病就
379	人笑话这家子的人眼里没有长辈了。"宝玉笑道："妈妈说的是。我不过是一
380	人?"婆子道："还有两盆花儿。"宝玉道："你出去说,我知道了,难为
381	起来么了?"袭人道："什么东西?"宝玉道："前日得的麒麟。"袭人道:
382	那福气穿就罢了,这会子又着急。"宝玉笑道："这话倒说的是。"说着
383	,再没人来接他,你只管放心罢!"宝玉道："凭他是谁,除了林妹妹,都
384	老爷不气,不时时刻刻的要打你呢?"宝玉笑道："再不说了。那是我小时候
385	尸倒骨的,作了药也不灵啊。"宝玉因向黛玉道："你听见了没有? 难道
386	,你自然知道。我如今要别过了。"宝玉道："好客易会着,晚上同散,岂
387	还要拣实在好的丫头才往你们家来?"宝玉听了,忙笑道："你又多心了!
388	既不知他来历,如何又知是绝色?"宝玉道："他是珍大嫂子的继母带来的
389	忙回身拦住,笑道："往那里去?"宝玉道："回太太去!"袭人笑道:
390	子又叫我做,我成了你们奴才了。"宝玉忙笑道："前日的那个不知是你
391	是李逵骂了宋江,后来又赔不是。"宝玉便笑道："姐姐通今博古,色色都知道
392	己倒不好意思的了,脸上方有三分喜色。宝玉便笑央道："好姐姐,你把那汤
393	他在大奶奶屋里,叨登的大发了。"宝玉道："怕什么,你们就快请去。"
394	开门合户的闹,倘或遇见巡夜的问?"宝玉道："怕什么! 咱们三姑娘也吃酒
395	回头道："当初怎么样? 今日怎么样?"宝玉道："暧! 当初姑娘来了,那不是
396	地下老婆们说:"下了这半日了。"宝玉道："取了我的斗篷来。"黛玉
397	生气要打骂人容易,何苦摔那命根子!"宝玉满面泪痕哭道："家里姐姐妹妹都没
398	黛玉道:香料壁上椒。舒风仍故故,宝玉道:"清梦转聊聊。何处梅花笛?"宝钗
399	没闻见。趁今儿我可是要开斋了。"宝玉道："这个容易。"说着,只见
400	说,让你说去。"说着便往外走。宝玉向晴雯道："你也不用生气,我也
401	"这怎么好呢? 明儿不穿也罢了。"宝玉道："明儿是正日子,老太太、太太
402	买卖人,都称他家是'桂花夏家'。"宝玉忙笑道："如何又称为'桂花夏家
403	头的簪子在地下抠土,一面悄悄的流泪。宝玉心中想道："难道这也是个痴丫头
404	翠,上面已结了豆子大小的许多小杏。宝玉因想道："能病了几天,竟把杏

续表

N	Concordance
405	云道:"如今我忘了,不会梳了。"宝玉道:"横竖我不出门,不过打几根
406	就写他做的诗。"众人都称道奇异。宝玉忙笑道:"好妹妹,你拿出来我们
407	急动,丧声歪气的,也是有的。"宝玉道:"想必是这个原故。等我回去问
408	要紧,我就做了主,打发他去了。"宝玉道:"很是。我已经知道了,不必
409	了四更一个更次,就再不能睡了。"宝玉又笑道:"正是有句要紧的话,这
410	呸!原来也是个'银样镴枪头'。"宝玉听了,笑道:"你说说,你这个呢
411	个是好的了,女人个个是坏的了?"宝玉发狠道:"不错,不错!"正说着
412	管房请的,这马钱是要给他的。"宝玉道:"给他多少?"婆子道:"
413	了,总没提起,我正想着问你。"宝玉道:"也没什么要紧,不过我想着宝
414	的就是贼,又没赃证,怎么说他?"宝玉道:"也罢。这件事,我也应起来
415	也就罢了,但问他:"疼的怎样?"宝玉道:"也不很疼,养一两日就好
416	谁敢管我不成!这也是他瞎气。"宝玉听了,点头笑道:"你不知道,他
417	,两个香袋儿,两个锭子药。"宝玉听了,笑道:"这是怎么个原故,
418	莺儿道:"葱绿柳黄可倒还雅致。"宝玉道:"也罢了。也打一条桃红,再
419	接茶吃了。因见麝月只穿着短袄,宝玉道:"夜静了冷,到底穿一件大
420	他生的也还干净,嘴儿也倒乖觉。"宝玉听了,忙道:"姐姐们这里,也竟
421	心较比干多一窍,病如西子胜三分。宝玉看罢,笑道:"这个妹妹我曾见过
422	不和他们去?"麝月道"没有钱。"宝玉道:"床下堆着钱,还不够你输
423	没妨碍的!"说着,眼圈儿就红了。宝玉道:"罢罢罢,不用提起这个话了。
424	搁在山门外头墙根下,别进门来。"宝玉道:"这是自然的。"说着,便
425	我们的笔墨,也不该传到外头去。"宝玉道:"这怕什么?古来闺阁中笔墨
426	了,要是这样闹,不如死了干净!"宝玉道:"我说自家死了干净,别错听
427	些的。心里只管酸痛,眼泪却不多。"宝玉道:"这是你哭惯了,心里疑惑,
428	:"姑娘们睡罢,明儿再说笑罢。"宝玉方悄悄的笑道:"咱们别说话了,看
429	有些警动他的好处,他才要会你。"宝玉道:"罢,罢,我也不过俗中又
430	去?"紫鹃道:"妹妹回苏州去。"宝玉笑道:"你又说白话。苏州虽是原
431	如何至四娘,必另有妙转奇句。"宝玉又念道:"纷纷将士只保身,青州眼见
432	得高低了。且通句转的也不板。"宝玉又念道:王率天兵思剿灭,一战再
433	了,撂下脸来说道:"你说什么?"宝玉笑道:"我何尝说什么?"黛玉便
434	家里未必找的出这么一个俗器来呢!"宝玉笑道:"俗语说:'随乡入乡'
435	我一头碰死了,也不出这门儿。"宝玉道:"这又奇了。你又不去,你
436	且问你,你们多早晚才念夜书呢?"宝玉道:"巴不得今日就念才好。只是他

续表

N	Concordance
437	："不好。倘或他们听见了倒不好。"宝玉道："这怕什么？等他孝满了，
438	！倒也有些意思。"便催宝玉快说。宝玉笑道："谁说过这个，也等想一
439	定了琴姑娘呢，不然，那么疼他？"宝玉笑道："人人只说我傻，你比我
440	是可惜了！"众人问："如何可惜？"宝玉道："此处蕉棠两植，其意暗蓄'
441	的？怪道穿上不象那刺猬似的。"宝玉道："这三样都是北静王送的。
442	这园子，把人的牙还笑掉呢。"宝玉道："这也算自暴自弃了。前儿我
443	忽有人回："环爷、兰哥儿问候。"宝玉道："就说难为他们，我才睡了，
444	："是不是？我来了他就该走了！"宝玉道："我何曾说要去，不过拿来
445	象那起挑脚汉了。"说毕，又笑。宝玉忙笑道："妈妈说的是。我每日都
446	字就是了。"众人道："怎么解？"宝玉道："他说'宝'，底下自然是'
447	这一个答道："打发宋妈瞧去了。"宝玉道："回来说什么？"小丫头：
448	，刀搁在脖子上我也不出去了。"宝玉忙笑道："你说那几件？我都依
449	第三日一早出去雇了两个人收拾好了。"宝玉说："怪道呢。上月我们大观园的池
450	入者。贾政因问："此闸何名？"宝玉道："此乃沁芳源之正流，即名'
451	笑问道："你几时又有个麒麟了？"宝玉道："前日好容易得的呢！不知多早
452	赌气花几两银子买进他们来就是了。"宝玉笑道："你说的话怎么叫人答言呢
453	看了，只管出神，心内还默默记诵。宝玉笑道："妹妹，你说好不好？"黛
454	："不值一坛，再唱好的来。"宝玉笑道："听我说罢，这么滥饮，
455	想病好，求其不添，也就罢了。"宝玉道："姐姐虽如此说，姐姐还要保重
456	，你如今大了，越发心直嘴快了。"宝玉笑道："我说你们这几个人难说话，
457	兆头的。"袭人忙问："何兆？"宝玉道："这阶下好好的一株海棠花，
458	赶上，在后面忙问："往那里去？"宝玉道："这条路是往那里去的？"
459	不用你操心。但只五儿的事怎么样？"宝玉道："你和柳家的说去，明儿真叫
460	个什么老爷……"说着，又想名姓。宝玉道："不拘什么名姓，也不必想了
461	你的头，教你必定说这些字样呢？"宝玉："如此说，则匾上莫若'蘅芷
462	也图不得，早睡了，晴雯还只管叫。宝玉道："不用叫了，咱们且胡乱歇一
463	！到底说句话儿，也象件事啊。"宝玉道："没有什么可说的么。"晴雯
464	又找去呢，多少你拿了去就完了！"宝玉道："你快叫焙茗再请个大夫来
465	亏了绊住，不然，早就飞了来了。"宝玉道："只许和你玩，替你解闷儿
466	床，袭人不得不问："今日怎么睡？"宝玉道："不管怎么睡罢了。"原来这一
467	姐姐，我再不敢了！"众人都笑起来。宝玉忙劝道："饶他罢。原该叫他们
468	省中十二冠首女子之册，故为正册。"宝玉道："常听人说金陵极大，怎么只十

续表

N	Concordance
469	他又牵肠挂肚的，没的叫他不受用。"宝玉道："不妨事，我回老太太，打发人
470	是哄你玩罢咧，你就认起真来。"宝玉道："你说的有情有理，如何是玩
471	说你是丫头，我只拿你当嫂子待。"宝玉道："你何苦来替他招骂呢，饶
472	怎么样的？"又要回贾母去请大夫。宝玉道："不用忙，不相干。这是急火攻
473	来，想起自己没有姊妹，不免又哭了。宝玉忙劝道："这又自寻烦恼了。你瞧瞧
474	熏香。好好儿的衣裳，为什么熏他？"宝玉道："那么着这是什么香呢"宝钗
475	，只单叫莺儿，如今就叫开了。"宝玉道："宝姐姐也就算疼你了。明儿
476	。吃毕，春燕便将剩的要交回。宝玉道："你吃了罢，若不够，再要
477	？若再多说两句，岂不蛇足了？"宝玉道："如此，底下一句兜转煞住，
478	儿的一件也做不着，那里认得呢？"宝玉道："你为什么不做眼面前儿的呢
479	'矣。"因命："再题一联来。"宝玉便念道：宝鼎茶闲烟尚绿，幽窗
480	些过来，又添了一个做诗的人了。"宝玉冷笑道："虽如此说，但只我倒替
481	这个名儿，明儿就叫人买些来吃。"宝玉道："这些药都是不中用的。太太
482	。凤儿嘴乖，怎么怨得人疼他。"宝玉笑道："要这么说，不大说话的就不
483	道，若回太太，我这人岂不完了？"宝玉道："你也不许再回，我便不说
484	："这又是一段了。底下怎么样？"宝玉道："明年流寇走山东，强吞虎豹势
485	你第几个？"蕙香道："第四。"宝玉道："明日就叫'四儿'，不必什么
486	跟来。其余老嬷嬷众丫鬟俱沿河随行。宝玉道："这些破荷叶可恨，怎么还不叫
487	又还了席，也请老太太赏菊何如？"宝玉笑道："老太太说了，还要摆酒还
488	红灯里'，用字用句皆入神化了。"宝玉道："叱咤时闻口舌香，霜矛雪剑娇
489	各色上用纱一百匹，金项圈四个。"宝玉道："这算什么？又不是帐，又
490	时候，叫袭人伏侍你吃了再睡。"宝玉道："从太太吩咐了，袭人天天临
491	这虽不很象，要补上也不很显。"宝玉道："这就很好，那里又找俄罗斯国
492	春笑道："你不敢，谁还敢呢？"宝玉道："这是一件正经大事，大家鼓舞
493	缸里呢。叫他们打发你吃不好吗？"宝玉笑道："既这么着，你不洗，就洗
494	击了，若鼓绝不成，又要罚的。"宝玉笑道："我已有了。"黛玉提起
495	把扇子搬出来，让他尽力撕不好吗？"宝玉笑道："你就搬去。"麝月道：
496	说道："这几天，老爷没叫你吗？"宝玉笑道："没有叫。"探春道：
497	"你又要死了！又这么动手动脚的。"宝玉笑道："说话忘了情，不觉的动了
498	"莺儿道："汗巾子是什么颜色？"宝玉道："大红的。"莺儿道："大红
499	弄鬼。趁早儿给我瞧瞧，好多着呢！"宝玉道："妹妹，要论你我是不怕的，
500	赶芳官，将杯内的子儿撒了一地。宝玉笑道："如此长天，我不在家里，

续表

N	Concordance
501	众人听了，都笑道："果然明白。"宝玉笑道："还是这么会说话，不让人
502	就说太太身上不大好，不得亲身来。"宝玉忙站起来答应道："是。"因问宝
503	么我去了，你不叫丫头开门呢！"宝玉诧异道："这话从那里说起？我要
504	菊》勾了，底下又赘一个"葡"字。宝玉忙道："好姐姐，第二个我已有了
505	湘云洗了脸，翠缕便拿残水要泼，宝玉道："站着，我就势儿洗了就完了
506	独你来了，我是不能给你吃的。"宝玉笑道："我深知道，我也不领你
507	长了个好胎子，真真是个傻东西。"宝玉笑道："人事难定，谁死谁活？
508	发不用去了。咱们两个说话儿不好？"宝玉道："咱们两个做什么呢？怪没意思
509	暗号，被那人知道了？你还不觉。"宝玉道："怎么人人的不是，太太都知道
510	，不觉昏昏睡去，竟到一座花园之内。宝玉诧异道："除了我们大观园，竟又有
511	歪着。"黛玉道："你就歪着。"宝玉道："没有枕头。咱们在一个枕头上
512	何苦来！这是我才多嘴的不是了。"宝玉向黛玉道："你只管铰！我横竖不
513	日你要哄我，也说我父亲就完了。"宝玉道："嗳哟，越发的该死了。"又
514	头疼脑热的！"说着，便真要起来。宝玉忙按他，笑道："别生气，这原
515	是好开交的。"说着笑着进去了。宝玉笑道："明儿你闲了，只管来找我
516	绢子？他又要恼了，说你打趣他。"宝玉笑道："你放心，他自然知道。"
517	不会喂人东西，等他们来了再喝。"宝玉笑道："我不是要你喂我，我因
518	不出来，又该罚了。"于是拿琵琶听宝玉唱道：滴不尽相思血泪抛红豆，开不
519	说道："前儿的丸药都吃完了没有？"宝玉答应道："还有一丸。"王夫人道
520	。黛玉不觉又红了脸，挣着要走。宝玉道："嗳哟！好头疼！"黛玉道
521	颤，明儿写不的字、拉不的弓。"宝玉道："没有吃冷酒。"凤姐儿笑道
522	不出去，你打发人前头说一声去。"宝玉道："上回连大老爷的生日我也没
523	"连环"、"梅花"、"柳叶"。宝玉道："前儿你替三姑娘打的那花样
524	。"黛玉方慢慢的起来。含笑让坐。宝玉道："妹妹这两天可大好些了？气
525	，在那里羞的脸红耳赤，低首无言。宝玉跺脚道："还不快跑！"一语提醒
526	字从'依依'两个字上化出来的。"宝玉大笑道："你已得了。不用再讲，
527	嫌他。象我们这粗粗笨笨的倒好。"宝玉道："美人似的，心里就不安静么？
528	玉正自日夜不安，此时见他又要回避，宝玉便上来笑道："好姐姐你瞧瞧，我
529	倒蹩，凤眼圆睁，即时就叫坠儿。宝玉忙劝道："这一喊出来，岂不辜负
530	二爷城外逛去，一会儿再回这里来。"宝玉道："不好，看仔细花子拐了去。
531	打急了，你好逃到南京找那个去。"宝玉道："那里的谎话，你也信了？偏
532	贾母那里请安去，只见黛玉顶头来了，宝玉赶上去笑道："我的东西叫你拣，

续表

N	Concordance
533	给你呢。"湘云道:"什么好东西?"宝玉道:"你信他!几日不见,越发高
534	能迎宾接客,老爷才叫你出去呢。"宝玉道:"那里是老爷?都是他自己要
535	,天之自成,不是人力之所为的。"宝玉道:"却又来!此处置一田庄,分
536	不说他们乐得不动,白冻坏了你。"宝玉道:"你放心,我自己都会调停的
537	"既这么着,我就叫人带他去了。"宝玉道:"只管带去罢。"说着要走
538	腰洗了两把。紫鹃递过香肥皂去,宝玉道:"不用了,这盆里就不少了。
539	,拆我这庙何如?只说出病源来。"宝玉道:"你猜。若猜得着,便贴得
540	差不多的人,就早作起威福来了。"宝玉道:"你不知道呢,他病着时,
541	秦钟连忙起来抱怨道:"这算什么?"宝玉道:"你倒不依?咱们嚷出来。
542	忽然那边来了几个女孩儿,都是丫鬟,宝玉又诧异道:"除了鸳鸯、袭人、平
543	叔在家里呢,我只当出门去了呢。"宝玉道:"你又淘气。好好儿的,射
544	有人来接,老太太也必叫他去。"宝玉道:"便老太太放去,我也不依。
545	听不听在你,也不值的这么着呀。"宝玉道:"你那里知道我心里的急呢?
546	才进来了,想是有事,又出去了。"宝玉跐跄着回头道:"他比老太太还受用
547	:"你请我请儿,包管就快了。"宝玉道:"你也不中用,他们该做到那
548	里,又不是客,等我自己倒罢了。"宝玉道:"你只管坐着罢。丫头们跟前
549	一面想,一面顺步早到了一所院内。宝玉诧异道:"除了怡红院,也竟还有这
550	起你来,可以细细问了底子才好。"宝玉道:"你原是个精细人,如何既许
551	了'姐姐',就把'妹妹'忘了。"宝玉道:"那是你多心,我再不是这么样
552	些人,也因出于不得已他方死啊。"宝玉道:"那武将要是疏谋少略的,
553	,该放我回去瞧瞧我们那一个去了。"宝玉道:"正是这话。我昨夜就要叫你去
554	巴巴的倒了两钟来,他又走了。"宝玉道:"那不是他?你给他送去。
555	了去。"黛玉道:"我死了呢?"宝玉道:"你死了,我做和尚。"黛
556	"我原叫芸香,是花大姐姐改的。"宝玉道:"正经叫'晦气'也罢了,又
557	女云儿。大家都见过了,然后吃茶。宝玉擎茶笑道:"前儿说的'幸与不幸
558	"小丫头说:"没有听见叫别人了。"宝玉道:"你糊涂。想必没有听真。"
559	,倒唬了一跳,道:"作什么?"宝玉道:"你梦里'嗳哟',必是踢
560	的呢,你也去斟一巡酒岂不好。"宝玉悄笑道:"再等一会再斟去。"
561	"贾珍便将里面无人的话告诉了他。宝玉听说,笑道:"这有何难,我荐
562	宝玉和探春来了,都入座听他讲诗。宝玉笑道:"既是这样,也不用看诗,
563	来。"宝玉等听了,也都出来看时,宝玉笑道:"我认得这风筝,这是大老
564	东小院儿里头拿环哥儿和彩云去了。"宝玉笑道:"谁管他的事呢!咱们只

续表

N	Concordance
565	日可别闹了,再闹就有人说话了。"宝玉道:"怕什么,不过才两次罢了。
566	啊,也不出门了,在家里高乐罢。"宝玉、薛蟠都笑道:"一向少会。老
567	出两件不大穿的衣裳,忙忙洗了脸。宝玉一旁笑劝道:"姐姐还该擦上些脂
568	常在一处,要存这个心倒生分了。"宝玉又笑道:"姐姐知道体谅我就好了
569	些,何不早说,带了来岂不便宜?"宝玉道:"糊涂东西,要可以带了来,
570	了。"秦钟说:"理他作什么?"宝玉笑道:"你别弄鬼儿,那一日在老
571	胡说。你好歹告诉我,他品行如何?"宝玉笑道:"你既深知,又来问我做
572	缘故。想是说,他那里配穿红的?"宝玉笑道:"不是不是。那样的人不配穿
573	,可是'白玷辱了好名好姓'的!"宝玉笑道:"你今儿还记着呢?"袭人
574	,里面盛着一盒,如玫瑰膏子一样。宝玉笑道:"铺子里卖的胭脂不干净,
575	得水。湘莲因问贾琏偷娶二房之事。宝玉笑道:"我听见焙茗说,我却未
576	插入瓶中。众人都道:"来赏玩罢!"宝玉笑道:"你们如今赏罢,也不知费
577	年,不过是这样,一点后事也不虑。宝玉笑道:"我能够和姊妹们过一日,
578	,一把拉着问:"你怎么来了?"宝玉笑道:"我怪闷的,来瞧瞧你作
579	:"我告诉你,你可不许告诉他。"宝玉笑道:"这个自然。"正说着,
580	到他房中来寻,只见黛玉歪在炕上。宝玉笑道:"起来吃饭去。就开戏了,
581	也不管,你只交给他快拿了去罢。"宝玉道:"自然如此。你那里和他说话去
582	话去了,姨太太就顺便叫我带来的。"宝玉道:"宝姐姐在家里作什么呢?怎么
583	:明儿叫你一个五更天进去谢恩呢!"宝玉道:"自然要走一趟。"说着,
584	!再一会子不来,可就都反了。"宝玉陪笑道:"你猜我往那里去了?
585	打个络子把玉络上呢。"一句话提醒了宝玉,便拍手笑道:"倒是姐姐说的是
586	个就好,那不知理的是太不知理。"宝玉道:"你们是明白人,担待他们是粗
587	你再批评。"黛玉道:"你说。"宝玉又诌道:"林子洞里原来有一群耗
588	外婆子说:"姑娘们的饭都有了。"宝玉道:"你们吃饭去,快吃了来罢。
589	"理他呢,过会子就好了。"宝玉向宝钗道:"老太太要抹骨牌正没
590	他,问道:"袭人到底多早晚回来?"宝玉道:"自然等送了殡才来呢。"
591	"贾母道:"原来是云儿有这个。"宝玉道:"他这么往我们家去住着,我
592	妈妈给史湘云送东西去的话告诉了宝玉。宝玉听了,拍手道:"偏忘了他!我
593	我的身子,我死我的,与你何干?"宝玉道:"何苦来,大正月里,死了活
594	而颤。茗烟见是宝玉,忙跪下哀求。宝玉道:"青天白日,这是怎么说!珍大
595	话,一个个都诧异,他竟这样有肝胆。宝玉忙笑道:"彩云姐姐果然是个正经人
596	我只记得有个'金刚'两个字的。"宝玉拍手笑道:"从来没听见有个什么'

续表

N	Concordance
597	风地里来哭,弄出病来还了得!"宝玉忙笑道:"谁赌气了!我因为听你
598	什么'庚黄'的。真好的了不得。"宝玉听说,心下猜疑道:"古今字画也都
599	雪,怪冷的,快替我做诗去罢。"宝玉忙笑道:"没有的事!我们烧着吃
600	把咱们熏臭了。"说着一径去了。宝玉纳闷道:"从来没人如此茶毒我,
601	年小……"一面说话一面咳嗽起来。宝玉忙道:"这里风冷,咱们只顾站着
602	接风,又可以做诗。你们意思怎么样?"宝玉先道:"这话很是,只是今儿晚了
603	儿弟兄。可惜他竟一门尽绝了后。"宝玉忙道:"咱们也别管他绝后不绝后
604	,如今又一暖,不觉打了两个嚏喷。宝玉叹道:"如何?到底伤了风了。"
605	这是怎么说,拿我的东西开心儿!"宝玉笑道:"你打开扇子匣子拣去,什么
606	"小巧而已。"湘云将手又敲了一下。宝玉笑道:"入世冷挑红雪去,离尘香
607	一首又不好,自然这会子另做呢。"宝玉笑道:"这正是'地灵人杰',老天
608	白芍等药,那分两较先也减了些,宝玉喜道:"这才是女孩儿们的药。
609	"小丫头道:"一夜叫的是娘。"宝玉拭泪道:"还叫谁?"小丫头说:
610	他说只说一句话,便道:"请说。"宝玉笑道:"两句话,说了你听不听
611	人忙问:"今日可丢了丑了没有?"宝玉笑道:"不但不丢丑,拐了许多东西
612	嘴儿。宝玉看时,见袭人和衣睡着。宝玉笑道:"好啊!这么早就睡了。"
613	袄便蹑手蹑脚的下了熏笼,随后出来。宝玉劝道:"罢呀,冻着不是玩的!
614	不依。你们是一气的,都来戏弄我。"宝玉劝道:"罢哟,谁敢戏弄你?你
615	扇子失了手掉在地下,将骨子跌折。宝玉叹道:"蠢才,蠢才,将来怎么样
616	这样的话,怎么是你读书的人说的?"宝玉叹道:"你们那里知道,不但草木,
617	:"休谬加奖誉,且看转的如何,宝玉念道:"眼前不见尘沙起,将军俏影
618	什么?"黛玉道:"我没说什么。"宝玉笑道:"给你个榧子吃呢!我都
619	夫人也道:"宝玉很会欺负你妹妹。"宝玉笑道:"太太不知道这个原故。宝姐
620	。"平儿笑道:"与你什么相干?"宝玉笑道:"我们弟兄姐妹都一样。他们
621	了,是我早起吃了冷香丸的香气。"宝玉笑道:"什么'冷香丸',这么好
622	吃饭了。"贾环等答应着便出去了。宝玉笑道:"可是姐姐们都过来了,怎么
623	几天戏来。宝姑娘一定要还席的。"宝玉冷笑道:"他还不还,与我什么相
624	原来你就是宝玉!这可不是梦里了?"宝玉道:"这如何是梦?真而又真的!
625	淇水','睢园'不是古人的?"宝玉道:"这太板了。莫若'有凤来仪
626	宝榻,悬的是同昌公主制的连珠帐。宝玉含笑道:"这里好,这里好!"秦
627	袭人。袭人忙赶了来,才夺下来。宝玉冷笑道:"我是砸我的东西,与你
628	在望'!又暗合'杏花村'意思。"宝玉冷笑道:"村若用'杏花'二字,

续表

N	Concordance
629	喜喜欢欢的,你又怎么这个样儿了?"宝玉冷笑道:"他们娘儿们姐姐儿们喜欢不喜
630	来了。白哭一会子,也无益了。"宝玉冷笑道:"原是想他自幼娇生惯养的
631	遇着叔叔欠安。叔叔如今可大安了?"宝玉道:"大好了。我倒听见说你辛苦
632	"偏这小狗攮知道,有这些蛆嚼!"宝玉冷笑道:"我只当是谁亲戚,原来
633	有金荣在这里,我是要回去的了。"宝玉道:"这是为什么?难道别人家来得
634	。宝玉不在家,我看有谁来救你!"宝玉连忙带笑拦住,道:"你妹子小,不
635	训他,倒没意思,便连忙替贾环掩饰。宝玉道:"大正月里,哭什么?这里不好
636	麝月笑道:"拿骰子咱们抢红罢。"宝玉道:"没趣,不好。咱们占花名儿
637	吃这一个梨,吃来吃去就好了。"宝玉道:"这也不值什么。只怕未必见效
638	:"不值一坛,再唱好的来。"宝玉笑道:"听我说罢,这么滥饮,
639	看了,只管出神,心内还默默记诵。宝玉笑道:"妹妹,你说好不好?"黛
640	想病好,求其不添,也就罢了。"宝玉道:"姐姐虽如此说,姐姐还要保重
641	你的头,教你必定说这些字样呢?"宝玉道:"如此说,则匾上莫若'蘅芷
642	,你如今大了,越发心直嘴快了。"宝玉笑道:"我说你们这几个人难说话,
643	叶之典故颇多,再想一个改了罢。"宝玉见宝钗如此说,便拭汗道:"我
644	,刀搁在脖子上我也不出去了。"宝玉忙笑道:"你说那几件?我都依
645	!倒也有些意思。"便催宝玉快说。宝玉笑道:"谁说过这个,也等想一
646	定了琴姑娘呢,不然,那么疼他?"宝玉笑道:"人人只说我傻,你比我
647	家里未必找的出这么一个俗器来呢!"宝玉笑道:"俗语说:'随乡入乡'
648	了,撂下脸来说道:"你说什么?"宝玉笑道:"我何尝说什么?"黛玉便
649	象那起挑脚汉了。"说毕,又笑。宝玉忙笑道:"妈妈说的是。我每日都
650	:"是不是?我来了他就该走了!"宝玉道:"我何曾说要去,不过拿来
651	这一个答道:"打发宋妈瞧去了。"宝玉道:"回来说什么?"小丫头道:
652	字就是了。"众人道:"怎么解?"宝玉道:"他说'宝',底下自然是'
653	。凤儿嘴乖,怎么怨得人疼他。"宝玉笑道:"要这么说,不大说话的就不
654	些过来,又添了一个做诗的人了。"宝玉冷笑道:"虽如此说,但只我倒替
655	又还了席,也请老太太赏菊何如?"宝玉笑道:"老太太说了,还要摆酒还
656	省中十二冠首女子之册,故为正册。"宝玉道:"常听人说金陵极大,怎么只十
657	!到底说句话儿,也象件事啊。"宝玉道:"没有什么可说的么。"晴雯
658	令比人唠叨!倒也有些意思。"便催宝玉快说。宝玉笑道:"谁说过这个,
659	政拈须寻思,因叫宝玉也拟一个来。宝玉忙问道:"老爷方才所说已是。但如今
660	是哄你玩罢咧,你就认起真来。"宝玉道:"你说的有情有理,如何是玩

续表

N	Concordance
661	意。贾政听了，便回头命宝玉拟来。宝玉道："尝听见古人说：'编新不如
662	着却好，不知你们的脾胃是怎样的。"宝玉道："你说好，把我的都拿了吃
663	人笑话这家子的人眼里没有长辈了。"宝玉笑道："妈妈说的是。我不过是一
664	"为你哥哥娶嫂子的话，所以要紧。"宝玉道："正是说的是那一家的好？只
665	替我炮制。我有的是那些俗香罢了！"宝玉笑道："凡我说一句，你就拉上
666	那福气穿就罢了，这会子又着急。"宝玉笑道："这话倒说的是。"说着
667	人？"婆子道："还有两盆花儿。"宝玉道："你出去说，我知道了，难为
668	老爷不气，不时时刻刻的要打你呢？"宝玉笑道："再不说了。那是我小时候
669	正为劝你这些个，更说的狠了！"宝玉忙说道："再不说这话了。"袭人道
670	去？"紫鹃道："妹妹回苏州去。"宝玉笑道："你又说白话。苏州虽是原
671	了，要是这样闹，不如死了干净！"宝玉道："我说自家死了干净，别错听
672	赌气花儿两银子买进他们来就是了。"宝玉笑道："你说的话怎么叫人答言呢
673	忽有人回："环爷、兰哥儿问候。"宝玉道："就说难为他们，我才睡了，

霍底本"宝玉……说"共现语境词

N	Concordance
1	了会子，都往后头不知那屋里去了。"宝玉说："大娘说'有话说'，不知是
2	丫鬟笑道："宝玉怎么跑到这里来？"宝玉只当是说他，忙来陪笑说道："
3	袭人等便搀至炕上，脱了衣裳，不知宝玉口内还说些什么，只觉口齿缠绵，
4	第三日一早出去雇了两个人收拾好了。"宝玉说："怪道呢。上月我们大观园的池
5	仗利害，留神天上吊下火纸来烧着。"宝玉笑回说："不往远去，只出去就
6	要睡觉？你闷的很，出去逛逛不好？"宝玉见说，携着他的手笑道："我要
7	在书房中和清客相公们说闲话儿，忽见宝玉进来请安，回说上学去。贾政冷笑道
8	《寄生草》，极妙，你何曾知道！"宝玉见说的这般好，便凑近来央告："
9	不见他，只当病了，忙使人来问。宝玉方去请安，便说："写字之故，因
10	猩毡斗笠一抖，才往宝玉头上一合，宝玉便说："罢了，罢了！好蠢东西，
11	听真。"旁边一个小丫头最伶俐，听宝玉如此说，便上来说："真个他糊涂！
12	软帘自往里间来。麝月只得跟进来。宝玉便推他出去说："不敢惊动。"麝
13	袭人。又问："这会子可好些？"宝玉一面道谢，说："好些了。"又让
14	湘云、宝琴、岫烟、惜春也都来了。宝玉忙迎出来，笑说："不敢起动。快
15	"林姑娘，姨太太叫我送花儿来了。"宝玉听说，便说："什么花儿？拿来我

续表

N	Concordance
16	口,平儿也打扮的花枝招展的来了。宝玉忙迎出来,笑说:"我方才到凤姐
17	调三窝四。"说着,大家都笑了。宝玉说:"关了院门罢。"袭人笑道
18	己为伴,时常大家讨论才能有些进益。"宝玉不待说完,便道:"正是呢!我们
19	玉心里原是再不理宝玉的,这会子听见宝玉说"别叫人知道咱们拌了嘴就生分
20	说着便向丫鬟手中接来亲与他带上。宝玉听如此说,想了一想,也就不生
21	有意,情沾怨笛送黄昏。大家看了,宝玉说探春的好,李纨终要推宝钗:
22	反引这浊物来污染清净女儿之境?"宝玉听如此说,便吓的欲退不能,果觉
23	此处如何?"众人见问,都忙悄悄的推宝玉教他说好。宝玉不听人言,便应声
24	!仔细明儿问你。才已发下狠了。"宝玉听如此说,才回来。一路打算:"谁
25	自己送他的。芳官便又告诉了宝玉,宝玉也慌了,说:"露虽有了,若勾
26	么'麒麟'可怎么好呢!"一句话又把宝玉说急了,赶上来问道:"你还说这
27	?可吃了什么没有?唬了没有?"宝玉只回说:"北静王的一个爱妾没
28	,又央告宝玉。先是他二人不肯,后来宝玉说:"不回去也罢了,只叫金荣赔
29	来。两个老婆子蹲在外面火盆上筛酒。宝玉说:"天热,咱们都脱了大衣裳才
30	便将墨笔等物拿着,随宝玉进园来。宝玉满口里说:"好热。"一壁走一面
31	伴,宝姑娘坐了一坐的话,告诉宝玉。宝玉听了,忙说:"不该,我怎么睡着
32	"是你要咒的,并不是我说的。"宝玉说:"我又有了,这一改恰就妥
33	色吃食,拣了命人送给薛姨妈去。宝玉便说:"雅坐无趣,领要行令才
34	我什么相干!"因问:"做什么?"宝玉说要吃茶。麝月忙起来,单穿着红
35	便走上来问紫鹃道:"你才和我们宝玉说了些什么话?你瞧瞧他去!你回
36	少受些辛苦,岂不念公子之德呢!"宝玉连说:"实在不知。恐是讹传也未见
37	,人倒疑惑起来,索性再等一等。"宝玉点头,因说:"我出去走走。四儿
38	散。佩凤、偕鸳两个去打秋千玩耍,宝玉便说:"你两个上去,让我送。
39	湘云说着笑着跑出来,怕黛玉赶上。宝玉在后忙说:"绊倒了!那里就赶上
40	将门锁上,把钥匙要了,自己拿着。宝玉忙说:"这一道门何必关?"又没多
41	哭,一行将方才莺儿等事都说出来。宝玉越发急起来,说:"你只在这里闹
42	他偷的呢,只管领他的情就是了。"宝玉听了,笑说:"你说的是。"袭
43	不信只问他!"说毕,指着宝玉。宝玉没好意思起来,说:"薛大哥,你该
44	这一点子好名还不会买去不成?"宝玉听了他方才说的,又陪笑抚慰他,
45	:"在南京收着呢,此时那里去取?"宝玉听了,大失所望,便说:"没福得
46	袜,两脚乱蹬,笑的喘不过气来。宝玉忙笑说:"两个大的欺负一个小的
47	了两三声,方见两三个老婆子走进来。宝玉见了,连忙摇手说:"罢罢,不用了

续表

N	Concordance
48	呢。"一面说,一面坐下吃茶。那宝玉便和他说些没要紧的散话,又说道
49	灯向地下一照,只见一口鲜血在地。宝玉慌了,只说:"了不得!"袭人见
50	了病,宝二爷怎么心里过的去呢?"宝玉听了这话,说到自己心坎儿上来,可
51	忙应是自己送他的。芳官便又告诉了宝玉,宝玉也慌了,说:"露虽有了
52	姨妈,也不好向着外人反说他的。怨不得宝玉说:'女孩儿未出嫁是颗无价宝珠,
53	有理,忙将宝玉抱下车来,送上马去。宝玉笑说:"倒难为你了。"于是仍进
54	的?这一赶,又赶出病来才罢。"宝玉回说:"不妨事。"宝钗、探春等
55	呢?等我把这个话告诉别人评评理。"宝玉自知说的造次了,后悔不来,登时脸
56	听如此说,只得且和众人吃酒去。这里宝玉又说:"不必烫暖了,我只爱喝
57	半。接着又听"嗤""嗤"几声。宝玉在旁笑着说:"撕的好!再撕响
58	"你的病可好了?跑来做什么?"宝玉不便说出讨情一事,只说:"来看
59	走进来,正听见湘云说"经济"一事,宝玉又说:"林妹妹不说这些混账话,要
60	里,那黛玉只一言不发,挨着贾母坐下。宝玉没什么说的,便向宝钗笑道:"大
61	炕上又又了一张桌子,方坐开了。宝玉忙说:"林妹妹怕冷,过这边靠板
62	了,自有许多好处。我且告诉你句话:宝玉常说,这屋里的人,无论家里外头的
63	正和王夫人众姐妹商议给史湘云还席。宝玉因说:"我有个主意:既没有外客
64	啊!"说着,催宝玉喝了两口汤。宝玉故意说不好吃。玉钏儿撇嘴道:"
65	替你作个生日,我心里才过的去。"宝玉、湘云等一齐都说很是。探春便盼
66	,原来是他。我可那里敢挑他呢?"宝玉不等说完,忙用话分开。湘云笑道
67	把海棠社改作桃花社,岂不大妙呢?"宝玉听着点头,说:"很好。"且忙
68	这里宝钗只刚做了两三个花瓣,忽见宝玉在梦中喊骂,说:"和尚道士的话如
69	得勉强笑道:"你这话说的是。昨儿宝玉还说:明儿怎么收拾房子,怎么做衣裳
70	,便说:"请安歇罢,我们走了。"宝玉还说:"再歇歇。"那林之孝家
71	觉亲密起来了。一时捧上茶果吃茶,宝玉便说:"我们两个又不吃酒,把
72	玉在旁,因问宝玉:"打那里来?"宝玉便说:"打宝姐姐那里来。"黛玉
73	宝玉,一面取了"败毒散"来敷上。宝玉说:"有些疼,还不妨事。明日老太
74	来。独有宝玉的美人儿,再放不起来。宝玉说丫头们不会放,自己放了半天,
75	自是山南海北干鲜水陆的酒馔果菜。宝玉因说:"咱们也该行个令才好。"
76	么?"原来黛玉知道史湘云在这里,宝玉一定又赶来,说麒麟的原故。因心下
77	福,只见宝玉醉醺醺回来,因问其原故,宝玉一一向她说了。袭人道:"人家牵肠
78	早说出来,我们也少些辛苦,岂不念公子之德呢!"宝玉连说:"实在不知。恐是讹传也未见得。"那长府官冷笑

续表

N	Concordance
79	干人？"只见那些丫鬟笑道："宝玉怎么跑到这里来？"宝玉只当是说他，忙来陪笑说道："因我偶步到此，不

霍译本"Bao-yu's"共现语境词

N	Concordance
1	he names of most of the principal females of Bao-yu's establishment. He knew at a glance t
2	other maid, too. Incidentally, the fact that Bao-yu's senior maids like Skybright and Musk
3	sin Shi's waiting for you!" She took hold of Bao-yu's hand and pulled him after her, to th
4	atitude for Bao-chai's kindness. Reentering Bao-yu's room, she found him lying back quiet
5	ai some distance ahead of her, just entering Bao-yu's courtyard. Continuing to amble on, s
6	days' convalescence had ended, not only were Bao-yu's health and strength completely resto
7	precaution Grandmother Jia called in some of Bao-yu's maids and told them that in future w
8	he girls. Lady Wang now proceeded to inspect Bao-yu's things. Anything which looked at
9	milady." Finding herself unable to shake off Bao-yu's attentions, Dai-yu got up from the k
10	er Jia's own maids. Her real name was Pearl. Bao-yu's grandmother, fearful that the maids
11	e sewing and other maid's-work, took care of Bao-yu's and the junior maids' pocket-money f
12	ppointment!" Jia Yun recognized the voice as Bao-yu's and hurried up the steps inside. He
13	pping round to the back, quietly called over Bao-yu's little page Tealeaf and whispered a
14	umped up from her spinning and hurried over. Bao-yu's spirits were quite dashed by her abr
15	d pointed to the self-propelling toy boat on Bao-yu's shelf. "Just get on that boat and go
16	demeanour admirably qualified him to become Bao-yu's study-companion, Grandmother Jia was
17	ck and get him to give you another beating." Bao-yu's pages came in next for her censure.
18	into the Garden. It may be recalled that when Bao-yu's sickness was at its height, it had b
19	bed inside the tent-like summer-bed, while Bao-yu's wet-nurse Nannie Li and his chief ma
20	Oh, and then she wanted to go and blow on Bao-yu's soup. Oh dear, I could have died
21	in a "lazy knot" and told her to go back to Bao-yu's room when she had finished dressing.
22	erchief as she said this in the direction of Bao-yu's face. "Ow!" he exclaimed—She had fli
23	nsense," she said. "You are more like one of Bao-yu's boys than one of the Master's." Erj
24	ght long under the bed-clothes. The day of Bao-yu's birthday arrived-the same day, it
25	ment. She made Tan-chun copy all ten poems-Bao-yu's and the girls' on to a sheet of fa
26	Aroma was about to retort; but the sight of Bao-yu's face, now white with anger, made her

续表

N	Concordance
27	rls alike are all agreeably unemployed, and Bao-yu's half-brother Jia Huan, on holiday li
28	lay back on the bed and closed her eyes. But Bao-yu's confidence was shaken. Had he a doub
29	ything to do with me. I managed to find this Bao-yu's room, but he was asleep. What I saw
30	ed in chorus, not daring to laugh. Presently Bao-yu's eye chanced to light on a little met
31	cted that he was in some way responsible for Bao-yu's misfortune. What Aroma had earlier o
32	had been composed. She told someone to take Bao-yu's share of the presents and go with hi
33	ually been offering herself as a fishwife to Bao-yu's old fisherman and wished the-remark
34	ts to the old lady before proceeding to take Bao-yu's pulse, mystified by the presence of
35	and made them sit down while she went off to Bao-yu's room to fetch some money. She weighe
36	ned in the evening they would be in time for Bao-yu's departure. The younger ones wormed t
37	mour. I can easily find out by asking one of Bao-yu's pages. But suppose it is only a ru
38	d Blossoms Pavilion when she caught sight of Bao-yu's old wet-nurse, Nannie Li, coming fro
39	ng their good-byes. A maid came forward with Bao-yu's rain-hat and he lowered his head sli
40	eported her." To Nenuphar in her desperation Bao-yu's appearance on the scene had been an
41	ho kept it, hardly less surprised to hear of Bao-yu's arrival than she would have been if
42	y'or whatever it was, there was a strain in Bao-yu's own nature which responded to it wit
43	rted at Partumee; but Parfumee dodged behind Bao-yu's back and clung to him. Bao-yu took S
44	irk on Dai-yu's face and knew very well that Bao-yu's rudeness must have pleased her. The
45	t of the lot is that Skybright that works in Bao-yu's room. Because she's a bit better-loo
46	at proud, peculiar girl Crimson who works in Bao-yu's room. If a girl like that knows that
47	and began talking nervously to someone else. Bao-yu's rudeness to Bao-chai had given Dai-y
48	ood-spot about the size of a small button on Bao-yu's left cheek. She bent over him to exa
49	the one whose birthday is on the same day as Bao-yu's." Lady Wang examined the girl closel
50	was evidently determined not to sit down in Bao-yu's presence, she took her by the hand a
51	ing to sleep, hoping by this means to engage Bao-yu's attention and provoke some coquetry
52	er, observing how numerous the maids were in Bao-yu's apartment and how light their duties
53	s tastes in it were decidedly peculiar. When Bao-yu's poem was praised earlier on, he had
54	n I am." She bustled off and began making up Bao-yu's bed. "Hail" said Skybright disgusted
55	the one whose birthday is on the same day as Bao-yu's?" she asked. Since the girl herself
56	Cousin Zhen to lead the way, and leaning on Bao-yu's shoulder, began the winding ascent o
57	k well of Bao-chai when you weren't around." Bao-yu's contribution to the conversation had

续表

N	Concordance
58	are most reliable to be on call at night in Bao-yu's room while she is away. And keep an
59	"Sh!" said Dai-yu, looking round crossly in Bao-yu's direction. "Can't you be a bit quiet
60	e Li on the rampage once more, taking out on Bao-yu's unfortunate maids some of the spleen
61	n her recent activities. "There is a girl in Bao-yu's room called Skybright," she said. "S
62	r with him, Aroma made her own bed up beside Bao-yu's in Skybright's place. Observing the
63	ects, it was natural for her to suppose that Bao-yu's acquisition of the gold kylin would
64	add something, but seeing the abject look on Bao-yu's face, she laughed and held her tongu
65	accident to happen. Another day went by, and Bao-yu's godmother, old Mother Ma, called rou
66	rived." She ordered a little maid to get Out Bao-yu's share of the things sent. There were
67	ittle of the demon's evil poison had entered Bao-yu's body and lodged itself in the innerm
68	t in my bedroom." A little smile played over Bao-yu's face and he nodded. The nurses were
69	The bowl was upset and hot soup spilled over Bao-yu's hand. Silver, startled, though herse
70	een them. This was something totally outside Bao-yu's experience. His heart started poundi
71	mpatiently. "And everyone else's, no doubt." Bao-yu's execrable pun had not amused him. "I
72	g out that to go in and ask for something on Bao-yu's behalf at the very moment when Tan-c
73	r floating speck of dust ever blown into it. Bao-yu's dreaming self rejoiced. "What a deli
74	me!" With these words she threw herself upon Bao-yu's body and, lifting up her voice, bega
75	her of the day before. Lady Wang, observing Bao-yu's dejected appearance, attributed it
76	"It's very overcast again," said Musk, when Bao-yu's toilet had been completed. "It looks
77	thout waiting to see more. Skybright noticed Bao-yu's vacant expression. His forehead was
78	into the house. The effect of this rebuff on Bao-yu's feelings was as if a bowl of icy wat
79	e the incense had almost burned itself out. "Bao-yu's failed to make the grade as usual,"
80	early youth Aroma had always been aware that Bao-yu's character was peculiar. His naughtin
81	Autumn offering." She got up and, leaning on Bao-yu's shoulder, led the way into the G
82	she said: "I think I heard someone say that Bao-yu's beating today was because of somethi
83	rief sojourn among them in the early days of Bao-yu's illness, Jia Yun had got by heart th
84	and inkstones in all directions and smashing Bao-yu's teabowl to smithereens so that tea f
85	should do so now that he knew she was one of Bao-yu's maids. He just said: "I'm sure you'r
86	seemed to remember something. "I hear young Bao-yu's been in trouble," he said. "What was

续表

N	Concordance
87	l fast asleep. Curious to know the sequel to Bao-yu's departure, Dai-yu, on the pretext o
88	saying "Don't write"; but partly because of Bao-yu's almost girlishly beautiful features,
89	rence. Well, let me tell you: Master Huan is Bao-yu's brother, whatever you may think of h
90	other's insistence that he had brought about Bao-yu's beating by means of a deliberate ind
91	sudden commotion arose from the direction of Bao-yu's room, and the three of them stopped
92	should be, she felt sure, when she heard of Bao-yu's excuse, that it must be a false one.
93	that?" Aunt Xue urged a less serious view of Bao-yu's derangement: "It's true that he is a
94	her and saw that she had spent the night at Bao-yu's side. She slipped off the kang hurri
95	e expenses I think we can just about manage. Bao-yu's bride-price and Miss Lin's dowry won
96	de you ill." This was a suggestion after Bao-yu's own heart. He had the watch called a
97	apable of scaring herself!" She emerged from Bao-yu's bedding now and crossed the room to
98	a Huan and Jia Lan had come to inquire after Bao-yu's health. "Tell them it's very kind of
99	ing and peeped through the gauze window into Bao-yu's bedroom. She saw Bao-yu, clothed in
100	and for all." The three girls went round to Bao-yu's room together. "Bao-yu," said Dai-yu
101	who had intended no more than a mild joke at Bao-yu's expense, realized too late that Suns
102	ord round Bao-yu's neck. Then, taking one of Bao-yu's hands in his own, he asked him how o
103	and all felt sorry for them. By this time Bao-yu's hundred days of convalescence had en
104	I remember one day she dressed up in one of Bao-yu's gowns and put a pair of his boots on
105	amps up from the floor below. By their light Bao-yu's face was seen to be covered all over
106	but won't you forgive her for my sake?" Bao-yu's sudden appearance at that moment was
107	umiliation in death OUR last chapter told of Bao-yu's delight at seeing the gold kylin aga
108	et in. Nightingale turned to listen: "That's Bao-yu's voice," she said. "I expect he has c
109	f they are left with nothing to do. No, It's Bao-yu's penalty we've got to think about, He
110	ing now made her mind up, Xi-feng acceded to Bao-yu's request in the following terms: "My
111	someone else take the blame!" Aroma grasped Bao-yu's hand and wept: "Because I offended o
112	that he was pleased and hastened to commend Bao-yu's remarkable ability. "That's the two
113	her, in guarded undertone, on the subject of Bao-yu's intentions. "Bao-yu really is a simp
114	ower-sprigged pale red trousers, which, like Bao-yu's, were unconfined at the ankles. Her
115	nized the foremost one as Li Gui, the son of Bao-yu's old wet-nurse) Nannie Li, and addres
116	began to examine the body she was clasping. Bao-yu's face was ashen, his breathing was sc
117	ked her in a low voice. "I want to ask about Bao-yu's and our allowances for this month. W
118	nds refastened its plaited silken cord round Bao-yu's neck. Then, taking one of Bao-yu's h

续表

N	Concordance
119	end of the north embankment, on a corner." Bao-yu's face beamed with pleasure. "Grannie
120	at cord up? If three parts of the blame was Bao-yu's, I'm sure at least seven parts of it
121	eir leader, who was perhaps thinking more of Bao-yu's demon-repelling talisman than of its
122	urst of angry shouting from the direction of Bao-yu's room. The occasion of it will be dis
123	She handed her the sheet of paper containing Bao-yu's gatha and the "Clinging Vine" poem.
124	ming with molten wax, toppled straight on to Bao-yu's face. There was a piercing cry, whic
125	g to say something. "Help me up!" Even with Bao-yu's assistance it cost her a good deal o
126	-spice touch all right!" Next they looked at Bao-yu's poem. White Autumn's sister stands
127	est had all gone, Aroma went and sat down at Bao-yu's bed-side and asked him, with tears i
128	though whether at Melilot's simplicity or at Bao-yu's improvidence is unclear, since just
129	o was able to guess what the real purpose of Bao-yu's early-morning excursion had been, tu
130	d even if they do, you've got a good excuse. Bao-yu's your elder brother; you can't do any
131	little refreshment, he turned round and saw Bao-yu's horse in the distance, jogging along
132	there was time for a meeting. But now it was Bao-yu's condition that prevented them. Liu X
133	i-feng smiled. "These would be old things of Bao-yu's," she said. "He and the girls here h
134	if you wanted her to be paid as a member of Bao-yu's establishment, to make it fair you'd
135	but also the youngest and least sensible of Bao-yu's pages. Jia Qiang told him how Jokey
136	anything, a shade more opulent. In answer to Bao-yu's questioning, Lady Zhen assured him t
137	were up in the air being flown successfully. Bao-yu's pretty lady was the exception. He sa
138	was kept busy running to and fro for news of Bao-yu's condition. By evening this was suffi
139	th you, and then we shall have some supper." Bao-yu's spirits began to revive a bit under
140	ng with extra-clothing for their mistresses. Bao-yu's Aroma sent him an old surtout lined
141	once more in their chairs. Lady Wang stroked Bao-yu's neck affectionately: "Have you finis
142	e guest who turned up was Lou-shi, mother of Bao-yu's former classmate, the intrepid littl
143	mission to purchase paper for the windows of Bao-yu's outer study, which had just been red
144	his illness. This, then, was the reason for Bao-yu's unseasonable melancholy—a melancholy
145	m for such emergencies. Having ministered to Bao-yu's wants, she rinsed her own mouth out
146	hat the others had now gone, led Oriole into Bao-yu's room to ask what it was that he want
147	ucted Aroma to pound up in wine and apply to Bao-yu's injuries in the evening. "This is a
148	Jia Zheng received a favourable report from Bao-yu's schoolmaster in which his creative a
149	hame-faced Nightingale, who, unable to leave Bao-yu's side, could only stand there and han
150	As soon as they had done so, Aroma reported Bao-yu's absence. The old lady was displeased

续表

N	Concordance
151	ntributions are of about equal merit. Except Bao-yu's, of course. He goes to the bottom of
152	instead and began to walk away. By the time Bao-yu's weeping was over, Dai-yu was no long
153	t's her or not." "Whenever I see anyone from Bao-yu's room, it's always either Aroma or Mu
154	quite different thought was running through Bao-yu's mind. "I would do anything—absolutely
155	ee was carrying, assumed that it was some of Bao-yu's West Ocean grape wine that she was b
156	you've forgotten that?" The scales fell from Bao-yu's eyes. "Good gracious, how stupid of
157	until the horse and its rider had passed by. Bao-yu's little party now issued out of the s
158	k again." Jia Zheng took the Magic Jade from Bao-yu's neck and handed it to the monk, who
159	you know where you are." At these words all Bao-yu's happiness drained away. Slowly he se
160	e knelt to answer it. "I don't often go into Bao-yu's room, madam, or see much of him, so
161	ing!" At the same time, Qin Zhong, struck by Bao-yu's rare good looks and princely beating
162	es, began to sing away for all it was worth. Bao-yu's day-dreaming took another turn. "Tha
163	n which he had come. Back home he remembered Bao-yu's invitation of the previous day, and

霍译本"said Bao-yu"共现语境词

N	Concordance
1	er what Papa Zhang has just said," said Bao-yu, "But I really have no use for th
2	h what you said just now, Father," said Bao-yu, "But on second thoughts it seems
3	leaf round to see you about that," said Bao-yu, "But you never seem to be at hom
4	before I come back again." "Why?" said Bao-yu in some agitation. "That's someth
5	red silk tunic. "You'll get cold," said Bao-yu. "Put my fur gown on." She picked
6	hed up again." "That explains it," said Bao-yu. "Last month, when the pods were
7	of all those new members!" "Yes," said Bao-yu. "What a happy inspiration of you
8	grandson." "That doesn't matter," said Bao-yu unconcernedly. "She ought to give
9	uch about writing poetry anyway," said Bao-yu. "Surely we can manage without he
10	uld take it regularly, every day," said Bao-yu. "If she can keep it up for two o
11	eady yet?" "I did have one ready," said Bao-yu, "But these three are so much bet
12	ll?" "Of course it isn't a dream," said Bao-yu. "It couldn't be more real!" Just
13	to blow her nose on. "How's that?" said Bao-yu. "Much clearer," she said. "But I
14	d in the morning." "Oh, anything," said Bao-yu. "Whatever comes first to hand. B
15	egin thinking about it. "I will," said Bao-yu; "But there's just one thing I wo

续表

N	Concordance
16	we may as well go the whole bog," said Bao-yu. "I expect we'll have you better
17	to me by the Prince of Beijing," said Bao-yu. "It's exactly like the one he we
18	?" "The rain makes no difference," said Bao-yu. "It's a horn lantern. They're no
19	er's side against Uncle and Aunt?" said Bao-yu. "Obviously someone was to blame;
20	nd laughed. "I've often said to Aroma," Bao-yu went on, "whoever gets you and yo
21	"I'm sure it will do very nicely," said Bao-yu. "At all events, we're not going
22	morrow, that's all. "But I must," said Bao-yu. "Tomorrow is his actual birthday
23	sited Qin Zhong's grave recently?" said Bao-yu. "Certainly I have," said Xiang-l
24	getting on." "Yes, you're right," said Bao-yu. "I was meaning to tell you last
25	normally feel that way about it," said Bao-yu, "It because I hate the silly, se
26	re you fill them." "Yes, Grandma," said Bao-yu, and proceeded from table to tabl
27	ling lies, it must be the parrot," said Bao-yu. The two girls were aghast. "You
28	eople outside." "What's the harm?" said Bao-yu. "If those famous poems written b
29	I must be going now." "Must you?" said Bao-yu. "I so seldom get a chance of see
30	s calls 'throwing yourself away'," said Bao-yu. "You shouldn't do that. The othe
31	ocked, I still ought to get down," said Bao-yu. "Quite right, sir," said Li Gui
32	ingale. "Thank the Lord for that!" said Bao-yu fervently. "If only she could sha
33	start making an outcry about it?" said Bao-yu, restraining her. "Why not accept
34	h do we give Dr Wang for-a visit?" said Bao-yu. "Ah, Dr Wang and Dr Zhang are ou
35	ad mark?" she said. "That's rich," said Bao-yu, "Your asking me! Anyone would th
36	way immediately." "But of course," said Bao-yu. "No one would expect you to spea
37	I can't do Linked Verses, anyway," said Bao-yu. "You have to make allowances for
38	o sit." "What a charming picture!" said Bao-yu. " 'A Bevy of Beauties Keeping War
39	p on the clothes-warmer, are you?" said Bao-yu. "I shall be scared, all on my ow
40	nette player". "You're all wrong," said Bao-yu, who had been grinning silently t
41	." "Oh, it was nothing important," said Bao-yu. "It's just that once you star
42	t have you got to be angry about?" said Bao-yu, amused. "You just concentrate on
43	the little pearl-inlaid cabinet," said Bao-yu. "I'll go along with you and have
44	ort. "We'd better keep this dark," said Bao-yu. "If my mother gets to hear of it
45	round." "Yes, I've got something," said Bao-yu. "Get ready to write." "Wine not
46	pass them on to you." "Thank you," said Bao-yu, "But I've got two pots of them a
47	hold." "In the world's eyes, yes," said Bao-yu. "But 'other countries, other wa

续表

N	Concordance
48	n't believe that rubbish, do you?" said Bao-yu. "How could there be another Bao-
49	as I used to." "I'm sure you do," said Bao-yu. "It's just that it's become so m
50	ction called 'Ying-ying's Reply'," said Bao-yu. "Since when did Meng Guang acce
51	have been deeply offended by it," said Bao-yu, "Yet now you say nothing." "It's
52	ith her when she was ill. "I see," said Bao-yu. "I needn't have been so puzzled
53	I hope you enjoy it, all-of you," said Bao-yu. "It took me enough trouble to ge
54	theme at our next poetry meeting," said Bao-yu. " 'Narcissus' and 'winter-sweet'
55	t a sick person in my room today," said Bao-yu. "My room is full of medicine-sme
56	s'!" "It is a good line, I agree," said Bao-yu. "We'll tell them that in future
57	got some. Snow Wave paper still," said Bao-yu. "It comes in large enough pieces
58	it?" said Aroma, instantly alert again Bao-yu said that he wanted some tea, so
59	eaves everywhere are rather ugly," said Bao-yu. "I can't think why they haven't
60	worry!" "I don't care who it was," said Bao-yu. "I don't want any Lins here, apa
61	t ten year!" "My dear young lady," said Bao-yu pleasantly, "You have all the tim
62	e mosquitoes?" "What mosquitoes?" said Bao-yu, mystified. "What are you talking
63	mistress. "I'm glad you've come," said Bao-yu, as she handed him the letter. "I
64	test at Green Delights. "Swallow," said Bao-yu, "You and your mother had better
65	-chun. "That's pretty unoriginal!" said Bao-yu. "Can't you do any better than th
66	fringes for sashes." "All right," said Bao-yu, "A sash-fringe." "What colour's
67	?" said Oriole. "Never mind that," said Bao-yu airily. "Do me some of every kind
68	hen it was Uncle She's birthday," said Bao-yu. "It will be a bit awkward if I g
69	ll over!" "Stop it, now! Stop it!" said Bao-yu, covering her mouth with his hand
70	ught to share with one's friends," said Bao-yu, "and not only furs and horses, b
71	," said Tan-chun. "What about me?" said Bao-yu. "Isn't anyone going to think of
72	complaining." "That's all right," said Bao-yu. "It's only twice. Anyway, we're
73	t here." "That's her, over there," said Bao-yu, removing one of the cups for him
74	because they had to?" "Nonsense!" said Bao-yu. "The soldiers among them lacked
75	very much for last night's party," said Bao-yu. "We'll have another one tonight
76	w did I …?" "I don't know either," said Bao-yu, laughing. "If I had known, I sho
77	ather eat with you today, Mother," said Bao-yu. "No, no, you can't," said Lady W
78	set him off," said Aroma, relieved that Bao-yu was only play-acting. "You should
79	iquette is that?" "I don't agree," said Bao-yu, smiling. "Adamantina is above et

续表

N	Concordance
80	t know what you are referring to," said Bao-yu in surprise. "Strike me dead if I
81	truly didn't know you had called," said Bao-yu. Cousin Bao came and sat with me
82	y you didn't think of it earlier," said Bao-yu. "We ought to have started a club
83	his is no time for false modesty," said Bao-yu. "Here is a serious proposition a
84	me of my youthful indiscretions?" said Bao-yu. "No, let me choose your name," s
85	hat cost so much?" "No, honestly!" said Bao-yu. "This prescription is a very unu
86	Yes, I'm sure that's what it was," said Bao-yu. "When I get back, I'll find out
87	are the sort of things you want," said Bao-yu laughing, "It's very simple. Just
88	one of those things are any good," said Bao-yu. "You give me three hundred and s
89	haven't been drinking cold wine," said Bao-yu. "I know, I know," said Xi-feng g
90	uestion." "That seems reasonable," said Bao-yu. "As I'm missing the patty all th
91	do with you. "We're all cousins," said Bao-yu. "What one of us does concerns al
92	o." "I wouldn't, even if she did," said Bao-yu. "I wonder," said Nightingale. "I
93	d out what they're talking about," said Bao-yu. "If I go out the back door and r
94	"So that's what was worrying you!" said Bao-yu, smiling. "Well, you are a simple
95	re, but there's a very fine moon," said Bao-yu. "Go ahead. we'll keep talking, d
96	when I was standing opposite you," said Bao-yu. "Now, apparently, it is all righ
97	"No, that's out of the question," said Bao-yu. "You've only just started gettin
98	omplete outfit I've been wearing," said Bao-yu. "There is a pair of pear-wood pa
99	ut the excellence of the person", said Bao-yu, misquoting slightly. "The lord
100	" "I've got one like that myself," said Bao-yu, "But I didn't bring it because I
101	alight!" "I'm not going very far," said Bao-yu. "I'll be back directly." Grandmo
102	those two women seemed very nice," said Bao-yu. "They were certainly very civil.
103	e lids off and let's have a look," said Bao-yu. The two women squatted on their
104	tears. "Don't be upset, Patience!" said Bao-yu consolingly. "I offer you an apol
105	Tell them it's very kind of them," said Bao-yu, "But not to come in here, becaus
106	easonably intelligent." "Tell me," said Bao-yu eagerly, "Is there another Bao-yu
107	those things: to test you." "You?" said Bao-yu in surprise. "What have you got t
108	veral mirrors in your vanity box," said Bao-yu. "Why don't you give me that litt
109	ht them with us?" "Stupid idiot." said Bao-yu. "Do you honestly think we could
110	ourite concubine died yesterday," said Bao-yu. "I went to condole with him. He
111	it seriously." "That was no joke," said Bao-yu. "It was too well-reasoned." Nigh

续表

N	Concordance
112	tience isn't that sort of person," said Bao-yu. "She wouldn't have known that yo
113	our mind without much difficulty," said Bao-yu, laughing. "You're afraid that as
114	ang Huo may have looked the same," said Bao-yu, "But they didn't have the same n
115	." "They can't he/p being stupid," said Bao-yu. "Being more intelligent than the
116	upposed to look the same as well," said Bao-yu. "That's not something you can fi
117	d much to amuse you there. "Good," said Bao-yu. "The more deserted the better." A
118	here and talk?" "What can we do?" said Bao-yu. "Just sitting here talking is go
119	! Isn't that stretching it a bit?" said Bao-yu with a laugh. "For eight bearers
120	k." "I should prefer to lie down," said Bao-yu. "All right, lie down then!" "The
121	room she has the sharpest tongue," said Bao-yu. Musk signalled to him agitatedly
122	ellow." "Man's life is uncertain," said Bao-yu. "Which of us knows when his time
123	ou're much too thin-skinned, Tan," said Bao-yu. "I'm always telling you: you sho
124	iends and close kin are kindest," said Bao-yu, coming over to where she sat and
125	now." "There's something in that," said Bao-yu laughing, and handed it to her. H
126	." "You can't if J won't let you," said Bao-yu. "I never heard of such a thing!"
127	ve when you say things like that," said Bao-yu. "I only said what a nice girl sh
128	nk there really are no more now," said Bao-yu. When she realized that Bao-yu mu
129	s very overcast again," said Musk, when Bao-yu's toilet had been completed. "It
130	." "Never mind how tired you are," said Bao-yu. "You'll do yourself much more ha
131	could see you coming towards me," said Bao-yu. "I knew it must be me you had co
132	s are enjoying themselves or not," said Bao-yu, "What concern is it of mine?" Ar
133	ourself ill." "I'll be all right," said Bao-yu. Bao-chai and Tan-chun, who happe
134	big ones against one little one," said Bao-yu, laughing. "I shall have to see a
135	I'm not much good at song-lyrics," said Bao-yu, "But I suppose I had better do w
136	you mean, "give and take a bit?" said Bao-yu in the same lack-lustre voice as
137	ou keep choosing plays like that?" said Bao-yu. "To hear you talk, it doesn't so
138	one else's expense!" "Never mind!" said Bao-yu. "When we hire a troupe for you,
139	o indulge her a bit." "Of course," said Bao-yu and ran off. He found Nannie Li l
140	ne only allowed to play with you," said Bao-yu, "And keep you amused? I just hap
141	example. Her Old Ladyship said that as Bao-yu was better now and there was to b
142	reform." "I've reformed already," said Bao-yu. "If I ever talk that way again,
143	middle of the New Year holidays?" said Bao-yu to Jia Huan, ignoring Bao-chai's

续表

N	Concordance
144	lling!" "I said if I were to die," said Bao-yu. "Don't twist my words. It isn't
145	I am." "And it's the way I feel," said Bao-yu, "That makes me the way I am! Do
146	ng away worse than ever!" "Right," said Bao-yu. "Right. I promise never to talk
147	ed for mercy. "In broad daylight!" said Bao-yu. "What do you think you're at? If
148	e girls here that really matters," said Bao-yu. "If I die, I die. What do I care
149	house¬ hold!" "How touchy you are!" said Bao-yu. "Having her to live with us does
150	right supposed to have committed?" said Bao-yu. "Maybe she isn't," said Aroma. "
151	l see you don't get into trouble," said Bao-yu. Reassured, Tealeaf fetched the h
152	p a moment, there's a good woman," said Bao-yu appealingly, just long enough to
153	re do you get 'green waxen' from?" said Bao-yu. "Tut, tut, tut!" Bao-chai shook
154	ieve that, do you?" "Indeed I do," said Bao-yu feelingly. "That's precisely what
155	"You only say that to humour me," said Bao-yu bitterly. "According to you I am
156	what has already been fore-told," said Bao-yu. "There was a portent of her comi
157	u, but you never notice." "Maybe," said Bao-yu, "But tell me this. How is it tha
158	autiful women are trouble-makers?" said Bao-yu. "There have always been lots and
159	deal with us three later." "You?" said Bao-yu, laughing incredulously. "The fam
160	's all very well for you to talk," said Bao-yu, mopping the perspiration from hi
161	l take the old girl so seriously," said Bao-yu. "Just leave her to do as she lik
162	" "I did watch for quite a while," said Bao-yu, "But I got rather deafened and c
163	ou shouldn't be too long, either," said Bao-yu with a smile. "I've got something
164	wear red." "No. On the contrary," said Bao-yu. "If she's not good enough to wea
165	ays dragging in things like that," said Bao-yu. "Very well, You will have to be
166	eat many mountains in this world," said Bao-yu. "You could hardly be expected to
167	it!" "I've only just let you off," said Bao-yu, "And here you go again, worse th
168	ay yet?" "There's still one left." said Bao-yu. "You must come for some more tom
169	af. "You don't even know her age!" said Bao-yu. "You can do this to her without
170	hout anyone knowing." "Too risky," said Bao-yu. "We might get kidnapped or somet
171	see him about. "Oh, nothing much," said Bao-yu. "He just wanted to say a few wor
172	k you where you were going?" "No," said Bao-yu. "Actually I changed because I wa
173	rse. "Thank you for your trouble," said Bao-yu with a winning smile as he rode i
174	can't think of anyone." "I know," said Bao-yu. "Why don't we go round to the Hu
175	has its pearl gone?" "I lost it," said Bao-yu. "I expect it fell off somewhere

续表

N	Concordance
176	unterfeit'!" "Well! You can talk!" said Bao-yu laughing. "Listen to you! Now I'm
177	ood-looking since I saw you last," said Bao-yu with a grin. "You could almost be
178	it down." "I recognize that kite," said Bao-yu. "It belongs to Uncle She's new g
179	s in West Lane." "Yes, of course," said Bao-yu. "I can't think what made me forg
180	dy, I don't. quite see the point," said Bao-yu wryly. "In any case, perhaps I'm
181	art." "I've already forgotten it," said Bao-yu. "If you go on talking about it,
182	firework?" said Jia Zheng. "Yes," said Bao-yu. Jia Zheng looked again, this tim
183	you?" "I'm the youngest." "Right!" said Bao-yu. "In future you will be called Fo
184	beyond what Tealeaf has told me," said Bao-yu. "I haven't been to see them. I d
185	water bright." "That's as may be," said Bao-yu, "But I don't believe Cousin Chai
186	rday and let it go." "Really!" said Bao-yu. "And I hadn't even flown it once
187	t be in time." "What other place?" said Bao-yu. Aroma smiled coldly. "Why ask me
188	to make fun of me." "Oh, really!" said Bao-yu. "Who would ever have the nerve t
189	tric Acid" and have done with it," said Bao-yu. "Citronella! How many girls ar
190	ortant I wanted to ask you about," said Bao-yu. "I've just remembered what it wa
191	ld!" "you're absolutely mistaken," said Bao-yu, laughing. "We're planning to roa
192	ll Aroma be away?" "I don't know," said Bao-yu, "But she certainly won't come ba
193	that's exactly what we should do," said Bao-yu. "The only thing is, it's a bit l
194	ty." "I think I've got something," said Bao-yu. Dai-yu picked up a writing-brush
195	o pay him ourselves." "How much?" said Bao-yu. "Well, you don't want to give to
196	nowing?" she asked him. "Not yet," said Bao-yu, "But it looks as if it will." Gr
197	me." "What's this lump here then?" said Bao-yu. "She's down in here getting warm
198	ll Tealeaf to go and get Dr Wang," said Bao-yu. The old woman took the silver an
199	w?" "That's all she was wearing," said Bao-yu. "You'll die before your time!" s
200	." "I wasn't thinking about that," said Bao-yu. "I was worried about your catchi
201	" "I suppose that's meant for me," said Bao-yu, "Since I'm the one who's always
202	is the finest smell in the world," said Bao-yu, "—far superior to the perfume of
203	myself with a pine or a cypress," said Bao-yu. "Confucius himself speaks highly
204	-qin mischievously. "River Queen," said Bao-yu. "Who else?" "Really?" said Bao-q
205	r one to hand." "Oh, what's that?" said Bao-yu. "We've all got this rose-coloure
206	ornamental, descriptive passages," said Bao-yu, "Otherwise it would seem too bar
207	ing legs on a snake!" "All right," said Bao-yu. "I'll try to make a quick change

续表

N	Concordance
208	to talk about Nightingale dying," said Bao-yu, laughing. "You started it," said
209	y." "I was only thinking of you," said Bao-yu in great agitation, "Yet now you
210	sion of laughter. "Dearest cuzzy!" said Bao-yu. "Won't you please make me anothe
211	d it," said Dai-yu. "I know what," said Bao-yu. "I've got a still better solutio
212	t she?" "Whether she does or not," said Bao-yu, "What concern is it of mine?" Th
213	!" "You'd better not imitate her," said Bao-yu. "It'll get to be a habit. You'll
214	ur bad luck for you!" "All right," said Bao-yu to the girl. "Go and fetch the bi
215	n't know how worried you make me," said Bao-yu. "So you feel worried, do you?"
216	u these flowers." "What flowers?" said Bao-yu. "Let me see!" He stretched Out h
217	rds." "I can't stand noisy plays," said Bao-yu. "I never could." "If you call th
218	esn't need very much doing to it," said Bao-yu. "I'm not going out anywhere toda
219	e by Cousin Zhen's mother-in-law," said Bao-yu. "How could I fail to know? Ravis
220	with Jia Lian. "Congratulations!" said Bao-yu. "You are a lucky man. She's a ra
221	of his face. "It does hurt a bit," said Bao-yu when she asked him, "But nothing
222	ct, I did." "I don't believe you," said Bao-yu, smiling back at her. "The tone o
223	m for you to look at." "Who have?" said Bao-yu. "What sort of poem?" "The young
224	, I have nothing to be afraid of," said Bao-yu. "But if I do let you look, you m
225	ve come just at the right moment," said Bao-yu, smiling at her. "Here, sweep the
226	t on with at all. "You go along I." said Bao-yu with a smile. "We shall be all ri
227	o, I'll continue as I've planned," said Bao-yu. "If not, it would be better to c
228	s." "I never made the comparison," said Bao-yu hotly, "And I never laughed at yo
229	ery point of view." "Don't worry!" said Bao-yu. "I'll tell Cousin Lian's wife pr
230	"I think it's an excellent idea," said Bao-yu. "May I see the poem?" "Let's all
231	ed to ring on in her head. "Well," said Bao-yu, "Is it good?" Dai-yu smiled and
232	d already given them your pledge," said Bao-yu. "You started off by saying that
233	the one they've chosen belong to?" said Bao-yu. "A family that was related to ou
234	may die out." "Spare your sorrow," Said Bao-yu. "What about this young lady? Why
235	sin Pan getting married." "I see," said Bao-yu. "Who did they finally settle on?
236	ent of autumn grief "Madam Fairy," said Bao-yu, whose interest had been whetted
237	ropes of pearls. "I like it here," said Bao-yu happily. "My room," said Qin-shi
238	should be so hard to pay. "I see," said Bao-yu to himself. "I wonder what the me
239	write poetry with!" "Hmn, maybe," said Bao-yu. "All the same, I am a bit worrie

续表

N	Concordance
240	" "What's a Cold Fragrance Pill ?" said Bao-yu with a laugh. "Won't you give me
241	ediately. " "Why worry about her ?" said Bao-yu over his shoulder, swaying slight
242	"So you have an inscription, too?" said Bao-yu pricking up his ears. "I must hav
243	no inscription." "Cousin, cousin," said Bao-yu entreatingly, "You've had a look
244	are in such a hurry to give her?" said Bao-yu. "It has to do with your Cousin P
245	re just saying that to humour me," said Bao-yu. "Where is Aroma?" he asked Skybr
246	fast asleep. "Just look at that!" said Bao-yu with a laugh. "It's a bit early f
247	ing there." "I have none to give," said Bao-yu. "Well, give me something to take
248	ing and giving him a nudge. "Why?" said Bao-yu. "We've finished." "She's finishe
249	I want to know about is jealousy," said Bao-yu. "Could one of your plasters cure
250	take responsibility for that too," said Bao-yu. "You can tell them I stole the b
251	ace and red hair!" "Useless dolt!" said Bao-yu angrily. "You can't even do a sim
252	nd I could do with a bath myself," said Bao-yu. "As you haven't had yours yet, b
253	hat's too great an honour for me!" said Bao-yu, laughing. Aroma nevertheless bro
254	ou have in mind?" "Try and guess," said Bao-yu. "If you can guess right, I shall
255	such great shakes after all then," said Bao-yu, smiling. "I said plasters couldn
256	ed." "I don't think much of that," said Bao-yu. "I can't see that working." "If
257	. " "What is this infusion called?" said Bao-yu. "How do you make it?" "It's call
258	y have done?" "Well, perhaps not," said Bao-yu, "But her face seems 80 familiar
259	s heard of the Cassia Xias." "Oh," said Bao-yu. "Why do they call them that?" "T
260	ways hearing about your plasters," said Bao-yu. "Tell me, what sort of things ar
261	you to tell me honestly, cousin," said Bao-yu. "Which of these three characters
262	k and have had my supper, cousin," said Bao-yu, "And I will give you a hand with
263	possible." "Sort it out nothing!" said Bao-yu. "I'm definitely going to report
264	u really ought to go," Bao-chai said to Bao-yu. "Whether you have lunch there or
265	you?" "Don't be upset, old chap!" said Bao-yu. "Tomorrow I'll treat you all." "L
266	ever you go, I shall go with you," said Bao-yu, taking up the purse and beginnin
267	nce. "You needn't have cut it up," said Bao-yu. "I know it's only because you ha
268	tifice." "There you are, you see!" said Bao-yu. "A farm set down in the middle o
269	"That's even more inappropriate!" said Bao-yu. " 'Refuge of the Qins' would impl
270	w they should sleep. "Oh, anyhow," said Bao-yu. "I don't mind." It should be exp
271	in the popular belief." "Surely," said Bao-yu, "It is much mote probable that p

续表

N	Concordance
272	s. "That's good!" "A lovely name!" said Bao-yu. But a moment later he added: "Ra
273	t say any more about it just now," said Bao-yu genially. "Wait until we are both
274	d permanently." "Dearest Grannie," said Bao-yu pleadingly, "I should be perfectl
275	t bother to heat the wine for me," said Bao-yu. "I prefer it cold." Good graciou
276	" "Who said anything about going?" said Bao-yu. "I just want them to have it rea
277	le plaster can do so many things," said Bao-yu. "I wonder if the trouble I am th
278	r wait a bit." "We wait for them?" said Bao-yu. "We have got the maids. We shall
279	-chun scornfully. "What if I did?" said Bao-yu. "There are lots of made-up thing
280	" "None of the girls has got one," said Bao-yu, his face streaming with tears a
281	stream we looked at earlier on," said Bao-yu. "We should call it 'Drenched Blo
282	ight' or 'islands' in this place," said Bao-yu, "If we are to make couplets in t
283	to quarrel with Miss Lin," she said to Bao-yu, "If only for the sake of this pr
284	ten. By the way," she said, turning to Bao-yu, "Mrs Lian asked me to tell you t
285	the ceremony." "What's the hurry?" said Bao-yu, a trifle pettishly. "I've not be
286	ally needs to be eaten with wine," said Bao-yu. Aunt Xue gave orders for some of
287	ou don't want to." "In that case," said Bao-yu, "I suggest 'The Garden of Spices
288	tly." "I can't think of anything," said Bao-yu, "Unless I did quite like that so
289	t rid of these." "Can't you wait?" said Bao-yu. "I shan't be a moment." "Oh, do
290	o talk about leaving this school," said Bao-yu. "We have as much right to come h
291	endants are from Academician Mei," said Bao-yu, "The ink-sticks and brushes are
292	or all they cared." "Don't worry!" said Bao-yu. "I know how to do it myself. And
293	his concern. "That's no problem!" said Bao-yu encouragingly. "I know just the p
294	"Didn't she call for anyone else?" said Bao-yu, brushing away a tear. "They didn
295	k you, but we have already eaten," said Bao-yu. "Here, or in the other house?" "
296	ong. "Now, now, stop play-acting!" said Bao-yu. "I saw you holding her that day
297	st?" "Shut up, or I'll clout you!" said Bao-yu, pushing him. During this muttere
298	d to pass through. "Here's Sappy," said Bao-yu with a meaningful smile. "Well, w
299	d wait for you." "You can't read," said Bao-yu, "so you wouldn't know about thes
300	e girl. "Oh, you're a silly girl!" said Bao-yu impatiently. "I'm sure you must h
301	hong. "No, give it to me, Sappy." said Bao-yu. She stood between them, pouting
302	up for you." "Oh, you're no good," said Bao-yu, "No more than any of the rest. T
303	me eating here with those clowns!" said Bao-yu. "No, back at home, with Grandmot

续表

N	Concordance
304	g Bao-yu to start. "Have a heart?" said Bao-yu. "I need a bit of time to think i
305	thing better than to begin today," said Bao-yu. "But what can I do if they won't
306	y badly" "Not so bad as all that," said Bao-yu. "A couple of days and it will pr
307	king that sort of stupid rubbish?" said Bao-yu. "I'd long since have fallen out
308	tion is not going to be much fun," said Bao-yu when the singers had been dispose
309	tent unless we do." "Hear, hear I." said Bao-yu and Xiang-yun. Tan-chun gave inst
310	you would." "I really don't know," said Bao-yu. "You must have been misinformed.
311	e verge of tears. "Now, now, now!" said Bao-yu. "Don't say things like that." "A
312	one's seal of office is nothing," said Bao-yu. Losing a thing like this is much
313	ang anxiously. "Not in the least," said Bao-yu. "Look at all the loot we've brou
314	id Xiang-yun. "Don't believe her," said Bao-yu. "Goodness! It's no time since yo
315	nt ones." "That's all right then," said Bao-yu. "I was going to say: my sister-i
316	do that knotting for you." "Yes," said Bao-yu. "I'm glad you reminded me." He r
317	said. "You're always so eloquent," said Bao-yu. "No one else gets a chance." "If
318	een going on while you were away," said Bao-yu. "While you were ill in bed, she
319	have you got wrapped up in there?" said Bao-yu. "The best present you could have
320	break it, by all means break it," said Bao-yu. "These things are there for our
321	ss I." said Tan-chun. "Not at all," said Bao-yu. He pointed smilingly at Aroma: "
322	get upset again." "No she won't," said Bao-yu. "She'll understand." Skybright-d
323	ing refined, thanks all the same," said Bao-yu. "I'm as common as dirt. And furt
324	" "I'm not asking you to feed me," said Bao-yu. "I'm just asking you to get it f
325	, Sunset, I always knew you were," said Bao-yu admiringly, "But there's really n
326	message didn't come from Father," said Bao-yu. "He'll have made it up himself."
327	up with scenes like this before," said Bao-yu. "What other reason can there be
328	grief." "I should become a monk," said Bao-yu. "Try to be a bit more serious,"
329	g-yun. "I'll tell you what to do," said Bao-yu. "Since there won't be any outsid
330	oor." "Now that's really strange," said Bao-yu. "You don't want to go, yet at th
331	ith us permanently." "Poor thing!" said Bao-yu. "How she must have cried and cri
332	you lot are difficult to talk to," said Bao-yu, "And I was certainly right!" "Do
333	nt. "You should have come sooner," said Bao-yu when they were indoors and Aroma
334	asked him. "Oh, several days now," said Bao-yu. "What a shame! I'll never get an
335	is exhausted." "Even if it does," said Bao-yu gaily, "I don't suppose you and I

续表

N	Concordance
336	out to you, shall I?" "All right," said Bao-yu. "If you're not having a bath you
337	y is terribly keen on good works," said Bao-yu. "There's nothing they like bette
338	them." "That's not spirit money," said Bao-yu hurriedly. "It's waste paper she
339	Ladyship won't suspect anything," said Bao-yu. "I shall tell her quite openly t
340	idn't mean to kick you, you know," said Bao-yu. "Who said you did?" said Aroma.
341	the names of most of those pills," said Bao-yu. "I expect he wanted her to take
342	se leave Number Two for me, Chai," said Bao-yu anxiously. "I've already thought
343	k quite different." "Stop moving!" said Bao-yu. "If you don't keep still, you'll
344	ing a mountain out of a molehill," said Bao-yu, returning her smile. "Why ever s
345	dentally treading on it. "Clumsy!" said Bao-yu reproachfully. "You won't be so c
346	end of all that." "So you shall," said Bao-yu. At that point a woman arrived fr
347	's a very neat bit of invective." said Bao-yu. "I can see I shall have to burn
348	ies when it's raining or snowing," said Bao-yu. "Why don't we wait until the fir
349	ber a name. "Never mind his name," said Bao-yu. "Don't try to remember it. Just
350	urn party for Cousin Shi herself," said Bao-yu, "And we are all invited. We'd be
351	sant." "You can't blame Parfumee," said Bao-yu. "Any departure from the straigh
352	've used up all your inspiration," said Bao-yu. "But instead of admitting that y
353	ghed. "I seem to be bottom again," said Bao-yu ruefully. "Though I must say I sh
354	Musk. "No, that's a boring game," said Bao-yu. "Let's play Choosing the Flower
355	?" "Are you another drinker then?" said Bao-yu. "Good! We'll have a real celebra
356	together." "Who cares about them?" said Bao-yu. "Let's talk about us." At this p
357	ok after this stuff for me, then," said Bao-yu to the servant, "And this evening
358	off straight away." "Quite right," said Bao-yu. "I already knew about it. There
359	make you se what is in my heart," said Bao-yu. "One day perhaps you will know.
360	moulded medicine-cakes." "Funny!" said Bao-yu. "I wonder why Miss Lin didn't ge
361	atter to you?" "You're right," said Bao-yu, laughing. "If you were to go for
362	nger ones manage to give so much?" said Bao-yu, pleased but a little concerned.
363	hey found out." "They won't mind," said Bao-yu. "As soon as her mourning's over
364	ed asking." "It'll be all right," said Bao-yu. "Ask Miss Tan too. She's fond of
365	ame. "Let's play a drinking game," said Bao-yu. "Yes, but let it be a nice, quie
366	ir elders." "You are quite right," said Bao-yu. "But in fact it is only once in
367	or trouble." "It'll be all right," said Bao-yu, "You see. Just ask her." Swallow

续表

N	Concordance
368	iss Bao must be very fond of you," said Bao-yu. "I expect later on when she gets
369	very hot samshoo." "We have some," said Bao-yu, and quickly ordered a kettle of
370	ng in judgement over her. "Right," said Bao-yu. "That's all settled. Let's all m
371	for nothing." "That's no problem," said Bao-yu. "I shall ask Her Old Ladyship to
372	Suncloud is a good, honest soul," said Bao-yu. "She certainly is," said Tan-chu
373	tent." "All right. Go and get it," said Bao-yu. "And be born a beggar in my next
374	r?" Dai-yu ignored him. "Oh well," said Bao-yu. "I haven't got time to worry abo
375	t be much good at writing poetry," said Bao-yu, "But she is jolly good at readin
376	ing of those slippers reminds me," said Bao-yu. "I happened to run into Father o
377	it for me." "Well, I don't know," said Bao-yu. "In the trips I make to bazaars
378	ke what now?" "Oh, the beginning!" said Bao-yu. "In the beginning, when you firs
379	he had been asking for you." "No," said Bao-yu, smiling at her concern. "Whoever
380	d. "Oh, Nenuphar is crazy." "Why?" said Bao-yu. "What do you mean?" "It was for
381	There's nothing crazy about that," said Bao-yu, "If they were friends." "Friends
382	llow-belly can push us." "Please," said Bao-yu exasperatedly, "Don't call her by
383	is itself a good theme for a poem, said Bao-yu. "I've already thought of one. Is
384	ch was ready. "Off with you then," said Bao-yu, "And come back as soon as you ha
385	ering." "What goes with viridian?" said Bao-yu. "Peach pink." "Mm. That sounds v
386	Oriole. "What patterns are there?" said Bao-yu. "There's stick-pattern, ladder-p
387	ou this to share with the others," said Bao-yu. "No," said Aroma. "They said it
388	what does!" "It's got no flavour," said Bao-yu. "Taste it yourself, if you don't
389	Yes, I think I've still got some," said Bao-yu. "Look, why don't you give her al
390	just ruined." "What's an old fan?" said Bao-yu. "Open up the fan box and get you
391	tched him the soup. "Silver dear," said Bao-yu, "If you still feel angry with me
392	d gracious! They mustn't do that!" said Bao-yu. "That's a terrible sin, knocking
393	t judgement, Green Boy?" "Oh yes," said Bao-yu. "It's a perfectly fair one. Mine
394	ught to have a name for the club," said Bao-yu. "We don't want anything banal,"
395	Now that's what I call sensible." said Bao-yu. "I can't stand set rhymes." Dai-
396	ere are so many girls in my room," said Bao-yu. "Please take any you have a fanc
397	ell, where am I going to go then?" said Bao-yu. "I just feel so bored." "Never m
398	Shen's party earlier this month," said Bao-yu. "I meant at the time to ask why
399	ly got anything much to give you," said Bao-yu. "Things like money and food and

续表

N	Concordance
400	time since we've seen you around," said Bao-yu. "How's the General?" "Fahver's i
401	ight." "I was going to send word," said Bao-yu. "Of course I was. But then old F
402	vous little blighter, aren't you?" said Bao-yu. "What do you want to go shooting
403	tter not waste time jawing, then," said Bao-yu, and left the young toxophilite t
404	me and we'll be quits." "Aiyo." said Bao-yu. "Worse and worse!" He turned to
405	ightingale came in. "Nightingale," said Bao-yu, "What about a cup of that excell
406	" "I shall share your vegetables," said Bao-yu. "Go on, you can go," He said, dis
407	"Won't you stay a little longer?" said Bao-yu. But Lin Zhi-xiao's wife was alre
408	e only a little smaller." "Funny!" said Bao-yu. "All the times she's been to our
409	shan't get started until morning!" said Bao-yu. "You know how I hate that kind o
410	my mouth shut." "Go on! Cut away!" said Bao-yu. "I shan't be wearing the wretche
411	eng with a scornful smile. "Well," said Bao-yu, "This is the first building our
412	ther a pity?" they asked. "Well," said Bao-yu, "There are both plantains and cr
413	"Fragrant Red and Lucent Green," said Bao-yu. "That takes account of both of t
414	, as for the name of the village," said Bao-yu scornfully, "'Apricot Village' is
415	beg of you, don't speak so loud!" said Bao-yu entreatingly. "I shouldn't really
416	ike to know what they are!" "Yes," said Bao-yu, "But they are too contrived." "Th
417	say what a big place Jinling is," said Bao-yu. "Surely there should be more tha
418	"None of the girls has got one," said Bao-yu, his face streaming with tears and sobbing hysterically.
419	ragrance?" "They certainly don't," said Bao-yu. "There are wild-fig and wisteria
420	in a single breath. "Now come on," said Bao-yu, "Let's hear about this "lucky ac
421	emember reading in some old book," said Bao-yu, "That to recall old things is b
422	else I want to discuss with you," said Bao-yu. "I'm not quite sure whether you
423	of them seems quite right to me." said Bao-yu in answer to the question. "In wh
424	nt to pour him a cup. "Good girl!" said Bao-yu. "If with your amorous mistress I
425	better one." "Now just a minute," said Bao-yu. "Just guzzling like this will ma
426	ets four." "Here, what is this?" said Bao-yu. "It isn't an invoice and it isn'
427	sit there, against the partition," said Bao-yu, while the guests were still arra
428	ts someone to play dominoes with," said Bao-yu to Bao-chai. "Why don't you go an
429	an mine." "If you really like it," said Bao-yu, "You're welcome to have mine." I
430	r her straight away." "Please do," said Bao-yu, and started to go. "Hey, come ba

续表

N	Concordance
431	tten." "You imagine these things," said Bao-yu. "It really isn't as you say." Ye
432	to give thanks." "Yes, of course," said Bao-yu inattentively, and gave Ripple in
433	don't you?" "Oh, leave her alone!" said Bao-yu. "She'll be all right presently."
434	t." "I've got to see Grandma now," said Bao-yu. "If you've got anything else to
435	if I had gone away." "Gone away?" said Bao-yu laughingly. "Where would you go t
436	ed, tea was served. "Now come on!" said Bao-yu, as he picked up the proffered cu
437	ang. "Eight Gem Motherwort Pills?" said Bao-yu. "Zhang's Dextrals? Zhang's Sini
438	urally weak constitution, Mother," said Bao-yu. "She takes cold very easily. The
439	of me!" "No, Mother, not stupid," said Bao-yu. "It's the strain. All those Vajr
400	d you round to my study that day," said Bao-yu, "A whole lot of things seemed to
401	ou've got to look after yourself," said Bao-yu. "You must try not to worry so mu
402	ily must have had some already?" said Bao-yu. Bao-chai shook her head: "Pan wa
403	our for myself!" "Oh do sit down!" said Bao-yu. "You don't have to be like that
404	an you expect me to believe that?" said Bao-yu. "The tears are still wet on your
405	you for the kind thought, though," said Bao-yu. "I decided to come back here par
406	gain when you can spare the time," said Bao-yu, and ordered Trinket to see him o
407	"When did I ever do such a thing?" said Bao-yu indignantly. "If you're referring
408	for that sort of thing nowadays," said Bao-yu. Now that we know the name of the
409	ook their leave. "I can't go out," said Bao-yu. "For heaven's sake don't let Aun
410	" "I wouldn't ask, if I were you," said Bao-yu, chipping in. "I thought it was r

杨译本"Baoyu's"共现语境词

N	Concordance
1	m the last chapter in which Jia Zheng tested Baoyu's literary talent, you may wonder to fi
2	next chapter. Chapter 57 Artful Zijuan Tests Baoyu's Feelings Kindly Aunt Xue Comforts Dai
3	respects to the Lady Dowager before taking Baoyu's hand to feel his pulse, while Zijuan
4	secretly got Qingwen and Venturina to enlist Baoyu's help. And as Yingchun's nurse was als
5	k gate, and there we will leave them. During Baoyu's absence, the maids in his apartments
6	ssed and lain down, she whispered to Daiyu: "Baoyu's heart is really true to you. Fancy hi
7	the old lady, ordering the servant carrying Baoyu's presents to accompany them. The Lady
8	d none of them but deplored it. By this time Baoyu's hundred days confinement was up and

续表

N	Concordance
9	Chapter 63 Girls Feast at Night to Celebrate Baoyu's Birthday Jia Jing Dies of an Elixir a
10	rs, eager to please him, hastened to commend Baoyu's remarkable talent. "The selection of
11	t it down, after which Xiren went to collect Baoyu's cup. He asked her, "Where's Fangguan?
12	chimed in, "Do make it up, both of you, for Baoyu's sake." "Not I!" cried Daiyu, "Are you
13	and when she discovered that she had shared Baoyu's bed she at once scrambled up. "How is
14	to see. Lady Wang observed, "The girls from Baoyu's place whom I see most often are Xiren
15	d that will take the wind out of your sails. Baoyu's just getting better, and we've all be
16	ile Xifeng had summoned two old nannies from Baoyu's quarters. "Xiren probably won't be ba
17	to Qingwen in looks, yet she's the best for Baoyu's chamber. Trustworthy, too, and honest
18	ns. Now all these kites were airborne except Baoyu's beauty, making him so frantic that s
19	y is the day for our club meeting. I suppose Baoyu's not here because he's forgotten this
20	nk are anathema to me." In Qin Zhong's eyes, Baoyu's striking appearance and ingenuous beh
21	brushes and ink over their desk and smashing Baoyu's teacup so that tea poured all over it
22	m writing eight-section essays, would follow Baoyu's example. This was why, whenever they
23	made no reply. Still Baoyu went on calling: "Baoyu's here!" Qin Zhong was at his last gasp
24	d spearhead that looks like silver." It was Baoyu's turn to laugh. "Now listen to you! I
25	with his account of the matter. Mingyan was Baoyu's most serviceable page but he was youn
26	that could wait until next they met. But as Baoyu's proposal was right she could hardly r
27	g their smiles at this, the others assented. Baoyu's eye now fell on a golden boat with an
28	ople say he's returned. I suppose we can ask Baoyu's pages to find out. If he hasn't come
29	enseless way you talk sounds as if you were Baoyu's servant, not Second Master's. Before
30	ress to give twenty herself plus Daiyu's and Baoyu's shares, and for Aunt Xue to give twen
31	panied Daiyu now to Green Gauze Lodge, while Baoyu's wet-nurse, Nanny Li, and his chief ma
32	her wrongly." Ouguan had been at a loss, and Baoyu's appearance had frightened her even mo
33	ehind his father's chair, to join them. When Baoyu's page brought him this invitation and
34	. It's only two or three times a month, when Baoyu's bored, that we all have a game togeth
35	nsense." So the three girls went together to Baoyu's rooms. Daiyu opened the attack by say
36	r occur to the old lady. This must have been Baoyu's doing." Since there was no hiding the
37	l the tea was cool. Fangguan held the cup to Baoyu's lips and he drank half of it. Then he

续表

N	Concordance
38	distress. Daiyu had been annoyed at first by Baoyu's immoderate language. Now, touched by
39	it. "What are you waiting for?" he roared to Baoyu's other pages Chuyao, Saohong and Moyu,
40	lady, and that was how she had later become Baoyu's maid. Having come here as a child, sh
41	age northwards away from the cortege and at Baoyu's orders went to invite Qin Zhong, who
42	up the sachet she had been making for him at Baoyu's own request. Baoyu, seeing that she
43	ay and I'll show you. Qin Zhong plucked at Baoyu's sleeve and whispered, "Isn't she fun?
44	ke it public for two reasons: partly because Baoyu's young, and if his father knew of this
45	d lady, so I've never paid much attention to Baoyu's affairs. But if you wish, madam, I sh
46	o one side. Now Jia Zheng had recently heard Baoyu's tutor speak highly of his skill in co
47	r incense." The old lady rose and leaning on Baoyu's shoulder led the way to the Garden. B
48	Li was on the rampage again, working off on Baoyu's maids her annoyance over her gambling
49	e made Jia Zhen lead the way and, leaning on Baoyu's shoulder, followed him up through the
50	ease go and beg Her Ladyship to let me off." Baoyu's heart bled for her. Tears started to
51	re taller than I am." She then went to make Baoyu's bed. "I was just nicely warm and you
52	now serious. All this was preying so much on Baoyu's mind that the honour conferred on Yu
53	hes-warmer above the brazier, Sheyue outside Baoyu's alcove. After the third watch had so
54	eshold by a subtle perfume which misted over Baoyu's eyes and melted his bones. "How good
55	sets off for the nether regions before long Baoyu's outer study was ready. He had agreed
56	ound for their inspection she fastened it on Baoyu's neck again, then asked her brother to
57	re was a row. And next she wanted to blow on Baoyu's soup, it's enough to make you split
58	s midspring, a whole series of misfortunes, Baoyu's loss of his friend Liu Xianglian, the
59	t it to somebody else." Xiren caught hold of Baoyu's hand and sobbed, "First you offend yo
60	e and went back to Bamboo Lodge. The news of Baoyu's disorder had made Daiyu suffer a rela
61	at she returned to her room. Qingwen noticed Baoyu's distraught look, the hectic flush on
62	r quilt, she secretly wept with rage. By now Baoyu's birthday had come round again, and th
63	he was studying. The clarity and fluency of Baoyu's answers made the prince turn to obser
64	eir respects. Recognizing Li Gui, the son of Baoyu's old wet-nurse, Jia Zheng de manded, "
65	n night duty. When the Lady Dowager heard of Baoyu's fright and asked the reason they dar
66	dy Wang had the whole house searched. Any of Baoyu's things which looked suspicious were t
67	tay in the Garden too. The more the merrier. Baoyu's face lit up. "That's a splendid idea,
68	cuse and quietly got hold of Mingyan, one of Baoyu's pages, to work on his feelings with h

续表

N	Concordance
69	money. Another order for wallpaper to paper Baoyu's outer study was read out and register
70	lady and her aunts and cousins, she took in Baoyu's costume. He was wearing a golden fili
71	nd finding her in a good mood she reported: "Baoyu's maid Qingwen has grown up row, and th
72	aiyu up. Just then, a commotion broke out in Baoyu's apartments and the three of them pric
73	f squabbling and angry shouting broke out in Baoyu's apartments. What it was will be discl
74	s not in her room but Mrs. Zhou found her in Baoyu's, trying to unravel the nine-ring puzz
75	n her for a few days. Don't let her sleep in Baoyu's quarters. We'll deal with her after I
76	he others had gone indoors, Li Gui led round Baoyu's horse and the boy mounted it and foll
77	ken cord, with his own hands he put it round Baoyu's neck. Then taking the boy's hand he a
78	cups with you and then we'll have our rice." Baoyu's spirits rose again at this. His nurse
79	Wang. "But do you know that minx Qingwen in Baoyu's place, madam? Because she's prettier
80	old lady was displeased when Xiren reported Baoyu's absence. She ordered him to be fetche
81	re they were going. The stewards' wives knew Baoyu's quirky ways and did not want him to p
82	ke that when you know how credulous he is?" "Baoyu's always been too trusting," put in Aun
83	rs. Hua and her son did not press the point. Baoyu's unexpected visit and the apparent int
84	se was nearly burnt up. The others laughed. "Baoyu's lost again," said Li Wan. "You'd bett
85	hey were much inferior. Besides, they lacked Baoyu's literary brilliance and poetic flair.
86	fallen short of her hopes. For these reasons Baoyu's inscriptions were adopted. Not all ha
87	stove, put its lid on again and placed it in Baoyu's lap. This done, she poured him some t
88	uld only move in her own bedding to sleep in Baoyu's room as in the old days. That evening
89	t a couple of them to keep watch at night in Baoyu's rooms. You must see to things too. Do
90	to give a truthful answer. "I seldom go into Baoyu's rooms or spend much time with him, s
91	the Palace. Daiyu glanced briefly at them in Baoyu's hand. "Am I the only one getting thes
92	knife at my throat could make me leave you." Baoyu's face lit up. "Well, what are your con
93	o taels a month are given to Concubine Zhao, Baoyu's to the old lady's maid Xiren; and Lan
94	elt, two pouches and a fan in a sheath, all Baoyu's old belongings. Wang Shanbao's wife.
95	studies; so let's wait a couple of years." "Baoyu's had one for two years already. Didn't
96	s frustrated, and slept. Now some time after Baoyu's abrupt departure Daiyu came, o
97	criptions in order to test him. And although Baoyu's childish efforts were far from inspir
98	poems specially written for these. Although Baoyu's couplets composed earlier are charmi

杨译本"said Baoyu"共现语境词

N	Concordance
1	musk, moon or islands here," said Baoyu. "If you want allusive couple
2	s much as you, third sister," said Baoyu. "I'm always urging you not t
3	write verses about this too," said Baoyu presently. "I've already made
4	den was given by some poet," said Baoyu, "Because this flower is as r
5	e. "If you're free tomorrow," said Baoyu to Yun, "Lust drop in and see
6	shan't be drinking any wine," said Baoyu. "Why not put a plate or two
7	ing her." "That's all right," said Baoyu. "I shall ask my grandmother
8	l laughter. "I'm last again," said Baoyu cheerfully. "But surely my W
9	"The moon's bright tonight," said Baoyu, clearing his throat. "We'll
10	ou astray?" "Leave it to me," said Baoyu. Then Mingyan brought round h
11	several times. "That'll do," said Baoyu. "Don't tire yourself. Taste
12	no good, that's quite fair," said Baoyu with a smile. "But you should
13	died out." "Never mind that," said Baoyu. "What's the girl like? How d
14	surprise. "That's all right," said Baoyu. "It's a horn lantern, and it
15	hink of a name. "Never mind," said Baoyu. "Names don't matter, just te
16	pirits." "There's some here," said Baoyu promptly. He told the maids t
17	keep out of his way. "I see," said Baoyu after a thoughtful pause. "We
18	uld bear with her." "I know," said Baoyu, and dashed off. Back in his
19	rop in any time you're free," said Baoyu, before telling Zhuier to see
20	we accuse her?" "Never mind," said Baoyu. "I'll take the blame for tha
21	yself." "Sit down, sit down," said Baoyu. "Why stand on ceremony with
22	ery decent of Sister Caiyun," said Baoyu. "But there's no need for you
23	ared at this point. "Zijuan," said Baoyu, "Pour a cup of that good tea
24	" "I suppose you won't stop," said Baoyu, "Till you've knocked out you
25	misses!" "Go and have lunch," said Baoyu, "And come back as soon as yo
26	aper. "I'm glad you've come," said Baoyu. "I'd quite forgotten, I mean
27	all the name." "I can guess," said Baoyu. "Just ginseng tonic pills."
28	ed to be having a good chat," said Baoyu to Xiren. "Why did Cousin Bao
29	i Gui. "So that's who he is!" said Baoyu scornfully. "Cousin Jia Huang
30	sed whenever people snub me," said Baoyu. "Well, now that you've stopp
31	hing." "Don't be too modest," said Baoyu. "The other day, when I was d
32	money instead?" "All right," said Baoyu. "We'll keep them and distrib

续表

N	Concordance
33	sh?" asked Yinger. "Scarlet," said Baoyu. "A black or slate-blue net w
34	Cousin Daiyu feels the cold," said Baoyu. "Come and sit by the partiti
35	that be fine?" "Don't worry," said Baoyu. "Let's go and tell your brot
36	g came in. "Look who's here," said Baoyu with a smile. "What about it?
37	hat's what I intended to do," said Baoyu, "But when I got there I foun
38	ll eat here with you, madam," said Baoyu. "No, no," Objected Lady Wang
39	pair it." "That explains it," said Baoyu. "Last month when the lotus s
40	ust have lost it out riding," said Baoyu. But when he went to bed and
41	e you're in." "You're right," said Baoyu, smiling. He handed the cape
42	d to fly into such a temper," said Baoyu to Qingwen. "I know what's on
43	that day? "Oh, nothing much," said Baoyu. "It simply occurred to me th
44	d Shenyue. "Oh yes, she did," said Baoyu. "You deserve to catch your d
45	h is no time for snivelling," said Baoyu. "If you don't like it here,
46	men should be treated alike," said Baoyu with a grin. "Why give me thi
47	ion. "Go ahead and enjoy it," said Baoyu. "You don't know the trouble
48	itality. "I've a suggestion," said Baoyu. "As we're not inviting outsi
49	s favourite concubines died," said Baoyu. "I went to offer condolences
50	e of Baoyu. "I can't go out," said Baoyu. "Whatever happens, don't let
51	u accept it." "That's right," said Baoyu. "It seems that you can't be
52	to look. "I know this kite," said Baoyu. "It belongs to Yanhong in th
53	n't show." "That's splendid," said Baoyu. "Where would we find a Russi
54	ne." "You don't know, madam," said Baoyu, "Cousin Lin suffers from an
55	ngs are no use to me, madam," said Baoyu, "Why not let my pages carry
56	ace is swarming with people," said Baoyu. "Take any of them you like.
57	inted out. "Don't be afraid," said Baoyu. "My Third Sister likes drink
58	d pouches, or sashes?" "Yes," said Baoyu. "One for a sash would be nic

附录三

薛宝钗人物形象语料库数据

霍译本"Bao-chai's"共现语境词

N	Concordance
1	heal the smart of a beating!" The nature of Bao-chai's reply will be revealed in the fol
2	ght upset her. He was puzzled, therefore, by Bao-chai's rejoinder, and even more puzzled w
3	usness of her own at Bao-chai's expense; but Bao-chai's brief explosion caused her to drop
4	-yun had collapsed, weak with laughing, upon Bao-chai's shoulder. The others had long sinc
5	tly tired when she went to bed at night, but Bao-chai's arrival and the lively conversatio
6	The clumsiness of his apology rapidly turned Bao-chai's weeping into laughter. Lifting her
7	myself." The person most gratified by Bao-chai's presents was Aunt Zhao. "I'm not s
8	rest had all contributed, were sent round to Bao-chai's. Our narrative supplies no details
9	e musings on the subject were interrupted by Bao-chai's voice: "Have you finished writing
10	wife Jin-gui reacted to Caltrop's defence of Bao-chai's intelligence with a toss of the h
11	iled himself of the opportunity presented by Bao-chai's arrival to slip quietly out again,
12	f Dai-yu's place and one in the direction of Bao-chai's. The senior maids, Aroma, Musk and
13	had finished reading it. Then they looked at Bao-chai's: Guard the sweet scent behind clo
14	ply, asked again. "I've just been playing at Bao-chai's. Oriole cheated me and Bao-yu turn
15	t of adding some facetiousness of her own at Bao-chai's expense; but Bao-chai's brief expl
16	about his reading it, he hesitated to answer Bao-chai's question for fear of giving Dai-yu
17	e others." She rose and went away. Presently Bao-chai's lunch arrived and Patience went in
18	m his looks and behaviour you'd think he was Bao-chai's brother. He's certainly more like
19	n to them. To her, therefore, these words of Bao-chai's were a source of tongue-tied embar
20	of turn, but who, suddenly catching sight of Bao-chai's expression, could not help laugh i
21	was roused from this reverie by the sound of Bao-chai's voice asking Aroma what it was tha
22	have been inside his mouth when he was born. Bao-chai's eye came to rest on the jade. "I a

续表

N	Concordance
23	te of Green Delights and in the direction of Bao-chai's courtyard. She was just passing by
24	, my friend." Bao-yu was still smarting from Bao-chai's testiness. To be set upon now by D
25	o Bao-chai as a birthday-present. Ever since Bao-chai's first arrival, Grandmother Jia had
26	is, coming from Li Wan, effectively silenced Bao-chai's objection. Some time was now spent
27	people fear the heat." The colour flew into Bao-chai's face. An angry retort was on her l
28	distance beyond the bank above. "Isn't that Bao-chai's place?" said Grandmother Jia. On b
29	t was stark and bare. The only decoration in Bao-chai's room was a vase of the cheaper kin
30	holidays?" said Bao-yu to Jia Huan, ignoring Bao-chai's excuses. "If you don't like it her
31	rther fear of quarrels and estrangements; if Bao-chai's heavenly beauty is discarded there
32	s done." After sitting for a while longer in Bao-chai's room, they got up and again moved
33	grown-up celebration," said Xi-feng. "But in Bao-chai's case she's neither exactly grown-u
34	king," said Xiang-yun, raising her head from Bao-chai's lap, it's more like a duel to the
35	court yard, her heart full of gratitude for Bao-chai's kindness. Re entering Bao-yu's roo
36	ing her out of the way? he sent her over to Bao-chai's place to borrow a book. As soon as
37	it will be remembered, bad been sent off to Bao-chai's for a book. When she got there, sh
38	efore," said Aroma. "I feel so embarrassed." Bao-chai's lips puckered up mockingly. "Embar
39	serve you right!" Dai-yu, blushing, clung to Bao-chai's hand. "Let's give her a year's lea
40	male tongue will cease from nagging. Discard Bao-chai's heavenly beauty, destroy Dai-yu's
41	s, Nightingale, Snowgoose and Delicate; then Bao-chai's maids, Oriole and Apricot; then Yi
42	to such ostrich-like avoidance of the issue. Bao-chai's strictures about fooling around'a
43	ut was urged by Grand mother Jia to wait for Bao-chai's birthday and not go back until she
44	e sat, thought how much better it looked for Bao-chai's attention, and wished that he had
45	g towards the summerhouse, intending to seek Bao-chai's company inside. Bao-yu would hav
46	a. As soon as she had gone, Patience-seized Bao-chai's hand and asked her, in a low and u
47	r faculties!" Before Li Wan could reply, Bao-chai's arrival was announced. Li Wan and
48	ving her to continue on her way there alone. Bao-chai's route took her past the House of G
49	Bao-yu—who still knew nothing of Dai-yu and Bao-chai's recent rapprochement was too fami
50	Lian halted and asked her what it was. "It's Bao-chai's birthday on the twenty-first," sai
51	o. "Where have you been?" she asked Bao-yu. "Bao-chai's." "I see (very frostily)." "I thou

杨译本 "Baochai's" 共现语境词

N	Concordance
1	a and Fangguan; and now Qingwen is dead, and Baochai's household has left. Though Ying-chun
2	" she said, "Fangguan in your place and Miss Baochai's Ruiguan. As you happened to spot me
3	verses, then remarked with a smile, "Cousin Baochai's and Cousin Daiyu's are specially go
4	ell them." With that she left. At this point Baochai's meal arrived and Pinger sent in to
5	and for Aunt Xue to give twenty herself plus Baochai's share. But it's not very fair for t
6	oqin. Her reactions to Xiangyun's remark and Baochai's answer were not what they would onc
7	if I found you short-handed." "Where's Miss Baochai's lunch?" asked Tanchun. Some girls h
8	re the daughter of my father's sister, while Baochai's a cousin on my mother's side — you
9	nyan, "Why not take your mother over to Miss Baochai's place to say a few kind words to Yi
10	praise of Baochai. "Everyone speaks of Miss Baochai's good manners and generosity," she g
11	rls hurried out to notify the matrons, "Miss Baochai's lunching here too. Have her food b
12	arch to our own family. We mustn't raid Miss Baochai's quarters." "Of course not. How can
13	l quieter. Didn't you notice how lonely Miss Baochai's place seemed after Xiangling went h
14	owager. As soon as she had left, Pinger took Baochai's arm. "Have you heard the latest new
15	rattle on a bit longer." Xiangyun, lying in Baochai's lap, was shaking with laughter. Bao
16	read poem after poem by lamplight, ignoring Baochai's repeated reminders to go to bed. S
17	ng to her distinctive temperament. Besides, Baochai's generous, tactful, and accommodatin
18	e relented. After that, Xiangling moved into Baochai's quarters and had no more to do with
19	rom Lady Wang's apartments, were laughing at Baochai's account of how Xiangling had been v
20	ing. You always insist that nobody can rival Baochai's looks but you should just see her
21	, Jia Lian stopped to ask what it was. "It's Baochai's birthday on the twenty-first," she
22	r home." "One can never be too careful," was Baochai's reply. "There's been all sorts of t
23	hat night, and so injure her health. Luckily Baochai's arrival and the lively conversation
24	k the poems out of his pocket and stepped to Baochai's side to read them with her. The poe
25	quick!" he urged Xiren, Sheyue and Qingwen. "Baochai's boy cousin looks and behaves quite
26	they left. Meantime Baoyu had taken Daiyu to Baochai's place to thank her. After the usual
27	gy; but you're not completely well yet. Miss Baochai's gift of these things today shows ho
28	e she had gone, her maids told him: "To Miss Baochai's place." Baoyu went then to Alpinia
29	ses. And I asked her, "Surely you knew about Baochai's leaving?" "She said yes, but Baoch
30	served tea, Miaoyu plucked at the lapels of Baochai's and Daiyu's clothes and they went o

续表

N	Concordance
31	d lady's place. We don't have to worry about Baochai's cousin it's settled that she's to s
32	shine others in every way. When she saw that Baochai's brother had brought all these thing
33	that he had not gone in person to ask after Baochai's recent indisposition, he decided to
34	" they urged Xiren. "Lady Xing's niece, Miss Baochai's cousin and Madam Zhu's two cousins
35	eded to be kept in order, Lady Wang enlisted Baochai's help as well. "The old serving-wome
36	e Lady Dowager urged her to wait until after Baochai's birthday and the performance of ope

参考文献

一 中文

（一）图书

陈福康：《中国译学理论史稿》，上海外语教育出版社1992年版。

陈可培：《译者的文化意识与译作的再生》，载刘士聪《红楼译评——〈红楼梦〉翻译研究论文集》，南开大学出版社2004年版。

陈宏薇、江帆：《难忘的历程——〈红楼梦〉英译事业的描写性研究》，载刘士聪《红楼译评——〈红楼梦〉翻译研究论文集》，南开大学出版社2004年版。

党争胜：《〈红楼梦〉英译艺术比较研究——基于霍克斯和杨宪益译本》，北京大学出版社2012年版。

方梦之主编《中国译学大辞典》，上海外语教育出版社2011年版。

冯其庸、李希凡：《红楼梦大辞典》，文化艺术出版社2010年版。

范圣宇：《〈红楼梦〉管窥》，中国社会科学出版社2004年版。

范圣宇：《中国名著汉外对照文库：红楼梦（The Story The Stone）》（套装共5册），上海外语教育出版社2012年版。

冯庆华：《红译艺坛——〈红楼梦〉翻译艺术研究》，上海外语教育出版社2006年版。

冯庆华：《母语文化下的译者风格》，上海外语教育出版社2008年版。

冯庆华：《思维模式下的译文词汇》，上海外语教育出版社2012年版。

冯庆华：《思维模式下的译文句式》，上海外语教育出版社2015年版。

郭豫适：《红楼梦研究文选》，华东师范大学出版社1988年版。

黄鸣奋：《英语世界中国古典文学之传播》，学林出版社1997年版。

洪涛：《〈红楼梦〉与诠释方法论》，国家图书馆出版社2008年版。

洪涛:《女体和国族——从〈红楼梦〉翻译看跨文化移植与学术知识障》国家图书馆出版社2010年版。

胡开宝:《语料库翻译学概论》,上海交通大学出版社2011年版。

黄立波:《基于汉英/英汉平行语料库的翻译共性研究》,复旦大学出版社2007年版。

刘梦溪:《传统的误读》,河北教育出版社1996年版。

吕启祥、林东海主编《红楼梦研究稀见资料汇编（增订本）》,人民文学出版社2006年版。

刘士聪:《红楼译评——〈红楼梦〉翻译研究论文集》,南开大学出版社2004年版。

林以亮:《红楼梦 西游记——细评红楼梦新英译》,台湾联经出版事业公司1976年版。

刘泽权:《〈红楼梦〉中英文语料库的创建及应用研究》,光明日报出版社2010年版。

刘宓庆:《文化翻译论纲》,湖北教育出版社1999年版。

刘宓庆:《翻译与语言哲学》,中国对外翻译出版公司2004年版。

林煌天:《中国翻译辞典》,湖北教育出版社1997年版。

李磊荣:《文化可译性视角下的〈红楼梦〉翻译研究》,上海译文出版社2010年版。

鲁迅:《中国小说史略》,人民文学出版社1973年版。

邱进、周洪亮:《文化视域及翻译策略:〈红楼梦〉译本的多维研究》,西南师范大学出版社2011年版。

任东升:《语篇翻译与译者的写作》,载刘士聪《红楼译评——〈红楼梦〉翻译研究论文集》,南开大学出版社2004年版。

孙艺风:《视角、阐释、文化:文学翻译与翻译理论》,清华大学出版社2004年版。

谭载喜:《翻译学》,湖北教育出版社2000年版。

王宏印:《〈红楼梦〉诗词曲赋英译比较研究》,陕西师范大学出版社2001年版。

王宏印:《英汉翻译综合教程》,辽宁师范大学出版社2002年版。

王宏印:《精诚所至,金石为开——为建立"〈红楼〉译评"的宏伟目标而努力〉》，载刘士聪《红楼译评——〈红楼梦〉翻译研究论文集》，南开大学出版社 2004 年版。

王宏印：《试论霍译〈红楼梦〉体制之更易与独创》，载刘士聪《红楼译评——〈红楼梦〉翻译研究论文集》，南开大学出版社 2004 年版。

王佐良：《英语文体学论文集》，外语教学与研究出版社 1980 年版。

吴世昌：《红楼梦探源外编》，上海古籍出版社 1980 年版。

王克非：《语料库翻译学探索》，上海交通大学出版社 2012 年版。

王克非等：《双语对应语料库：研制与应用》，外语教学与研究出版社 2004 年版。

肖家燕：《〈红楼梦〉概念隐喻的英译研究》，中国社会科学出版社 2009 年版。

许钧：《文学翻译的理论与实践——翻译对话录》，译林出版社 2001 年版。

严苡丹：《〈红楼梦〉亲属称谓语的英译研究》，外语教学与研究出版社 2012 年版。

杨宪益：《银翘集》，（香港）天地图书有限公司 1995 年版。

杨义：《中国古典小说史论》，中国社会科学出版社 2004 年版。

《脂砚斋重评石头记》（庚辰本），文学古籍刊行社 1955 年朱墨套印本。

赵长江：《霍译红楼梦回目人名翻译研究》，河北教育出版社 2007 年版。

赵世开主编《汉英对比语法论集》，上海教育出版社 1999 年版。

周振甫：《小说例话》，江苏教育出版社 2005 年版。

（二）期刊

陈琳：《〈红楼梦〉"看官"英译与中国古典白话小说西渐》，《红楼梦学刊》2011 年第 1 期。

陈曜：《〈红楼梦〉英译史及其在英语文学中地位初探》，《湖北成人教育学院学报》2007 年第 3 期。

冯其庸：《红楼论要——解读〈红楼梦〉的几个问题》，《红楼梦学刊》2008 年第 5 期。

葛锐：《英语红学研究纵览》，《红楼梦学刊》2007 年第 3 期。

洪涛：《评"汉英经典文库本"〈红楼梦〉英译的疏失错误》，《红楼梦学刊》2006 年第 4 期。

洪涛：《〈红楼梦〉翻译研究与套用"目的论"、"多元系统论"的隐患——以〈红译艺坛〉为论析中心》，《红楼梦学刊》2010年第2期。

贺显斌：《英汉翻译过程中的明晰化现象》，《解放军外国语学院学报》2003年第4期。

胡开宝、朱一凡：《基于语料库的莎剧〈哈姆雷特〉汉译文本中显化现象及其动因研究》，《外语研究》2008年第2期。

胡显耀：《基于语料库的翻译小说词语特征研究》，《外语教学与研究》2007第1期。

黄立波、王克非：《翻译普遍性研究反思》，《中国翻译》2006年第5期。

黄立波、王克非：《语料库翻译学：课题与进展》，《外语教学与研究》2011年第6期。

姜其煌：《〈红楼梦〉霍克斯英文全译本》，《红楼梦学刊》1980年第1期。

柯飞：《汉语"把"字句特点、分布及英译研究》，《外语教学与研究》2003年第12期。

柯飞：《翻译中的隐和显》，《外语教学与研究》2005年第4期。

刘泽权、朱虹：《〈红楼梦〉中、英文本中刘姥姥形象的对比——以刘姥姥话语的人际功能分析为例》，《翻译季刊》2007年第44期。

刘泽权、田璐、刘超朋：《〈红楼梦〉中英文平行语料库的创建》，《当代语言学》2008年第10期。

刘泽权，田璐：《红楼梦叙事标记语及其英译——基于语料库的对比分析》，《外语学刊》2009年第1期。

刘泽权、赵烨：《〈红楼梦〉人物"哭态"探析》，《河北学刊》2009年第29期。

刘泽权、侯羽：《国内外显化研究概述》，《中国翻译》2008年第5期。

刘泽权、闫继苗：《基于语料库的译者风格与翻译策略研究》，《解放军外国语学院学报》2010年第33期。

刘迎姣：《〈红楼梦〉英全译本译者主体性对比研究》，《外国语文》2012年第1期。

刘军平：《从跨学科角度看译者主体性的四个维度及其特点》，《外语与外语教学》2008年第8期。

陆丙甫：《"的"的基本功能和派生功能——从描写性到区别性再到指称性》，《世界汉语教学》2003 年第 1 期。

李希凡、李萌：《"可叹停机德"——薛宝钗论》，《红楼梦学刊》2005 年第 2 期。

欧阳健：《眼别真赝 心识古今——和蔡义江先生讨论〈红楼梦〉版本》，《红楼梦学刊》1994 年第 3 期。

宋华、刘晓虹：《〈红楼梦〉人物外貌英译的审美建构》，《红楼梦学刊》2008 年第 2 期。

卫乃兴：《基于语料库的对比短语学研究》，《外国语》2011 年第 4 期。

文军、任艳：《国内〈红楼梦〉英译研究回眸（1979—2010）》，《中国外语》2012 年第 1 期。

魏瑾：《从文学文体视角看林黛玉形象在翻译中的再现》，《安徽文学》（下半月）2007 年第 5 期。

吴昂、黄立波：《关于翻译共性的研究》，《外语教学与研究》2006 年第 5 期。

吴篮玲：《言外意、弦外音、境外味——简析〈红楼梦〉语言的橄榄美》，《修辞学习》1997 年第 7 期。

王丽娜：《〈红楼梦〉在国外的流传、翻译与研究》，《国家图书馆学刊》1992 年第 1 期。

王克非：《英汉/汉英语句对应的语料库考察》，《外语教学与研究》2003 年第 6 期。

王克非、胡显耀：《基于语料库的翻译汉语词汇特征研究》，《中国翻译》2008 年第 6 期。

王克非、黄立波：《语料库翻译学的几个术语》，《四川外语学院学报》2007 年第 6 期。

王克非：《翻译：在语言文化间周旋》，《中国外语》2010 年第 5 期。

许国璋：《借鉴与拿来》，《外国语》1979 年第 3 期。

闫敏敏：《二十年来的〈红楼梦〉英译研究》，《外语教学》2005 年第 4 期。

姚琴：《〈红楼梦〉文字游戏的翻译与译者风格——对比 Hawkes 译本和杨宪益译本所得启示》，《外语与外语教学》2009 年第 12 期。

姚琴：《基于平行语料库的〈红楼梦〉意义显化考察——以霍译本林黛玉人物特征为例》，《外语教学与研究》2012年第3期。

郑向前：《〈红楼梦〉早期抄本研究综述》，《红楼梦学刊》1991年第3期。

查明建、田雨：《论译者主体性——从译者文化地位的边缘化谈起》，《中国翻译》2003年第3期。

张美芳：《利用语料库调查译者的文体——贝克研究新法评介》，《解放军外国语学院学报》2002年第10期。

张娅丽：《近十年薛宝钗研究述评》，《龙岩学院学报》2012年第1期。

（三）学位论文

付红丽：《跨文化视角的〈红楼梦〉中涉及人物塑造的隐喻研究》，硕士学位论文，湖南师范大学，2011年。

江帆：《他乡的石头记：〈红楼梦〉百年英译史研究》，博士学位论文，复旦大学，2007年。

黄生太：《〈红楼梦〉拟声词及其英译研究》，博士论文，上海外国语大学，2011年。

陆梅：《〈红楼梦〉人物描写及其翻译中的隐含的语用分析》，硕士学位论文，广西大学，2004年。

梁艳：《美的传达——论〈红楼梦〉杨译本中的人物外貌描写》，硕士学位论文，上海外国语大学，2009年。

孙洋：《霍克斯〈红楼梦〉人物话语翻译艺术研究》，硕士学位论文，山东大学，2012年。

田婧：《从语境对等论〈红楼梦〉两英译本中王熙凤的性格塑造》，硕士学位论文，广东外语外贸大学，2005年。

徐文臻：《〈红楼梦〉中个性化人物语言风格在译文中的再现》，硕士学位论文，中国石油大学，2008年。

二 外文

（一）图书

Lefevere Andre, "Mother Courage's Cucumbers: Text, System and Refraction in a Theory of Literature", in Lawrence Venuti (ed.) *The Translation*

Studies Reader, London and New York: Routledg, 2000.

Altenberg, B., "Adverbial Connectors in English and Swedish: Semantic and lexical Correspondences", in H. Hasselgard and S. Oksefjell (ed.), *Out of Corpora*, Amsterdam: Rodopi, 1999.

M. Baker, "Corpus Linguistics and Translation Studies: Implications and Applications", in M. Baker, G. Francis and E. Tognini-Bonelli (ed.), *Text and Technology: In Honor of John Sinclair*, Philadelphia & Amsterdam: John Benjamins, 1993.

M. Baker, "Corpus-based Translation Studies: The Challenges That Lie Ahead", in H. Somers (ed.), *Terminology, LSP and Translation*, Amsterdam: John Benjamins, 1996.

Baker, Mona (ed.), *Routledge Encyclopedia of Translation Studies*, Shanghai: Shanghai Foreign Language Education Press, 1998/2004.

Bassnett, Susan & André Lefevere, *Constructing Cultures: Essays on Literay Translation*, Shanghai: Shanghai Foreign Language Education Press, 2001.

S. Bernardini & F. Zanettin, "When is a Universal not a Universal? Some Limits of Current Corpus-based Methodologies for the Investigation of Translation Universals", in A. Mauranen and P. Kujamaki (ed.), *Translation Universals – Do They Exist?* Amsterdam: John Benjamins, 2004.

S. Bernardini, "Reviving Old Ideas: Parallel and Comparable Analysis in Translation Studies—With an Example from Translation Stylistics", in K. Aijmer & C. Alvstad (ed.), *New Tendencies in Translation Studies. Selected Papers from a Workshop G teborg 12 December* 2003, G teborg: Acta Universitatis Gothoburgensis, 2005.

Blum-Kulka, S., "Shifts of Cohesion and Coherence in Translation", in J. House & S. Blum Kulka (ed.), *Inter-lingual and Intercultural Communication. Discourse and Cognition in Translation and Second Language Acquisition Studies*, Tübingen: Gunter Narr Verlag, 1986.

A. Chesterman, "Beyond the Particular", in A. Mauranen and P. Kujamaki (ed.), *Translation Universals: Do They Exist?* Amsterdam: John Benjamins, 2004.

A. Chesterman, "Hypothesis about Translation Universals", in G. Hansen, K. Malmkjar and D. Gile (ed.), *Claims, Changes and Challenges in Translation Studies. Selected Contributions for the EST Congress, Copenhagen, 2001*, Amsterdam: John Benjamins, 2004.

Croft, W., *Typology and Universals*, Cambridge: CUP, 1990.

Damrosch David, *What is World Literature?*, Princeton & Oxford: Princeton University Press, 2003.

Englund-Dimitrova, B., "Explicitation in Russian-Swedish translation: Sociolinguistic and pragmatic aspects", in B. Englund-Dimitrova & Al. Pereswetoff-Morath (ed.), *Swedish Contributions to the Thirteenth International Congress of Slavists, Ljubljana, August 2003*, Lund: Lund University, 2003.

Birgitta Englund-Dimitrova, *Expertise and Explicitation in the Translation Process*, Amsterdam/ Philadelphia: John Benjamins Publishing Company, 2005.

Hansen, G., K. Malmkjar & D. Gile (eds.), *Claims, Changes and Challenges in Translation Studies*, Amsterdam: John Benjamins, 2004.

Hawkes David (trans.), T*he Story of the Stone* (Volume I – III), London: the Penguin Books Ltd., 1973, 1977, 1980.

Hawkes David, "The Translator, the Mirror and the Dream-Some Observations on a New Theory", in John Minford & Siu-kit Wong (ed.), *Classical, Modern and Humane Essays in Chinese Literature*, Hong Kong: The Chinese University Press, 1989.

Hawkes, David, *The Story of the Stone: A Translator's Notebooks*, Hong Kong: The Center for Literature and Translation, Lingnan University Hong Kong, 2000.

Hunston, Susan, *Corpora in Applied Linguistics*, Cambridge: Cambridge University Press, 2002.

Johansson, S., *Seeing through Multilingual Corpora: On the Use of Corpora in Contrastive Studies*, Amsterdam: John Benjamins, 2007.

Kennedy, G. D., *An Introduction to Corpus Linguistics*, London/ New York: Longman, 1998.

D. Kenny, *Lexis and Creativity in Translation: A Corpus-based Study*, Manchester: St. Jerome, 2001.

D. Kenny, "Parallel Corpora and Translation Studies: Old Questions, New Perspectives? Reporting that in Gepcolt: A Case Study", in G. Barnbrook, P. Danielsson & M. Mahlberg (ed.), *Meaningful Texts: The Extraction of Semantic Information from Monolingual and Multilingual Corpora*, London & New York: Continuum, 2005.

Kinga Klaudy, "Back-translation as a Tool for Detecting Explicitation Strategies in Translation", in Kinga Klaudy, José Lambert and Anikó Sohár (ed.), *Translation Studies in Hungary*, Budapest: Scholastica, 1996.

K. Klaudy, "Explicitation", in M. Baker (ed.), *Routledge Encyclopedia of Translation Studies*, London: Routledge, 1998.

S. Laviosa, "The English Comparable Corpus: A Resourceand a Methodology", in L. Bowker, M. Cronin, D. Kenny & J. Pearson (ed.), *Unity in Diversity? Current Trends in Translation Studies*, Manchester: St. Jerome, 1998.

S. Laviosa, *Corpus-based Translation Studies: Theory, Findings and Applications*, Amsterdam: Rodopi, 2002.

A. Lefevere, *Translation, Rewritiing, Marl the Manipulation of Literary Fame*, London and New York: Poutledge/Shanghai: Shanghai Foreign Language Education Press, 1992/2004.

Geoffrey Leech, "Teaching in Language Corpora: A Convergence", in Gerry Knowles, Tony. McEnery, Stephen Fligelstone & Arme Wichman (ed.), *Teaching and Language Corpora*, London: Longman, 1997.

A. Mauranen & P. Kujamaki (eds.), *Translation Universals: Do They Exist?* Amsterdam: John Benjamins, 2004.

McEnery, Tony and Andrew Wilson (eds.), *Corpus Linguistics*, Edinburgh: Edinburgh University Press, 1996.

Nida, E. A., *Toward a Science of Translating*, Shanghai: Shanghai Foreign Language Education Press, 1964/2004.

Nida, E. A. & C. Taber, *The Theory and Practice of Translation*, Leiden: E. J. Brill, 1969.

Nord, Christiane, Translating as a Purposeful Activity-Functionalist Approaches Explained, Shanghai: Shanghai Foreign Language Education Press, 2001.

M. Olohan, *Introducing Corpora in Translation Studies*, London & New York: Routledge, 2004.

Papai, Vilma., "Explicitation: A Universal of Translated Text", in A. Mauranen & P. Kujamuki (ed.), *Translation Universals: Do they Exist?* Amsterdam/Philadelphia: John Benjamins Publishing Company, 2004.

T. Puurtinen, "Nonfinite constructions in Finnish Children's Literature: Features of Translationese Contradicting Translation Universals", in S. Granger, J. Lerot & S. Petch-Tyson (ed.), *Corpus-based Approaches to Contrastive Linguistics and Translation Studies*, Amsterdam: Rodopi, 2003.

J. Schmied & H. Schffler, "Explicitness as a Universal Feature of Translation", in M. Ljung (ed.), *Corpus-based Studies in English*, Papers from the 17th International Conference on English Language Research on Computerized Corpora (ICAME 17) Stockolm, May 15-19, 1996, Amsterdam: Rodopi, 1997.

Serpellet, Noelle, "Mandative Constructions in English and Their Equivalents in French: Applying a Bilingual Approach to The Theory and Practice of Translation", in Bemhard Kettemann and Georg Marko (ed.), *Teaching and Learning by Doing Corpus Analysis. Proceeding of the Fourth International Conference on Teaching and Language Corpora*, Amsterdam & New York, 2002.

Shuttleworth, Mark and Cowie, Moira, *Dictionary of Translation Studies*, 上海外语教育出版社 1997 年版。

Shlesinger, M., "Interpreter Latitude vs. Due Process: Simultaneous and Consecutive Interpretation in Multilingual Trials", in S. Tirkkonen-Condit (ed.), *Empirical Research in Translation and Intercultural Studies*, Tübingen: Gunter Narr Verlag, 1991.

Stubbs, Michael, "British Tradition in Text Analysis from Firth to Sinclair", in M. Baker, G. Francis & E. Tognini-Bonelli (ed.), *Text amd Technology: In Honour of John Sinclair*, Amsterdam & Philadelphia: John Benjamins, 1993.

W. Teubert, "Directions in Corpus Linguistics", in Halliday, M. A. K., Wolfgang Teubert, Co-lin Yalop & Anna Germakova (ed.), *Lexicology & Corpus Linguistics*, London & New York: Continuum, 2004.

Toury, G., "What are Descriptive Studies into Translation Likely to Yield A-part from Isolated Descriptions", in K. M. van Leuven-Zwart & T. Naaijkens (ed.), *Translation Studies: State of the Art*, Amsterdam: Rodopi, 1991.

Toury, Gideon, "Probabilistic Explanations in Translation Studies. Welcome as They Are, Would they Qualify as Universals", in Anna Mauranen & Pekka Kujamaki (ed.), *Translation Universals: Do They Exist?* Amsterdam: John Benjamins, 2004.

Tirkkonen-Condit, S., "Unique items—Over-or Under-represented in Translated language?", in Anna Mauranen & Pekka Kujamaki (ed.), *Translation Universals: Do They Exist?* Amsterdam: John Benjamins, 2004.

Vanderauwera, R., *Dutch Novels Translated into English: The Transformation of a "Minority" Literature*, Amsterdam: Rodopi, 1985.

Vinay, Jean-Paul & Jean Darbelnet, *Comparative Stylistics of French and English: A Methodology for Translation*, Translated and edited by Juan C. Sager & M. J. Hamel, Amsterdam & Philadelphia: John Benjamins, 1958/1995.

Williams, Donna, *Recurret Features of Translation Features in Canada: A Corpus-based Study*, Ottawa: School of Translation and Interpretation, University of Ottawa, 2005.

Wilss, Wolfram, *The Science of Translation: Problems and Methods*, Tübingen: Gunter Narr, 1982.

Yang, Hsien-yi & Gladys Yang, *A Dream of Red Mansions* (Volume I-III) (trans.), Beijing: Foreign Languages Press, 1978–1980.

（二）期刊

M. Baker, "Corpora in Translation Studies: An Overview and Some Suggestions for Future Research", *Target*, Vol. 7, No. 2, 1995.

J. B. Casagrande, "The Ends of Translation", *International Journal of American Linguistics*, Vol. 20, 1954.

Ewa Gumul, "Explicitation in Simultaneous Interpretation: A Strategy or a By-product of Language Mediation", *Across Language and Cultures*, 2006, Vol. 7, No. 2, 2006.

Halverson, S., "The Cognitive Basis of Translation Universals", *Target*, Vol. 15, No. 2, 2003.

H. Hasselgard, "Using Parallel Corpora in Contrastive Studies: Cross-linguistic Contrast of Future Referring Expressions in English and Norwegian", *Foreign Language Teaching and Research*, Vol. 1, 2012.

D. Kenny, "Creatures of Habit? What Translators Usually do with Words", *Meta*, Vol. 43, No. 4, 1998.

K. Klaudy & Krisztina Károly, "Implicitation in Translation: Empirical Evidence for Operational Asymmetry in Translation", *Across Languages and Cultures*, Vol. 6, No. 1, 2005.

S. Laviosa, "Core Patterns of Lexical Use in a Comparable Corpus of English Narrative Prose", *Meta*, Vol. 43, No. 2, 1998.

S. Laviosa, "The Corpus-based Approach: A New Paradigm in Translation Studies", *Meta*, Vol. 43, No. 4, 1998.

Noel, D., "Translation as Evidence for Semantics: An Illustration, Linguistics", Vol. 4, 2003.

M. Olohan & M. Baker, "Reporting that in Translated English: Evidence for Subconscious Process of Explicitation", *Across Languages and Cultures*, Vol. 1, 2000.

M. Olohan, "Spelling out the Optionals in Translation: A Corpus Study", *UCREL Technical Papers*, Vol. 13, 2001.

M. Olohan, "Leave it Out! Using a Comparable Corpus to Investigate Aspects of Explicitation in Translation", *Cadernos de Traducao*, Vol. IX, 2002.

M. Olohan, "How Frequent are The Contractions? A Study of Contracted Forms in the Translational English Corpus", *Target*, Vol. 15, No. 1, 2003.

L. Øver as, "In Search of the Third Code: An Investigation of Norms in Literary Translation", *Meta*, Vol. 43, No. 2, 1998.

Elisa Perego, "Evidence of Explicitation in Subtitling: Toward a Categorization", *Across Languages and Cultures*, Vol. 4, No. 1, 2003.

T. Puurtinen, "Syntax, Readability and Ideology in Children's Lliterature", *Meta*, Vol. 43, No. 4, 1998.

T. Puurtinen, "Genre-specific Features of Translationese? Linguistic Differences between Translated and Non-translated Finnish Children s Literature", *Literary and Linguistic Computing*, Vol. 18, No. 4, 2003.

Saldanha Gabriela, "Translator Style: Methodological Considerations", *Translator*, Vol. 17, 2011.

Seguinot, Candace, "Pragmatics and the Explicitation Hypothesis", *TTR Traduction, Terminologie, Redaction*, Vol. 1, No. 2, 1988.

Tirkkonen-Condit, S., "Translationese—A Myth or an Empirical Fact? A Study into the Linguistic Identifiability of Translated Language", *Target*, Vol. 14, No. 2, 2002.

M. Tymoczko, "Computerized Corpora and the Future of Translation Studies", *Meta*, Vol. XLIII, No. 4, 1998.

(三)学位论文

Wong, Laurence, *A Study of the Literary Translations of the Hong Long Meng: with Special Reference to David Hawkes's English Version*, Graduate Department of East Studies, University of Toronto, 1992.

(三)网络

A. Frankenberg-Gacia, "Are Translations Longer than Source texts? A Corpus-based Study of Explicitation", http://www.academia.edu/3260827.

Mc Enery, T. & A. Wilson, "Corpora and Translation, Uses and Future Prospects", http://ucrel.lancs.ac.uk/papers/techpaper/vol2.pdf.

M. Olohan, "Comparable Corpora in Translation Research: Overview of Recent Analyses Using the Translational English Corpus", http://www.iff.unizh.ch/cl/yuste/postworkshop/repository/molohan.pdf.

Pym, Anthony, "Explaining Explicitation", http://www.fut.es/-apym/welcome.html.

后　　记

　　本书是在博士论文的基础上修改而成的。完成此书稿的时刻，我的心中涌起的不仅仅是喜悦，更多的是无限的感激。回顾自己的学术历程，深感老师和亲人对我恩重如山，是他们无私的支持和厚爱，使我在严寒酷暑中能坚持学习，使我能在远离祖国的异国他乡能将此书稿修改付梓。

　　首先，我要感谢我的恩师——上海外国语大学的冯庆华教授。正是在先生的指引下，我跨进了《红楼梦》翻译艺术研究的大门。先生不仅在学术上给予我指导，为我提供宝贵资料，耐心地帮我修改论文，及时地帮助我解决学术研究上的困难，还鼓励远在异乡的我继续学术探索，可以说，先生是我学习、工作和生活中的引路人，是我心中永怀感激和敬佩的人。

　　聆听上海外国语大学的戴炜栋、李维屏、汪小玲、许余龙、乔国强、虞建华、俞东明、张健、查明建、肖维青、郑新民、王恩铭等诸多教授的课程和讲座让我获益良多，他们的治学方式给了我种种启迪。他们博学敏锐、宽容严谨和一丝不苟的治学精神及处世态度潜移默化地影响着我，并成为我终生受用的宝贵财富。

　　同时，我还要感谢各位同门、学友给予我的帮助和支持，特别感谢李崇月、苏建红、毛卫强、张雯、杨惠莹等，感谢他们毫无保留地分享自己的观点，与他们的讨论给了我许多灵感和启发，也让我的学术生涯平添许多温暖和乐趣。他们率真的个性和对学术的执着追求也不断激励着我。

　　感谢江苏大学外国语学院的领导和同事。陈红院长在生活上给予我悉心关怀，在学术上给予我细心指导，在我松懈倦怠时给予我精神上的鼓励；华厚坤主任、徐慧霞和田红副主任为我从事学术研究提供了方便，并一直关心我的工作和学习；吴转利老师完全承担了我的教学工作，他们的无私帮助为我赢得了更多的学习、研究时间。感谢刘洪兰主任为我求学创造的良好条件。感谢外国语学院各位关心、支持我的同事。

感谢父母和兄长陪伴我在学术的道路上一路成长，一直给予我支持、理解和不求回报的关爱；感谢我的先生和公婆，一直无怨无悔地支持我的学习和工作；感谢我的儿子，你的勤奋好学，给予我奋斗的勇气和信心。

感谢国家留学基金委，给了我实现剑桥梦的机会，让我能在宁静的典藏云集的剑桥大学图书馆中完成此书稿。

感谢中国社会科学出版社的编辑们，特别是我的责任编辑王琪老师，她们的人文情怀、学术态度和敬业精神时时熏陶着我、鞭策着我，让我不敢懈怠。

感谢所有关心和帮助我的人。

谨以此书献给他们。

姚 琴

2017 年于英国剑桥大学